W9-BBL-723

146525

L
F
VIC

A Victorian Christmas tea

DATE DUE		APR 23 2002
AUG 19 2000	JUL 05 2001	MAY 13 2002
		JUN 13 2002
OCT 10 2000		JUL 15 2002
JAN 04 2001	SEP 19 2001	
MAY 09 2001	OCT 23 2001	SEP 14 2002 / SEP 30 2002
MAY 25 2001		JAN 29 '03
		MAY 22 '03
JUN 06 2001	NOV 29 2001	DEC 05 '03
	APR 01 2002	JUN 30 '04

JUN 28 2000

JUL 28 2000

MAY 16 2005

A VICTORIAN CHRISTMAS TEA

This Large Print Book carries the
Seal of Approval of N.A.V.H.

A VICTORIAN CHRISTMAS TEA

Catherine Palmer
Dianna Crawford
Peggy Stoks
Katherine Chute

Thorndike Press • Thorndike, Maine

Published in 1998 by arrangement with
Tyndale House Publishers, Inc.

Thorndike Large Print ® Christian Fiction Series.

The tree indicium is a trademark of Thorndike Press.

The text of this Large Print edition is unabridged.
Other aspects of the book may vary from the original edition.

Set in 16 pt. Plantin by Rick Gundberg.

Printed in the United States on permanent paper.

Library of Congress Cataloging in Publication Data

A Victorian Christmas tea / Catherine Palmer . . . [et al.].
    p. cm.
  Contents: Angel in the attic / Catherine Palmer — A daddy
for Christmas / Dianna Crawford — Tea for Marie /
Peggy Stoks — Going home / Katherine Chute.
  ISBN 0-7862-1541-0 (lg. print : hc : alk. paper)
    1. Christmas stories, American. 2. Historical fiction,
American. 3. Christian fiction, American. I. Palmer,
Catherine, 1956– .
  [PS648.C45V53   1998]
  813'.0108334—dc21   98-8443

CONTENTS

Angel in the Attic

CATHERINE PALMER

PROLOGUE

December 1880
Silver City, New Mexico

"If I so much as catch a glimpse of a single hair on your scrawny hide, I'll pull the trigger. You hear?" Fara Canaday lowered the shotgun and flipped her blonde braid over her shoulder. Her latest suitor was scurrying away across Main Street, his hat brim tugged down over his ears with both hands — as if that might protect him from a blast of pellets.

"And stay gone, you ol' flea-bit varmint!" she hollered after him.

"Ai, Farolita, you got rid of that one." Manuela Perón, the housekeeper at the red-brick Canaday Mansion, shook her head. "And the one before. What did you do to that poor man? Spill hot tea into his lap?"

"He tried to kiss me!"

"Is that so terrible? You have twenty-four years, señorita. Long ago, you should have

9

been kissed, wedded, and made into a mama."

Fara shrugged. "They're all after Papa's fortune, Manuela. Why should I let some greedy, no-good, money-grubbing —"

"It's *your* fortune, Farolita. Your papa has been gone almost a year now. If you wish to do well by his memory, you will marry and bear an heir. What use is a daughter to a wealthy gentleman? None. None but to marry a wise man who can manage the business and bring heirs to his line."

"*I* can manage the business. I looked after Papa's affairs all five years he was ill — and we didn't lose a single silver dollar. In fact, the Canaday assets grew by leaps and bounds. We bought the brickworks. We cut a wider road to the silver mine. We invested in two hotels and a restaurant. Manuela, the Southern Pacific Railroad is on its way to Deming, and if I have my say, Silver City will join it with a narrow gauge branch line. In a couple of years, we'll have telephones and electricity and —"

"Ai-yai-yai!" Manuela held up her hands in a bid for peace. "These are not the words of a lady. Why did your father send you away to that school in Boston? To learn about telephones and electricity? No. He sent you to learn elegant manners. To learn

10

the wearing of fashionable clothes. To learn conversation and sketching and sewing!"

Manuela ignored Fara's grimace and rushed on. "Why did your papa want you to learn these things? So you can marry well. Look at you now, Farolita. Have you been riding the horses again? If I lift your skirts, will I see those terrible buckskins from the *Indios?* Your hair is wild like an Apache. Your skin is brown from the sun. You never wear your bonnet! And you put on men's boots! You pick your teeth with hay stems — and you spit!"

"If I learned one thing in Boston, it's that housekeepers aren't supposed to lecture their mistresses." Fara let out a hot breath that quickly turned to steam in the chill December air. "For three months now, Manuela, I've been giving you lessons from the Boston lady's book. You're supposed to wear your black-and-white uniform — not that flowered mantilla. You're supposed to knock softly and introduce your presence with a little cough. You're supposed to insist that all visitors put a little calling card in the silver tray by the front door . . . and *not* let them come barging into the library where I'm making lists for the Christmas tea!"

"But . . . but . . . that man didn't have

a calling card." Manuela's brown eyes filled with tears. "I don't know where is the silver tray. I think it went the way of the crystal goblets — with Pedro, the thieving butler. And the black uniform you brought me is so . . . tight. I have ten children . . . and . . . and . . ."

"Oh, Manuela, I'm sorry." Fara wrapped her arms around the woman who had served her family with love so many years. "It's just these confounded gentleman callers. They come courting and wooing, and they get me so riled up I start hollering at you."

"*Sí,* Farolita, my little light. I know. I know." Manuela hugged Fara, calling her by the pet name that evoked images of the soft yellow candles set out in bags of sand on Christmas Eve to light the way of the Christ child. "We must have peace in this house."

"Peace and goodwill," Fara said.

"Goodwill to all — even men."

Fara crossed her arms and fought the grin tugging at the corners of her mouth. "Not to men with marriage on their minds," she said firmly. "Godspeed but not goodwill."

Touching the housekeeper lightly on the cheek, Fara started back into the house. As she shut the door behind her, she heard Manuela whisper to a throng of imaginary

12

suitors, "God rest ye merry, gentlemen. Let nothing you dismay."

Fara chuckled and added, "But don't have dreams of marriage — not to Fara Canaday!"

⚜

Phoenix, Arizona

The memory of the previous night's choking nightmare swept over Aaron Hyatt as he strode through the lobby of the Saguaro Hotel in downtown Phoenix. He had dreamed he was going to marry Fara Canaday. Stopping stock-still on the burgundy carpet and staring up at the hideous gargoyle that had reminded him of the nightmare, he ran a hand around the inside of his collar.

Marriage? What a despicable thought. What a gut-wrenching, spine-chilling, nauseating idea.

"Evenin', mister." A young bellboy peered up at Hyatt. "You look a little pale, sir. Are you all right?"

Hyatt's attention snapped into focus. "Why am I going to New Mexico?" he demanded of the lad. "I've been sitting in my room most of the day pondering the question — and I still don't have a good answer.

13

Why would a sane man travel across mountains and deserts — give up two good months of his life — just to meet a woman?"

The bewildered boy swallowed. "Maybe . . . maybe she's a beautiful woman?"

"She's not. If I were a gambling man, I'd wager half my fortune she's plain faced, oily haired, dull witted, and lazy. She'll be all done up in silks and ribbons. She'll giggle and mince around the parlor like a little lap dog. She'll have nothing in her brain but bonbons and fashions. I know the type. Know them well, trust me. So why am I going?"

"Because . . . because you were told to?"

"Asked. Asked by my father on his deathbed." *Go and find Jacob Canaday, the best man I ever knew. Honest. Hardworking. Loyal. A Christian man. Go and find him. He has a daughter. If you can, marry her, Aaron. She'll make you a good wife.*

"She might make a good wife," the boy ventured.

"Pah! You have no idea. None whatsoever. She'd nag me to death. The rich ones always do. They've had life too good. Too easy. She'd want everything she doesn't have — and twice as much besides. She'd make my life a sludge pool of misery. Well, I'm not going. I'm a praying man, young

14

fellow, and I surely believe the Lord speaks in mysterious ways. That dream must have been a sign." He reached into his pocket for a coin. "Send word to the livery stable for me, will you? Tell them Aaron Hyatt wants to be saddled and out of town by six."

"Hyatt? Are you Mr. Hyatt?" The boy's eyes widened. "There's a gentleman's been lookin' for you. He's waitin' upstairs with his pals. They've been drinkin' whiskey for hours, but he says he'd wait all day and all next year if need be. Says he's been expectin' you to track him down these fifteen years."

"Fifteen years? I was no bigger than you fifteen years ago — and sure as summer lightning I wasn't tracking anybody but Sallie Ann, the girl next door with the pretty red pigtails." Hyatt glanced up the staircase. "Who is the man?"

"It's Mr. James Copperton, of course. He's famous. He owns the biggest saloon in Phoenix and half the trade in loose women. Maybe he wants to do business with you."

Hyatt scowled. "I wouldn't do business with a man like that if my life depended on it. But I reckon I'll have to speak to him. Run up and tell him I'm here." He glanced at the gargoyle again. "Then hotfoot it to the livery, boy. Tell them I'm riding out tonight."

"Tonight?"

"I'm not one to waste a single minute once I've made up my mind. The more miles I can put between Miss Fara Canaday and me, the happier I'll be." He flipped the coin to the boy. "Hop to it."

"Yes sir!"

The lad raced up the curving staircase, taking the steps two at a time. Hyatt pondered the gargoyle a moment longer. *Spare me, Lord,* his soul whispered in silent prayer. *If I must take a wife, give me one with fire in her spirit, brains in her head, and the smile of an angel. Amen.*

As he started up the stairs, the young bellboy flew past him. "They're waitin' for you, Mr. Hyatt," he said. "I'm on my way to the livery."

"Good lad." Hyatt reached the landing and turned the corner to start up the second flight of steps. As he placed his hand on the banister, a strangled cry echoed down.

"It's him! It's him!"

Hyatt looked up — straight into the barrel of a trembling six-shooter. *Ambush.* Fire shot through his veins, tightened his heart, stopped his breath. The small pistol tucked under his belt seemed to burn white-hot. Could he reach it in time?

"You sure it's him, boss?" someone shouted. "He looks awful young."

"It's him. It's Hyatt!" The man holding the pistol swayed at the top of the staircase. Hyatt had never seen the drunkard in his life. "Fifteen years you've been after me, Hyatt! Every time I look over my shoulder there you are, haunting me like a devil. I'll stop you this time —"

"Now just hold on a minute, mister —"

"Is your name Hyatt?"

"Yes, but —"

The pistol fired. The pop of a firecracker. Pain. Blood. The smell of acrid black smoke. Gasping for air, Hyatt flipped back his jacket, drew his pistol, aimed, and fired.

"I'm hit! I'm hit!" the man moaned.

A bullet struck the mirror on the wall beside Hyatt. Glass shattered. Screams erupted in the lobby below. Hyatt jammed the pistol under his belt and grabbed his left forearm. Searing purple pain tore through him as he turned on the landing.

"After him! After him, boys. Don't let him get away!"

Another shot splintered the wooden balustrade. Hyatt hurtled down the steps, his pursuers' feet pounding behind him. *The livery. Get to the livery.*

He raced through the lobby. A woman fainted in front of him, and he vaulted over her. He burst through the double doors. Dashed out into the chill darkness. Down an alley. Across a ditch. He could hear men running behind him. Shouting.

His head swam. The livery tilted on its side, lights swaying. The smell of the stables assaulted him, made him gag. In the doorway, the bellboy's face looked up at him, white and wide-eyed.

"You're bleeding, mister!" he cried. "What happened?"

What happened? What happened? Hyatt didn't know what happened. Couldn't think. His horse. Thank God, his horse! He wedged his foot in the stirrup. Threw one leg over the saddle. The stallion took off, hooves thundering on the hollow wood floor of the ramp. Galloped past the men. Past mercantiles. Houses. Foundries. Corrals.

Hyatt cradled his scorched and bleeding arm. He no longer heard his pursuers. He turned the horse east. Mountains. Caves. Tall pine trees. Fresh springs. Better than desert.

Yes, he would head east.

CHAPTER ONE

Holly. Ivy. Cedar wreaths. Pine swags. Hot apple cider. Cranberry trifle. Plum pudding.

Oh, yes. And mistletoe.

Fara Canaday dipped her pen into the crystal inkwell and ticked the items on her list one by one. She had planned and organized the sixth annual Christmas tea for the miners' children as carefully as she always did. Each item on the list was in order, and in two weeks the anticipated event would go off without a hitch.

Tomorrow, a fifteen-foot pine tree would be cut, brought down from the forested ranch near Pinos Altos, and erected in the front parlor of Canaday Mansion. Already, piñon logs lay in neat stacks beside the seven fireplaces that heated the large brick home. The silver candelabras had been polished, the best china washed and dried, the white linens freshly pressed. Twelve plump turkeys hung in the smokehouse, ready to be garnished and set out on silver trays. The only thing remaining was to post the invitations. The housekeeper would see to the task.

Leaning away from her writing desk, Fara kneaded her lower back with both hands. The lady's maid had the morning off, and Manuela had laced Fara's corset far too tightly. Born in the mountains of Chihuahua, Mexico, Manuela possessed a flat face, bright brown eyes, and an indomitable spirit. She approached her labors like a steam locomotive on a downhill run. She polished silver-plated bowls straight through to the brass. She dusted the features right off the Canaday family portraits. And when she laced a corset, strings broke, grommets popped out, and ribs threatened to crack.

Fara sucked a tiny breath into her compressed lungs and tugged at her collar. The ridiculous lace on the dress just in from New York threatened to choke her to death. And these silly shoes! The pointed little heels poked through the carpet. That morning they had nearly thrown her down the stairs. If it weren't for a business meeting at the brickyard, a trip to the bank, and dinner with the Wellingtons still to come,

Fara felt she would tear off the abominable gown and shoes and fling them down the coal chute. With a sigh, she tossed her pen onto the writing desk. Black inkblots spattered across the Christmas list.

"Confound it," she muttered. If only she could escape this sooty town and her ink-stained lists. She would pull on her buckskins, saddle her horse, and ride up into the hills.

"Letters," Manuela announced, barging into the library and dumping a pile of mail on the writing desk. "Invitations mostly, señorita. You'll be here all afternoon answering these."

Fara restrained the urge to remind her housekeeper to knock. To announce herself. To use all the polite manners so painstakingly covered in the manual Fara had brought from the Boston school for young ladies.

"Did you already go to the post office, then?" she asked.

"Sí, señorita. You didn't have anything you wanted to mail, did you?" Manuela eyed the large stack of invitations.

"Just these two hundred letters."

"Ai-yai-yai."

Fara let out her breath. "Manuela, please. When you're going into town, let me know.

I need a new bottle of ink, and we have to get some red ribbons —"

"Look at this packet, Farolita!" Manuela was sifting through the mail on the writing desk. "It's from California. I wonder who it could be? Do you know anyone in California?"

Fara grabbed the thick envelope. "Manuela, I asked you not to look through my mail. It's private, and you're . . . you're . . . well, you're supposed to be the household staff. It's not proper."

"And who is to say what is proper?" Manuela sniffed. "I have been with your family since I was four years old. I knew your mama before she was married. I knew your papa back when he was working in the mines. I used to change your diapers, *niñita*. I am not household *staff*. I am Manuela Perón."

"Yes, but at the school in Boston —"

"*Now* you decide to follow the rules of the school in Boston? After you have chased away all the men who want to make you a wife?"

"I'm trying to honor Papa. I know he wanted me to have a family of my own. Children. A husband."

"Pushing a man out the window will not get you a husband."

"That lamebrain had climbed up the rose trellis!"

"You broke the other man's nose with the bust of George Washington."

"You didn't hear what he had suggested."

"What about that poor fellow in church? You stuck out your foot and tripped him!"

"He had passed me a note saying he wanted us to marry and move to Cleveland, where he would buy a shoe factory with Papa's money."

"Maybe you would have liked this Cleveland. These days all you do is make your lists and go to meetings. Even the Christmas tea you run like a big project at the brickyard or the silver mine." She gave a sympathetic cluck. "What has happened to my happy Farolita? My little light?"

Through the window over her desk, Fara studied the pine-dotted Gila Mountains with their gentle slopes and rounded peaks. Outside, soft snowflakes floated downward from the slate-gray sky to the muddy street. At the Pinos Altos ranch, it would be snowing on Papa's grave.

The black-iron window mullions misted and blurred as Fara pondered the granite headstone beneath the large alligator juniper. This would be her first Christmas without her father. Though she had managed her own affairs — and many of his — for years now, she missed him. The house felt empty. The days were long. Even the prospect of the Christmas tea held little joy.

A portly Santa Claus in his long red robe and snowy beard would not appear this year. Instead, the gifts of candy canes and sugarplums would lie beneath the tree. The miners' children would ask for the jolly saint, and Fara would have to tell them he had already come — and gone away.

When had life become so difficult? Where was the fun?

In the mountains, that's where. At the old ranch house at Pinos Altos. The stables. The long, low porch. The big fireplace.

"Open the packet from California," Manuela said. "Maybe it's a Christmas present to make you smile again."

Fara broke the seal and turned the large envelope up on her lap. A stack of letters tied with twine slid out, followed by a folded note. She opened the sheet of crisp white paper and began to read.

Sacramento, California
Dear Miss Canaday:

As evidenced by the enclosed correspondence, my late father, William Hyatt, was

24

a close friend to your father, Jacob Canaday. I understand they once were gold-mining partners in a small mountain town called Pinos Altos. Perhaps you have heard of it. My father moved to California before the New Mexico silver strike of 1870 — an event that proved to be of great benefit to your family.

In compliance with my father's wishes, I am traveling to Silver City to discuss with you possible business and personal mergers. I shall arrive in New Mexico two weeks before Christmas and will depart after the start of the new year.

Cordially yours,
Aaron Hyatt

Fara crumpled the note. "Of all the pompous, arrogant, conceited, vain —"

"What is it?" Manuela asked. "What does the letter say? Who is it from?"

"Another complete stranger with the utter gall to impose himself on my hospitality at Christmastime! Another moneygrubbing attempt to get at my father's fortune! Oh, I would like to wring this one's ornery neck." Fara stood and hurled the balled letter into the fire. " 'Possible business and personal mergers,' he says! 'Our fathers

25

were close friends,' he says! As if I would give such a man the satisfaction of calling on me. Manuela, I tell you, they're all alike. They catch the faintest whiff of money, and they come wooing me with flowers and chocolates. Fawning all over me. Calling me *darling* and *dearest*. Proposing marriage left and right."

"Mrs. Ratherton next door is telling everyone you have run off seven men in the last two months."

"If Mrs. Ratherton and all her gossiping cronies would keep their snooty noses in their own affairs —"

"There is a rumor in town, Farolita, that you will shoot the next man who tries to court you."

Fara pondered this. "Well . . . not through the heart."

"Señorita!"

"If I thought even one of those men had the slightest warm feeling in his chest for me — for *me,* not my money — I'd listen to him."

"Would you?"

"I want a family. I want children." Fara's shoulders sagged. Truth to tell, she was tired of having sole responsibility for the business. Tired of meetings and schedules and lists. Sometimes . . . sometimes she ached for a gentle word, a tender touch. Even a man's kiss.

"But you've seen all those scoundrels who come calling on me!" she exploded. "You know what they're after as well as I do. Now here comes a con artist from California. Sniffing after silver. Trying to use these letters from my father to attach himself to me. *Personal merger.* Of all the ridiculous, scheming contrivances. And he's coming all the way from the West Coast. He must be scraping the bottom of the barrel to be that desperate."

"When does he arrive?"

Fara glanced at the ashes of what had been the man's letter. "Two weeks before Christmas."

"Two weeks? But that's now!"

"I'm not going to see him."

"You'll have to see him." A small smile crept over Manuela's lips. "It's *proper.*"

Fara crossed her arms. "I won't see him. Even if he calls, I won't speak to him."

"Maybe he will have a white calling card to put into the silver tray."

"I won't come down. If I have to see one more fawning suitor in the drawing room, I'll choke."

"How can you avoid him?"

"I . . . I just won't be here, that's how.

I'll go away. I'll go up to the old ranch house, Manuela. I've been wanting to visit Papa's grave. I want to see it before Christmas. So I will."

"You can't do that, *niña!* You have so much to do here. You have to plan the tea."

"Done." Fara whisked the ink-stained list from her desk. "You take care of the details, Manuela. Put those etiquette lessons I gave you into practice. Decline my dinner invitations. Call off my meetings. Turn away my callers. Give me two weeks of rest, and I promise I'll come back to Silver City in time for the children's tea."

"But the brickyard meeting this afternoon —"

"Cancel it." Excited at the sudden prospect of escape, Fara picked up her skirts and marched out of the library. "I'm going to pack my bag. Tell Johnny to saddle the sorrel."

"But you will not have any food at the ranch house, Farolita!" Manuela puffed up the steps after Fara. "And what about firewood? You will freeze! You will starve!"

"I can chop my own firewood. I'll shoot a deer."

"*Farolita!* What would your poor papa say?"

In the bedroom doorway, Fara swung

around and took the housemaid by the shoulders. "He would say, 'Good show, Filly, old girl! I taught you to chop wood, build a fire, and hunt for your food. Now, go to it!' That's what Papa would say — and you know he would."

"*Si,* you are just like him. Just as stubborn . . . impatient . . . contrary . . . headstrong —"

"Don't worry. Old Longbones will be there. He'll help me."

"That Apache? Ai-yai-yai!" Muttering to herself, Manuela went off to alert the household.

Fara began stripping away the clothes that had confined her. She tossed petticoats, skirts, and the hated corset onto the bed. Then she rooted in her cedar chest until she found the buckskins given to her by the half-breed, Old Longbones.

Often she wore the soft, buttery leather leggings under her skirts. But not so the warm moccasins and the beaded suede tunic. Now she slipped them on, reveling in the scent of wood smoke and musk that still clung to the warm garments. The cone-shaped silver ornaments that dangled on leather fringes clicked as she moved.

After unpinning her bun, Fara wove her thick hair into a long golden braid that snaked down her back to her hips. Then she turned to the gilt-framed mirror that stood in one corner. The woman who looked back from the silvered glass was no longer the gangly teenager who had first worn the buckskins. This was no half-grown child. Angles had transformed into curves. Shapely arms and long legs now warranted the modest covering of skirts and bodices.

The matrons at the Boston school for young ladies would swoon, Fara thought as she settled her favorite battered leather hat on her head. She stuffed a nightgown, a few simple dresses, her Bible, and the local newspaper into a traveling bag and left the room.

As she walked toward the carriage house, Fara took note that the snow was coming down heavily now. Cotton puffs blanketed the piñon branches. White icing trimmed rooftops. Thin ice sheeted puddles on the path.

Fara threw back her head and stared straight up at the swirling, dancing flakes. *Father God!* The prayer welled up inside her like a song. *I praise you for snow, for fresh air . . . for hope! Take me away, Lord. Away to the mountains, to the pine trees. To Papa's grave. Take me away from city streets and business meetings. Most of all, dear Lord, take me away from witless, greedy, cold-hearted suit-*

ors. *Amen and amen.*

Buoyed by the promise of freedom, Fara spread her arms wide and turned in giddy circles. Two weeks! Two weeks alone! Hallelujah!

Old Longbones dozed in the rocking chair beside the roaring fire. He and Fara had made a feast of fiery tamales and Indian fry bread, washed down with hot apple cider. They had spent long hours reminiscing about the old days when Jacob Canaday was alive and silver fever filled the air. When the ranch house bustled with prospectors and miners. When mud caked the wooden floors and men swapped tales while fiddles played the night away.

Fara was tired from the six-mile ride up the mountains to Pinos Altos, but she couldn't remember when she'd felt so good. The spicy scent of piñon wood crackling in the big fireplace filled her heart with wonderful memories. Many involved her friend Old Longbones. In the passage of years, his face had grown leathery and wrinkled, and silver threads mingled in his long black hair. But the half-breed's heart had not changed.

Wounded in an Apache attack on the Pinos Altos settlement, he had been abandoned by his Indian comrades. His blue eyes, left-handedness, and tall frame — all inherited from his fur trapper father — made Longbones suspect in the mind of his own tribe. Though an enemy to the white miners, he had been taken in by Jacob Canaday and nursed back to health. During the 1861 raid of Pinos Altos by Cochise and Mangas Coloradas, the famous Apache warriors, Longbones had stood faithful to his adopted family. Now he lived alone in the big, empty ranch house — and Fara knew she could not be in better hands.

She shut her eyes and drifted, disturbed only by the barking of her two dogs, Smoke and Fire, who had followed her horse up from Silver City. As she snuggled beneath a thick blanket in her chair, her white nightgown tucked around her toes, Fara listened as Old Longbones's half-coyote joined the yapping. Then she heard the unmistakable howl of a wolf.

She sat up straight.

Old Longbones opened one blue eye. "They are down by the log cabin of Jacob Canaday. Maybe they have found a raccoon."

Fara knew no raccoon in its right mind would come out of hiding in the middle of a blizzard like this — and so did Old Longbones. If the animal wasn't in its right mind . . . hydrophobia? Fara didn't want to lose her dogs to that dreaded disease.

"I'll go check things out," she said.

"You will get cold in that dress."

Fara glanced down at her nightgown. "I'll take my blanket."

"Better take the rifle, too, Filly."

"Yes, sir." Since her father had died, Old Longbones was the only person who called Fara by her pet name. She smiled, realizing how typical it was of the Apache not to fret too much about Jacob Canaday's daughter and her impulsive actions. He had watched her grow up. He knew she could take care of herself.

Fara tugged on her boots and wrapped the big blanket tightly around her head and shoulders, allowing the hem to trail behind her. Then she took the rifle down from the rack over the door, lifted a lantern from its hook, and stepped outside. Snowflakes flew at her in a blinding white fury. Following the barks and howls, she walked across the porch and tromped down the familiar path toward the cabin.

Jacob Canaday had built the little log house in 1837 when he was a young prospector and gold had just been discovered in Pinos Altos. Fara had been born in that cabin, and there her mama had died. After that, she and Papa had moved up to the big new ranch house. It wasn't until the silver strike in 1870 that they started spending time in Silver City, and not until '76 that they built the tall brick mansion. By then, Papa was already sick, and the business had begun to consume his only child.

Despite the chill, Fara took a deep breath of snow-filled air. The lantern lit the tumbling flakes and cast a weak light across the virgin snow. She cradled the rifle as she approached the tiny snow-shrouded house. The commotion came from the front yard, and she peered around the cabin's corner to see what sort of creature had disturbed the dogs and drawn a wolf.

"Lord have mercy!" she gasped.

It was a man. He lay prone in the snow, face up, and spread-eagled as though a giant hand had dropped him from the sky.

A pair of wolves circled him, yapping and snarling, held at bay only by the three dogs. Fara set the lantern down and cocked the rifle. Stepping into the open, she fired a single shot into the air. The animals started. The lead wolf crouched as if to spring at her. Fara moved first, leaping at the predators.

"Hai! Hai!" She waved her arms, fanning the huge blanket around in the air. The dogs went wild, barking and snapping at the wolves. Fara reloaded, fumbling in the semi-darkness. Her second shot — just over the wolves' heads — scattered them. Breathing hard, she watched their silver forms melting into the thicket of pine trees, blending with the snow, vanishing to nothing.

Tails wagging, the dogs bounded toward her. She gave each a quick pat as she strode forward to kneel at the fallen man's side. Was he dead? She cupped his face in her bare hands and turned his head. Sightless, his blue eyes stared up into the falling snow.

God rest his soul, she prayed. Fara dusted off her hands and assessed the situation. She couldn't very well leave the body out in the blizzard. The wolves would be back. Maybe she could wrap it in the blanket and roll it under the cabin porch. When the snow melted a little, she and Old Longbones could bury the poor fellow.

Shivering, Fara threw the blanket across the snow beside the body and gave the large shoulders a shove.

"Thank you kindly, ma'am, but I never touch the stuff," the corpse mumbled.

Fara let out a squawk and sat down hard. "What?"

"Six times three," he muttered.

Grabbing the lantern, she held it close to his face. The man's blue-tinged lips moved, words barely forming on his thickened tongue. "Out of my way, buzzard-breath . . . the capital of South Carolina . . ."

Fara shook her head. He was alive. Barely. Now what? She brushed the snow off the stranger's cheeks and slipped her palm under the shock of thick brown hair that lay on his forehead. His skin was cold, clammy. She lifted his big hand and felt for a pulse. Sure enough, he had one.

She sighed. The last thing she wanted to do was spend her precious holiday looking after a big galoot who didn't have sense enough to stay out of the weather. But if she left him in the snow, the cold would kill him in a couple of hours, though it would be a painless death. The man was delirious already.

Fara ran the lantern light down the stranger. *He must weigh two hundred pounds. All of it muscle.* His left arm had been clumsily bandaged. She held the light closer. He'd been wounded. Looked like a gunshot. Blood caked the white rag. She bent over and sniffed. Putrefaction. After caring for horses, dogs, and cattle all her life, she would know that odor anywhere.

Even if she tended the man, he was likely too far gone to live long. Warmed up, he'd only suffer. Why make him go through the agony? Kinder to let him go. He was a stranger . . . probably a no-gooder . . . wounded . . . maybe even wanted by the law.

By now, Old Longbones would be wondering where she was. She stood, turned, and took two steps toward the ranch house. *Be not forgetful to entertain strangers. . . . I was a stranger, and ye took me in. . . . I was sick, and ye visited me. . . . Verily I say unto you, Inasmuch as ye have done it unto one of the least of these my brethren, ye have done it unto me.*

"Confound it!" Fara stamped her foot. What a time for a bunch of Sunday school verses to come pouring into her head. She didn't want to take care of the scoundrel. She gave her tithes at church, donated her old clothes to the charity closet, and hosted the Christmas tea for the miners' children. Wasn't that enough?

Now which of these three, thinkest thou, was neighbor unto him that fell among thieves? . . . He that showed mercy on him. . . . Go, and do thou likewise.

Fara turned around and eyed the man in the snow. This was no poor innocent who had fallen among thieves — he'd been shot! And she was no Good Samaritan. She deserved her two-week rest. She had a right to some peace and quiet!

"The capital of Missouri," he muttered. "St. Louis."

"It's Jefferson City, you cabbage head!" she snarled and stalked back across the snow to his side. Letting out a hot breath, she grabbed his big shoulders again and heaved them onto the blanket. Then she hooked her fingers into his belt loops and rolled his midsection over. Finally, she picked up his booted feet and flopped them to join the rest of him.

"Filly?" Old Longbones's voice echoed down from the ranch house porch. Belying the distance, his words carried clearly down the mountainside. "Filly, you OK?"

"I'm all right, Longbones," she hollered back. "I'll be up in a few minutes. Go on back to the fire."

Now . . . where to put the lunker? Fara eyed the cabin. If she stashed him in there, she could maintain her haven in the big house. She could build a fire to warm him up, pile blankets over him, and then head back to her toasty sanctuary. Maybe Old Longbones would have a look at the man in the morning. The Apache knew effective Indian treatments for illnesses and injuries. Once the stranger was alert enough, Fara could strap him onto a horse and send him down the mountain to a Silver City doctor.

Shuddering in the freezing air, she took the loose end of the blanket and dragged her two-hundred pound load across the yard and up the cabin steps. By the time she had wedged him through the front door, she was sweating. The dogs bounded in and out of the chilly room, alternately sniffing their mistress's strange bundle and yipping at her for attention.

"Eighteen forty-seven," the man mumbled.

"It's 1880," Fara said, hanging the lantern on the wall nail. "It's almost Christmas, and I was hoping for a little peace and quiet. Instead, I've got you. And you stink."

"Pink lemonade," the man said.

"Stink, not pink!" Fara threw open the blanket and drew in a breath. Well, now. Bathed in the golden lamplight, the man didn't look half bad. He was so big he filled up half the little room, his shoulders broad and his legs long and lean. He had big hands and thick, muscular arms. If he hadn't been such a healthy specimen, he probably wouldn't have lasted as long as he had.

Beneath his black, unshaven whiskers, his face was square-jawed and chiseled into rugged angles and planes. He had a straight nose, thick hair, and eyes the blue of a New

39

Mexico summer sky. His lips were firm, but they were about as blue as his eyes, and that was all the attention Fara decided to give them. After all, the man was clearly a bad apple.

"So, who shot you?" she asked as she walked over to the woodstove. "You sure have on some fancy duds there. Stole 'em, I bet. Was that who plugged you? Some fellow you robbed?"

"Corn on the cob," he mumbled.

Fara opened the stove's firebox, draft regulator, and all the dampers. Then she stoked the box with split wood and struck a match. Good thing the apple pickers and sheep shearers still used the cabin in the summer and fall. It wouldn't take long to make the place habitable, and then she could get back to her fireside chair.

As the wood crackled into flame, Fara checked the rolled sleeping pallets stacked along one wall. When she was a little girl, this room had held a single big bed for her papa and a little trundle for his only child. Their dining table still stood near the stove, and a ladder led up to the loft. Fara ran her hand over the smooth wood of the tabletop. Papa hadn't been the greatest cook, but they'd managed to enjoy many a wonderful meal in this cabin. Now she had a chef and china and a table made of fine cherry wood. She would trade them all to have Papa back.

"Sphinx," the wounded man said, his half-frozen tongue garbling the word. "Finx . . . Phoenix."

Fara studied him. Eyes closed now, he was stirring a little. Just as she'd suspected. Warm him up, and he'd start to feel the pain in his arm. His feet and fingers would thaw, and those would hurt, too. Then he'd want water . . . food . . . a chamber pot.

"I'm not going to take care of *that* for you," she said, setting her hands on her hips. "I reckon I've done my part as a good Christian should. I've done more than my fair share, to tell you the truth. I'll let you stay here till you're warm and rational, and then you can head back to Phoenix or wherever you came from. I brought you in out of the snow, but I don't have to know who you are . . . or learn anything about you . . . or care what becomes of you. You're not my responsibility, you hear?"

"Thirty-eight plus . . . sixteen . . ."

Fara sighed. "This is not a schoolroom," she said, bending over and shaking the stranger's solid shoulder. "Wake up, sir. Wake up. You're in Pinos Altos. This is New Mexico."

41

He grimaced in pain and cupped a hand over his wounded arm. Fara fought the sympathy that tugged at her heart. Her papa had taught her a man didn't often get shot at unless he was up to some shenanigans. This fellow in his fine leather coat and gray wool trousers looked exactly the part of a scalawag — a confidence man, a gambler, a saloon keeper — or worse.

"I'm going up to get you some blankets," she said, shaking him again. "Blankets. So you'll be warmer."

He lay unmoving on the floor, so she grabbed the lantern and headed for the ladder to the loft. Many long winter days, the loft had been her childhood hiding place. She had played for hours with her cornhusk dolls. In the late afternoon sunlight, she loved to read her mother's copy of *The Pilgrim's Progress*. Over and over, she read favorite passages until she knew many of them by heart. The pilgrim's stopping places — the Slough of Despond, Doubting Castle, Vanity Fair — were as familiar to her as Pinos Altos and Silver City. When the pilgrim stood at the foot of Christ's cross and his heavy burden dropped from his shoulders, Fara always wept with joy. Such blessed relief. Such peace.

In the attic, she lifted the lid of the old

storage trunk. Quilts lay stacked to the brim, their bright colors muted in the lamplight. Fara tucked several under her arm. She would drape the blankets over her own frozen pilgrim and leave him to seek his peace. As she stepped onto the top rung, she looked down.

Blue eyes wide, he was sitting straight up, staring at her. Wounded arm cradled, he breathed hard. "You . . ." he said, his voice husky. "You're . . . am I . . . am I . . . dead?"

Fara's heart softened. "No, sir."

"But . . . but . . . you're an angel. Aren't you?"

CHAPTER TWO

"I'm no angel," the ethereal creature said as she descended from the ceiling in a wash of pale amber light. Hyatt blinked. He could have sworn she had a halo. A gown of pure white drifted to her feet, its hem swaying and fluttering in the warm air. Spun gold hair hung around her shoulders, thick and wavy like a costly cape. He squinted, straining to see if wings grew out of her shoulder blades. Wait a minute, weren't all the angels in the Bible men? Gabriel . . . Michael . . .

But this creature! She was so beautiful. Translucent. Celestial. Now she hovered over him, draping him in her warm glow. Her pale hands moved across his icy skin. Long lashes framed her dark eyes. He longed to speak to her. There were so many questions. But his tongue was thick and his brain felt foggy.

"Angel . . . ," he managed.

"I told you — I'm not an angel. Now lie down before you keel over."

He frowned as the creature pushed his shoulders onto the soft surface. If not an angel then . . . he glanced up, suddenly alarmed. Satan was known as the father of lies. Deceit was his primary weapon. Maybe this angel of light was really a demon of the darkness! Had Hyatt died and gone to . . . to . . .

"I believe in Jesus Christ," he muttered.

"Sure you do. And you think St. Louis is the capital of Missouri." The creature smiled — a smile so entrancing, so stunning that Hyatt's heartbeat sped up, and his skin actually began to thaw. "Comfortable?"

He tried to nod, but his neck was so stiff it wouldn't move. "Am I . . . am I dead?"

"Not yet, fella, but if I hadn't come along, you'd be wolf meat. What did you do to your arm?"

"Arm?" Was that the source of the pain that raged like wildfire through him? He tried to look at his arm, but the creature had bundled him to the chin. "Where? Where am I? Pinks . . . Phoenix?"

"New Mexico. Pinos Altos, to be exact."

New Mexico. That's where he'd been headed days ago. Before Phoenix. Before the hotel shooting. Snatches of memory drifted across his mind like wisps of smoke. Riding a narrow trail through the trees. Sleeping in a cave. Drinking water from a stream. Moving east toward Silver City and the woman . . . daughter of his father's friend. Maybe a man his own father had regarded so highly could help him now. Was Silver City far? How would he travel without his horse?

"Leg," he said. "Horse."

"You didn't have a horse, buckaroo," the angel said. "When I found you, you were on foot . . . or, more exactly, you were on your backside."

"My horse . . . leg broke."

At that her face softened. "I'm sorry. Was it a good horse?"

He managed a nod.

"Well, don't trouble yourself too much. You'd better concentrate on that arm of yours. Looks septic to me. What happened?"

"Finx."

"Phoenix?" She shrugged. "You've come a long way. Look, I'd put you up on the bed there, but I'm just about done in. You're a deadweight. So I'm going to leave you right here on the floor to rest. I've stoked up the stove and bundled you in blankets. Get some sleep now, and I'll check on you in the morning."

The angel slowly rose above him, her long white gown shimmering in the light. As she turned to go, he worked a hand out from under the quilts and clutched at her hem.

"Angel," he murmured.

When she turned, her hair billowed out in a golden cloud around her face. A halo. She had denied it, but Hyatt knew the truth. God had sent him an angel.

"Angel . . . thank you," he whispered.

She tugged her hem from his fingers. "Save your breath. You just get yourself well enough to get off my property, and that'll make the both of us a lot happier."

As the creature drifted away, Hyatt turned the vision over in his mind. She looked like an angel. She had the touch of an angel. She had the melodious voice of an angel. But the words she spoke put him in mind of a spitfire. What had God wrought?

Fara yawned and rolled over on the warm featherbed. The pink light of dawn glowed on the flowered wallpaper across the room. It was too early to wake up on her first day of freedom. Unlike Old Longbones, whose confidence in God's protection had given him the peace of mind to doze straight through her adventures, Fara had hardly slept all night. Her mind had churned with thoughts of the missed meeting at the brickyard, the canceled dinner invitations with clients, the details of the Christmas tea. And that *man*.

The wounded stranger had haunted her dreams with his feverish blue eyes. Why had he ridden all the way from Phoenix? How had he ended up at the Canaday ranch? Should she have tried to save him? What if he died? What if he were already dead?

Fara sat up in bed. She should go down and check on him. Maybe the fire in the stove had gone out. Maybe she had forgotten to bolt the door, and the wolves had returned. What if he had wandered away in his delirium?

Never mind about him, Fara. Relax. This is your holiday. You deserve a rest.

Yes, that was true. If anyone had earned the right to a few days of peace and quiet, it was Fara Canaday. Listening to the voice inside her head, she picked up the newspaper she had brought from Silver City. She tucked a second pillow under her head and stared sleepily at the tiny printed text. Her Christmas tea was the talk of the town — as always.

Miss Fara Canaday, one of Silver City's

finest citizens, once again brings the joy of the season to our society. The annual Christmas Tea for the children of local silver miners will take place on December 24 at four o'clock in the afternoon at the Canaday Mansion.

"We're inviting the children of two hundred families," Miss Canaday said. In hosting this delightful event, she will be joined by the matrons of Silver City's most upstanding families. Mayor Douglas lauded Miss Canaday's generosity. "In the tradition of her beloved father, Jacob Canaday . . .

Fara let her eyes drift shut. Papa had always gotten such a chuckle out of his role as a leading member of Silver City's high society. He remembered well his days as a poor prospector with no education and little more to call his own than a mule and a pickax. Like her father, Fara had learned to use the relationships with the wealthy to further the Canaday family businesses. But she preferred the company of her horses.

Remembering the sadness in the stranger's blue eyes as he had spoken of his horse, Fara felt concern prickle her awake again. Confound it, she wasn't going to think about him! She was going to relax.

After the sun came up and she ate a good breakfast, she would stroll down to the cabin and check on the man. Until then, the time was hers. She glanced again at the newspaper.

PROMINENT PHOENIX CITIZEN STILL CRITICAL AFTER GUN BATTLE

Mr. James Copperton, owner of five Phoenix business establishments, was gunned down late on the evening of December 4. A former associate by the name of Robert Hyatt stands accused in the incident. Copperton remains in grave condition with a bullet wound to the upper right shoulder. Also injured in the gun battle, Hyatt escaped and was last spotted riding east from Phoenix.

"He's been trailing me for years," Copperton said. "We had a falling out some time ago, and he swore revenge." Copperton, who maintains a four-man bodyguard at all times, said he had been expecting the attack. "I always keep a watch on the hotels around Phoenix. When I heard that Hyatt had checked into the Saguaro, I knew the time had come. I was ready for him, but he's a sharpshooter."

Hyatt, who is wanted for train robbery in Kansas and horse rustling in Texas, is known as a gunslinger. He stands six-foot-three and weighs two hundred pounds. He has brown hair, blue eyes, and should be considered armed and desperate. Injured in the left forearm, he may be dangerous. Anyone with information on Hyatt should contact the sheriff.

Fara swallowed and read the article a second time. Then she sat up and looked out the window toward the little cabin. Six-three. Two hundred pounds. Blue eyes. Brown hair. Wounded in the left forearm. Phoenix. She tried to make herself breathe. A wanted gunslinger was lying in Papa's cabin!

Throwing back the covers, she slid out of bed onto the cold pine floor. She quickly pulled on her buckskin leggings and warmest flannel skirt, knowing she would need all the protection she could get for a ride into Pinos Altos in all the snow. After buttoning on a blouse and jacket and pinning up her hair, Fara headed down the stairs.

The scent of frying venison wafted over her.

"You slept a long time, Filly," Old Longbones said. He gave her a snaggletoothed grin. "Look, I have your breakfast ready. Venison steak. Eggs. Oatmeal."

"I'm going to have to ride down to Pinos Altos," she said. "It's an urgent matter, Old Longbones. Breakfast will have to wait."

"*You* will have to wait." He gestured to the window. "Still snowing. No trail."

Fara bit her lower lip. She had to get to the sheriff before the man escaped . . . or died. Maybe he was dead already. In some ways, that would be a relief. Then she wouldn't have to fool with the situation.

"Sit down, Filly," Old Longbones said. "I will fill your plate."

"No, really. I can't. Not right now." Should she tell him? What if her old friend wanted to go down to the cabin? She couldn't put him in any danger. *Armed and desperate,* the article had said. In her hurry to get back to the warmth of the ranch house, she had neglected to check the man for weapons. As for his level of desperation, only time would tell.

"What's the matter, Filly? You're usually so hungry in the morning — just like your papa. The two of you could —"

"There's a man," she blurted out. "I found him last night in the snow. You remember the dogs barking?"

"When I called down, you told me you were all right."

"It was nothing. This fellow was lying out by the cabin. Wounded. But now I know he's a desperado, Old Longbones. He's wanted in three states. I have to get to the sheriff."

"A desperado? He told you this?"

"I read about him this morning in the Silver City newspaper I brought with me. He's a train robber."

The Indian let out a long, low whistle. Fara knew he wouldn't be too troubled by a man who robbed trains — those long black snakes, he called them. Apaches rarely spoke of snakes, creatures they feared and hated. When they mentioned the reptiles, they used only mystical terms, as though serpents were unfathomable spirits from another world. In Old Longbones's mind, trains fell into the same category.

"He's a horse rustler, too," Fara said. She knew that to an Apache, horse thievery was a different matter altogether from train robbery. Rustling was an offense that deserved the most severe punishment.

"What man did he steal horses from?"

Old Longbones asked.

"I don't know. But I do know he hunted down and shot a prominent citizen in Phoenix. The poor gentleman is near death at this very minute."

"Filly, are you sure this desperado in the newspaper is the same man you found in the snow last night?"

"Absolutely. It's Hyatt, all right. I dragged him into Papa's cabin. He's lying down there half frozen and sick to death with a putrefied gunshot wound."

"Putrefied?" Old Longbones looked up from the skillet. "Is it infection — or gangrene? I had better check him."

"But you don't understand. He's a terrible man. He might harm you."

"Filly." The Apache gave her a long look. "Once I was the enemy of your people. My friends and I raided the White Eyes' towns and attacked your settlements. Like that desperado in your papa's cabin, we stole guns and horses. Sometimes, Filly, we killed. But in my time of greatest need — when I lay wounded, abandoned by my friends, and near death — Jacob Canaday took me in."

"I know the story, Longbones. But this is very different."

"It was not easy for your papa to do this

54

thing." The old Apache went on speaking as if he hadn't heard her. "The White Eyes of Pinos Altos were very unhappy with Jacob Canaday. It was a great risk. For all he knew, when I came back to health, I might kill him . . . and his little golden-haired daughter. But Jacob Canaday always followed the teachings of that Book."

He pointed to the well-worn Bible on the mantel. "In the Bible there is a command we Apaches have never understood," he said. " 'Love your enemies.' That is not our way. To us it seems foolishness and weakness. But Jacob Canaday showed me the great strength of those who can follow that command. Jacob taught me about God's love by loving me enough to take such a risk. Because of the love of Jacob Canaday and his God, I learned to accept the White Eyes as my brother. And I learned to love the Son of God as my savior — the one who freed me from the consequence of my many wrongs. Now tell me, Filly, shall we let that desperado with his putrefied wound go to his death? Or shall we love our enemy?"

Fara averted her eyes. She had been brought up reading the Bible while nestled in her papa's lap. Many times his gentle voice had spoken that command: *Love your enemies.* She had always believed it — in the abstract. It had come to mean tolerating her nosy neighbors or inviting the owner of the competing brickworks to her Fourth of July picnic. But to really put herself out for someone else? someone who might harm her?

"Old Longbones," she said softly, "I hear your wise words. But if this Hyatt fellow were to hurt you —"

"He told you his name was Hyatt?" The Apache set the skillet away from the fire and picked up his leather coat. "I am surprised a wanted desperado would tell you his true name."

"He didn't, but —"

"Then how can you be sure? Come on, Filly. We will examine this wounded man of yours."

Before Fara could press her argument further, Old Longbones had placed a pot of hot oatmeal into her arms. He shrugged on his coat, grabbed the steaming skillet of eggs and venison, and headed out the door. "Maybe some warm food in his stomach will revive our desperado," he called over his shoulder.

Hugging the oatmeal, Fara stumbled behind Old Longbones through the foot-deep snow. Almost blinded by swirling flakes, she could barely make out the Apache, who was scuttling along as spryly as any teenager. It did her heart good to see her friend so animated. From the time Fara and her father had moved down to Silver City, Old Longbones seemed to wither before their eyes. When Jacob Canaday died, the Indian's mourning had been as intense as Fara's.

"Where are the horses the desperado rustled?" Old Longbones asked as he stepped onto the porch of the old cabin and stomped the snow off his moccasins. "Did he bring them into the mountains? Do they have shelter?"

"He was on foot. He told me his horse had snapped a leg."

"That is bad." Old Longbones winced as he pushed open the door and called out, "Are you still alive, desperado?"

Fara swallowed before stepping inside. Memories of the stranger's blue eyes had disturbed her all night. In spite of his ramblings, she had sensed his strength — a strength that fascinated her. Few of the men who courted her spent their time out of doors. They loved ledgers and lists and money — Fara's money. But Hyatt seemed different. Intriguingly different.

Telling herself not to be silly, she slipped

into the small room. The man lay on the floor, unmoving. At the sight of his still form, her heart constricted in fear. She set down the oatmeal and fell to her knees.

"Sir? Are you all right?"

She laid a hand on his hot forehead, and his blue eyes slid open. "Angel," he said. "You came back."

She glanced at Old Longbones. "He's delirious."

"Maybe . . . maybe not." The Indian frowned and crouched beside her. "You are still with us, White Eyes, but maybe not for long. Do you feel pain?"

"My arm," the man grunted.

"Will you let me look at it?"

Hyatt nodded, and Old Longbones directed Fara to stoke the fire in the stove. Thankful to escape, she hurried across the room. Why did the sight of the stranger's bright eyes double the tempo of her pulse? Why had the thought of his death suddenly terrified her? He was a gunslinger — the worst sort of human being. One whiff of her gold and silver fortunes would elicit his most despicable traits. Greed. Selfishness. Ruthlessness. Treachery.

"Filly," Old Longbones called, "I will need your help now."

She shut her eyes. So much for lying

around the ranch house reading books and relaxing by the fire. She was going to have to participate. She was going to have to reach beyond herself and touch this man's life. Letting out a deep breath, she lifted up a prayer. *Father God, I confess I don't want to do this. I don't want to be around this disturbing man. Give me strength.*

"We need to move our friend onto the bed," the Apache said as Fara approached. "Then we will have to work some strong medicine. What is your name, White Eyes? Where are you from?"

Fara stiffened. *Don't let him be the Phoenix gunslinger, Lord. If he's anybody else, I can do this. But don't let him be Hyatt.*

"My name's Hyatt."

Old Longbones glanced at Fara. She shook her head. "Let me take him down to Pinos Altos," she whispered. "The sheriff can handle him."

"No, Filly. God has given this man to us." He placed a gnarled hand on the man's brow. "Mr. Hyatt, we are going to take care of you. Me and this . . . this angel."

Fara rolled her eyes as Old Longbones bent over Hyatt. She had never been angelic in her life — and she wasn't about to start now. There was nothing for it but to slip her arm around those big shoulders and begin to heave. Hyatt did his best to help, coming to his knees and staggering to his feet.

Leaning heavily against Fara, he lurched toward the narrow bed beside the stove. As she grunted under his weight, she wondered how long it had been since she'd allowed any human to come this close. Even though the man smelled of his illness and his many days' travel, he was warm and solid. His big hand tightened on her shoulder.

"Angel," he murmured.

"My name is —" She stopped herself, realizing the penalty for revealing her true identity to such a man. "I'm Filly."

He looked into her eyes as she lowered him onto the bed. "Filly. That's like . . . like a horse."

"Papa gave me the name. He said I was too feisty and high-spirited for my own good." She drew the blankets up to his chest. "He thought about calling me Mule."

Hyatt's face broke into a grin. "Stubborn, are you?"

"Just don't push me, Mr. Hyatt."

"Ready, Filly?" Old Longbones asked. With a pair of tongs, he carried a glowing ember from the stove. "You help me hold him still."

"Whoa there," Hyatt said, elbowing up.

"What are you planning to do with that coal?"

"You have a gunshot wound in your arm, Mr. Hyatt," Longbones explained. "The bullet went through, but the powder burned your skin, and the wound has become infected. I think some of the flesh may even be dead. You know the meaning of dead flesh? Gangrene. If you want to live, we must burn away the sickness in your arm. Then God will begin to heal it."

Hyatt clenched his jaw and nodded. "All right. Do your work."

Fara could hardly believe a low-down horse thief would submit so willingly to the ministrations of an Indian. But Hyatt drew his injured arm from under the covers and laid it across his chest. Not wanting to witness the terrible burning, Fara looked up into the desperado's eyes. *Help me, Angel,* they seemed to plead. She hesitated for a moment, then she took both his hands in hers.

"I can't carry a tune in a bucket, Mr. Hyatt," she said softly. "But you need distracting." She kept her focus on his and began to sing:

"When peace like a river attendeth my
    soul;

61

when sorrows like sea billows roll;
whatever my lot, thou hast taught me
    to say —"

"It is well," Hyatt ground out as the red-hot ember seared his festering wound. "It is well with my soul."

Surprised the gunslinger knew the words, Fara continued to sing. "It is well."

"With my soul," he forced the words.

"It is well . . . with my soul. It is well, it is well with my soul."

The cabin filled with the stench of charred hair and scorched skin, but Hyatt barely winced. Instead, he gripped Fara's hands with a force that stopped her blood and made her fingertips throb. Beads of perspiration popped out on his forehead and thick neck. The blue in his eyes grew brighter and hotter as he stared at her.

"Angel," he said in a choked voice.

"I'm here," she murmured. "I'm with you."

When she thought the burning could not go on any longer, Old Longbones rose. "Enough," he said. "There will be a scar, Mr. Hyatt. Perhaps your hand will move stiffly in the years to come. But if God wills it, you will live. Now I will go and search for nopal."

"Let me go," Fara said. "You shouldn't be out in the blizzard."

The Apache dismissed her with a wave of his brown hand. "I know where the nopal grows, Filly. I can find it even under the snow. You stay here and feed this man some breakfast."

"But Longbones —"

"And wash him, too. He stinks."

The Apache shut the door behind him, and Fara could hear him moving across the porch. Glancing at Hyatt, she saw he had finally shut his eyes and was resting again. But when she tried to detach her hands, he tightened his grip.

"Don't go, Angel."

"I told you I'm no angel. I'm a headstrong, stubborn —"

"You're an angel." His lids slid open, and his eyes found hers. "You ran off the wolves. You hauled me out of the snow. You took me into your cabin. You brought the old Indian to heal me. I owe you my life."

For half a second, she was drawn into the music of his words. All her adult life, she had longed to hear a man speak to her with such sincerity, tenderness, warmth. And then she remembered Hyatt was a con man. A desperado. A gunslinger.

"You sure are a smooth talker," she said,

pulling away. "But I ought to warn you that a silver tongue won't get you far with me. I respect a man who speaks straight and tells the truth."

"I am telling the truth," he said. "I'm grateful to you. You saved my life."

"And you twisted mine up in knots. It's almost Christmas, and I've been looking forward to a few days of rest. Now you're here, and Old Longbones is ordering me to give you breakfast."

"And a bath."

"Not a chance." Flushing, she walked over to the stove. The very idea of touching him again flustered her. Maybe the Apache would take it upon himself to tend the wounded man. He needed something to do, and this would fill the bill nicely. But could she trust the gunslinger not to harm the old man?

Fara filled a plate with eggs and venison. Then she ladled a large dollop of oatmeal into a bowl. She was as hungry as an empty post hole, but she didn't like the idea of eating with Hyatt. It smacked of acceptance. She wanted him to understand that — as a good Christian — she would see to his welfare. But she would never consider him an equal. She would tolerate him, but she would never like him.

"Here you go," she said, holding out the plate.

He eyed the steaming eggs. "They smell good."

"Better than you."

He smiled. "I think I can manage the eggs, but I won't be able to cut the steak."

"All right, I'll do it." Fara sat on a rickety stool near the bed. "But just this once."

She sliced off a chunk of steak, speared it with the fork, and placed it in his mouth. He let out a deep breath and began to chew. "You know how long it's been since I ate a hot meal?"

"Since Phoenix, I reckon."

His brow narrowed. "How did you know I'd been in Phoenix?"

Fara's blood chilled. She mustn't let Hyatt know she was aware of his crimes. It would put her — and Old Longbones — in grave danger. All the same, she wasn't about to let him off the hook. He was a criminal, and he had committed a heinous crime. Never let it be said that Fara Canaday would let a villain get away easy.

"You kept muttering about Phoenix," she said. "Last night."

"What did I say?" He had stopped chewing. "Did I talk about the shooting?"

"Nope." She popped another bite of steak

into his mouth. "So, who pegged you?"

He shook his head. "Don't know. Can't remember his name."

Sure, Fara thought. *You'd only been tracking that poor Mr. Copperton for years.* "Seems strange that a man you didn't know would take it upon himself to shoot you."

Hyatt leaned back on his pillow, eyes shut and brow furrowed. "It happened so fast," he said. "I turned on the staircase landing, and there he was. He . . . he was aiming to kill."

"Lucky for you he missed. Did you shoot back?" She waited, wondering if he would tell the truth.

"I shot at him," Hyatt said. "He hollered out he was hit. But his men came after me."

"So you ran?"

The blue eyes snapped open. "Wouldn't you?"

"Depends. I'm not walking in your shoes. Maybe you had some kind of a history with the fellow. Maybe you held something against him that needed settling. In a case like that, only a yellowbelly would run."

"A yellowbelly?" Hyatt's eyes crackled with blue flame, and his good hand snaked out and grabbed her by the wrist. "I'm no coward. I never saw that man in my life. I was ambushed."

She leaned close and jabbed a forefinger into his chest. "You swapped lead with him, buckaroo. Then you took off like a scorpion had crawled down your neck. Doesn't sound to me like you've got enough guts to hang on a fence. And you're a sinner besides."

"Now listen here, lady." He elbowed up until they were nose-to-nose. "I'll have you know I'm a Christian man —"

"Trying to get yourself out of trouble by taffying up the Lord?"

"I'm as straight as a —"

"You're so crooked —"

"I got the nopal." Old Longbones stepped into the cabin carrying an armful of the flat, fleshy stems of the prickly pear cactus. At the sight of the man and woman, he stopped, his brown eyes darting back and forth. "Filly?"

She straightened, clutching the plate of now-cold eggs. "You found the nopal."

"Yes. But I see you have already brought color to our patient's cheeks. And a sparkle to his eyes."

CHAPTER THREE

Hyatt knew the woman didn't trust him. He studied her busily heating water and fussing with the Indian. She wasn't an angel, she informed the old man, and she didn't take kindly to a stranger pinning such labels on her. Especially a stranger who had showed up in the middle of the night with a gunshot wound. The Indian didn't pay her much heed, just went about his work on the prickly pear stems.

Hyatt felt as though the devil himself had been gnawing on his arm. His wound burned with a pain so intense he could hardly concentrate. Yet for some reason, the woman's distrust of him was a greater torment. He could understand her doubts about the character of a man with a bullet hole through his arm. But to call *him* — Aaron Hyatt, owner of one of the most profitable gold mines in California, builder of two mercantiles, a hotel, a grocery, and a church, and a good bronc buster to boot — a coward . . . and crooked?

He might not have minded the insults if she'd been a creature of little brain and less beauty. But this woman — this Filly — was intriguing. On the one hand, she clearly was poor. She lived in a run-down cabin, and she dressed like the prospector's daughter she probably was. That flannel skirt obviously had been on horseback more than once, and Hyatt had glimpsed the buckskin leggings at her ankles. The only friend she seemed to have was the Indian. Not that the old man was bad company, but he certainly wasn't the high society type who consorted with Hyatt's usual female acquaintances.

On the other hand, Filly was a dazzler. Her thick gold hair gleamed in the early morning light, and those brown eyes of hers put Hyatt in mind of sweet blackstrap molasses. More than her fine figure and slender waist, her spunky spirit beckoned him. Had a woman ever stood up to him the way this Filly had, poking him in the chest, calling him names, putting him in his place? Not a one. This golden angel had him downright mesmerized.

He came to a decision. While he was here

in her cabin, he would do more than tend his arm and get back on his feet. He would convince this woman of his kind, generous, intelligent — and equally stubborn — nature. Maybe he'd even win a kiss for his trouble.

"I won't wash him!" Filly announced, setting her hands on her hips. "It's not proper."

"Just wash his face and that arm, Filly," the Indian said. "He can take care of the rest himself. You start with the arm, and then I can put on the nopal."

Jaw clenched, she turned those big brown eyes on Hyatt. "I don't suppose you're well enough to wash your own arm, are you?"

He held back a smile. "I'm feeling a mite poorly, Miss Filly," he said. "I'd be much obliged if you could do it."

Pursing her lips, she heaved the bowl of steaming water over to the stool and knelt beside it. "Hold out your arm, Mr. Hyatt," she said, dipping a clean rag into the water. "I doubt this will hurt any more than what Old Longbones did to you a few minutes ago."

As she pushed up his sleeve and began trickling warm water over his splotchy skin, Hyatt took a closer look at her face. Long dark lashes framed her eyes. A pair of perfect eyebrows arched beneath the fringe of soft golden bangs she wore. When she cradled his arm to dab the wound with clean water, a look of concern flashed across her brow.

"Don't cry out or jump now," she said.

"I reckon I've broken more bones than you ever knew a man had. You won't hurt me, Miss Filly."

She looked at him, her brown eyes serious. "How'd you break those bones? Jumping off trains?"

Hyatt scowled. *Trains?* What on earth made her think he'd want to jump off a train?

"Horses," he said.

She nodded. "I guess keeping a remuda just ahead of the law could be dangerous work."

"What? Why, I never stole a horse in my life," he exclaimed, propping himself up on his good elbow. "I may have pulled a few wild tricks in my younger days — and I came out the worse for my foolishness. But I'm a breeder now. And I enjoy breaking a high-strung stallion . . . or a filly."

Ignoring the bait, she dropped the rag into the pot of water. "A breeder, are you? Then why don't you tell me what a bitting rig does?"

"It teaches a horse to flex at the poll . . . that's the top of his head just back of his ears."

"I know where the poll is." She leaned closer. "What's a hackamore?"

"A bitless bridle."

"Mecate?"

"A hackamore lead rope. You aren't going to trip me up, Miss Filly. I've been breaking horses since I was a colt myself." He studied her face, the elegant tilt to her nose, the fine paleness of her skin. "How do *you* know so much about horses?"

She shrugged and called over her shoulder. "Old Longbones, I've washed him. He's all yours."

"You fed him, too?"

"She's been talking too much to feed me," Hyatt said. "Chatty little creature you've got on your hands, sir. Would you be the one who taught her about horses?"

"No." The Indian took Filly's place on the stool. Hyatt tried to hide his grin as she strode toward the door to dump the wash water. For some reason, he was enjoying their give-and-take immensely.

"Filly's father taught her to ride," the Indian said. "He was a good man."

"Was?"

"He has been dead almost a year. Filly

covers her sorrow with much talk and busyness. But her pain is great. Her father was the joy of her life."

Hyatt let his focus follow the young woman as she returned to the stove to pour more hot water into the bowl. Though Filly was clearly his opposite in education and social standing, he felt her sadness as though it were his own. His father's death had been a hard blow, and one he would not easily set aside. He had loved, admired, and learned so much from the man. Respect for his father had driven Hyatt from California on this ill-fated journey. He knew the elegant Fara Canaday awaited him in Silver City, and having come this far, he would complete his dreaded mission. But he already regretted the moment he would leave the presence of the fiery Miss Filly.

"The nopal will bring you healing," Old Longbones said as he laid the fleshy disk of split cactus stem on Hyatt's wound. "We Apaches have used the prickly pear for many years. It is good medicine."

"And you're a good man to take such care of a stranger."

"Filly's father once cared for me when I lay near death. His love brought more than healing to my body. It was healing to my empty heart. Perhaps here you will find such healing."

"I thank you, sir, but I don't believe my heart is empty."

The old man grunted. "Something drove you into the mountains with a bullet hole through your arm. Were you not following your heart?"

Hyatt pondered the Indian's question. "Not long ago, my father died," he answered in a low voice. "Before his death, he asked me to travel here. He wanted me to find someone."

"Was that someone God?"

Hyatt shook his head. Years ago, he had surrendered his life to Christ, and since then he had tried to walk the straight and narrow. He was honest and truthful and fair. Though he didn't associate with the outcasts of society, he gave charity to the poor and brought tithes to his church to be used in ministering to the needy.

"I found God a long time ago," Hyatt said.

"Then your heart is not empty. And you have opened it to love all people."

"Well, I . . . I do my best."

"And you have found the love of a godly woman to be your wife?"

"No, I can't say as I have. To tell you the

truth, I don't particularly want to get married —"

"Empty." The old man laid his hand on Hyatt's chest. "Our love of God is shown through our love for all people. And a wife? 'Whoso findeth a wife findeth a good thing, and obtaineth favour of the Lord.' "

"Preaching again, Longbones?" Filly bent over and softly kissed the Indian's leathery cheek. "You'll have to forgive him, Mr. Hyatt. I'm afraid my friend can't hold in the joy of his salvation the way most of us do."

"It doesn't bother me," Hyatt said. In fact, the Indian's words made more sense than anything he'd heard in a long time. If a man loved God — really loved him — maybe that man ought to reach out beyond what was comfortable.

Hyatt surveyed his Spartan surroundings. He had been brought up in the lap of luxury. His father's gold fortunes had built brick mansions and bought gilt-framed mirrors, goose-down bedding, and fireplace mantels that soared to fifteen-foot ceilings. Did that wealth make Hyatt any greater in God's eyes than the old Indian and the young woman who lived in this humble cabin?

"Come on, Old Longbones," Filly was saying. "You've tormented this poor tumbleweed enough. Let's go get ourselves some breakfast before we keel over."

"Wait —" Hyatt called out. "You two don't live here?"

"There's another house," the Indian said. "Up the trail."

As they started again for the door, Hyatt felt a pang in his gut. The angel would leave. He'd be alone. Then his arm would heal, and he would go away. For good.

"Miss Filly," he said. "You forgot to wash my face."

She crossed her arms and tilted her head to one side. "There's hot water on the stool, Mr. Hyatt. You'll manage."

Hyatt swallowed, thinking hard. He wasn't ready to let her go. Not just yet. He glanced at the Indian. The old man lifted a hand, touched his chin, and winked.

Hyatt smiled. "But Miss Filly," he said. "I'm in terrible need of a shave."

Fara pulled her father's watch from her skirt pocket and checked the time. Almost four. Why had she ever agreed to shave that renegade's chin this afternoon? And why had she looked at her watch every fifteen minutes — all through breakfast, washing dishes, chopping firewood, fixing lunch, baking, and playing checkers? She didn't want to shave Hyatt, that's why. She was dreading the moment worse than a trip to Dr. Potter, the tooth extractor.

"Time to go yet?" Old Longbones said.

Fara jumped and jerked the watch from her pocket again. As the long chain dangled to her lap, she looked up sheepishly. "I just checked the time, didn't I?"

The Apache nodded as he jumped his king over three of her men. "You have not been paying attention, Filly. Usually, we fight to the death. But today . . ." He spread his hands over the stack of red checkers he had accumulated.

"I'm going to shave his chin and get it over with," she announced, scooting back from the table. "There's nothing worse than a job you don't want to do just hanging over your head. Better to tackle it."

"Take the bull by the horns," Old Longbones said.

"That's right."

"Especially when the bull has a very strong chin and very blue eyes."

Fara clamped her mouth shut and stared at the Indian. Despite herself, she could feel the heat rising in her cheeks. She didn't find anything attractive in that horse rustler! That train robber! That would-be assassin! How could Old Longbones think otherwise?

77

"Go on, Filly," he said. "Maybe after you clean him up, he won't disgust you so."

"I doubt that," she said, lifting her chin. But the release she felt that it was *finally* time to go down to the cabin sent her striding across the room for her coat. "I'd better change the nopal," she added. "And I'll take him something to eat. Maybe he'd enjoy some of that bread I baked this afternoon. I wonder if he likes honey. The sugar would do him good, you know. I'll take this jam, too, just in case he prefers it. Did you know he told me the answer to every question I asked him about breaking horses? For being such a villain, he does have some intelligence. I've got Papa's best razor in this bag. You don't suppose it would be wrong to use it on him, do you?"

Old Longbones was smiling. "Did you put in the soap?"

"Yes, I thought a thick lather would help. I've never shaved any man but Papa, and I —" She stopped in the middle of the kitchen floor. "He wouldn't use that razor against me, would he?"

"If he tried, would you let him succeed, Filly?"

She thought of Hyatt's weakened condition and wounded arm. He wouldn't be much of a match for her. In fact, she might make the shave something of a test. If Hyatt turned villain and tried to hurt her, she would know once and for all the blackness of his heart. But if he didn't . . .

"Don't worry about me, Longbones," she said. "I can take care of myself."

Grabbing the basket she had filled with goods, Fara headed out the door. The two dogs bounded after her, eager to be outside in the snow. Evening was already creeping across the mountains, painting hollows blue and the hillocks pink. A set of double tracks across the trail told her a rabbit had come out of hiding to investigate the scenery. After a blizzard such as the one that had blanketed Pinos Altos, not much else was moving. In the nearby town, wagons would be bogged down, shutters drawn, and fires crackling. Families would sing and sew and tell stories — all waiting for the blessed coming of Christmas.

An ache filled her heart as Fara stepped onto the porch of the little cabin. She could almost hear her own laughter as she and Papa had roasted piñon nuts or strung popcorn around a tree or built a snowman in that very yard. A Christmas tree . . . Maybe she should bring Hyatt a small tree. Not that he deserved such charity, of course. But after all, this was the season of goodwill. She really ought to be kind, even though he was beneath her in status and probably beyond all hope of redemption.

Inasmuch as ye have done it unto one of the least of these my brethren, ye have done it unto me.

"Confound it," she said aloud. Not another Sunday school memory verse! Hyatt was nothing like Fara's idea of a charity case. It was one thing to donate money to clothe the poor or to plan a Christmas tea for the miners' children. But to actually associate with a man of Hyatt's reputation? To actually minister to him?

Be not forgetful to entertain strangers: for thereby some have entertained angels unawares.

Hyatt was no angel. Fara scoffed at the notion that God would send an angel in the form of a scruffy, unshaven, wounded gunslinger. Hardly. Angels were messengers sent from heaven to warn . . . or teach. What could Fara possibly learn from a desperado like Hyatt?

She pushed open the door to find the man seated at the table by the stove. He more than filled Papa's chair, his long legs stretching across the floor and his shoulders reaching higher than the slatted chair back.

"Good afternoon, Mr. Hyatt," she said,

motioning the dogs to wait outside. "How's your arm?"

He picked up a gold pocket watch and dangled it by the chain. "You're late."

Bristling, she marched into the room and kicked the door shut behind her. So much for angels. "I beg your pardon, but I am not a minute late. Your timepiece must be fast."

"My father gave this watch to me before he died, and it's never been a second off."

Fara set the basket on the table. She pulled out her father's watch. "The correct time is four o'clock, sir," she declared, and snapped the lid.

"Four-o-five."

"Four exactly." She glared at him. But the harder she looked into his blue eyes, the more she began to wonder why he had been waiting for her so eagerly . . . and why both of them had been checking their watches to the last second . . . and how both had come to acquire a watch by a father's death.

"Your father died?" she asked.

"This past October." He slid his watch into his vest pocket. "He was more than a father to me. He was my closest friend."

"I'm sorry." Fara lowered her focus, ruing her harshness. It was odd to think that a man like Hyatt would have tender feelings. "I lost Papa in the spring. Doesn't seem much like Christmas, does it?"

"I thought by getting away . . . by coming out here . . . I wouldn't think about it so much. My mother died years ago, but the house was never quiet. Until now."

"I know just what you mean." She sank down into a chair and began taking the bread, honey, and jam from the basket. "Papa used to sing all the time. He knew all sorts of silly songs from his mining days — some of them not so nice. He used to change the words so I wouldn't be corrupted."

Hyatt smiled. "My father recited limericks."

"Oh dear. Papa would never go that far with me around. He was very sensitive to the notion that he had charge of a girl. He felt he should have done better by me. I grew up wild, you know. Riding horses, hunting with Old Longbones, climbing trees, swimming in the river. To this day, I can hardly walk in a skirt."

"I noticed your buckskins."

She lifted her head, startled. "Mr. Hyatt! It's not proper to look at a lady's ankles. Don't you know that?"

His mouth twitched. "I beg your pardon.

It looks like your father taught you manners after all."

"Some." She had learned the rest at the Boston ladies' school, but Hyatt didn't need to know about that. After all, if he sensed he was in the presence of a woman who mingled in the highest circles of Silver City society, he might see an opportunity for gain. And then he'd be just like all the other men she'd ever met.

But he wasn't, was he? Fara stopped her slicing and studied Hyatt for a moment. Other men put on airs. They preened. They spoke false words of affection and admiration — the language of courting. But the desperado was just a regular fellow. Easy to talk to. Even interesting.

"Ever read a book, Mr. Hyatt?" she asked, handing him a slice of bread spread with honey. It might be entertaining to talk to him about some of her ideas while she shaved him. "Surely you've read the Bible and *The Pilgrim's Progress.*"

He seemed to be struggling with some emotion. Was he trying not to bemoan his lack of education — or was this laughter dancing in his eyes?

"I don't mean to offend," she said. "I realize there are those who have had little opportunity for education. I myself never went to a proper school. But I did learn the things I needed to get along."

He took a bite of the bread and chewed for a moment. "I can read," he said. " 'I seek an inheritance incorruptible, undefiled, and that fadeth not away.' "

Fara caught her breath at the familiar words from John Bunyan's allegory. " 'And it is laid up in heaven,' " she continued, " 'and safe there, to be bestowed, at the time appointed —' "

" 'On them that diligently seek it,' " he joined her to finish the passage.

She stared into his blue eyes. Who was this gunslinger who liked to break horses and could quote from *The Pilgrim's Progress?* "I believe you must have been brought up well," she said.

"I was."

Then what went wrong? she ached to ask. *What had led him into a life of crime?* She shook her head. It would never do to know too much about a man like Hyatt. If she understood his past, she might come to feel a measure of sympathy for him. Then his sins might seem forgivable.

Forgive us our trespasses as we forgive those who trespass against us.

"Confound it!" she snapped.

"What's wrong?"

"I am plagued, Mr. Hyatt." She pushed away from the table. "Positively plagued. A man brought up well ought to behave well, don't you think? He shouldn't commit sins."

"I reckon everyone is a sinner in one fashion or another. Even you."

"I'm talking about big sins. Great ones."

"As I recall, Christian in *The Pilgrim's Progress* was carrying on his shoulders a very great burden. Yet he was seeking that incorruptible inheritance laid up in heaven. When he came up to the cross 'his burden loosed from off his shoulders, and fell from off his back, and began to tumble —' "

" 'And so continued to do, till it came to the mouth of the sepulchre, where it fell in, and I saw it no more,' " she finished. "Yes, I know the story, Mr. Hyatt."

"If Christ can forgive very great sins, why shouldn't we?"

Fara stared at him. *Was* this man an angel sent to test her? Or was he a demon sent to tempt her with his blue eyes and clever words? Was he a desperado — a gunslinger — or was he just a man?

"I brought a straightedge," she said, laying the razor on the table. "And some soap. There's hot water on the stove."

Hyatt reached out and laid his hand over hers. "Miss Filly," he said, "I can barely bring this slice of honey bread to my mouth. Left to my own devices, I'll have to grow a beard that reaches my knees before I'm able to use a razor. I would be much obliged if you were to do me the honor of giving me a shave."

Fara slipped her hand from beneath his. "Mr. Hyatt," she said, squaring her shoulders. "Prepare to become the best-shaven gentleman this side of the Gila River."

She set the razor, a towel, and a bowl of hot water on the table. Behind him, she began whipping the soap into a white lather. She watched his movements, anticipating the moment when he would reveal his true character. He would grab the razor, leap to his feet, hold the blade to her throat, and demand money, horses, a rifle. But he made no move toward the razor. Instead, he sat contentedly eating the bread and sipping coffee from a tin cup.

"Did you bake this?" he asked. "I've never tasted better bread."

Fara felt as vanquished as if he *had* used the razor. Her image of the fierce desperado evaporating, she flushed and nodded as her pleasure at his compliment spread in a warm glow through her chest. She had been praised as a businesswoman. Honored for her charity work. Admired for her fine gowns and elegant hairdos. But her bread?

"It's the cinnamon," she confided as she drew the towel over Hyatt's shoulders and tied it behind his neck. "I use just a pinch. It brings out the flavor of the honey."

"Cinnamon, huh?"

"It's a spice. It comes from the bark of a tree."

He chuckled. "I know what cinnamon is, ma'am. I just never thought of putting it in bread."

She wished she could tell him about the goodies she loved to bake for her Christmas tea — the Mexican wedding cakes, the *biscochitos,* the piñon nut logs. This year she had left the baking to the cooks at Canaday Mansion. But maybe . . . maybe she would just whip up a few *biscochitos.* If he liked the taste of cinnamon, Hyatt would love those.

Fara used her papa's big brush to lather the desperado's chin and jaw. "You sure managed to sprout some tough-looking whiskers," she said. "Lucky thing I'm good with a razor."

"I trust you. You're my angel."

At that, Fara's heart sped up so fast she wondered if he could hear it. Telling herself not to be silly, not to give his words a second thought, and certainly not to tremble, she began to draw the razor's straight edge down the side of his face.

As the rough stubble came away, she saw that his skin was smooth and taut. Though the Western sun had bronzed him, Hyatt bore none of the craggy lines and leathery wrinkles of the miners and cowboys she so often passed on the streets of Silver City. The more bristle she shaved away, the less he looked like a desperado and the more he transformed into a square-jawed, clean-cut, elegant gentleman.

"Gracious," she said as she dipped the towel in the warm water and rinsed off the last of the lather. "Mr. Hyatt, you look absolutely . . . positively . . . decent."

He laughed, and for the first time she realized what straight white teeth he had, and how fine his lips were, and how very brightly his blue eyes sparkled. When he slipped a comb from his pocket and ran it through his hair, she stared transfixed. Could gunslingers be so handsome? so mannerly? Again she thought back to the article in the newspaper. Six feet three inches tall. Two hundred pounds. Blue eyes. Brown hair. Shot through the left arm.

"May I ask how much you weigh, Mr. Hyatt?" she asked.

A flicker of curiosity crossed his brow. "Two hundred pounds before I went on my starvation ride into New Mexico."

"And your arm," she whispered. "Where did you say you were when you were shot?"

"Phoenix. A hotel." His eyes grew distant, as though he was seeing through her to that other place and time. "I was walking through the lobby of the Saguaro Hotel. A boy said something to me. 'Someone's waiting for you.' Who? Who was it?"

Copperton, Fara wanted to say. *You know who it was. You'd been tracking him for years.*

"I started up the steps," Hyatt continued. "I turned on the landing. There he was . . . with a six-shooter . . . shouting, waving the gun. . . ."

"So you shot him," Fara said.

The blue eyes snapped back into focus. "No! He shot first."

"Are you sure?"

"Positive."

"And you don't remember his name?"

He shook his head. "I'd never heard it before in my life."

You, Mr. Hyatt, are a handsome, intelligent, mannerly gentleman, Fara thought. *You are also a low-down, conniving snake. And the biggest liar in New Mexico Territory.*

CHAPTER FOUR

Fara made up her mind to let Old Longbones tend the desperado. The Apache knew more about healing than she did, she reasoned. Besides, she wasn't comfortable with the way she felt in Hyatt's presence. He was too slick. He spoke with such an honest light in his eyes and such frank words on his tongue, that she slipped easily into trusting him.

Worst of all, she actually liked the low-down gunslinger. Hyatt laughed easily. He knew about horses and good books. And he enjoyed her baking.

So Fara stayed up at the big ranch house and sent Old Longbones down to the cabin to change the nopal dressing and check on the wounded man. She spent most of the following day riding her horse through the forest and visiting her father's grave. The dogs played in the deep snow while Fara sat on a fallen log and stared at the head-stone.

Jacob Canaday. How could a man once so alive be dead? The cold granite belied the warmth of the man whose name was carved on its surface. Fara wept. Then she cut branches of pine and juniper and laid them around the stone. Then she cried some more.

The sun was setting as she climbed the porch and entered the big house. Old Longbones looked up from the rocker beside the fire. He had been dozing in the warmth.

"How's our desperado today?" Fara asked.

"Better." The Apache scratched his chin and gave a yawn. "You know, Filly, that dangerous gunslinger of yours . . . he doesn't have a gun."

Fara pondered that for a moment. "He's a very confusing man."

"Yes."

"You think he'll live?"

"Oh, yes. He grows strong — especially after eating all that bread you baked."

She took a step toward the fire. "He ate it all?"

"Mmm." The Apache leaned back in the rocker and shut his eyes again. "He says

91

you are the best baker of bread he ever knew."

A smile tugged at Fara's lips. "Wait until he tastes my *biscochitos*," she whispered.

"I don't believe I've ever had something truly melt in my mouth before," Hyatt said as he watched Filly pour him a second cup of tea the following afternoon. "Who taught you to bake these *biscochitos?*"

"Manuela," the young woman said. "She's my . . . my friend. In town."

He nodded. Filly was holding back. That afternoon — in spite of her obvious reluctance to spend more than a few minutes in his presence — they had sat together in the little cabin for hours. He had lured her into reading *The Pilgrim's Progress* to him while he sat beside the stove. Then she had ordered him into a pair of her papa's old denims and a flannel shirt so she could wash his traveling clothes. She returned with a batch of cookies she'd baked that morning, and they'd shared a pot of tea. It had been the best afternoon of his life.

If it weren't for the vast gulf between their upbringings, Hyatt would have vowed Filly was his perfect match. She was smart, witty, and beautiful. Equally important, she didn't have the least compunction about giving him a piece of her mind when she thought he deserved it. He'd never met a woman with as much spunk.

When she went away that evening, he found the solitude of the little cabin almost unbearable. Though the pain in his arm was intense at times, the wound was beginning to heal. But his hand was stiff and difficult to flex. He didn't sleep well. He had little energy. Worse, he found himself anticipating his own future with a measure of dread.

It was bad enough to think of returning to California — the empty mansion, the rounds of insufferable parties, a business he had organized so efficiently it could almost run without him. But before he could return to those wearying occupations he would be obliged to complete his mission. The idea of spending time in the presence of a stuffy heiress like Miss Fara Canaday was enough to send chills down his spine. He might have tolerated the woman had he not grown so enchanted by the high-spirited filly who had dragged him out of the snow and saved his life.

When she knocked on the cabin door the following morning, he jumped to his feet like a kid at Christmas. His gift — the beautiful golden-haired angel of his dreams — swept into the cabin wearing a pair of buckskin trousers, a red flannel shirt three sizes too big, and a shearling coat that hung down to her knees.

"Checkers," she announced, sliding a wooden game board onto the table. "Old Longbones won't play with me. Guess I'm stuck with you, buckaroo."

Hyatt set his hands on his hips. "I come in a poor second, do I?"

"I reckon you do. Ever played before?" She flashed those molasses eyes at him as she thunked the bag of checkers on the table.

"Checkers is child's play to me. How about chess?"

Her mouth dropped open, and he had to laugh. Within minutes they had devised a set of chess pieces from a collection of saltshakers, wood chips, and leftover biscochitos. Filly proved herself a worthy opponent. All morning and most of the afternoon, they battled over the game board. Just when Filly would crow she had him cornered, Hyatt would wiggle out of her trap. As the shadows grew long, he finally managed to box her in.

"Check," he announced.

"What!" She stared at the board. "Are you sure? Are you positive?"

"Look at my bishop. You're done for."

"Don't count on it. Just give me a minute here. I'll figure this out."

Chuckling, Hyatt stood and walked over to the stove. One day at chess with Filly had been as much fun as he'd had in years. As he pushed split wood into the firebox, he thought again about his bleak prospects. A trip to Silver City to meet a pompous heiress. A long journey back to California to resume his duties. He had friends, gold, and all the entertainment money could buy — and he'd much rather play chess in a run-down cabin with a poor prospector's daughter.

Was he ungrateful? God had blessed him so richly. He had been given more than any man could ask for. Why did the old Apache's words now ring so true? *Empty. Your heart is empty.*

"Checkmate," Filly announced in triumph.

Hyatt swung around. "What? How can that be?" He studied the chess board. Sure enough, she had him cornered. But wait . . . "Where's my bishop? Hey, what did you do with my —"

He looked up to find Filly smiling innocently at him, a hint of powdered sugar dusting her upper lip. "Your what?" she asked.

"You *ate* my bishop!" he shouted.

She began to giggle. "I was hungry. You said yourself they were delicious *biscochitos.*"

"That was my bishop!" He started toward her, and she leapt from the table. "You can't eat the chess men. That's not in the rules."

"Rules, rules!" she said, dancing out of his reach. "Who said we had to play by the rules?"

"I always play by the rules." He lunged for her long blonde braid.

"Boring, bor— ! Oh!" Captured, she whirled toward him and stopped, her face less than a breath from his.

Hyatt swallowed. The fragrance of pine and cinnamon drifted over him, and he realized it came from the woman's skin. Her braid hung like a silk rope in his hand. Her eyes shone brighter than any two stars, and his voice caught in his throat. He lifted his injured arm and brushed the sugar from her lip with a fingertip.

"Checkmate," he said.

"A person should always play by the rules," Fara told Old Longbones as they walked toward the barn to check on the horses the following morning. "It's foolhardy to buck against the order our society has put on things. Take that desperado, for

96

example. The Bible tells us to love our enemies. To be hospitable to strangers. To minister to the sick and the imprisoned. But it's just not wise to become too friendly with the likes of such people."

"Why is that, Filly?" The Indian lifted the bolt that barred the barn door. "Are you afraid you might start to see the desperado as a human being? You might start to care about him? Once you know him, you might begin to truly love him?"

Fara stopped just inside the barn door and crossed her arms. On any other day, she would have enjoyed this moment. The banter with Old Longbones. The rich scent of hay, oats, and leather in the barn. The soft nickering of the horses. But ever since Hyatt had come into her life, she had felt off-kilter and confused. Once, her world had been so well ordered. She had known the rules — and followed them. Now her heart was in chaos.

"Jacob Canaday was a breaker of rules," Old Longbones said as he began filling a bucket with oats. "Did he not take me into his home?"

"But you're different, Longbones. You've always been loyal to us. You're our friend. We can trust you."

"Only because your Papa's love changed

me. I came to Pinos Altos to raid, to steal, to burn — even to kill the White Eyes. But I stayed because I had found a man who cared about me. His acceptance opened my heart. I gave my life to the Son of his God, and I became a new man."

"Because Papa took the risk of caring for you."

"Of *knowing* me." The Apache beckoned to her. "I think it may be better to care deeply for one gunslinger, Filly, than it is to make a Christmas tea for the children of two hundred miners whose names you will never know."

Stung, Fara leaned over a stall door and ran her fingers through the coarse red-brown mane of her favorite mare. Old Longbones didn't understand the risk she felt in reaching out toward the man in the cabin. How could he? The Apache might speak of the importance of marriage and family, but he had never had a wife of his own. He had never known the strange, driving force that was propelling Fara toward Hyatt.

Mysterious and powerful, the compulsion was headier than anything she had ever felt. She thought about the man every waking moment. He walked through her dreams at night. She had memorized the sound of his voice, the nuances of his smile. Everything about him drew her — from their recitation of John Bunyan to their teasing over the chess board. She wanted to do more than tend to the healing and salvation of a wayward gunslinger. The moment when he had caught her braid she had wanted him to kiss her.

Could she possibly care about Hyatt with nothing more than Christian charity? Could she minister to him as a child of God in need? Could she like him . . . without loving him?

"Be the daughter of Jacob Canaday, Filly," Old Longbones said. "Break the rules."

Fara shut her eyes and let her mare's soft nose nudge her cheek. *Father God, help me. Help me to care . . . to really care, as Papa cared. Help me love as you loved. And please . . . please protect me from my own wayward heart.*

In the days that followed, Fara watched the snow begin to melt and the creek beds fill with icy, rushing water. Determined to do right by her father's memory, she made the gunslinger her missionary priority. She gave up her much-deserved rest and filled her days with cooking hot meals, changing nopal bandages, and reading long passages from the Bible to the object of her Christian ministry.

Hyatt responded by making her days a form of torture. He was as delightful a man as she had ever met. He teased her, complimented her, and challenged her at chess, checkers, and dominoes. He debated every philosophy she tossed at him. He told stories that had her laughing until tears ran down her cheeks, and he sang songs that made her heart ache. When she mentioned cutting down a little Christmas tree, he accompanied her into the woods. Together, they hauled back a little sapling and set it up in the cabin. Then they trimmed it with strings of popcorn, bright red chiles, and bows fashioned of straw.

As the snow melted, the days ticked by. Christmas approached, and Fara's heart grew tighter and the lump in her throat more solid. The prospect of her Christmas tea held scant joy. The anticipation of business meetings and sloppy mud streets made her positively morose. But she knew her emotional turmoil had little to do with Christmas and everything to do with Hyatt.

She had utterly failed in her missionary project, she thought one bright afternoon as she carried his lunch from the big house down toward the cabin. All her Bible reading had elicited no tearful remorse over train robberies and horse rustling. Hyatt had confessed to no dastardly crimes. He had never spoken of the man who had shot him with the least measure of vengeance in his voice. In fact, Hyatt seemed as good and as kind a man as had ever lived.

If anyone had been changed in the two weeks of her campaign, it was Fara herself. She had laughed harder, prayed more fervently, and enjoyed herself more thoroughly than she had since her papa had died. She had been eager to start each day and sorry to go to bed each night. And Hyatt — always Hyatt — had filled her thoughts.

Things couldn't go on this way. The night before, Fara had made up her mind. It was time. Past time.

"Tomorrow's Christmas Eve," she said softly as Hyatt held the door open for her. "Old Longbones says the trails are clear and almost dry."

Hyatt watched her in silence as she spread a white cloth and set out dishes and spoons. She could feel his eyes following her around the room, and she knew he sensed the tension in her movements. Her hand trembled as she dipped out a ladle of hot soup. The lid clanged against the pot. She sank into her chair and turned to him.

"Your arm is better now," she said.

He nodded. Joining her, he sat in the chair near the stove. She led them in a brief prayer, then she stirred at her soup. "I reckon you'll be wanting to head on out," she said.

His hand paused, spoon halfway to his mouth. "Out?"

"Back to Phoenix . . . or wherever."

"Are you running me off?"

She sipped at her soup. "I won't be around to tend you after today," she said. "I'm going to town. I have things to do."

"Things?"

"Christmas things."

They ate in strained silence. Finally Hyatt cleared his throat. "I guess I always knew this time would come. I thank you for your care of me. I owe you my life."

"You don't owe me a thing. I've done what any Christian woman should."

"My angel."

"Don't call me that!" She blinked back the unexpected tears that stung her eyes. "I've failed — failed at what I thought I should do for you. I don't have the strength of heart my father had. I'm weak. Willful."

"Human?" He reached toward her, but she drew back.

She couldn't stay with him. Not a moment longer. If she did, she would be the one confessing — blurting out how much joy he had brought, how deeply she had come to care for him, how empty her heart would feel when he went away. She pushed back from the table and stood.

"I'm going now," she said. "I won't see you again."

"Wait —" He caught her hand. "Where are you going?"

"To visit Papa's grave for a few minutes. Then I'll be leaving for town. Old Long-bones is saddling my horse. He's getting one ready for you, too. You're welcome to take it — my gift."

"Filly —" He followed her to the door.

"Please don't." She held out a hand, touching him lightly on the chest. "Give me this time alone."

Before he could restrain her, she hurried out of the cabin and flew down the steps toward the path that led to the lonely grave. Tears flowing now, she lifted her heavy skirts and ran until the chill air squeezed her breath, and her heart hammered in her chest. When the little granite stone came into view, she fell on her knees and buried her face in her hands.

I love him, Lord. I love him! Make me strong enough to let him go.

Hyatt strode down the muddy path, his conviction growing with every step. Filly was wrong! She had not failed her father's memory. Strength and kindness lived in her heart. Her tender ministrations had taught Hyatt more than Filly would ever know. For the first time in his life, he understood what it meant to truly care about another human being — no matter her wealth, her education, her pedigree, or her circumstance.

As he marched after her, he hardly noticed the bright blue sky or the green juniper and piñon branches that stretched toward it. He didn't care that his boots were caked with mud and the sleeves of his borrowed shirt barely came to his wrists. He didn't feel the chill wind, and he gave the ache in his injured arm no heed. Pride had held him in its bondage — pride that informed him he was too good for a prospector's daughter. But now he knew he had important business. Business he should have taken care of before now.

"Filly?" He spotted her crumpled on the ground by a smooth gray headstone. "I have to talk to you."

She swung around. "Hyatt." Coming to her feet, she motioned him away. "Don't come here. Please. Go back to the cabin. I can't talk to you. Not anymore."

"Filly, wait." He caught her arm as she brushed past him. "There's something I must say to you."

"No, Hyatt. Old Longbones is waiting. I'm expected in town."

"Listen to me." He gripped her arms and forced her to stop. Turning her toward him, he met her eyes. She had been crying — and he sensed that this time her tears had little to do with her father's death. If he was right — *Dear God, let me be right* — she felt exactly as he did. If she accepted him, he would have a woman who loved him for the man he was — and not for the riches he could give her. And she would have a man who longed to give her the treasures of his heart.

"Filly," he said. "Two weeks ago, you found me half dead in the snow. These hours we've spent together have been the sweetest . . . the brightest . . . of my entire life. In many ways, I feel I've known you forever. If I tried, I couldn't invent a better companion — at chess, at storytelling, at debate — than you. I couldn't wish for a more beautiful woman to sit beside me at my dinner table —"

"Hyatt, please."

Her brown eyes filled with tears again, but

he went on, determined to have his say. "We know so much about each other — hopes and dreams. Even fears. But there's something you don't know about me. Something I've kept hidden. I . . . I am not . . . not completely . . . the man you believe I am. I have not wanted to tell you the truth. But Filly . . . I love you. I must tell you —"

"No," she cut in, distress shuddering her voice. "I don't want to hear it. Leave things as they are, Hyatt. Leave us with good memories. With the days of joy we've spent together. Don't talk. Don't tell me your secrets. I can't bear it."

"But, Filly —"

"No, Hyatt. I can't love you. Not in the way you mean. Not in the way my heart demands. I can't."

She pulled away from him and began running down the path. He watched her go. The fringes of her buckskins swung around her ankles beneath her heavy skirt. Her blonde braid thumped against her back. The piñon trees closed in, and his angel — the gold and shining beauty of his life, the joy of his heart — vanished in the thick forest.

Fists clenched, Hyatt turned on his heel and stared at the place she had been kneeling. The patch of bare ground was strewn with juniper branches. The little granite headstone rose from the mud. *Papa.* Her papa. He walked toward the grave. Then he stopped and stared at the name carefully carved in the cold gray stone.

Jacob Canaday

CHAPTER FIVE

"What is the matter with you, Farolita?" Manuela leaned over Fara's shoulder. "Ever since you came down from Pinos Altos yesterday night, you have been so quiet. You do not even fight me when I try to lace the corset."

Fara picked up a hand mirror and held it behind her head to evaluate her chignon. "A little tighter, please, Manuela," she said. "The ribbon loops, not the corset."

Sighing, the housekeeper fussed over the satin bow that held Fara's bun high on her head. "Did that old *Indio* treat you poorly?" she asked. "When I saw that you had brought him down to Canaday Mansion, ai-yai-yai, I could not believe my eyes. What will the poor children think of that Apache? He will frighten them half to death!"

"Old Longbones couldn't scare anyone if he tried. He's going to be my Santa Claus."

"Him? A Santa Claus with long black hair and skinny legs? A Santa Claus who once came to these mountains to murder everybody?"

"Manuela," Fara said softly. "That was years ago. People change, you know. They . . . they're not always what they seem."

For the hundredth time, Hyatt's blue eyes flashed into her thoughts. Fara swallowed, forcing away the memory of the last moment she had seen him. *I love you*, he had told her. *I love you.* And she had pushed him away, run from him, fled the truth she knew he must confess.

As she rode down the mountain, she had turned his words over and over in her mind. Always, she came to the same conclusion. To care, to minister, to love with the love of Jesus Christ — that was right. But to give her heart to a man who had chosen a life of crime, a man who had shown no indication of remorse or intent to change? No, she could not do it.

She had made the correct choice in walking away from Hyatt. She had done her part to care for him as her father had cared for Longbones. But it would be wrong to yoke herself to a man whose life contradicted what her father had taught Fara was right and good. No matter how much she had come to love him.

Lord, help me, she prayed as Manuela fastened the twenty tiny buttons that ran up the back of her velvet gown. *Help me let him go. Help me to do your will always — no matter the consequences.*

As she stood to pull on her long white gloves, she could hear the children pouring through the mansion's wide front doors. Giggling, chattering, exclaiming in joy over the decorations and tables groaning with treats, they scattered down the halls. Fara smiled.

"The *ratóncitos!*" Manuela cried. "They swarm, they nibble, they make holes in the carpet and leave crumbs in the settee."

Chuckling in spite of herself, Fara started down the long winding staircase. Below her, she could see that the little mice were indeed stuffing their faces with pecan tarts and bite-sized sandwiches. A group of rag-tag boys chased each other through the foyer, their muddy boots thudding on the white marble floor. A tiny girl with a mop of tangled red curls was the first to spot their hostess.

"Miss Canaday!" she cried. "It's Miss Canaday! Here she comes!"

Fara continued her descent amid a chorus of cheers. The children swarmed around the foot of the stairs to touch her skirt and gawk at the pearls dripping from her necklace. Fara sank to her knees among them and gave each grimy hand a little squeeze and each ruddy cheek a kiss. "Merry Christmas!" she whispered. "And what's your name, my little man? Oh, that's a fine ribbon you have, young lady. Have you tried the mincemeat pies?"

Laughing with delight, the children took her hands and dragged her toward the large living room. As she passed the dining room, she spotted Old Longbones, the sack of toys and goodies at his feet. He and Manuela were arguing over the correct way to wear the long red robe and white beard, and Fara shook her head and smiled.

In the living room, the fifteen-foot pine glowed with a hundred tiny white candles, each perched on a branch and held by a silver clip. Blown glass balls from Germany and Bohemia glistened in the golden light. Paper fans, feathered doves, and tiny angels twirled on the thin red ribbons. In the fireplace, piñon logs crackled and snapped, sending off a spicy fragrance that filled the room.

"Merry Christmas, Mrs. Auchmann, Mrs. Tatum, Mrs. Finsch," Fara called as she approached the group of society matrons gathered in a clump to observe the city's annual charity tea. They had positioned themselves perfectly beside the tree for the newspaper's photographer to capture their benevolent actions.

"Mrs. Ratherton," she said, clasping the hand of her nosy next-door neighbor. "How good of you all to come. This year I'd like all of you to help me with the children. Mrs. Auchmann, you'll take charge of the tart table. I've already spotted a little fellow who will make himself ill if he doesn't restrain himself. Mrs. Tatum and Mrs. Finsch — how lovely you both look. Please go down to the kitchen and help the cooks bring up the pies. And Mrs. Ratherton. My dear Mrs. Ratherton. Won't you assist in carving the turkeys?"

"Turkeys!"

Fara gave them her most gracious smile as she strolled over to the photographer. "Mr. Austin, thank you for coming. Please keep your focus on the children this afternoon."

"Anything you say, Miss Canaday." He whipped the daily paper from his pocket and held it open. "Your tea is the headline story, Miss Canaday," he said. "I had to fight the editor to rank it over the capture of the gunslinger who shot that fellow in

Phoenix. But I knew our local charity event was —"

"Gunslinger?" Fara grabbed the paper.

"Frank Hyatt. They caught him in West Virginia three days ago."

Fara stared at the blur of words. But Hyatt had been in her cabin in Pinos Altos three days ago.

"Hyatt claims he never shot anybody in Phoenix," the reporter said. "Claims he has an alibi. Though Hyatt did confess to the train robberies and the horse rustling, he says James Copperton must have plugged another man. Probably a fellow with the same name — poor old cayuse."

Another man. Who? Hardly able to breathe, Fara handed back the newspaper and drifted to the tea table. Taking her place among the servants, she began pouring out tiny porcelain cups of the finest black tea laced with frothy milk and sugar. The children lined up to receive their tea with both hands outstretched.

Who had been in the cabin in the forest? Whom had she dragged out of the snow? *Hyatt.* But who was Hyatt? Who was the man she had grown to love?

"Thank you, Miss Canaday," a child said, drawing her attention.

"God bless you," she murmured in return. "William, one lump of sugar or two?"

"She knows my name!" The boy laughed as he and his companions retired to the hearth to sip the sweet beverage.

Yes, Fara thought, trying to order her thoughts. *Papa, I know his name. And I will reach out beyond my Christmas tea to touch his family and his life.*

The ache and confusion in her heart mellowed as the town choir began to sing carols and the children settled down, balancing on their knees plates heaped with turkey, cranberries, potatoes, and hot rolls. Fara slipped out her pocket watch and opened the lid. Five o'clock — almost time for Santa Claus. She wondered if Manuela had managed to tie the white beard on Old Longbones's chin.

When she closed the lid on her papa's watch, she remembered Hyatt's snapping blue eyes as he had chastised her for being late. Her focus misted, but she swallowed at the gritty lump in her throat and stepped out into the midst of the children.

"Boys and girls," she said. "Every year, we come together at Christmastime to remember the precious gift God sent to earth so many years ago."

"Baby Jesus!" a husky voice called out.

"That's right, William. God sent his own

son to be born on Earth. Jesus grew up to teach us that we must all learn to love each other — no matter what kind of food we eat, or the color of our skin, or the clothes we wear, or the words we speak. We must love each other as much as Jesus loved us. And do you know how much that was? He loved us enough to die for us."

She looked around at the shining eyes and wondered how many of these children had ever heard the message of Christ's saving grace. "At Christmas, we remember God's gift to us by giving gifts to each other." Recognizing the signal of what was to follow, the children began to elbow each other and whisper. "And do you know who has come to visit us tonight? Right here at Canaday Mansion?"

"Santa Claus!" they began to shout.

"Santa Claus! Santa Claus!"

Fara turned and held out a hand. "Santa Claus," she said.

Into the room walked a tall, brown-haired man clad in a fine black suit, a bright red tie, and a jaunty top hat. His blue eyes twinkled as he swept the hat from his head and gave Fara a deep bow. She caught her breath as he swung the sack of toys from his back and set it on the floor. Before the children could move, he bent down on one knee and took Fara's hand.

"Miss Canaday," he announced. "I am Aaron Hyatt, the son of William Hyatt of Sacramento, California."

"Of the Golden Hyatts!" Mrs. Ratherton whispered loudly to Mrs. Auchmann. "He's worth a fortune!"

"Before his death, my father asked me to travel to Silver City to meet you — the daughter of Jacob Canaday, his oldest and dearest friend."

Fara clutched her throat, unable to speak. *Him?* This was Aaron Hyatt, the man she had dreaded meeting so much she had run away to Pinos Altos? The man she had tended so faithfully — whose clothes she had washed and whose arm she had nursed — was Aaron Hyatt? *This* was Aaron Hyatt?

"I come to you now on bended knee, Miss Canaday," he said. "I want you to know I love you with my whole heart. Filly . . . will you marry me?"

Mrs. Ratherton let out a muffled shriek. "Run for cover, Mrs. Finsch!" she cried. "It's another suitor. She'll go for that shotgun!"

In the midst of the confusion, Fara looked down into blue eyes that mirrored a love so deep and true she could not have believed it, had she not felt it in her own heart. Smiling, she fought the tremble in her lips.

"Mr. Hyatt," she said softly. The room fell so still not even a child wiggled. "Your love has made me the happiest woman in all the world. Yes, I will marry you."

The crowd erupted into cheers. The children leapt to their feet. The choir began to sing "Jingle Bells." Mrs. Ratherton fainted, and Mrs. Finsch, Mrs. Tatum, and Mrs. Auchmann drew out their ostrich-feather fans and tried to revive her. The photographer snapped wildly, sending puffs of black smoke through the room. Old Longbones wandered into the chaos, the white beard dangling from the back of his head, and began doling out presents.

"Merry Christmas," Fara said, drawing Hyatt to his feet.

Strong arms slipped around her and folded her close. Fara drifted in the heady security of a future bright with glad tidings of comfort and joy. When she lifted her head to gaze into the blue eyes of the man she loved, Hyatt's warm lips brushed against hers.

"I love you," he whispered. "My Christmas angel."

RECIPE

Dear friend,

I tasted my first biscochito many years ago when I lived in the mountains of southern New Mexico. Nothing is better than the scent of a piñon log fire, the crisp promise of Christmas in the air, and the sugar-and-cinnamon taste of warm biscochitos.

This seventy-five-year-old recipe was sent to me by Myra Simons of Albuquerque. It belonged to her great-grandmother. Myra assures me these are New Mexico's best biscochitos, so try the recipe — then snuggle up with a loved one and enjoy!

Catherine Palmer
Jeremiah 29:11

BISCOCHITOS

From the Kitchen of Grandma Rufina and Aunt Tillie

1 lb lard (or margarine)
1½ cups sugar (granulated)
2 eggs
1–1½ tsp anise seeds

6 cups flour
3 tsp baking powder
1 tsp salt
⅓ – ½ cup sweet red wine (or grape juice)
½ cup sugar mixed with 1 tsp cinnamon
(can be adjusted to taste)

Cream sugar and lard (or margarine) until light and fluffy. Add eggs and anise seeds. Mix well. Sift flour with baking powder and salt. Add to sugar and egg mixture a little at a time (4 to 5 additions). Knead until dough holds together. (Avoid overmixing as this makes dough tough.) Add wine (or grape juice) as needed to help hold mixture together. Roll out dough to about ½ inch thick. (Cookies should be thick.) Cut using seasonal or traditional fleur-de-lis shapes.

Bake at 350 degrees for approximately 10 to 12 minutes. Note: Cookies do *not* brown.

Remove cookies from cookie sheet and allow to cool. Dust both sides of the cookies with the cinnamon and sugar mixture. Store in an airtight container. Cookies freeze well.

A Daddy
for Christmas

DIANNA CRAWFORD

CHAPTER ONE

Off the coast of Maine, 1870

Another huge wave crashed over the bow and swept across the deck. Lovett Keegan tightened his grip on the wheel and braced himself against the sea's fury. Would this storm never end?

Timber splintered ominously, and Keegan looked up. Above the first boom the center mast had snapped. Spars, sails, and lines screeched and groaned as they spilled crazily toward the deck.

"Look out above!" he shouted.

With relief, he saw his yellow-slickered men already diving out of the way as the mast smashed across the aft railing. It dipped into the dark rolling water, taking with it a tangle of canvas and rope.

The schooner listed dangerously. The crewmen raced for the high side, grabbing onto anything tied down as they scrambled upward, the howling wind stealing their shouts and cries.

Another wave rushed over the deck, and beneath his feet, Keegan felt a further tilting. Any second, the ship would capsize.

The ax — he had to get to the ax. Free the ship from the tangled mass pulling them over, or they were doomed.

Keegan tied down the wheel and made a staggering dash to the toolbox next to the cabin wall. Snatching out the ax, he started chopping on a nearby spar caught between the cabin and a stack of crates.

Someone was beside him, pulling on his arm. His first mate, Mr. Gosset.

"Start cutting the ropes!" Keegan yelled close to the man's ear.

"It's too late!" Gosset shouted back. "She's lost! Abandon ship!"

"*No . . . I'll lose everything.*" Keegan started chopping again.

"Don't be a fool, Cap'n. We're lowering the skiff. Come with us."

Keegan glanced behind him and saw one man at the winch and two others guiding the rowboat over the rail.

"You get the men to safety. I can't leave while there's a chance to save her."

"This ship's not worth your life. Come with us . . . *now*." Mr. Gosset grabbed Keegan's arm and pulled.

He jerked free. "*Let go.* I've got too much invested. The cargo . . ."

A crashing wave sent them both sliding across the deck.

Catching an edge of downed sail, Keegan worked his way back to the spar. "Get out of here! Meet me in Boston. Griffin's Wharf."

Keegan started wielding ax to spar again, glancing back until he saw the men were launched and away from the ship, their little boat bobbing over a giant swell like a fisherman's cork. "See them to safety, Lord," he called through the driving rain, then put his back into his swing. No second could be wasted. He had to save the ship. He'd worked too many years to lose everything now.

Tess Winslow heard the clatter of freezing rain against glass just as she finished packing freshly baked scones into her carrying basket. Dismayed, she pushed aside ruffled chintz and looked out the window over the kitchen sinkboard.

For the past two hours she'd watched the sky and hoped and prayed the weather would abate, to no avail. The full force of an ice storm was upon them, slanting in from the northeast. She turned from the window and glanced across the room at her young daughters. Both lay belly down on the rag rug before the hearth with their heads close together, drawing chalk pictures on their slate boards. Six-and-a-half-year-old Sarah, and Elizabeth, a tender four, looked so darling with their ruffled pantalets peeking out from beneath their hooped skirts. They'd been dressed in their Sunday best and fidgeting since noon, waiting for the moment Tess would say it was time to go. She really hated having to disappoint them. Aside from the new rag dolls she'd made them, the festivities at the church would be the only Christmas celebration her children would get this year.

The mantel clock struck the half hour. Two-thirty. The play would start promptly at three, and it was almost a mile into Moon Bay Harbor. If they were going, they'd have to leave now.

Another blast of wind whined past, rattling the windows. Tess knew it would be pure folly to take two small children outside in this kind of weather, no matter how urgent the reason, particularly with the storm steadily growing more fierce. In fact, she realized as she assessed the wood supplies by the fireplace and the cookstove, she'd better gather in a cartload from the woodshed before it got any worse. At the front door she plucked her galoshes from a flat-topped chest, then sat on the lid to pull them on over her shoes.

Sarah, with the wide blue eyes and silky brown hair so like her own, looked up from her slate. "Is it time now?"

Not wanting to dash her child's eagerness — something she'd seen so seldom of late, Tess hedged. "I need to bring in wood for tonight."

Tess took her navy cloak from its hook above the chest and wrapped it around her. She shoved her way out a door being driven against her by biting rain and wind — a wind that whistled around the curved wall of the lighthouse as if the tall stone structure weren't attached to the cottage.

Her head bent and skirts whipping between her legs, she started for the wood-shed. In the blur of the downpour, the few yards seemed like a hundred. Tess could scarcely hear the waves crashing on the rocks below the bluff, but the vibration beneath her feet told her more than she cared to know. Peering into a foggy gray void where the sea should have been, she was grateful all the fishing boats of Moon Bay were in port for Christmas Eve.

A spray of water misted her face. It tasted of salt. *Waves couldn't come all the way up the bluff, could they?*

Of course not, she told herself flatly. Just a spray borne on the wind. She absolutely refused to let fear get the best of her. It mattered not if this was her first major storm since moving out here on the point to be the lighthouse keeper. She'd lived in Maine long enough to know that winters on the coast were oftentimes quite violent, and the lighthouse had never washed away yet.

"I'll not be scared off," she affirmed aloud as she gained the protection of the shed. The position of lighthouse keeper included a snug two-bedroom house and a small salary. With the income she already brought in sewing for the neighborhood ladies, she and the children would do just fine. And by next year, she would have enough put aside to give the children a Christmas with all the trimmings.

Pulling the cart close to the stacked logs, she began to fill it. Refusing to be bullied by the gale, she lifted her voice above the roar of the storm. "Howl all you want, wind. I'm staying."

On her return to the house, Tess's bravado began to wane. Despite the stinging sleet, she dreaded the moment she would enter the dwelling — the moment she'd have to tell the children they wouldn't be going to the church. What could she possibly do to make up for not being there with the other children, not seeing the play with the actors all in costume, the singing, the sweet treats?

Tess paused as an idea began to take form. "Maybe . . . just maybe."

Both of her darlings stood just inside the door, already in their galoshes and gloves when she entered into a warmth that burned her chafed cheeks. She walked past the children toward the fireplace with an armload of wood.

They chased after her, their rubber overshoes slapping against the planked floor. When she dropped the logs into the box and turned back, they blocked her path.

"Sarah says the clock says it's time to go." Elizabeth's fists were knotted at her waist, and her small round face had a determined set. She looked almost comical, considering her mischievous green eyes and her wild halo of blonde hair. Tess and Sarah had come to call Elizabeth their busy little Bitsy.

Dropping into her rocker, Tess gathered her daughters close. "Please listen to me, and don't say a word until I've finished. I think you'll be pleased."

Bitsy perked up, but not Sarah. Her face took on that expression of stoic suffering the child had come to make her own since Tom had died, leaving them with few resources.

Tess knew she somehow should have done a better job of shielding her young worrier from the realities of their finances. "I'm sorry, dears, but the storm has grown much worse. See the sleet beating against the window? We can't possibly walk to church in that. We'd freeze to death on the way, even if we could find the village. So I have another idea. A grand idea. We'll have our own tea party right here."

Bitsy crinkled her button nose. "*A tea party?* What's fun about drinking tea?"

Tess brought forth her brightest voice. "Obviously you've never attended a stylish tea party. We'll have to get dressed up in our fanciest hats and our frilliest dresses."

Bitsy's lips pressed into an angry line. "But I don't have a fancy hat."

If Tess couldn't even entice her four-year-old with the novel idea, how would she ever win over Sarah? "Well, silly girl, we'll have to drag out my store of summer clothes, of course. And we'll just try them all on until we find the perfect costumes, right down to

130

the gloves and shoes."

"Really?" Sarah asked, but the question didn't lighten her porcelain-blue eyes.

Tess gave her own nose a haughty hike. "Absolutely. If we're going to invite Her Royal Majesty, Queen Victoria, to come all the way from London for our oh-so-elegant tea, everything must be correct. Flawless."

Bitsy, beginning to warm up to the notion, crowded between her mother's legs. "The queen is coming here? To our house? When?"

"Oh, Bitsy," Sarah said with older-sister disdain. "Don't be such a baby."

Tess caught Sarah's fine chin in her hand. "And don't you be such an old stick-in-the-mud. Right over there is London *and* Queen Victoria." She pointed toward the dress-maker's form standing in the corner by her Singer sewing machine. "Her highness is merely wearing a disguise at the moment. The proper clothes, a stylish bonnet — and a head to put it on — and you'll recognize her in a snap."

Sarah slanted her gaze away, but there was a smile tickling the corners of her mouth.

"And," Tess added for good measure, "you'll want to invite Princess Daisy and Lady Morning Glory."

"Princess?" Bitsy's brow crinkled. Then her eyes popped wide, and she hooted. "Oh, you mean our dolls, Daisy and Glory."

"And where is old Romeo?" Tess asked as she searched the room. She spotted their fluffy black tomcat curled in front of the cookstove. "He'll need a bit of dressing up, too."

That did it. Bitsy emitted an ear-shattering squeal and jerked on Tess's hand. "Come on, Mama. Can I wear that yellow dress you wore to Miss Mandy's wedding?"

"No, me," Sarah cried, finally joining in. "I'm the oldest. I should be the one to wear it."

"No. Me!"

Laughing, Tess pulled both squirming bodies into a hug. For once, she loved hearing them argue. Maybe this wouldn't be such a bad Christmas after all.

Shivers, violent shivers, convulsed through Keegan. His teeth chattered until he thought they would chip away. But he would not give up. In the belly of the ship, by the flickering light of a single lantern, he shoved on the handle of the bilge pump as icy water sloshed around his calves. Out . . . back. Out . . . back. He braced his legs against the pitch of the deck and shoved again for the thousandth time. Most of his more costly cargo was in watertight containers. If he could pump enough water from the hold, the old girl might ride out the storm.

And he would.

"Push," he told his numb hands, his aching shoulders.

He'd cut the mast free. Righted the ship. "Pull."

This was his big chance. Big chance. "Push."

How could this happen on the first voyage of his own ship? "Pull."

All the way to India and back. Hold filled with Oriental riches. "Push."

Shouldn't have tried to make Boston by Christmas. "Pull."

Should have stayed in Halifax. "Push."

A loud scrape shook the planks beneath Keegan's feet, the ripping of wood. A mighty shudder, and torrents of water gushed past his legs. With no one on deck to steer the ship, she must have hit a rock. *A blasted coastal rock.*

She was going down. His big chance gone. He took a last look at chests and crates that were even now breaking from their constraints and bobbing in the flooded hold, then dove for the ladder. He had to escape before the ship sank and sucked him down with it.

Reaching the upper deck, a stinging sleet blasted his face. He gasped for breath and clutched his slicker more tightly over his drenched clothing. *Freeze or drown. Which would be worse?*

The sky had turned dark, but not too dark to see that his vessel rode dangerously low in the water. It would be only a matter of minutes. Or less.

Fear and a gripping dread seized him. *God's punishment. That's what this was.* Ever since he ran off to sea at fifteen, he'd been living a sinful, carnal life. And now he would pay. And with more than just his life, if those pulpit thumpers were right.

The frightening thought infused Keegan with new energy. "Forgive me, Lord Jesus, for going my own selfish way all these years," he cried as he ran to the toolbox. "Forgive this sinner." He dug furiously through the tools until he found a crowbar. He pried the lid from the nearest crate and tied himself to the flat surface with a length of rope. "God help me!" he cried, and threw himself over the rail.

The bitterly cold sea churned over him.

They'd been having a "high old time," as

Tess's mother used to say. The children hadn't laughed so much in ages and neither had she — despite the fact they'd left her bedroom strewn with discarded clothing and accessories of every description. Scarcely an article she owned had been left untouched, untried.

Now, at the kitchen table covered with a colorful piece of floral calico, Tess lighted the half-dozen candles for which she'd managed to find holders and surveyed their handiwork. Place settings of the rose-trimmed children's tea set Tom had brought back from Holland for Sarah's first birthday surrounded the tapers. On each small plate rested one of the cranberry scones she'd baked for the church party, along with a dollop of honey butter. Even the dolls and "Queen Victoria" had one of the treats before them.

The dolls, draped in beads and feathers, occupied the only vacant chair, while the "queen" stood at one corner, a pillow for a head, her form swathed in all manner of lace and fringed scarves.

Poor old Romeo appeared none too pleased with his inclusion in the festivities. Shawled and beaded, he lay pinned to Bitsy's lap, his tail swishing angrily across the velvet of her dusty rose gown — a gown

135

that pooled in great folds on the floor all around the four-year-old.

"When's the tea gonna be ready, Mama?" Bitsy asked as she tightened her grip on the cat.

"Ladies having tea don't ask dumb questions," Sarah said in a superior tone as she sat absolutely straight in her chair — a posture, Tess suspected, more needed to keep the scoop-necked blue dimity on her shoulders than anything else. And of course, Sarah had her bonnet to balance. She'd chosen the widest-brimmed hat Tess owned — with an ostrich feather added for good measure.

"When the kettle whistles, milady," Tess said, staying in her snooty character. "It won't be but a few moments. I should have time to run up to the top of the castle tower to light yet another candle . . . one to announce to whomever it may concern that our tea is about to commence."

"Do you have to go up now?" Disappointment rang in Sarah's voice.

"Just a quick check, milady. A sneaky wind may have gotten in and blown out some of the lamps. But remember, if the kettle whistles before I get back, don't touch it. Promise?" She eyed both girls until each nodded in agreement. Without bothering with her cloak, she scooped up the flounced and bustled yellow frock both children had originally wanted to wear and hurried down the hall, past the bedrooms and through the door to the tower.

Refracted light from the mirrors above reflected on the stairwell walls, creating a pleasant glow by which Tess ran up the circling staircase as fast as her breath and legs would allow. Only her duty as light-house keeper could have taken her away at such an inopportune moment.

The wicks and lamps were in perfect order, shining brightly among cuts of mirror cocked in every conceivable direction — for all the good it would do this night. The beacon didn't penetrate into the sleet more than a few feet past the tower windows.

Re-entering the hallway, Tess heard the tea kettle whistling. "I'll be right there," she yelled, making a last-second decision to give her girls their Christmas presents tonight instead of in the morning. The gifts would lift their spirits again if they had started bemoaning the church party while she was out of the room. She snagged the two paper-wrapped dolls from the top of her closet, then hurried on to remove the complaining kettle from the heat and pour boiling water into the prepared teapot.

"Lady Theresa," Sarah called from the table. "Mistress Elizabeth took a bite of her scone. And we haven't even said grace yet."

"Just a little longer," Tess said, turning back toward them. She was struck by how really lovely everything looked. The summer colors, so colorful and lively, glowed in an amber circle of light. "I thought now would be the perfect time," she said as she placed a gift beside each child's plate. "While I serve tea. Merry Christmas, my beautiful daughters."

With excited cries, they ripped away the paper.

Tess had no doubt they would be thrilled by the dolls. She'd saved scraps from the brightest materials, along with bits and pieces of trim and lace from the dresses she'd sewn for her customers all year. If nothing else, the dolls would be dressed with as much gaudy flair as their mistresses.

As high-pitched squeals of delight nearly shattered her eardrums, and Romeo leapt from Bitsy's lap to Queen Victoria's shoulder, Tess knew she was right. The girls hugged their new play-pretties and fussed with their clothing while she poured tea spiced with cloves from her precious stash. Then, plucking her own summer straw hat from her chair seat, she tied a flowing bow beneath her chin and joined them.

"Now, gentle ladies and kind sir," Tess began, directing her last word to the black cat wrapped around the queen's shoulders. "I do believe this occasion calls for a very special prayer. I think, dear hearts, we should each thank the Lord for something good that happened to us this year. By your leave, I'll begin." She bowed her head and folded her hands. "Dear heavenly Father, I want to thank you for Mr. Patterson's willingness to give a woman the job of lighthouse keeper so I can always stay home with my little ones. And thank you for providing us such a cozy little cottage to live in." Tess then lifted her gaze to her firstborn. "It's your turn, Sarah."

The child pressed her long delicate fingers together and bowed her head with her most serious expression. "Dear Lord, you know Mama worried about money for a long time. I thank you that we don't have to worry anymore. I hope. Oh, yes. Thank you for the doll. Amen," she finished in a rush, then glanced at her sister. "You're next, Bitsy."

"Mmm." Bitsy squeezed her eyes tight. "Thank you for the most prettiest doll I ever saw. And for the tea party. And getting to wear Mama's feather hat. And . . . and I'm so happy, there's only one more thing I want in the whole world. My own daddy."

Tess's throat closed, she was so surprised. And disappointed. She'd tried so hard since she received word last year of Tom's death. So hard. A moment passed before she realized Bitsy wasn't finished. "I want a daddy like Mary Beth has. She says they don't ever have to worry about anything, and he won't let nobody pick on her. And he kisses her and plays with her. So that's the mostest thing I want for Christmas. Thank you, Jesus, and *a—men.*" Her eyes popped open like merry little jacks-in-the-box. "Can I eat my scone now? With honey butter on it?"

Tess had to swallow hard before she could answer. All the joy of this night was gone for her. "Yes, dear."

"Bitsy," Sarah said in her reprimanding tone.

Tess cringed. She didn't know if she could endure one of their spats right now.

Sarah leaned within inches of Bitsy's face. "Daddies aren't Christmas presents. You can't wrap a daddy in tissue paper and give him to someone."

"Can too."

"Cannot."

"Girls, I —"

The door crashed open, banged against

the wall. Someone filled the opening, then stumbled forward. A man, drenched to the bone.

"Look!" Bitsy cried. *"It's our daddy!"* She leapt from her chair. And tripped over yards of skirt.

The man stared with wild, stunned eyes. Then, as if he'd been struck with a club, he dropped to his knees and fell forward with a thud.

CHAPTER TWO

Keegan felt a tugging at his shoulder. Something moved his body. But his arms, where were his arms?

Though it was a struggle, he managed to raise his eyelids a fraction to a blur of light. In the center of which loomed a large black spot. He blinked hard to clear his vision. The black spot had yellow eyes. A head.

A huge cat, shawled in green, peered down at him from above.

"Sarah, Elizabeth, grab his other arm. Help me with him." The voice was not the cat's. At least, he hoped it wasn't. Keegan tried to search for the origin of the sound, but he couldn't muster the strength to lift his head.

Something brushed across his face, blocking the light. A kind of cloth. *A burial shroud?* It moved past and came into focus.

A lacy flounce at the bottom of a pale blue skirt.

His gaze moved up the fabric until he discovered a small child swathed in an oversized dress. Over her head, a huge hat floated at a crazy angle.

She tugged on an arm. His . . . which, thankfully, still remained attached to his body. Relief washed over him.

When another baby, swimming in a sea of pink velvet, came to the aid of the one in blue, he couldn't feel her hands on him any more than he could the other's. Yet by the scrape of his boots across the boards, he knew he was being dragged someplace.

Then he became aware that the tiniest one's hair frothed into a golden halo. *A cherub. They're cherubs. I've died. Drowned at sea.*

The realization shuddered through him. He hadn't seen the light in the mist, after all. Hadn't made his way through the waves and rocks toward it. Hadn't climbed the slippery cliff on frozen legs, stumbling, falling, to find a lighthouse with every window glowing, drawing him. Drawing him home. *This must be heaven.*

"Pull harder. Toward the fire."

Fire? He was — *Oh, no!* The cherubs, for all their innocent beauty, were dragging him to the fires of hell. His mind railed against the terrifying thought. But his body refused to stop even the frailest of the tiny beings.

The warmth of flames began to burn against his cold cheeks. Was this to be his punishment for the cavalier way he'd treated females his whole life? For thinking of them as being there solely to entertain him?

And what about his grandmother? Such a good woman. She'd tried so hard to raise him right, keep him on the true path. And what thanks had she gotten? He'd run off to the sea the first chance he got, to wild adventures and sinful pursuits.

"Sarah, go into my bedroom and bring the covers off my bed. Elizabeth, you fetch my teacup. Be careful not to spill it."

The woman's voice again. And, Keegan realized, they'd stopped dragging him . . . *short of the fire.* Maybe they didn't plan to toss him in. *Maybe I'm not dead.*

In a summery yellow dress and wide-brimmed straw hat, this woman with the soothing voice knelt beside him.

But wasn't it winter? Christmas eve? Wasn't the wind howling in the distance even now?

Yet she had eyes as light as an August sky. And hair the deeper shade of sand when shimmering beneath the surf. In swift moves she unbuttoned and stripped off his shirt. Then she moved toward his feet. More tugging. He heard one boot clunk on the floor, then the other.

The smallest child wended her way toward him, a mass of unwieldy skirts hoisted over one arm and a cup in her other hand. "Here, Mama," she said in a small high voice as she held out the fancy little cup.

"Good." Her mother, now beside her, took it. "You go to his feet and start rubbing them — hard."

"I have the covers," came another child's voice.

Beneath a pile of blankets that appeared to be moving toward him, Keegan spied snatches of light blue fabric.

"Sarah, put the gray woolen one over him, then go warm his other foot as your sister is doing." The woman sat down, lifted his head onto her lap, and tilted the cup to his mouth.

Hot liquid burned his lips but felt so good as he swallowed. It slid down his throat in a warm streak.

A violent tremor seized him.

A child let out a frightened squeal. "Mama, why's he shaking like that?" It was the one in blue. "Is he dying?"

"I don't think so. Perhaps the shaking will

help warm him." The woman lifted one of his lifeless hands and began to massage it. "I pray it does."

"You two are being such ninnies," said the child with the halo of blonde curls. "Don't you know Jesus isn't mean? He's not going to bring us our own daddy, then let him die."

Daddy? In the hazy reaches of his memory, Keegan thought the child had called him that before.

Where on earth was he? Could he have a family? Had he hit his head? Forgotten them?

And who were these people? They looked real . . . yet didn't. They certainly were comely enough. And the youngest one had green eyes like his. Hadn't his hair been just as blond and curly as hers when he was small?

No. He'd never forget anything as important as a family. There must be another explanation. Could it be that God Almighty *had* heard his plea for forgiveness? Had sent him the light, and it led him to heaven? Brought him to the life he was meant to have?

So much he needed to ask. If only his mouth would form the words.

The low soothing voice came again.

"Sarah, dear, bring me another cup of tea."

Soon more liquid passed his lips, silky warm . . . and the woman's lap was so cozy . . . the familiar scent of roses swam around him . . . his eyelids, so heavy . . . so sleepy . . .

Late into the night Tess sat in her rocker. Wrapped in her heaviest knit shawl, she was unwilling to walk away from the man lying on the rug at her feet. A mug of hot chocolate and the crackle of the hearth fire were her comfort in this lonely vigil. The children were bedded down, and the lighthouse cottage was muffled in white silence. Several hours before, the wind had stopped, and the sleet had turned into light, fluffy snowflakes. Snow for Christmas. That would please the girls.

A soft groan came from the man nestled among the covers on the floor. She glanced down at him. Not the slightest quaking remained, only quiet breathing. She'd succeeded in bringing up his body temperature. He would live, she was sure of it now. She had proved to herself and, hopefully, to all the town, that she was capable of the task the federal lighthouse administrator had given her. Despite the fact that she was merely a woman.

The man's wet clothing lay draped on the two small rockers beside Tess. Beneath them, puddles of water reflected the firelight. There could be no doubt he'd come from the sea. Yet on a night like this, how could any man have survived being thrown overboard or shipwrecked? Had his clothes not been sopping wet, and his body numbed by icy seawater, she would have assumed he'd come from town.

Perhaps he *was* from Moon Bay Harbor and happened to be on the beach when a wave caught him by surprise. Leaning forward in her rocker, she took a moment to assess his face. No longer plastered to his head, his hair was short with a tendency to curl. The sun had streaked it with gold, like her husband's had been after a voyage to the southern climes. The planes of the man's weathered face had a strength and honesty about them, though softened by laugh lines around his mouth. She liked that. But not his mustache. It drooped pitifully. Picturing it waxed and curled upward in the fashion of the townsmen, she tried to match his looks to someone around Moon Bay. She couldn't think of anyone resembling him.

The man stirred. His lids fluttered, and he stared blankly for a moment. Then his gaze drifted to her and lingered, though he didn't seem to focus. His eyes appeared to be either green or hazel. She couldn't be sure in the capricious firelight.

Slipping to her knees, Tess lifted the stranger's head and gave him a drink from her mug. His hand came out from his blankets and covered hers.

He made a conscious move. Marvelous. "Good evening," she ventured softly.

Instantly his face came alive. "You *are* real." His gaze shifted past her, then came back. "There were children, too. A cat. Dolls and dummies. All sitting around a table in frilly clothes. Having an afternoon tea. At night, by candlelight."

Tess burst out laughing. No wonder the man had passed out. He must have thought he'd fallen down a rabbit hole to join Alice in Wonderland. "I'm so sorry," she managed past her mirth. "I can only imagine the spectacle we made. Because of the storm, I couldn't take the children to the Christmas play in town. So, we had our own impromptu celebration."

He chuckled, a deep friendly rumble that seemed genuine. Tess, however, suspected he thought her a touch daft.

"Little ones need that kind of thing now and again," she said.

"Not just little ones." The man propped himself on an elbow. "My whole crew was ready to keelhaul me when they realized we weren't going to reach Boston before Christmas Eve."

"Your crew!" Tess started to rise.

He caught her hand. "No need to look. They abandoned ship hours before I did. They would've landed farther up the coast."

"I pray they did."

"They're competent seamen." He glanced around the room. "Where exactly am I?"

"The lighthouse on the point of Moon Bay Harbor. I'm Tess Winslow, the lighthouse keeper."

He gave no outward sign of surprise at her occupation. Instead he shrugged and said, "Moon Bay — that doesn't sound familiar."

"It's a fishing village about sixty miles northeast of Portland. It's become even smaller since the continental railroad was completed last year. A good half of the young people have sold out and gone west. After the gentler winters and fertile valleys, they said. Some of the older folks left, too. My in-laws were among them."

"You can't blame them for wanting an easier life. Maine has a way of cutting a man down to size . . . and then some." He

150

flashed an uneasy grin.

"It certainly does." Already Tess could see a humility about the man and an understanding nature.

"And what about your husband? I don't recall seeing him."

He apparently didn't realize he was the guest of a lone woman with two little girls. She hesitated to tell him, but considering his weakened condition, he posed no present threat. "My husband was a seaman like you. He was killed about a year and a half ago." In some Caribbean port, she was tempted to add. Killed in a senseless brawl in a strange land when he should have been home.

"A seaman spends so little time in his home port. That's why I've never considered marriage." He paused. "Things must be hard for you and the children."

"We're getting by. Here." She raised the cup, offering him more hot chocolate.

He took the proffered drink with a hand as tanned as his face. When he'd finished, he settled back onto his pillow with a lazy smile. "Good. Hot chocolate after all these years. You truly are a saint." That said, he closed his eyes and rolled onto his side, facing the glowing embers.

Tess settled back in her rocker to savor

the compliment. The man was proving as charming as he was handsome.

But it wasn't long before she came to her senses. He was probably just another sweet-talking sailor, all promises one day and gone the next. The way her husband had been.

She was no more a saint than any other good Christian woman. She was the lighthouse keeper merely doing the job the town paid her to do. And no grateful eyes or boyish smile was going to woo her into thinking otherwise. She'd already been that kind of a fool when she'd eloped with Tom.

Her mother had never let her forget how reckless she'd been. Every letter came with some reminder of her bad choice, no matter how subtle.

Tess took a cleansing breath. Many times this past year when she didn't know how she would scrape together another month's rent, she had come very close to taking the children home to her family. But now with an adequate home and salary, she would never have to go back to Connecticut in defeat. Wouldn't have to hear her mother say, "I told you so." Even if her mother had been right.

A great yawn overtook Tess, and she looked up at the mantel clock. Twenty past two. She rose and stretched. The girls would be waking up in just a few hours. She needed to go to bed, get some sleep.

Picking up the hem of her voluminous yellow skirt, she stepped carefully between the chair and the man on the floor. Pausing, she took one last look at the sleeping form. He might be just another sweet-talking sailor, but it did seem much less isolated with him here . . . less lonely.

CHAPTER THREE

"Is not."

"Is too."

Tess groaned as she came awake. Her children were already arguing. She reached for covers to pull over her head but found only her thick wool cloak. The man in the front room had her bedding.

A man in her front room! That certainly brought her fully awake.

A patter of bare feet, and the girls raced into her room, their ruffled flannel nightgowns flying out behind them. They crashed onto her bed, their wiggly bodies crawling up on either side of her pillow.

"Tell Bitsy, Mama. Tell her she's being just a stubborn ninny."

"Am not."

"Are too."

Weary of the incessant arguing that had been going on since the weather had turned cold and they'd been staying inside so much, Tess pulled herself into a sitting position and looked from one to the other. "What is it this time?"

"Bitsy says the man in the front room is going to be our new daddy." With a huff, Sarah flipped her long night braid off her shoulder.

"He is," Bitsy railed with determination.

"Is not. We don't even know his name. Do we, Mama? Or where he came from."

A valid point. It hadn't been until Tess retired that she'd realized she hadn't learned the man's identity. But that would soon be remedied. "We'll ask him as soon as he wakes up." Bitsy, however, had to be dealt with before that. She turned to her youngest. "I told you last night, he's just some unfortunate soul who washed ashore. No more, no less."

"See," Sarah added in a snide tone.

Bitsy reared back her thin shoulders. She wasn't one to give in that easily. "I prayed for him, and he came. *So there.* Mama always says we're supposed to pray for what we need. And God hears us, day or night, no matter how loud the storm is. Huh, Mama? Huh?"

Tess was stumped for an answer. She didn't want to shake her child's faith, but

. . . Swinging her feet off the bed, she opted for the coward's way out and changed the subject. "It's Christmas morning. I need to start a fire in the cookstove because I'm fixing you a special breakfast. Eggs and biscuits and ham and —"

"And lots of it," Bitsy cried, wrapping her arms around Tess's neck. "Daddies — I mean men — eat lots more food than we do."

The child was such an imp. Tess pecked her on the cheek, then pulled the small hands away. "Yes, dear, lots of food." Reaching for her chenille robe at the foot of her bed, she saw bright light peeking around the edges of her damask drapes — the promise of a sunny day. The dimness below the window revealed the mess from last night's dressing-up still lying in heaps. Both her commode and chest of drawers were buried beneath the frocks of her carefree youth, along with every inch of the floor — a good hour's straightening at the very least. More, if the girls insisted on helping her. "You two put on your warmest clothing. It snowed last night, and I'm sure you'll want to go out and play in it today."

"Oh, goody." They both jumped up and down on their knees, causing her bedsprings to squeak.

But not a second passed after she'd left the room than the arguing resumed.

"He is not."

"Is too."

Tess turned back to the door and adjusted the ties of her salmon-colored robe. As impetuous as her Bitsy could be, she might just take the dispute to the man in the main room. "Girls, don't you pester our guest with this 'daddy' business. It would be most impolite." Not to mention embarrassing. A shiver crawled up her spine at the very thought. "Do I have your promise on this?" she said with a pointed stare.

Sarah shrugged and nodded nonchalantly.

Not Bitsy. "Yes," came hissing out only after several seconds of clenching her teeth and knotting her fists.

Tess hadn't taken two steps down the hall when she heard Sarah trumpet her triumph.

"*See.* I told you so. Besides, he's got that droopy old mustache. Our daddy didn't have one. I don't like them. And neither does Mama."

That stopped Tess again. Why would Sarah think that? Mustaches were the height of fashion.

"Who says?" Bitsy sounded dubious, justifiably so. Tess waited out of sight, wondering what Sarah would come up with to convince her younger sister this time.

"Remember when Mr. Spencer came calling? He had a mustache, and Mama wouldn't even let him kiss her."

"How do you know?"

Yes, Tess thought, *how did Sarah know that?*

"At our old house, I sneaked down the stairs one night and watched 'em. He tried to, and she pushed him away."

"Why didn't you let me watch, too?"

"You were already asleep. And besides, you're too young."

"Am not."

"Are too."

What a pair. With a smile, Tess shook her head and walked on. That Sarah. She was far more aware of happenings than Tess had known, though not quite correct in her assessment. Mr. Spencer's mustache hadn't offended Tess. It had been the man himself, with his uppity, self-important ways.

Emerging from the hall, Tess looked beyond the clothes-draped rockers and the sleeping man to see a few embers glowing in the fireplace. She tiptoed to the wood box and pulled out the last two pieces. As quietly as possible, she placed the logs over the coals. She'd certainly fed a lot of the fast-burning pine last night, keeping the room warm for the stranger. More would be needed before she could start breakfast.

Tess watched the steady rise and fall of the big man's chest while she pulled on her galoshes and tossed her cloak over her robe. Spent as he'd been last night, this morning he would probably have the appetite of a horse. She doubted she had enough of her precious eggs to satisfy that hunger. A double batch of biscuits was in order. And plenty of the smoked ham.

The cat leapt off the settee and trotted over to brush against her leg. She swooped him up. "Time for you to go out, too." Yes, somehow she would make the food stretch. She had had plenty of practice.

Keegan was awakened by something tickling his lip. Groggily he swiped with his hand. It brushed against something metal. A knife? Pistol?

Instantly he opened his eyes to find a small child stooped beside him — one of the lighthouse keeper's daughters. The one with the bouncy blonde curls. He relaxed.

Her gaze collided with his, and her mouth opened in surprise, then she looked away with what he'd have sworn was a furtive expression. Probably just shy.

"Good morning," he said to ease her fear.

Her expression changed in an instant as she grinned so wide every baby tooth sparkled. "Merry Christmas, Mr. Sailor." She had one hand tucked behind her back.

She couldn't be hiding anything of his. He'd arrived with only the clothes on his back. Even his rain slicker had been lost in the surf. "Call me Keegan," he said, hoisting himself onto his elbow. "And what's your name?"

"Elizabeth. Elizabeth Louise Winslow. But everybody just calls me Bitsy. Don't you want to go back to sleep again? We'll be real quiet."

The nickname fit perfectly. "If it's all right with you, I'd like to call you Bitsy, too." Keegan looked past her for her older sister or that fine-looking mother of theirs. He saw only the dress form, standing in the corner in front of a treadle sewing machine and a cutting table. It now was devoid of its head and hat, but scarves and lace flounces still draped it. "Where's the rest of your family?" he asked, chuckling at the remembrance of his first sight of them all.

"Oh, Sarah's in the bedroom dressing her new doll. And Mama went to the shed for wood." Bitsy reached out with her one exposed hand and pulled his covers up more snugly. "You need to go back to sleep."

The child was as persistent as a mother hen. But Keegan wasn't sleepy now. He sat up and discovered quite a few sore spots. All in all, he'd taken quite a beating yesterday. But, he thought bitterly, his ship had fared far worse. And his cargo. The profit from the Oriental silk fabrics alone would have been enormous. Enough to purchase a second ship. But now he had none. Nothing. For eight years he'd saved for that ship. Eight wasted years.

Keegan heaved a sigh. *Buck up, old man. This isn't the first time you've been penniless.*

He stretched the kinks from his arms and back . . . and suddenly he found his chest was bare. He wore no shirt — not even his undershirt. Where were his clothes? Spotting them draped over the rockers, he grabbed the closest, but he couldn't reach his dark trousers. "Bitsy, would you please hand me the rest of my clothes?"

Still in a stoop beside him, she looked from him to the trousers with no change of expression. "You sure you don't want to sleep some more?"

"No, Bitsy. I do *not* want any more sleep. My long underwear, if you please."

"Oh, all right." Using her free hand, she pushed off the floor while keeping the other tucked secretively behind her. "Just a minute." Twirling away, she ran to the kitchen area and opened the drawer of a worktable. A clunking sound followed just before she slammed the drawer shut.

What on earth could a child that small have to hide?

Bitsy then dragged, more than carried, the remainder of his clothes to him. "Keegan?" She crouched beside him again.

"Yes?" he grunted while working a foot into a leg hole.

"You don't have a little girl like me, do you?"

"Afraid not. I've been out to sea mostly. I don't come home often enough to have a wife and children."

"You must be very sad, then. Not to have any little girls to give you hugs and kisses. Daddies love hugs and kisses."

Hugs and kisses from big girls had always been more to his liking. With his trousers on, he searched for his undershirt.

She found it first and flung it to him. Still in a squat, she was all smiles, her toes peeking out from her ruffled nightgown hem. Her eagerness to please tugged at Keegan's heart, and he realized the little scamp looked more huggable than he'd ever imagined a small child could.

"And at Christmas," she continued as he

dressed, "if you had a little girl, she'd make you plenty of presents. I'm giving Mama lots of pretty shells for bowls and things. Rocks, too. Smooth shiny rocks I found all by myself. Down in the tide pools."

He couldn't help returning her grin. He remembered doing the same at her age, giving useless gifts to his grandmother. And she'd fawned over them as if he'd given her some store-bought prize. More. And the hugs . . . she'd been lavish with them.

Donning his black sweater, he began to feel some of Bitsy's exuberance. Children were what made Christmas fun. He hoped he would be around when Bitsy handed her mother the presents. "When are you giving them to her?"

"Prob'ly after breakfast. Mama's fixing us a special one with lots of food. 'Cause you're here. You being so big and all."

Another pleasure — a home-cooked meal. Now, that was a real Christmas present.

He found his boots still drying on the hearth and rose on stockinged feet. One hip protested a bit. He remembered slamming against a rock last night when his makeshift raft broke up a few yards from shore. Considering how close he'd come to death, a few bruises were a welcome exchange. He still couldn't believe he'd survived both the cold and the rock-strewn surf.

Keegan picked up his bedding and laid the pile on a rocker except for a patchwork quilt he kept to fold.

"Don't!" Bitsy sprang to her feet. "You won't be able to take another nap if you do that."

"I don't take naps," he said, raking his fingers through his thatch of short curls.

The child let out an impatient sigh. "Let me help you then." She grabbed a corner of the quilt and shook it worse than a dog does a rag.

Some help, Keegan thought, thoroughly amused as he joined her in their assault on the quilt. The folding took twice the time it would have without the child's assistance, but letting the squirt help was much more fun. He chuckled. All in all, this promised to be a good morning. He'd worry about the rest of his life later.

The whining squeak of a wheel and the crunch of ice came from the front yard.

"Mama, with the pushcart."

"Sounds like she's having a hard time. I'd better help."

On legs still a tad wobbly, Keegan reached the door and swung it open to find Mrs. Winslow gathering logs from the two-wheeled cart. The woman looked as good in the morning as she had by firelight, and as her attention was occupied he studied her. The cold had blushed her cheeks — a striking contrast to the navy blue of her cloak and the brilliant white snow. Her night braid nested in the hood of the cloak, just a few tempting inches at its tip spilling out.

It was all Keegan could do not to reach out and give it a playful tug. "Good morning, ma'am," he said.

She looked up with a start, and then she smiled — a warm smile that went all the way to her eyes. "When I heard the door open, I thought it was one of the girls. It's good to see you up and about."

"And ready to help. Here, let me take that."

Her mouth fell open for a moment, but just as quickly she flashed a grin with as much exuberance as any of Bitsy's.

Relieving her of the wood, Keegan found it hard to believe she would be so amazed when a man offered to assist her. As pretty a young woman as she was, men should have been lined up at her door. He started into the house.

"Mister —" she said on a light laugh.

He turned back. "The name's Keegan. Captain Keegan, if you'd prefer."

"Captain." She took a step closer, obviously trying to suppress her laughter, yet a smile still played at the corners of her mouth and across her light blue eyes.

He had misread her completely. She hadn't been amazed — she was amused.

"I have to ask," she barely managed, "if you were going to rid yourself of your mustache, why did you cut off only one side?"

Mustache? His magnificent mustache that had taken years to grow? That he waxed into perfectly balanced curlicues whenever he made port? The one all the lasses fawned over? He dropped the logs and raised a hand to his upper lip.

One side was nothing but stubble.

Suddenly he remembered being awakened by a tickling lip. And Bitsy. Hovering over him, hiding something behind her back. *Scissors.*

He wheeled and charged into the house, his furious gaze sweeping the room. *"Bitsy!"*

But the little scamp had disappeared.

CHAPTER FOUR

Keegan turned when Mrs. Winslow caught his arm.

"I'm terribly sorry," she said. "I can't imagine what got into Bitsy."

He saw he had frightened her with his roar. She probably thought he intended to eat the sprout — which didn't seem like such a bad idea at the moment. "I suppose kids can be a handful," he acknowledged.

"I'm sure Bitsy didn't do that out of spite." The woman sounded sincere. "That child can get the oddest notions. I'll speak to her as soon as I start a fire in the cookstove." She released his arm and reached down to pick up the logs.

Keegan knelt beside her. "Let me do that. I'll get a fire going for you if you'll loan me a razor and some soap. I need to finish what the little —" he cleared his throat — "*child* started."

"Yes, of course." She held open the door for him, her gaze not quite meeting his.

Keegan caught that haunting whiff of roses again as he passed her.

"What in heaven's name was Bitsy thinking —" her glance targeted his upper lip, and she couldn't quite squelch her amusement — "to cut off your mustache?"

"I know why she did it." The older child, Sarah, stood near the entrance to the hall, staring up with her mother's light blue eyes. "You know what a dumb baby she is — and how set she is on him being our new daddy."

Daddy? The word rocked Keegan.

"I told her you don't like kissing men with mustaches, so . . ." She shrugged, then nonchalantly started toying with her doll.

Keegan wasn't sure he had heard correctly until he spotted Mrs. Winslow's face glowing like a tropical sunset. "I — uh — I don't know what to say." She rushed past the kitchen table to the stove and started tossing kindling into the firebox.

Keegan didn't feel any too comfortable himself. The cozy room with its plump cushions and ruffled curtains began to look like a man-trap. Blast, he wished his boots were dry. The air pulsed with unspoken words as he waited until his hostess moved away from the stove so he could put in a couple of split logs.

"I suppose it's more my fault than hers," Mrs. Winslow said as she lifted the kettle onto one of the stove's heating lids.

So she had actually put the man-trapping ideas into her child's head? Keegan headed for the door to fetch more wood, feeling a sudden impulse to just keep on going.

When he returned, Mrs. Winslow had placed everything he needed for a shave on the table — a mug, brush, and razor . . . most likely her late husband's. He wasn't quite sure what to say.

"You'll need a looking glass," she said. "I'll fetch a hand mirror from my bedroom."

Was she being apologetic or merely coy? Either way, he'd have to be on his guard around such an attractive young woman.

He felt a tugging on his sleeve. Sarah had sidled up beside his chair. "It's not Mama's fault. It's Bitsy's. Just yesterday Mama said we're doing fine on our own now that the town has let her be the lighthouse keeper. And even before, when she sewed for Mrs. Pritchard and the other ladies, it didn't matter how sore Mama's fingers got, or her eyes. She'd stay up all night if that's what it took. We never went hungry, not once. It's Bitsy who wants a daddy — ever since last month when she saw Martha Jane's daddy tossing her in the air. Martha Jane laughed so hard, I thought she'd split her seams." The thin-boned child, whose eyes were more expressive than her words, sniffed with disdain. "But she's just a silly baby like Bitsy and loves that sort of thing."

Keegan knew he shouldn't let the little girl affect him, but the way she pretended not to care tugged at his tender spot. He cupped her fragile chin. "Yes, I can see you're much too grown up for that."

She stepped back from him. "Mama and me are doing fine without a daddy around. But last night when Bitsy prayed for one, and then you came crashing through the door, well . . . she's being just plain stubborn, thinking God sent you here to us. Just plain stubborn."

"Sarah, dear," Mrs. Winslow called as she walked from the hall. "I really don't think Captain Keegan wants to hear about Bitsy's Christmas wishes." She propped a hand mirror against the oil lamp on the table. "Captain, your water should be hot soon. I'll go find Bitsy. She needs to face what she's done and apologize."

A vision of Bitsy's expectant face flashed before Keegan, and he felt a rush of need to soften her disappointment as well as her punishment. "Let me explain. I don't want her to get into trouble over some whiskers — fine though they were. But first," he said, picking up the mirror and viewing the butchery, "I'd better get rid of this one-sided spectacle." As ridiculous as he looked, small wonder Mrs. Winslow couldn't keep from laughing.

"You do look peculiar," Sarah said, eyeing him solemnly.

"*Sarah*," Mrs. Winslow censured as Keegan burst out laughing. The child had a knack for blunt honesty.

Her mother spread her hands helplessly. "I don't know what to say. The girls aren't usually like this."

Sarah, the snitch, had given away Bitsy's hiding place — the top of the lighthouse tower. Keegan started up an enclosed staircase that spiraled as high as a clipper ship mast. Climbing the narrow steps in his stocking feet, he gritted his teeth against the pain in his bruised hip, a reminder of yesterday's losses.

After years of crewing for others, he'd finally managed to save enough from some personal cargo investments to purchase a merchant schooner. And then, only then, for the first time in his life did he get caught in a storm so fierce, so violent, it tore a ship he sailed asunder. Sank it. And his dream.

He pondered the situation as he climbed. It couldn't be worse than the day he arrived in this world, killing his mother and sending his father packing.

The picture of his grandmother's plump cheeks, dimpled smile, and cushiony bosom floated into his thoughts. Never once had she complained about having to raise her grandchild for her drifter of a son. But now she was getting too old to be running that wharf-side inn. With some of his profits, Keegan had planned to open a bank account for her and make sure she spent her last days in comfort.

He reached the top of the stairwell and studied the layout. Beacon lamps and mirror assemblies took up most of the platform. A narrow walkway circled them, and halfway around it Bitsy stood on a stool. Still in her pink flannel nightgown, she pressed her face against one of the windowpanes that circled the tiny room, oblivious to his presence.

Small wonder. The view of sea clashing with the rugged Maine coast was a sight to behold. A gray-and-white seagull soared across the blue sky toward the open water. Along the bluffs on each side of the tower, windblown pines dripped sparkling snow.

So beautiful, so peaceful, one would never know all of nature had been on a rampage just hours ago.

He could've stood there all day, but he and Curly Top had a couple of things to get straight.

"Bitsy, I thought this would be —"

"Oh!" She whirled, startled. The stool teetered.

Keegan snatched her up just as the stool crashed to the deck. Dangling from his arms, she twisted around and crawled up his chest like a Madagascar monkey, then pointed to something below. "Look! Christmas presents! A daddy *and* Christmas presents!"

Keegan glanced down to where she indicated. On a thin strip of sand sat a chest. Then he spotted another. Farther down, he saw a third. Chests. Part of his cargo!

"Come on! Come on!" Bitsy cried as she bounced up and down in his arms. "Let's go see what the three wise men brought us."

Tess smiled as she flipped sizzling ham slices in the frying pan. She couldn't believe how well Captain Keegan had taken Bitsy's mischief. She didn't know a single man in Moon Bay who would have been that kind about having his mustache mutilated. Except maybe old Tobias. The elderly bachelor had been the one who'd spoken in her favor when the lighthouse administrator was considering her request for the job.

Perhaps men without families of their own were more inclined to treat females with charity.

Tess turned to her ever-willing helper, Sarah, who was setting the table. "Dear, why don't we put the candles from last night on the table again? With the calico cloth, they'll make everything more festive."

The child's face brightened. "Like another party." In a nightgown that was already inches too short, she skipped to the candle drawer.

How fast her children were growing, Tess thought with a sense of loss. Her babies would be half-grown before she knew it.

"I think Cap'n Keegan looks a lot friendlier without his mustache. Don't you, Mama?"

"I suppose," she replied in a nonchalant tone that belied a surprising fluttering of her heart. As handsome as he looked after he shaved, Tess was amazed some enterprising lass hadn't snatched him up long ago. But then, she mused while moving ham slices from the pan to a plate, he'd chosen the sea — and the free life — over a wife. Tom, too, should have remained a bachelor. Although he'd never said the words, Tess knew he came to regret the responsibility of marriage. After Bitsy came along, he rarely took leave from Dorsey's Shipping to come home.

Poor little Bitsy. Suddenly her smallest one's fixation became crystal clear. She wanted that father she never really had. Glancing to the hallway, Tess wondered how the four-year-old was taking the news that the captain had not come here to be her father. She hoped his explanation didn't upset Bitsy too much and ruin Christmas for her.

The tower door rattled open, and Captain Keegan entered. He strode into the room with Bitsy sitting in the crook of his arm. Both sported similar grins — two curly-headed peas in a pod.

Undoubtedly, the discussion had gone well. Far better than Tess would have imagined.

"Mama, we gotta go down to the beach," Bitsy cried, her cheeks flushed with excitement. "They left our Christmas presents there."

Wiping her hands on a towel, Tess stepped toward the pair. "Who? What?"

"The wise men, Mama. Remember?

They're the ones who bring the gifts." Still clinging to the captain's neck, Bitsy swiveled toward her sister. "Come on, Sarah. Come see what they brung us. There could be lots and lots of things."

"Cargo chests." With a conspiratorial wink at Tess, Captain Keegan lowered Bitsy to the floor. Some of his merchandise must have washed ashore, she realized.

"I've got to put on my boots first, and you have to get dressed." He gave the child a light pat on the back. "Now, scoot. You, too, Sarah. I'll bet there's a present down there just for you."

Sarah looked doubtfully from the captain to Tess — too serious, too skeptical for a child her age. "But I haven't finished setting the table."

Tess took linen napkins from Sarah's hand. "Run along and get dressed. I'll do it for you. You don't want Bitsy to beat you down there, do you?"

As both girls ran out of the room, Tess caught the aroma of baking biscuits and turned back to the stove.

"Would we be delaying breakfast if we go?" the captain asked over his shoulder as he padded to the hearth for his boots.

"It won't be ready for fifteen minutes. Take more time if you need. I'm pleased some of your cargo washed ashore. I pray there won't be too much water damage."

"The chests were caulked and sealed tight. As long as they aren't punctured, the merchandise should be fine. In fact, if these made it to shore, there could be others. I'll need to get all of them off the beach before the tide comes in . . . *and* before someone else finds them and claims them as salvage."

Tess offered a reassuring smile. "Since it's Christmas day, most folks will be at home celebrating with their families. Oh, and Captain Keegan, you'll need something larger than my wood cart to take your chests from here to the harbor. After breakfast, I'll hike up the road to McCann's place. He's got a good-sized wagon."

The captain stood and came toward her. He seemed taller in his boots, straighter, stalwart in his bearing, and almost intimidating as he held her eyes in his unwavering gaze. He stopped directly in front of her. "You are a godsend," he said just above a whisper. "Saving my life last night, and now helping me with my cargo."

Tess's heart fluttered again, and she felt suddenly uneasy at his nearness. She would have stepped back, but the stove stood behind her. *"Godsend,"* she said. "To hear Bitsy tell it, you're the godsend."

Deftly, she slipped to one side of him and opened the cold box mounted in the outside wall. She removed a small basket of eggs and faced him again.

He was still there, much too close for clear thought. "By the way," he said, laugh lines creasing deeply on either side of his mouth, "I haven't spoken to Bitsy yet about that *father* business. We got too busy with the gifts of the magi."

A much safer topic, she thought with relief.

Tess brought a bowl down from a shelf beside the stove. "Don't let that little wheedler talk you out of more than a trinket or two." Cracking an egg into the bowl, she remembered her older daughter. "Thank you for including Sarah. Lately she's lost her zest for fun. If she and Bitsy didn't argue so much, I'd forget she was a child."

The captain nodded. "Maybe while we're down there, she'll find something that will put the spring back in her step." He moved past her to the stove. "Coffee smells good," he said, serving himself a cup from the enamel pot. "And so does everything else around here."

By his tone, Tess had no doubt that everything included her. Typical sailor. The man was flirting *outrageously* before they were even on a first-name basis.

CHAPTER FIVE

"Ready!" Bitsy shouted. She charged into the front room, her blonde curls bouncing wildly about her face.

Tess was grateful the child had interrupted the awkward moment between her and the captain. Yet she felt a twinge of disappointment when his attention left her for the child. Was she still susceptible to the flirtations of a sailor?

Sarah entered at a more dignified pace, but Tess caught a hint of anticipation in her eyes. The lure of the treasure. Or the captain. Maybe all three Winslows were caught up by the mariner's charm.

"Put on your galoshes and button up. Are your mittens in your pockets?" There was nothing like the responsibilities of motherhood to bring a woman back to her senses.

Once the front door slammed behind the adventuring threesome, the house fell into an empty silence. Tess wished she'd gone with them. Breakfast could have waited. But biscuits were in the oven.

She hurried to the window above the deacon's bench for a last glimpse as they headed toward the path that would take them down the rocky cliff. After all the previous night's slash and roar, no more than three inches of snow impeded Bitsy as she danced around Captain Keegan, flapping her arms. Laughing and talking nonstop, she puffed vapor clouds in every direction.

The captain, towering above the child in his black sweater and trousers, looked thoroughly amused. He was favoring one leg, though. Probably because of the bruised hip Tess had noticed the night before.

Then Sarah caught her mother's eye. The elder daughter merely trudged along behind the others. The contrast between the two girls tugged at Tess's heart.

At that moment Captain Keegan paused and turned back. He said something to Sarah and held out his hand. She stopped and stared at him.

Tess held her breath, clenched the chintz curtain, and prayed.

Slowly, hesitantly, the child's mittened fingers stretched out. As the captain took her hand and brought Sarah alongside him,

Tess released her breath. Hand in hand, the two followed "butterfly" Bitsy toward the edge of the bluff.

Watching them go, Tess couldn't hold back her tears. Never before had she realized how deprived her children were. She'd seen to their everyday needs and their spiritual training, but this one need she could never fulfill. Every little girl craved a father who would make her feel cherished and beautiful . . . like his very own princess, just as her father had Tess. That was special — something she hadn't felt in a long, long time.

The threesome disappeared below the cliff, and Tess returned to the eggs, all the while wondering if maybe Captain Keegan truly might be an answer to Bitsy's prayer. The man seemed to be everything those little girls could ask for. For today.

Even if he would be on a ship headed for Boston tomorrow, he was doing a pretty good imitation of a daddy for this one morning . . . a daddy for Christmas.

Picking up a fork to scramble the eggs, Tess dwelled on Keegan's face. Shaving off that mustache had revealed lips fuller than she'd expected. Very nice lips. And they spread so easily into a friendly smile.

Suddenly Tess realized she still had on her robe. And her hair! She quickly checked on the biscuits, then ran for her bedroom, ripping the ties from her chenille wrapper as she went.

On her return to the kitchen after dressing, Tess glanced at the clock and knew she'd spent too much time primping. She quickly tied her fullest apron around a waist now cinched by her corset. She couldn't afford a single drop of grease on her best day gown. Below a V neck filled with white lace, the burgundy velvet bodice fitted smoothly. Just below the waist, a swag trimmed with ribbon and lace dyed to match met in the rear to form a generous bustle, one the women at church had especially admired. The upswept chignon at the crown of her head was no less elaborate, and she'd left just enough tendrils to wisp about her face and neck to soften the formal severity.

Undeniably, she'd overdressed for a simple breakfast with her family, Christmas or not. Nor could she deny she'd gotten all decked out for the man.

But what harm could there be, she mused as she poured the eggs into the skillet. Keegan would be gone tomorrow.

She looked across to the window where she'd last seen him. He'd be coming back any minute with the children. And no matter how hard she tried to make herself think more soberly, the years seemed to slip away, leaving her as excited and lighthearted as a young girl.

In fact, as soon as the eggs were done, she would fetch her cameo to pin at her throat for a final touch. The family heirloom that one day would be Sarah's was her last item of value. She'd sooner swallow her pride and take the children back home than sell the cherished cameo.

When the eggs were done, Tess set the skillet at the back of the stove to keep warm with the other food. She started for her bedroom but was stopped when she spotted flashes of movement outside. They were returning.

She dashed across the room for a closer look.

A child perched gaily in the crook of each of Captain Keegan's arms. And they were all laughing uproariously. Even Sarah.

Tess's eyes misted again. She stepped away from the window and hurried to the table to light the candles and put on the food.

The three didn't enter the front door. Instead she heard noise at the back of the hall — they'd come through the tower door. Giggles and whispered shushings. Then another door opened and closed. Such a high time they were having.

Everything for breakfast was on the table by the time the group came to the front of the house, and only with the greatest effort did the little ones contain their enthusiasm. The captain himself grinned like a little boy as he looked from the children to Tess.

All three secreted a hand behind their backs as the girls thrust forth their other wrists. They wore sparkling chains dangling with the tiniest of bells that tinkled airily.

"Aren't they the most beautifulest bracelets you ever saw?" Bitsy cried.

Seeing the joy in her children's eyes, Tess's throat tightened, and those blasted tears started pooling again. "Be seated, everyone," she said, hastening out of the room. "I forgot something."

Keegan had never considered high-necked, bustled-up dresses attractive — until he watched Mrs. Winslow sweep from the room. The woman was downright inspiring. And that fresh scent of roses mixed with the morning's fare — he was beginning to see how easily thoughts of settling down could creep up on a man.

"Wonder what Mama forgot," Bitsy said, climbing onto her chair and hiding her cloth-wrapped present beneath a fold of her plaid skirt.

"Nothing," Sarah answered. The smile that Keegan had worked so hard to bring to her lips was gone. "Mama was about to cry. And she never lets us see her do that."

Why? What would make a woman cry when everything was going so well? Glancing at Sarah, Keegan saw a sheen of tears misting her eyes, too.

"Mama don't cry," Bitsy said. "Only babies cry."

When Sarah shot Bitsy a weary look, Keegan asked, "Does she cry often?"

Sarah solemnly shook her head as she slipped onto her slat-backed chair. "No. I only saw her twice. Once when the man from the bank came and said we had to move. Then when Mrs. Pritchard refused to pay her 'cause a dress Mama sewed for her didn't look the same on her as it did in the magazine." Sarah frowned. "But I thought Mama was happy today."

Keegan had thought the same. The candlelit table was heaped with biscuits, ham, and eggs, looking as festive as the woman herself.

The food! Of course. She must have used food stores she couldn't spare just to provide him with a hearty breakfast. Maybe he should just wait until she returned and make some plausible excuse. Then he could thank her for her hospitality and take his leave.

But he hadn't eaten since yesterday morning, and his gnawing hunger wasn't letting him forget it. Plus everything smelled so good — almost as good as Mrs. Winslow.

"This is your chair here," Bitsy said, patting the one next to her own. She then rested a hand on the lump in her lap again.

Keegan sighed. "I'm waiting for your mother to come back." Then he'd go, but not before the little ones gave her their presents. He couldn't leave before that.

A moment later Mrs. Winslow returned, her damp lashes a telltale sign that Sarah had been right. "Sorry. I — uh — forgot to remove my apron. And this being such a special day . . ." Her gaze only briefly skimmed across his face before she glanced elsewhere. As she pulled out her chair, she turned to Keegan. "Please, don't stand on ceremony. Be seated."

His grandmother's instructions came to the fore, and he rushed to help her into her seat . . . a feat made more difficult by her cumbersome bustle.

"Why, thank you, Captain Keegan."

As she settled her skirts around her, he managed to take in several discreet whiffs of her cologne, all the while wishing he could run his fingers along the sides of that silky white neck. But that was not to be. He had to leave.

"I really should get back down to the beach. Other chests may have washed ashore farther up . . . I need to see they aren't swept out again with the tide."

"Mr. Keegan," said Mrs. Winslow, turning in her chair. "I'm sure as an expert seaman you know the tide won't start to turn again for a couple of hours. Please, do join us for our Christmas breakfast. Then, just as soon as we're through, we'll all go down and help you scout the beach." She smiled at each of her daughters in turn. "I've a couple of pretty good hide-and-seekers here."

Bitsy clutched his hand and squeezed. "Don't go without us, Keegan. *Pleeease.*"

Those pleading eyes. How could he refuse her? And her mother seemed equally sincere. He'd just have to trade some of his goods at the village store to replenish her larder before he left for Boston.

No sooner had Keegan sat down than Bitsy cried, "Can we do it now, huh? Can we?"

At the first hint of a nod from him, Bitsy brought from hiding her present, which she'd wrapped in a gingham scrap. She slammed it down on her mother's plate.

Not to be outdone, Sarah did the same. "Open mine first."

"No! mine!"

"My goodness," their mother said. "How can I choose?" Then with a wink at Keegan that made his heart do the craziest leapfrog, she said, "I suppose I'll open the one that's about to teeter off my plate." She picked up Sarah's narrow-shaped gift and untied the bow at each end. Then she lifted out one of the many silk fans Keegan had bought while in Bombay. They were said to be from the Japans. "Oh, Sarah," she said, flipping it open. "This is exquisite. Such a delicately painted picture."

"It's for hot days at church. Now *you'll* have the prettiest fan there."

"I most certainly will. I'll treasure it always." Laying the fan across the top of her plate, she unwrapped Bitsy's gift, a carving of an animal.

Bitsy leapt to her knees. "See? It's a — a —" She swung to Keegan. "A what?"

"An elephant."

"Yes, that's what it is. Look at its nose, Mama. Did you ever see anything like it?"

Mrs. Winslow held the gold-trimmed miniature in her open palm for everyone to view. "I can't say that I have. I'll display it on the mantel so that whenever anyone comes to visit, they'll see what a grand gift my Bitsy gave me. You've both brought me the most wonderful presents. Through the kindness of Captain Keegan, of course."

She turned to him with appreciation shining in her eyes — all that he could ever hope for. He saw where the little girls got their engaging charm. No wonder his heart kept acting up. The only response he managed was a quick nod.

"Time to eat," Bitsy said and grabbed a biscuit.

"Not yet." Sarah, sitting on the other side of Keegan, placed her little girl hand on his. "Keegan hasn't given Mama his present."

All eyes were on him as he withdrew a small parcel from beneath his sweater.

"Really, Captain Keegan, you've given us so much already."

Ignoring the young widow, he placed a folded square of black velvet on her plate. "This is merely a token for saving my life. And, personally, I think my life is worth quite a lot."

"Yes, of course." She sounded flustered. "But still, I think —"

"Don't. It's Christmas. Simply enjoy."

Looking a bit guilty, she acquiesced and

spread open the fabric to display a heart-shaped pendant of gold set with a ruby — one of the most costly items he'd bargained for on his travels.

She gasped. "Good heavens!" Picking it up, she tried to hand it back. "I couldn't possibly. This is much too beautiful. Far too valuable."

He closed her fingers over the chain-strung heart. "Mrs. Winslow, do you think my life is worth less than this bauble?"

"No — I —" She looked at her daughters, whose shining faces said, "Keep it!"

Keegan continued to hold her hand around the necklace until at last her expression changed to one of gracious acceptance. "Very well. But only if you'll call me Tess."

The smile that accompanied her last words was so encouraging, he knew if he wasn't careful he'd be offering himself as her next present. Instead he mumbled some inane nonsense about how the name suited her . . . all the while feeling the need for some fresh air.

"Now can we eat?" Bitsy asked as she took a bite of her biscuit.

"Not yet, dear," her mother said. "We haven't given thanks to the Lord."

Bitsy put down her biscuit and turned to

Keegan with an exuberant smile. "That's the daddy's job."

Tess shot Keegan a disturbed glance.

He shrugged and turned to Bitsy's baby-round face. It was time — past time — to set her straight. "Bitsy, I'm having grand fun playing with you today. But, I'm afraid it is *just for today*. Tomorrow or the next, I'll be on my way again. To Boston."

Bitsy said nothing, only stared at him. Then, cocking her head, she stared longer. Finally she spoke. "Say the prayer, Captain Keegan. I'm hungry."

Then it struck him. They expected him to say grace. *To pray out loud!* Him, Lovett Josiah Keegan. He hadn't done that since he left his grandmother's house. Nor had he seen the inside of a church. But what kind of an example would he be for the children if he confessed that? All eyes at table were on him. Waiting.

Buck up, he told himself. *Be brave. It's just a few simple words*. But his heart started pounding, and heat rushed to his head. His hands turned clammy.

He wiped them on his trousers and took a deep breath. His throat was dry. He cleared it. Took another breath. "Almighty God . . ."

CHAPTER SIX

"Almighty God, thank you for this good food and the wonderful family who took me in during my hour of greatest need. Amen." At the finish of the short prayer, Keegan almost collapsed with relief.

"And the chests," Bitsy whispered urgently as she peeked around her folded hands. "Don't forget to pray about them."

Couldn't the child ever leave well enough alone? Keegan cleared his throat again. "Yes, Father, thank you for bringing some of my cargo ashore undamaged."

Keegan took a deep breath, deciding to thank the Lord for the rest of the miracle before Bitsy interfered again. "And, Lord, thank you for causing a break in the storm last night long enough for me to see the beacon light and to find my way here to this warm and welcoming haven. In the name of Jesus, Amen."

Bitsy leaned toward him. "That's the way Christmas is, you know. God's special star brought the wise men to Baby Jesus, and our light brought you to us. And you brought gifts just like them." She jiggled the bracelet around her wrist. "Don't we have the bestest God?"

Such simple clarity. From Keegan's childhood memory a Bible verse emerged. *Out of the mouth of babes and sucklings thou hast perfected praise.* In that moment, he also had no doubt that his grandmother had never ceased holding him up to God in prayer. Even yet, after all these years God had honored her petitions by saving his life. He suddenly felt unworthy, humbled.

"Eggs, Captain?" Tess casually held out the platter as if neither he nor the child had said anything unusual.

Grateful, he took them from her. He appreciated everything he'd seen and heard from his hostess thus far. Hard to believe he'd stumbled onto someone so extraordinary in such a remote setting. He loved the way her slender fingers wove around her fork, and the way every time he glanced at her eyes they startled him with their almost transparent blue, and how her soft full lips parted —

"Keegan." Sarah's thin voice broke into

his musings. "Is that your first name or your last?"

"My last. But that's what everyone calls me."

"Why?" she pressed.

"Because I prefer it."

"Why?" Bitsy chimed in.

"Biscuits, Captain?" Tess offered.

He took the plate and busied himself buttering a couple of biscuits, hoping the subject of his name would be forgotten.

"Keegan," Bitsy said flatly, "I thought you liked us."

"I do," he said, wondering where that had come from.

"Then why don't you want us to call you by your first name like you do us?"

"I'm just not all that fond of it."

"I'll bet I'd like it."

"Elizabeth, stop pestering the poor man. If he wanted you to know, he would've told you." Tess then looked squarely into his eyes. "For reasons of their own, sailors quite often don't give their full names."

Was the woman accusing him of being just one more sailor looking for a night of fun in port before weighing anchor? True as that had been more times than he could count, having her confront him with it grated. "It's Lovett," he shot back, returning

194

her direct gaze with one of his own. He turned to Sarah with a forced smile. "Lovett Josiah Keegan."

"*Love it?*" Bitsy asked at a shattering pitch.

"No, Bits, Lov-*ett*. But you're not the first one to make that mistake. When I was a little older than you, the kids at school had a fine time making all kinds of mistakes with it. So," he said, addressing her mother again, "I'd just as soon be called Keegan."

A grin swept Tess's face. "Lovett. I do *love* the sound of that. Have some ham, Lovett."

Tess knew any good impression she'd made on her guest by donning her finest clothes for breakfast was ruined. Now wearing men's overalls, galoshes, and heavy gloves, she stood at the edge of a rocky cliff as she bent and pulled along with him on a rope.

She had volunteered to help haul up the chests — insisted, really. He couldn't have found other assistance before the tide turned, especially on Christmas Day.

The captain hadn't been as fortunate in his search as he had hoped. Although debris from the ship was plentiful, they'd found only two more chests among the tide pools and along the narrow beaches — beaches that soon would be under several feet of water.

"Just a little more," Keegan called from behind her.

She gripped the thick hemp rope tighter and gave a final tug as the last of the five watertight containers bumped and scraped over the top of the craggy edge.

"You can crew with me anytime," he said, taking the rope from her. He began coiling it as he walked toward the chest.

Tess had mixed feelings about the compliment. She was glad he thought her as much help as any of his seamen, but being one of the boys did nothing to bolster her sense of femininity. She pulled off the heavy gloves. "The job's only half done. I'd better round up the girls and go fetch the McCanns' wagon." Blocking the glare from sun and snow with her hand, she scanned both directions along the jagged precipice, but with no success. "Did you see which way they went?"

He glanced up from untying the crate. "North." He leapt onto the nearest boulder. "I think I see one of them. Aye, they're coming from behind that pile of rocks." He waved his arms. "Over here!"

Hearing Keegan, the children ran toward

them, gesturing with their own arms as they came. About halfway they halted. Bitsy cupped her mouth with her hands and yelled, "Come see! The ocean — it's magic! It's changing colors. Red! Yellow! Purple!"

"The child does have a vivid imagination." Tess exchanged a glance with a man whose eyes couldn't decide the shade they wanted to be. Right now, they were a warm gray-green.

He grinned and snatched her hand. "Let's go see."

Racing along the cliff top with Keegan, Tess hadn't felt so carefree in years. He had a way of making everything more fun and exciting. When they reached the children, both girls pointed to the surf below them.

A kaleidoscope of brilliant colors spilled and tumbled among the waves, while more snaked and swirled around the crusted boulders of a flooding tide pool and ripped boards from the wreckage.

"One of the crates of silk must have broken open." Keegan's expression turned grim. "Worth hundreds of dollars. What a waste."

Tess gave Keegan's hand an empathetic squeeze before removing hers. "It can't all be ruined."

He slowly shook his head. "Barnacles,

splintered wood, salt water."

"Surely some can be salvaged."

Bitsy grabbed a handful of Keegan's trousers. "Can I have it then? Can I? Please?"

Tess pulled her away. "Mind your manners." She looked out again at the delicate silk being ground into the sand and scraping against millions of crustaceans. "I know it looks bad, Keegan, but there might be enough undamaged lengths for some blouses or scarves."

"No one on the docks of Boston is going to pay two cents for wads of wet smelly cloth." Desolation edged his voice.

"Mama," Sarah said, her face thin and solemn. "You know how we save the scraps from the ladies' dresses and make quilts and dolls and things? Couldn't we cut out the good pieces and make lots of pretty stuff?"

"Didn't you hear Keegan, dummy?" Bitsy said, sticking out her chin. "It stinks."

Sarah wheeled to face her. "Not if you wash it, dumber than a bunny."

Just as Tess started to reprimand them both for name-calling, Bitsy began jumping up and down. "Yes! Yes! A quilt with a beautiful picture like the Baby Jesus story Mrs. Driscoll made for the church. You know, the one where his mama and daddy are in the stable, and the animals, and the wise men. But *we'll* make one that shows how Keegan's ship sank, and how he saw our light and swam to us. And then we took him in and made him all warm again. And we wrapped him up just like they did Baby Jesus. And the chests — we have to show the chests floating to us, bringing our presents, and . . ." She gulped a breath, her eyes all a-sparkle. "And we have to show how the sea turned into all the colors of the rain-bow!"

With a burst of laughter, Keegan swooped her up. "All of that in one picture? Well, I certainly wouldn't want to deprive you of that. Let's go get some more rope and the grappling hook. Everything we catch is yours. And your mama's, of course."

The idea of silk patchwork quilts intrigued Tess. What woman wouldn't want such an elegant and colorful counterpane for her bed? Tess caught Keegan's arm. "Why don't you and the girls go ahead with your fishing. I think I'd rather hike over to Mr. McCann's for the wagon by myself anyway. It probably wouldn't do my reputation much good for them to learn a man as fit as you look today spent the night in my house. And you know how painfully honest the girls can be."

"Aye, that I do," he said knowingly and smiled, the mischief in his grin unmistakable. Then he sobered. "And I'd appreciate it if you wouldn't mention my ship wrecking just yet. More of my cargo might wash ashore on the next tide or two. I don't want the whole town heading out here for a scavenger hunt. The more I recoup, the fewer seasons I'll have to crew for someone else before I can purchase another ship."

"What does re-pu-ta — reputa-ton mean?" Clinging to Keegan's neck, Bitsy brought her nose within inches of his as they headed for the small cart loaded with the grappling hook and rope.

He dodged the little girl's face as he watched Tess departing the rocky ledge for the path into town. In a velvet dress or men's overalls, front or back, the woman was a pleasure to behold.

"*Keegan,* what does repu-ta-ton mean?"

"Reputation, ninny," Sarah corrected as she traipsed along holding Keegan's free hand.

Reputation? Kids could ask the stickiest questions. He stopped and shifted Bitsy's weight. "Your reputation is what people think of you. It's whether they think you're a good person or one not so good."

"Huh?" Bitsy scrunched her face. "But why would your staying the night at our house be bad for Mama's repu — repu —"

"Re-pu-ta-tion." Sarah back-stepped in front of Keegan and glowered up at her little sister. "You can't never remember anything, can you? Remember when Madge Carlson snuck out of her house and spent the night with Bender Hatfield? Remember what Nancy Sue told us? Nancy Sue said that justice of the peace, Mr. Butler, came and made 'em get married. 'Cause if they didn't, Madge's reputation would be *ruined for life.*"

Sarah really was a bright little thing. Too bright. She never seemed to miss a thing. He took her hand and started walking again. "I don't think you two need to worry about such things for years and years. Especially when we have a rainbow to go catch."

The bright sun had turned the snow to slush by the time Tess neared the clearing to the lighthouse on her return from McCann's place. *Afoot.* More than a mile round-trip in floppy galoshes. What a long day this had been after an almost sleepless night. Yet the sun still rode high in the southern sky. And Christmas dinner hadn't even been started.

Walking out of the shadows of a stand of pines, she came upon a delightful surprise that put a lively spring back into her step.

Great long ribbons of color were strung across the sparkling white clearing leading to her cottage. Yards and yards of silk of every hue covered close to an acre of the uneven terrain.

Sarah and Elizabeth stood on a knoll a good hundred feet apart, stretching out a piece of Chinese red fabric, while Keegan, favoring his sore hip, walked behind a strand of apple green, folding it as he went. Perhaps he'd decided the fabric was worth taking with him after all.

No one noticed her until she was almost upon them. "Hi, there," she called, coming up behind Keegan.

He wheeled around.

"I'm sorry to tell you — no one was home at the McCanns'. They must have gone visiting for Christmas."

He glanced toward the bluff, where one of his chests sat. "I'd better trek on into Moon Bay, then, and see about renting one from the livery."

"I thought about that. But it'll be closed. And with folks gathering with their families for their Christmas feasts, I doubt if you'll find anyone willing to conduct business this afternoon. Why don't we just store the trunks in the lighthouse until tomorrow?"

"You're right. I probably wouldn't find a

fishing boat captain willing to take me south till then either." With a lopsided smile, he shrugged his broad shoulders. "And, who knows, maybe more of my merchandise will float in on the next tide."

"We did it," Sarah called from the top of the knoll. "We got 'em all laid out."

Keegan spread his arm to encompass the vast array of silk streamers. "And you did a great job. Thank you."

Tess watched the girls come running down the hill hopping over every color of the rainbow and more. She turned back to Keegan. "I see you found the silk worth saving after all."

"For you, Tess. I'm folding them up until you have time to wash and dry them. As long as the weather stays cold, they should keep for awhile without souring."

"This piece looks pretty good," she said, scanning several yards of the light green. "Are you sure you want to leave them?"

"Even if I had time to bother with all of this, I could never dry scores of these bolts aboard a ship."

Tess glanced about her again. What a financial boon — this rainbow on her hill. A sight as welcome as Noah's rainbow must have been to him after the flood. "I have to do something for you in return."

Keegan motioned toward the lilac strip lying beside the green. "Start folding."

"Yes, of course." She picked up an end. "If you haven't grown too weary of us females, and if you can abide the idea of having lobster for Christmas dinner, I'd be most pleased if you'd join us. We all would. Girls," she called to her daughters, who had nearly reached them. "Shall we ask Captain Keegan to stay for dinner?"

Their answer was a resounding yes, as they both crashed into Keegan, almost toppling him in their zeal.

He glanced from the beaming faces staring up at him. "Are you sure, Tess? I've already imposed on your holiday. I'd better go into town and find a room for the night. But if you don't mind, I'd like to come back later this evening when the tide ebbs. Check the beaches again for salvage."

"Stay until after we check the beaches tonight. It makes no sense to put that much needless strain on your bruised hip."

"You have to stay!" Bitsy cried. Jumping up and down, she clung to his arm. "We got lotsa lobsters. You gotta come see 'em. They're in the lighthouse, crawling around in a big water barrel. They got big long pinchers and everything."

"And we still have the cranberry scones I

helped Mama make," Sarah sang out.

"Then how can I refuse?" He brandished a grin that matched theirs. "I can't think of anything I'd love more than to have lobster and Sarah's cranberry scones with —" he glanced up, his grin becoming more of a tease — "with the three fair ladies of Moon Bay Point."

CHAPTER SEVEN

Tess finished drying the last plate and hung her dish towel on a peg above the drain board. She was tired but content. Dinner had gone well, her only regret the fact that she had remained in her unflattering overalls. But it would have been foolish to change and then don them once more when the meal was over. Besides, it wasn't as if she'd ever see Lovett Keegan again after tomorrow.

And that fact she must not forget — no matter how pleasant it was to pretend otherwise. No matter how much he'd charmed her and the girls throughout the meal.

She moved aside the floral curtain and looked out. Dusk came early this season of the year, and sundown was fast approaching, marking the end of a most enjoyable day — the kind of day memories were made of.

She sighed. Time to wake Keegan.

Turning toward the glow of the hearth, she gazed upon him lying on the rag rug with one of the striped deacon's bench pillows under his head, and her two little girls cuddled close — all three so quiet in their slumber after such an exciting day. The only sound besides their slow breathing came from the occasional hiss and crackle of embers behind the fire screen.

Just a short while before, all had been noise and laughter. A smile lifted the corners of her mouth as she remembered the lighthearted fun when Keegan regaled the children with tales of tigers and elephants and monkeys, replete with gestures and outlandish roars and screeches. It was hard to believe this was the same man who had stumbled in last night almost dead, the same one who'd lost almost everything he'd worked years to attain. How many men would be able to put aside their own tribulation to entertain a stranger's children?

Tess knelt at his head and touched his arm. His thick lashes lifted, and his gaze found hers. He smiled, a warm sleepy smile that turned her insides — not to mention her tongue — to mush.

Rather than risk speech, she pointed to the mantel clock, a reminder that the tide was on the ebb and soon it would be dark. She then gingerly moved each sleeping child away, giving Keegan space to rise without disturbing them.

While he quietly gathered his boots and put them on near the door, Tess fetched her oldest blanket and cut a hole in the center for his head. Nights were always colder after a storm, and though she hated to sacrifice any of her covers, she would have done no less for any man bereft of all but the clothes on his back.

"Here," she whispered, bringing it to him. "Put this on."

He pushed it away. "You shouldn't ruin a blanket for me."

"It's done. Put it on."

"I'll replace it."

He always seemed so concerned about being a burden. Did her circumstances appear so humble? Or was it his pride? Most likely, he didn't want to be obligated, she thought with disappointment. Sailors loved their freedom. She'd learned that from Tom.

Outside, a breeze had picked up, adding an extra chill to the late afternoon. Tess pulled her cloak tighter as they strode toward the path down the bluff.

The wind tossed Keegan's blanket, twisting it around a leg. He chuckled as he straightened it. "Nothing shy about the Maine coast. And this point of yours sticks out there like the prow of a ship, braving anything the North Atlantic has to offer."

Tess paused and looked out across the water, now dark and moody and studded with whitecaps. Wisps of hair whipped across her face as she breathed in the briny air. "I know there's a wildness about this coast. Every tree that's managed to take root is a testament. Look how the trunks and branches are gnarled and bent. But I love it here on the point. When I'm up in the tower, the sea on three sides, I can imagine what a sailor high up a mast must feel."

She glanced at Keegan, so tall and sturdy, yet so like the wind. Blowing through her life today, tugging relentlessly at her heart, and gone tomorrow.

Suddenly, she wished she hadn't spoken to him of her private thoughts. They must have sounded quite foolish and dull. "Of course, my ship lacks the danger, the adventure of one of yours." She tucked a bothersome strand of hair behind her ear and hurried on.

Keegan's long legs easily kept stride. "There's a lot to be said for having a steady deck under your feet. After yesterday, I'm appreciating the feel of solid ground beneath mine for a change."

As they started down the zigzagged path, Tess couldn't help but notice how much more of the schooner's debris now littered the narrow strip of beach. "It must have been frightening, having your ship break apart like that. Was it the only ship in your fleet?"

"*My fleet?*" That easy chuckle rumbled out again. "That *was* my fleet. I ran off to sea as a cabin boy when I was just a lad, for that high adventure you mentioned. Years passed before I had the forethought not to fritter away my earnings and start investing in foreign goods to sell in our domestic ports. I was sailing with a good-hearted captain who always spared me a little space in the cargo hold. Then last season, I managed to scrape enough together to buy my own schooner."

"Surely, you have insurance."

"A luxury I couldn't afford."

"Then these chests truly are all you have."

"Aye. That and my health, thanks to you. I'll have to start again. The money I get for the merchandise will help." He stepped past her and leapt from a last boulder onto the sand, then reached up and lifted her off.

She had her health, too, and easily could

have jumped down on her own, but she liked the feel of his strong hands at her waist, hers on his muscled shoulders . . . liked being taken care of for a change.

After her feet touched ground, he maintained his grip, and his gaze did not express the usual mischief, the usual humor. His eyes had grown as dark as the sea, and as alluring. And his mouth, only a breath away. So close, so tempting . . .

Her heart hammered within her chest.

Anticipation? What in heaven's name was she thinking? She stepped out of his grasp. To come down here alone with a man she scarcely knew. "It'll be dark soon. We'd better split up if we want to search both sides of the point." Without giving him a chance to disagree, she started across an outcropping of rocks that led to the north side.

Only after she hopped down on the far side of the barnacle-encrusted pile did she look back to see if he followed her. He hadn't. If anyone should be accused of inordinate desire, it was she. Her lips tingled even now, wanting to be kissed. By a sailor.

Swiping hard at her mouth, she forced her attention back to the purpose at hand, the search for salvage between rocks, in crevices and among the bobbing scraps of his ship.

Keegan couldn't shake the woman from his mind. She'd run away, leaving him far more chilled than the nip in the air. Yet he'd read in her eyes how much she wanted to be kissed. As much as he wanted to kiss her. He was sure of it. But she'd pulled away so abruptly, one would have thought his hands were firebrands.

He tried to shift his thoughts from that moment when her eyes turned into tempting pools of blue, tried to concentrate on searching the small cave gouged into the sheer stone cliff. But the image would not be banished . . . those needy eyes of the lonely widow. A widow, he reminded himself, of another sailor. A woman who'd been a part-time widow long before her husband died. No, he couldn't blame Tess for pulling away. To her, the temptations of a merchant seaman probably *were* akin to playing with fire.

Tess needed a man who would come home to her at night. She deserved that. And so did the children. They needed a daddy for every day. Not just one for Christmas.

"Lord, you have to help me," he whispered into the wind. "Please help me not to be any more of a trial to this woman than I already have been." Keegan remembered the silk that had washed ashore. "And I pray that Tess will find enough undamaged fabric to make her life better, easier — to make her taking me in a blessing instead of a curse."

Daylight faded away, leaving Keegan in the inky darkness beneath the beacon light and forcing him to abort his search on the south side of the point. He spied a handy crevice and climbed to the top of the bluff, wondering if Tess had found anything of worth to the north. As he approached the lighthouse, he saw her slim figure trudging through the snow from the opposite direction. A real trooper, she'd stayed out in the cold and deepening darkness as long as he had. She would be a fine catch for some landlubber. He was amazed she hadn't been reeled in by some lucky fellow already.

Walking toward the light on the wind-swept bluff, he heard his crunching footsteps. They reminded him how quickly in these northern climes an afternoon's slush could turn to ice. He slowed his pace so he would reach the entrance at the same time as Tess.

"Any success?" he asked as she drew near.

Her face was shadowed by her hooded cloak, depriving him of its loveliness. "Sorry, no. You?"

"No." With a shrug, he stepped closer, hoping to catch a glimpse of her face. "Maybe in the morning."

Like blue flames, her eyes reflected the light from the window. And, like a moth, he was drawn to them. "Thanks for all the help," he said, managing barely more than a hoarse whisper. "You're a —"

The door to the cottage opened, spilling a streak of light across them both.

"It *is* you!" Bitsy charged outside, with her older sister close behind. "Sarah said you'd gone." Bitsy was upon him in seconds. She flung her arms around one of his legs. "See, Sarah, I told you he wouldn't go without saying good-bye. Would you?" she added, peering up at him.

"Girls," Tess scolded. "You're out here in your house slippers. They'll be soaked through."

His intimate moment with Tess shattered, Keegan plucked up the warm, fidgety children and carried them into the house. How very much he would miss them when he was gone. But as young as they were, they'd probably forget him within the month.

That hurt.

He hugged them closer. He'd find some special little bauble for each of them when he docked in Boston. And after that, he'd send them something from wherever he made port. He wouldn't let them forget their "Christmas Daddy" any more than he'd forget them — or their beautiful mother.

Keegan deposited the girls onto the hinged bench just inside the door. "I *am* leaving now, for Moon Bay Port. But I'll be back in the morning to check the beaches one more time and fetch my chests."

Sarah stared up at him with mournful eyes, Tess's eyes, and he found her gaze disconcerting. "It's too dark and cold. Stay here like last night," she begged. "I'll go with you in the morning to get the McCanns' wagon. I know the way."

"Me too. Me too!" Bitsy shrilled while trying to pull the gray blanket off of him. "Please stay."

Tess, Keegan could see, disapproved. It was one thing to take in a frozen half-dead stranger. It was another thing entirely to invite in a healthy full-blooded man — one who clearly found her irresistible.

"I'm sorry, kitten," he said, removing Bitsy's thin arms.

Taking up where Bitsy left off, Sarah shoved at his blanket. "If you'll stay, we won't make you sleep on the floor like last night. Mama can sleep with us, and you can have her bed."

"Yes." Bitsy nodded frantically. "Like Mama does when I have a nightmare. Besides, you don't have a real coat or mittens or nothing."

"And your boots are all wet. Your toes'll freeze off. Won't they, Mama?" Sarah turned those heart-melting eyes on Tess.

She looked down at boots that an unexpected wave had soaked a few minutes earlier. "Oh, my, the children are right. I didn't spend half the night warming you up . . ." She paused, and her gaze flitted away. The woman did have a distracting habit of putting her foot in her mouth. . . . "to have you getting lost in the dark the very next night and freezing to death."

"But I —"

"No buts. It's settled. So, if you'll excuse me, I need to straighten your room a bit." She turned around and strode into the hall, trying to appear far more assured than she was.

"Keegan, will you make us some cocoa?" Bitsy asked with an all-too-bright grin. "Cocoa makes you real sleepy. Don't it, Sarah?"

"Oh, yes." Sarah, too, now sported a smile that didn't seem genuine. "I'd like some, too. I'll help you, Keegan. I know where everything is."

Bitsy gave an exaggerated yawn, then grabbed his hand and started pulling him toward the stove. Keegan let her draw him along, charmed as usual by the tyke. She intended to do everything possible to get him settled in for the night. And he couldn't say the prospect wasn't appealing compared to going back out into the cold.

"Tell you what," he said. "I'll fix the cocoa *if* you promise not to take the scissors to the rest of my hair while I'm asleep."

"Wake up."

Keegan opened his eyes.

Lamplight close to his face blinded him.

He blinked hard. *Tess. Coming to him.* He must be dreaming.

"Get up. *Please!*" She sounded urgent.

He glanced toward the window. "It's still dark out. What is it? What's happened?"

"*The girls — they're gone.* I woke up, and they weren't in bed."

He sat up. "Did you look in the front room?"

"They're not there. They're nowhere in the house. Not the tower either. They were sleeping right next to me. I can't believe I didn't hear them."

"You were tired. You were up most of last night. Do they run off a lot?"

"Never." She glanced out into the hall. "I'm afraid the lure of the treasure was just too enticing."

"Climbing those cliffs at night?" He leapt from bed and started pulling trousers on over his long underwear. "They could get hurt."

CHAPTER EIGHT

With a lantern held high, Keegan jogged along the swiftly disappearing shoreline, splashing through several inches of water even after a wave receded. *God in heaven, where are those girls?* With the tide coming in, there soon would be nothing but deep water and waves battering the cliffs.

A deep crack appeared in the rock wall. He swung the lantern toward it. Searched upward to the top.

Nothing.

"Sarah! Bitsy!" he shouted, as he'd done a hundred times already.

Still no answer. Nothing but the relentless churn of waves among the rocks as the sea came to claim them. Even the wind had disappeared, sucked into the darkness beneath the eerie beams of the beacon light.

He had to be a good mile from the lighthouse now. Where were they? As he'd done earlier this evening, he'd taken the south side of the point while Tess took the north.

A frigid wave crashed into him, soaking him to the waist, nearly knocking him off his feet. He was a grown man. What would it do to the girls? They were just babies.

"Sarah! Bitsy!" His voice was becoming hoarse, and fear bound his chest so tightly that each breath was a strain. What would he do if he found them floating facedown? How would he tell their mother? Or bear it himself?

He heard something. A dull thumping.

He ran toward the sound. Toward several rocks sticking up from the undulating waves. Then he stopped short. A chest. Thank God, just another chest bumping between two rocks like a docked boat.

Remembering to inhale again, Keegan forced in a lungful of air. He'd never felt so frustrated, so helpless in his life. Even when his ship was sinking in the torrential storm, even when he was dashed about in the icy sea, he hadn't known such consuming fear.

He started jogging again, his lantern's light dancing crazily across the shallow water. He ran until he neared a point similar to the one with the lighthouse. With the tide up, it jutted out into the sea and could no longer be circumvented without a boat. He was blocked. He turned back in defeat.

"God in heaven, I beg you. Let the girls be with Tess. Please. Surely you wouldn't save me and some worthless cargo, then take the children. You wouldn't be that cruel. You wouldn't send me to them, make me love them, then snatch them away."

Another light appeared, flickering orange and yellow across the inky water.

Keegan looked to the top of the bluff and spotted a glowing circle about a hundred yards away. Tess's lantern?

Please, let her have the children, he repeated over and over as he found the nearest crevice and started climbing.

By the time he mounted the top, Tess had reached him.

She searched past him as frantically as he peered into the darkness beyond the sphere of their lamps. Her eyes as wild as her voice, she clutched the front of his sweater. "You don't have them! Did you see anything? Hear anything? This can't be happening."

She was falling apart. He pulled her to him. Her breathing came hard, labored. Her body trembled. His own heart, too, was near bursting. He drew her closer, tighter, until her face was buried in the hollow of his shoulder. "Don't give up. We'll find them."

"How? Where?"

"We won't stop till we do. We *will* find them." The words sounded hollow even to him. "The lighthouse! I'll wager they went back to your house while we were searching."

She lifted her face and sought his eyes. "Oh, Keegan, I pray so. I do pray so."

"So do I." With the most encouraging smile he could muster, he turned her in the direction of the beacon, and they hurried toward it, arms tightly clasped around each other, circles of lamplight guiding their feet toward their fervent but fragile hope.

"This is all my fault," Tess panted between breaths. "I should never . . . have brought two small children out here to the point . . . rugged cliffs . . . ocean on three sides. I was stubborn. Full of pride. When Tom died, I should have taken the girls home to my family in Connecticut. They would have been safe there. And poor little Sarah . . . she wouldn't have turned into such a worrier."

Keegan stopped, turned her to face him. He couldn't believe what he'd just heard. "You have family? Why didn't you go?"

She pressed her lips into a thin line, and her eyes glistened with unshed tears. Swallowing, she looked away. "Because I would have gone home a failure — the fool who ran away with a ne'er-do-well sailor only to return penniless, with two children." Her chin began to quiver. "And now look at what my pride has earned me. I've lost my precious babies."

He caught her chin between his fingers and thumb. "Don't do this to yourself. You're a wonderful mother. All anyone has to do is look at your daughters to know that. We'll find them. If God would listen to this sinner's prayer and save me, how could he not heed yours? They'll be at the house."

Tess wanted to be brave, to trust, but her whole body was so knotted with fear she could barely stand. She clutched on to Keegan's sweater, desperately seeking some of his strength.

"Look, Tess!" He spun her toward the inland woods, where a glow moved through the trees, dancing off snowy branches. Coming from the path to town.

"We were looking in the wrong direction!" he nearly shouted.

Filled with new hope, she sprinted across

the uneven terrain as fast as her rubber boots would carry her. Keegan ran right beside her.

As they neared, Tess realized there were two lights — lights being held much too high for children to be carrying. Panic again gripped her.

Two mounted riders emerged from the trees, one carrying a lantern. A second lamp swung from a horse-drawn sled.

Tess reached the party and halted, taking in large gulps of icy air. Her fear mounted when she recognized one of the riders as Moon Bay's only officer of the law. Mr. Butler was the justice of the peace. The other man was Cameron Hall, a large beefy fellow who assisted Mr. Butler whenever there was trouble. "My children — have you seen my children?"

From the sled came a woman's voice. "They're right here. As if you really cared."

The older woman's reply stopped Tess in her tracks. What was Mr. Butler's busybody wife doing with Sarah and Elizabeth?

Before Tess had a chance to ask, Keegan strode to the sled, tore away the blankets covering the girls, and scooped them into his arms. They clung to him as he hugged them close. And they looked fine. Her darling daughters looked just fine. Weak with relief, Tess moved toward them on trembling legs.

"What on earth were you two thinking?" Keegan scolded. "Running out of the house in the middle of the night. Do you have any idea how worried we were?"

Hiram Butler and Cameron Hall shoved past Tess, each grabbing one of Keegan's arms.

"We know precisely why the girls came to us," Mr. Butler said in angry clipped words, his bony face looking all the more skeletal in the shadows cast by the lanterns.

"Precisely," his wife echoed.

"No child would run out into the freezing night to fetch me unless something was terribly amiss." Mr. Butler tightened his grip on Keegan's arm. "Now, unhand those children."

Tess couldn't believe what she heard. "You girls did *what?*"

The girls avoided Tess's gaze as Keegan lowered them to the ground. Elizabeth for once was not only silent, she hid behind Sarah. Left to face her mother alone, Sarah's eyes almost doubled in size. She gulped like a pelican.

"Uh . . . Bitsy and me . . . we went to get the justice of the peace so you and Keegan would have to get married."

Tess grabbed her by the shoulders. "*Married!* What are you saying?"

Sarah hunkered down as if she wanted to disappear. "Like Madge Carlson and Bender Hatfield. They spent the night together, and Mr. Butler made them get married."

"I see." Tess released Sarah and stood back from the girls. "Elizabeth. Come out from behind your sister."

Bitsy peeked around Sarah.

"So, girls, this is how you repay Captain Keegan for his many kindnesses to you? By setting the law on him? Besmirching his good name? Dragging these good people out into the bitter cold on Christmas night? And do you have the slightest idea where Captain Keegan and I have been for the past hour? We've been on the beach getting soaked to the bone searching for you. Now, go on back to the house. And when I get there, I'd better find you in bed, where you belong."

They didn't have to be told twice. They took off like frightened rabbits.

It took every ounce of courage Tess possessed to face the others. This was beyond embarrassment. She could only imagine the story Mrs. Butler would weave from the events of this night. And Keegan. The children had offended him unforgivably.

"My deepest apologies, Captain," Tess said. "I must take full blame for this fiasco. I was too lax with Bitsy. I should have been firm with her about her fantasies from the start. I should have made her understand that you had not been dropped down from heaven just to be her daddy."

The law officers released their hold on him, looking apologetic. But the angry dip of Keegan's brows did not ease.

Who could blame him? Her daughters had just tried to make him the leading man in a shotgun wedding. Tried to push him off on their mother. On *her*. Her mortification was beyond blushing — the blood drained from her face. She turned to Mrs. Butler. "I'm so sorry that you've been forced out of your warm bed on a fool's errand. That, too, is my fault. It matters not that the captain has been a perfect gentleman. I was a poor example to my girls. As a widow with impressionable daughters, I should never have extended the hospitality of my home to the captain, even if he had lost his ship, and had no coat, and had his boots soaked through. As it's turned out, the poor man spent far more time out searching for the children than he ever would have on a walk into the village. Not to mention the embarrassment we've caused him."

No one spoke. A chasm of silence stretched between her and the others. Between her and Keegan.

There was nothing left she could say or do. Without making eye contact, she took her extra lantern from Keegan. It was over, and the Butlers no doubt would give the abused man a ride into town. "I need to see to my children, so I bid you all a good night."

When Tess entered the girls' bedroom, both pretended to be asleep, and that suited her just fine. Let them stew in the mess they'd stirred up for a while. Closing the door behind her, she went to her own room, but with little hope of getting any rest.

How would she ever face the people of Moon Bay after this? Or Keegan when he came to fetch his chests?

Worse even than the embarrassment was the emptiness the man had left in his wake. Her room now seemed twice as large, the walls twice as bare as they'd been before the jaunty sailor tramped through her house, filling it with his tall tales and boisterous laughter — before he'd looked at her and made her feel beautiful again. And wanted.

Tess placed the lantern she still carried on

her nightstand. It cast a bright circle across her bed — across covers thrown back when Keegan had sprung up from a sound sleep. The pillow remained dented where his head had lain. The manly smell of him would still be on it, left there to remind her through the night of how alone she was.

She snatched up the lantern and left the room, left for the warmth of her children.

The next morning when the mantel clock chimed eight times, Tess dragged her stiff body from bed. Glancing back, she saw that both girls remained sound asleep, which was understandable considering the past day *and* night. Tess still found it hard to believe the extent of grief and trouble those two had instigated. Yet now they looked so young and sweet, so innocent, locks of hair and arms flung across their pillows.

But she'd have to wake them. Time stopped for no man — or child, for that matter. And she wanted them to understand fully what would be expected of them today. No more Christmas wishes. Life as it really was.

"Girls." She shook the foot of the bed, near where the black cat lay peacefully curled. "Wake up." Seeing them stir, she continued. "I expect Captain Keegan to come soon to fetch his chests."

That roused them. Four huge eyes flew open. No doubt they remembered the mischief they'd done.

"I want you dressed and your breakfast eaten before the captain arrives. And a talk — we'll be having a very serious talk about last night's mischief."

"But, Mama," Bitsy wailed as she bounded up to her knees. "Keegan wasn't supposed to go away last night. That's not how it was supposed to happen." She stuck out her lower lip as if she were the one who'd been wronged. "Mr. Butler was supposed to make him marry us. Make him stay here with us. He's the daddy I prayed for." A fat tear rolled down her cheek. "And now he's sailing away."

How could Tess stay mad? She sat down and pulled her youngest into a healing hug. Feeling Sarah's weight against her shoulder, she included her in the embrace.

When everyone was breathing normally again, Tess held them at arm's length . . . her sweet-faced cherubs. "Yesterday we had a wonderful time with Captain Keegan — so special, it was almost magical. But it was also a day for learning hard lessons."

"Like in school?" Sarah asked, her delicate features displaying mild confusion.

"Not exactly. More of a lesson about us and God. You know how you'll ask me if you can do something? And how sometimes I say no?"

"Like when we want to go down to the beach without a grown-up?"

"Yes, Sarah, because it's too dangerous for you there alone. And when we pray for something, sometimes God says no, because he loves us and knows better than we do what's good for us and what's not. And sometimes we simply have to wait until the Lord feels it's the right time to say yes."

"Like when we had to wait for hours and hours for you to finish Mrs. Dabney's dress so we could go on a picnic?" Bitsy chirped.

"Exactly." Tess smiled, pleased they both understood. "And, Bitsy, when you prayed for a daddy the other night, God *did* hear you. Our heavenly Father knows better than anyone who will be the best daddy for you." She tapped her youngest on her pug nose. "So I don't want you going out again trying to make some unsuspecting man marry me. Do you understand?"

"But I couldn't just let Keegan get away."

"*Bitsy,*" Tess chided. "You *will* stop trying to trick people into doing what you want."

The child mashed her lips tight and huffed, "Oh, I guess."

"I'll take that for a yes. And for now, we'll all just have to be patient and wait until the Lord decides who your and Sarah's new daddy will be." *If you're to have one,* Tess added to herself. And instantly she felt her own wretched wanting.

Sarah reached up and touched Tess's face. "What's the matter, Mama?"

Forcing a smile, Tess rose. "Nothing, dear. But it's getting late. I need to dress, and so do you."

As Tess left her children's room, she knew exactly what her prayer would be tonight . . . whether to move back to Connecticut. Her daughters might never have another father, but they did have a grandfather who would shower them with that special kind of love. Her own desires she'd get over. She had before.

By the time Keegan finally drove up to the lighthouse in a sled-fitted wagon, it was 10:23 A.M., according to the mantel clock. Too long a wait for someone as jumpy as Tess felt, knowing she'd have to face him after last night's humiliation.

Be brave, she told herself. Then she opened the door, determined to act polite and businesslike. She would put from her mind that she'd sat up all Christmas Eve saving his life. That she'd laughed and then cried all over him yesterday. And she prayed he had forgotten, too.

Keegan wore a new green plaid coat that complemented his eyes, his tan, and his sun-streaked hair.

Tess's heart leapt. "Good morning," she called, wishing the mere glimpse of him didn't affect her so.

"Good morning," he returned with an easy grin, hopping down as if he hadn't parted from her last night with a look of utter disdain. He moved to the rear of the wagon and unloaded a small crate.

She felt movement at the back of her gray wool skirt. The girls. Too shy to show themselves, they peeked around, nonetheless.

Toting the crate on one shoulder, Keegan approached Tess. "Where do you want me to put these foodstuffs?"

"Food?" She surely looked as dumb as she sounded when she stepped back to let him pass, her mouth gaping and two "monkeys" hanging on to her skirt.

"Just replacing some of what I stuffed myself on yesterday." He walked to the kitchen area and set the box on the drain board.

Of course. Paying his debt. Businesslike. "That was most thoughtful of you, Captain."

His brows crimped in a slight frown. "I thought we'd settled on Keegan. Isn't that right, girls?" He tipped his head and stared down at them.

From behind her, Tess heard one thin yes, and then another.

"That Cameron Hall who rode out here last night has been a big help," Keegan continued in a confident voice. "He gave me a place to spend the night, then introduced me to one of your local fishermen this morning. Buck Kiley. Buck is taking me down to Boston on the evening tide."

Tess's heart sank. He'd said the words. He was leaving. As intent as Tess was not to show her disappointment, she couldn't stop the tightening in her chest, the lump in her throat.

Bitsy flung herself from behind Tess. "You're really, really gonna leave us?"

"Aye." He dropped down on one knee. "The sooner I go sell my merchandise, the sooner I'll be back."

"*You're coming back?*" Bitsy said the words for Tess.

"Aye. That I am."

Before he could say another word, both girls flew into his arms.

And Tess turned away so he wouldn't see her cry.

But he wouldn't let her hide. With the children hanging on to his coattails, he turned her to face him. "Tess, I thought you'd be pleased. I thought we'd become . . . friends."

She snatched up her apron hem and swiped at her tears. "I am. We are."

"Then I also hope you'll be pleased that I've struck a deal with Buck to buy one of his boats from what I earn selling my merchandise. I've decided to become a fisherman. I may not be in port every single night, but it sure beats being gone half a year at a time. Sundays, maybe I can sit with you at church. And Tess, I'm hoping you and the girls will invite me out here for supper now and then."

Was he saying what she thought she was hearing? Her skirt was being tugged on again.

"Mama, say yes," Sarah demanded in her most grown-up tone.

Holding her in his gaze, Keegan stood so close that Tess could manage only a nod as she swallowed down the emotion clogging her throat.

"That's good," he said, his own voice becoming a rough whisper. "Because . . . last night I never felt so robbed in my life. Or more alone than when the children were taken from me. I had to just stand there with no right to speak. Then you turned and walked away, too."

"But I thought . . . you just stared at me as if . . . I was so ashamed. I thought you no longer wanted to have anything to do with us."

His grip tightened on her shoulders. "Well, I'm speaking now. And I'm saying I want to come calling more than I've ever wanted anything in my life."

"Are you sure you won't regret giving up the sea, the high adventure?"

"I won't be giving up the sea. And as for high adventure, I have a pretty fair notion I'll have all I can handle right here on Moon Bay Point."

"Mama, Mama, does that mean he's going to be my daddy?" Bitsy yanked on Tess's apron pocket.

"That depends," Keegan answered for her, one side of his mouth lifting in a lopsided grin, "on whether your mama likes me enough to let me kiss her one of these fine days."

"Course she will. Remember, we got rid of your mustache."

"Do it, Mama," Sarah urged. "Kiss him now."

"Yes, Mama, kiss me now." Keegan's

smirk was irrepressible.

She could play that game. "So, it's a kiss you want, *Lovett.*" Grabbing two handfuls of Keegan's springy curls, she pulled him to her. And by the time his lips met hers, there wasn't a trace of that smug smile left.

His arms came around her, pulling her close. In no time at all, Tess knew he was as good at kissing as he was at grinning and talking. Perhaps God didn't intend for Bitsy to wait so very long for her answer after all.

"See, Sarah. Didn't I tell you he was going to be our new daddy?"

"Did not."

"Did too."

Recipe

Dear reader,

This recipe came highly recommended from a friend. The Cranberry Walnut Scones had become a tradition in her family, as they now have in ours. I serve them as part of our Christmas morning brunch. Enjoy!

Dianna Crawford

CRANBERRY WALNUT SCONES

3 cups flour
½ cup sugar
1 tbs baking powder
½ tsp baking soda
½ tsp salt
¾ cup butter cut into small pieces
1 cup fresh cranberries (or frozen)

½ cup chopped walnuts
1½ tbs grated orange peel
1 cup buttermilk
1 tbs cream or milk
1 tbs sugar mixed with:
   ¼ tsp cinnamon
   ⅛ tsp allspice

Stir together flour, sugar, baking powder, baking soda, and salt. Rub butter into mixture until coarse crumbs form. Stir in cranberries, walnuts, and orange peel. Add buttermilk and mix with fork until evenly moistened. Gather into a ball and place on a floured board. Pat into a circle ¾" thick. Using a biscuit cutter, cut into rounds and place 1½" apart on a greased baking sheet. Brush tops with cream or milk and sprinkle with sugar/spice mixture. Bake on lower rack of oven at 400 degrees for 14 to 16 minutes.

Optional topping:
   8 oz cream cheese
   2 tbs honey
   1 tbs orange peel
Whip together until smooth.

Tea for Marie

PEGGY STOKS

*For Mary Strand
I didn't forget.*

CHAPTER ONE

Grandma Biggs sniffed with disdain, stretched herself to her full four feet, ten inches, and thumped the wide oak planks of the porch with her cane. "Marie Katherine Biggs! Were you out driving with that Farrell boy?"

"Goodness, Grandma," Marie replied. She watched the stylish black carriage retreat down the country lane, drawn by a perfectly matched set of bays. A cloud of dust rose in its wake in the golden October sunshine. Still tingling with excitement, the nineteen-year-old danced up the three steps to the porch and removed her bonnet. "A person would think you didn't care for Chadwick Farrell."

"I don't. The boy galls me." Grandma's snapping brown stare met her own as the cane struck the porch again for good measure. "He's good-lookin', I'll grant you, but he's got nothin' more inside him than hot air and horsefeathers."

"He's got so many wonderful ideas, Grandma."

"Oh, I imagine the boy can talk pretty enough. He always did. I'm also certain his term at the university only made that worse. I'm just wondering what he's all about. All these years, he comes, he goes. We see him, we don't. It's no proper courtship, Marie." She lifted slender, snow-white brows. "I'm wondering, too, what he tells you about his family — and why you're never invited over there."

Marie sighed and set her hand on her grandmother's shoulder, her pleasure at the afternoon drive through the countryside beginning to fade. "I think the least I can do is give him a chance. He's very nice."

A wrinkled yet still strong hand came up to cover her own. "He comes from money, Marie; don't let that be goin' to your head. 'Tain't no secret his mama threatened to jump right into the Minnesota River when she found out her boy had taken a fancy to you. 'Imagine,' " she said in a high tone dripping with mock disdain, her pinched expression mimicking the one Imogene Farrell wore as a matter of fact, " '*my son taking an interest in a farmer's daughter. It is simply not acceptable.'*"

"I'd best help Mother with supper," Marie said. The remainder of her enjoyment of the afternoon's outing had dissipated. Several uncomfortable questions about Chadwick Farrell once again arose in her mind, questions she'd worked so hard at putting aside during the drive.

"Now take Harald Hamsun there, across the way," Grandma continued, hooking her cane over her wrist and tugging Marie's arm until she was forced to turn around. The fair Norwegian farmer was barely visible, leading a team of oxen and a heavily loaded wagon from his fields. "A nice, honest man, he is. Hardworking. Just like his uncle Einar, afore he took sick." She nodded with approval, a mischievous twinkle appearing in her eyes for just a moment. "A set of fine, broad shoulders the young man has, too."

"Yes, ma'am," Marie agreed, hoping her grandmother had finally finished rendering her opinions. "I'd best go help Mother now," she offered once again, wanting nothing more at that moment than to occupy herself with some task and quell the busy debate her reason was waging regarding Chadwick Farrell.

"Go on and help your mama, then." Grandma's voice softened, and she gave

Marie's arm a gentle squeeze before shifting her cane back into her hand. "I think I'll just enjoy a little of this weather before it turns nasty for good. Prob'ly only a handful of decent days left." With that, the elder Mrs. Biggs adjusted her shawl and made her way down the porch steps. Somewhat relieved, Marie stepped into the kitchen, not entirely trusting she'd heard the last of her grandmother's opinions concerning her choice of suitors.

By the time the Biggs family sat down for supper, much of Marie's pensiveness had yielded to her normally optimistic disposition. The good-natured banter of her younger brothers and sisters, combined with the delicious aromas wafting from the kitchen, did much to settle her disordered thoughts. The issue of Chadwick Farrell seemed much further away, and a feeling of peace stole over her while Father asked the blessing.

"How was your ride with young Mr. Farrell today, Marie?" Father inquired in a genial tone, as he sliced the roast pork and passed the platter. Strands of gray battled evenly with the rich chestnut color of his hair and beard. His deep brown gaze sought hers. "He seemed to leave in a hurry."

"He always leaves in a hurry," twelve-year-old Hugh commented, bumping Marie's elbow to indicate that she should take the bowl of mashed potatoes.

"The way he flies out of here." Anthony, two years older than Hugh, spoke in a voice already much lower in timbre than it had been a year ago. "I think maybe he doesn't like us."

"Well, he likes Marie," Sarah, nine, chimed in. "And he sure has a fancy carriage. If you marry him, Marie, will you have fancy things, too?"

"Hush, Sarah," Mother admonished gently. "No one said anything about Marie marrying Mr. Farrell. Now take some corn and pass it on." She glanced around the table at her brood, giving them a wordless warning not to tease their oldest sister. "How *was* your ride, dear?" she asked. "We didn't get much of a chance to talk when you came in."

"Oh, it was . . . fine," Marie replied, scooping a small spoonful of potatoes onto her plate. She felt the eyes of all upon her. "The sun was actually very warm."

"Maybe that's why she suddenly got a sunburn on her cheeks." The musical voice of Rosemary, nearly seventeen years old, was laden with laughter.

Good-natured giggles, chuckles, and chortles broke out around the table. Seated between Hugh and Rosemary's twin, Raymond, Grandma Biggs loudly cleared her throat. "Well, you people can hee-haw all you like." She glared at her son. "I do not understand, William, why you let Marie say no when Mr. Hamsun called, askin' to court her. I'm tellin' you, that Farrell boy is nothin' but a skunk."

"Does he stink, Gramma?" Three-year-old Julia's innocent question produced another round of laughter from everyone but Marie.

"To high heaven, child," Ruth Biggs replied, nodding approvingly while Hugh pinched his nostrils and pulled a face.

"That will be enough," Father said. His voice was stern enough, though a trace of a smile lingered at his lips.

"I think we should change the talk from skunks to squirrels," Mother offered diplomatically, with a slight nod toward her mother-in-law before turning to her husband. "I'm quite certain I've been hearing more activity on our roof than I ought to, William. I'd like you to go up there and take a look. . . ."

"May I please be excused, Mother?" The peace that had settled over Marie during

Father's prayer had long since fled. A lump had lodged itself in her throat, and unshed tears burned in her eyes.

"Yes, you may," her mother answered. "Would you go out and put the hens in for me? I'll keep a plate for you, dear."

There was a hush at the table as Marie pushed back her chair and rose. When she reached the back door, she heard a sudden buzz of conversation start up at the table. Julia's piping voice asked, "Is Marie going to cry?"

No, she wasn't going to cry, she vowed, closing the door quietly and stepping out into the evening. The temperature had cooled dramatically in the past few hours, making her regret she hadn't taken a wrap. Walking toward the hen yard, she wished her family would be more receptive toward Chadwick. Mother and Father had allowed him to pay call again since he'd returned from the university, but she could sense their reservation, no doubt having to do with the on-again, off-again manner in which he'd called upon her over the past several years.

They were from two different worlds, she and Chadwick, but if only her family could know the Chadwick she knew. A restless but bright-minded thinker, he flew through his high school courses and embarked upon his higher education with relish. He was an exciting person to be around, bold and so certain of himself.

The Chadwick her family didn't know worked hard at his father's bank and spoke eloquently about all the plans he had for social improvement and reform. He wanted to improve the Mankato area in south-central Minnesota and progress someday throughout the state and country. Even in high school he had talked of such things, but since he had returned from the university, he seemed so much more determined to carry out his altruistic ideals.

With twilight approaching, the hens were only too happy to run into their coop and roost. As Marie closed the door and latched it, her mind's eye recalled the afternoon's events. Her heart did a little flip-flop as she remembered the way Chadwick's lean, neatly manicured fingers had lingered over her hands when he'd passed the reins to her. Briefly, she allowed herself to wonder if he was ever going to kiss her. He'd exhibited nothing but gentlemanly behavior toward her, but she sensed his interest. He liked her first of all, he'd told her many times, because she had such a pretty smile, but he liked her most of all because she was a good listener and asked intelligent questions.

Shivering, she crossed her arms and rubbed her palms over her upper arms as the chilly breeze intensified into a gust. Glancing up at the sky, she was surprised to see the setting sun almost entirely obscured by a layer of gray clouds. Rain tonight, maybe snow if the mercury dipped below freezing. The month had already been visited by one good frost, which had nipped many tender vines.

The glow of yellow light was visible from the Hamsun farmhouse, warm and beckoning against the deepening shadows. Einar Hamsun had built his sturdy home many years before on an *L*-shaped plot of two hundred acres in the heart of Blue Earth County. Graced by a mix of woods and fields, the land lay just south of the twisting Le Sueur River.

Long-ago widowed with no surviving children, the elder Mr. Hamsun had suffered a severe stroke just two years before, succumbing to death a short time later. Within a few weeks his nephew Harald had come from Illinois to take over the farm. As Marie understood things, he had bought out all interests from Einar's two surviving brothers.

Harald Hamsun was a nice enough man, she supposed, though she really didn't know him very well. He was typically Scandinavian in appearance with blond hair and blue eyes, and she guessed him to be somewhere in his mid-twenties. He wasn't as tall as Chadwick, and whereas the younger man's lines were long and lean, everything about Harald seemed broad — his face, his shoulders, his hands. He was a quiet man, unassuming, yet Father held a great opinion of him.

The only places she saw him were about his farm, in church, and occasionally at the table when Mother invited him for Sunday dinner. How he could make up his mind that he wished to court Marie based on the small amount of interaction they'd had made no sense to her at all. He was just lonely, she decided, living over there all by himself.

"Ooh, it's gotten cold! Looks like it might rain, too." Lost in thought, Marie hadn't heard Rosemary's approach. "I'm awfully sorry for teasing you, Marie," Rosemary continued, linking her arm through Marie's. "We were only having fun, but things just seemed to go too far at your expense. Everyone's sorry . . . well, except for Grandma. Mama's still talking on about squirrels, but now Grandma's decided Mr. Farrell is closer to a ferret than a skunk."

"It's all right," Marie said, feeling a crooked smile steal across her lips. Exasperating as her family was, she loved them dearly.

"Are you in love with Chadwick?"

"I'm not sure," Marie answered slowly. "I know I feel excitement when I'm with him, but it doesn't feel like the kind of love I have for you or Mother or Father."

"It's not supposed to, silly." Laughter bubbled up from deep inside the slender, dark-eyed young woman, and she gave Marie a playful shove, knocking her off balance.

"And just what do you know about that?" Straightening, Marie planted her hands on her hips and gave Rosemary a searching look.

"Maybe more than you do," Rosemary answered coyly, tossing her dark braids. "Race you to the house." With that, she was off.

Shaking her head yet unable to resist the challenge, Marie picked up her skirt and outraced her younger sister by three whole steps.

Lying in bed listening to Rosemary's deep, even breathing beside her, Marie sighed and turned from her side to her back. She'd said her prayers and asked the Lord for his peace, but her mind simply wouldn't rest. The unpleasant questions about Chadwick had come back, as they always did.

What *were* her feelings for Chadwick? And if he liked her so much, then why didn't he invite her to spend time with his family? Mama was always inviting him to stay for a meal, though he scarcely did. Was it really true that Imogene Farrell disdained her as much as Grandma said?

Eventually, fatigue overtook her, and she dozed.

Coughing and choking, Marie awakened, disoriented. Beside her, Rosemary was coughing too. Someone was shouting frantically, a surreal, bizarre sound, accompanied by muffled crackling noises. Shrieks of terror came from elsewhere in the house as her lungs struggled for pure, clean air.

"Everybody out! The house is on fire!" Father burst through the door, a lamp in one hand. Thick black smoke whirled about his hurried movements like a horde of writhing demons. "Get outside, now! Don't stop for anything. She's going fast."

The house is on fire? The terrible commotion registered in Marie's mind as she and Rosemary stumbled from their bed. Panic beat in her breast as she watched Father pull a limp Sarah out of her bed and toss her over his shoulder. The fumes were thick and acrid, and the crackling sound grew louder. Clinging to her sister's arm, choked by fear and smoke, Marie made her way to the door, wondering if they would all get out alive.

CHAPTER TWO

There was no chance of saving the house.

"Look at that, would you?" Grandma Biggs's normally outspoken tone was subdued as she stared at the conflagration before her. "You'd think the rain might slow it down even a little."

"The rain's what's keeping everything else from going up right along with the house," Father responded, his voice dull. "There's that to be thankful for."

"And that we're all safe, William." Mother threaded her arm around Father's waist and nestled close, unmindful of his soggy, soot-blackened union suit. "That's the most important thing of all."

Father remained standing as if at attention, not giving any reply. The animals were noisy and restless, but the group of survivors huddled just inside the barn door, their panic spent, watching in silence as the fire destroyed their home and possessions. For Marie, the feelings she experienced during this night were a curious dichotomy. Though all her worldly goods perished before her eyes, she was overwhelmed with thankfulness for the gift of life itself.

Thanks to Father's alert, everyone had made it out of the house safely, and in the cold, light rain Sarah had revived at once. Harald Hamsun, awakened by the disturbance, had responded nearly immediately to their plight. He and Father and the boys had been able to make a few trips back inside to salvage some items on the ground floor, but once the flames had licked up through the ceiling and ignited the roof, they'd dared not chance more.

The heat from the burning building was incredible. Dressed in their bedclothes, soaked by the cold rain, not one of them felt anything but hot. The glow from the blaze painted their faces eerie shades of red while they stood soberly, silently, save the coughing of several sets of offended lungs.

"Hullo! William! Can I bring my team inside?" Once it was clear that everyone was safe and unharmed and that there were no efforts that could be made to save the house, Harald had returned to his home. Now he approached once again, this time leading a pair of workhorses pulling a wagon. The beasts were noticeably nervous near the heat and flames, yet he guided them with skill into the barn.

"That's it, girls. Whoa." Patting each horse, he turned toward the huddled family. "There is food and cider in the wagon," he said simply. His broad face, tinted crimson by the flames, was etched with concern. "Dry blankets if you wish."

"Thank you, Harald." Mother stepped forward to take his hand. Her smile was genuine, though stress showed in her eyes and about her mouth.

Raymond, Anthony, and Hugh wasted no time in converging upon the large covered basket in the back of Harald's wagon. Grandma Biggs was now seated on an old stool that someone had found for her, and Julia was snuggled securely in Marie's arms, her head resting on Marie's shoulder.

Marie watched with growing concern as Father stepped away from Mother's side, away from all of them, to stand by himself. He had barely spoken since they fled the house. His posture was tense, stiff, his expression as unyielding as stone. Such uncharacteristic behavior unsettled Marie, and by the way the others acted, she was not alone.

Only Harald seemed undaunted. He approached Father without hesitation and placed his hand on the older man's shoulder. "You will all come to my house," he said quietly, only a trace of his musical native accent evident in his voice.

"I can't accept such an offer," Father said through tensed jaws. A long moment later he added, "There are ten of us. . . . I couldn't ask it of you."

Harald waited an equally long moment before replying, nodding slightly. "You didn't ask it, William."

Father stood, unmoving, while Harald waited patiently beside his friend.

"Would you have us sleep in the barn, son?" Grandma asked with only a little of her usual spunk, her voice husky from coughing.

"Others have done it."

In Marie's arms, Julia suddenly tensed, her head snapping up so fast it bumped the side of her older sister's face. "Mama! I don't *want* to sleep in the barn!" she wailed, tears springing to her eyes. "My house burning . . . and my dolly gone," she sobbed, despite Marie's attempts to calm her, "and now I wanna go to Mr. Hamsun's."

"Oh, it's late, my darling," Mother soothed, taking her youngest child from her eldest, "and you must be very tired. Just as soon as your father makes a decision, we'll make you up a nice bed. Things won't seem so bad in the light of morning." Though she cast her husband a troubled glance, she hummed softly, rocking the quieting child back and forth in her arms.

Maybe Mother thought things would be better by morning, but Marie feared things might be much worse by the light of day, especially if Father continued to behave in this peculiar manner. Would he really insist that they all stay in the barn — even Grandma and Julia? When the fire died down, the temperature inside the barn would fall . . . and they were all dressed in their nightclothes.

Nightclothes.

With a downward, horrified glance she realized she was standing before Harald Hamsun clad only in her nightdress, her shoulders and torso covered by a damp quilt. Good heavens! Instinctively she tightened her grip on the quilt, wishing she still held Julia in front of her. With embarrassment she lifted her gaze to see if he had noticed her immodest attire.

A relieved sigh escaped her when she saw that Harald's attention was still on Father. They were conversing now, voices low.

Taking a moment to study their benevolent neighbor, Marie decided he wasn't a handsome man, not in the strictest sense of the word. His head was a little too big, she thought, yet it matched the rest of him. Though he stood just an inch or so under Father's height, he seemed bigger than the taller man, probably because his shoulders were thicker and wider.

His jaw was strong, his face clean shaven, but it was her opinion that his eyes tended to be a little on the narrow side. In fact, she remembered once thinking that when he laughed they seemed to crinkle up entirely out of sight. Since entering the barn he had removed his hat and oilskin, and his light-colored hair was plastered to his head. His clothing was wrinkled, rough, intended for hard work. . . .

Marie stopped her musings, more than a little ashamed of herself. Here she stood in her barn in a damp, dirty nightdress, her own hair looking unimaginably horrid, thinking critical thoughts of this kind man who'd come out into the rain and offered them his assistance and virtually everything he had — his food, his blankets, his home. He really did have a good heart.

She wondered what Chadwick would say if he could see her in this bedraggled state.

Thank goodness he never would! Her heart beat a little quicker knowing how he would doubtless be moved to great compassion to see her home burnt, her family displaced. He always spoke in such a stirring way of his great care for others, looking toward the future and conceiving of ways in which he could help his fellow man.

An enormous crash startled Marie from her thoughts. The house had just collapsed. It seemed unreal to see what little was left of their two-story frame home. Father had worked so hard just a few years ago, building a splendid addition onto the small house that had originally stood on that spot. Judging from the expressions on the others' faces, they were experiencing the same feelings. It was really true: They had nothing left but the clothes on their backs.

But we've all got our lives, thank the Lord for that.

"You all go on over to Hamsun's," Father spoke, his voice sounding flat. "I'm going to stay here and . . . and watch over things."

There was a chorus of voices volunteering to stay with him, but Father was firm in his bidding. Harald nodded, stepping toward his wagon. While Raymond and Anthony assisted their grandmother from her stool, Mother transferred Julia from her arms back to Marie's. Taking a blanket from the back of Harald's wagon, Mother wrapped it around her shoulders and went to stand next to Father.

"I'll be staying with you, William," she announced in a tone of voice that brooked no argument. "A wife's place is by her husband's side, and I'll not let you spend the night here by yourself."

Marie felt relief run through her when she saw her father's brief nod. If there was anyone who could help him, it was Mother. Many times she had marveled at how intuitive her mother was, how she just seemed to know how another person was feeling. Mother's words were always just right, too. Marie wished she could be only half as sensitive. Then she would never put her foot into her mouth ever again.

"May I take this bundle from you?"

Marie started at the sound of Harald's voice, not having noticed his approach. He smiled and held his arms out for Julia.

Goodness, they were large at this close distance. Or was it that his chest seemed so immense? And his hands were much bigger than Chadwick's. Marie knew it was rude to stare at him so, not to mention not replying immediately. But she was faced with the dilemma of standing before this neighbor man with only a bit of quilted fabric separating her body from his if she relinquished her youngest sister to him.

In the end, Julia made the decision for Marie as she unclasped her arms from around Marie's neck and lurched toward Harald. Easily cradling the three-year-old in one powerful arm, he extended his other hand toward Marie.

"Will you come to my home, Marie?"

It was as if he sensed her awkwardness and embarrassment and wanted to put things at ease between them. Nothing but kindness and concern shone from his face as he gently took her hand, enfolded it in his, and led her to the wagon. There he set Julia back in her arms and tucked a blanket around them.

"Let's go, Harald," Hugh said, his fingers already wrapped around a bridle. Raymond and Anthony waited near the row of stalls after helping Grandma Biggs take a seat between Rosemary and Sarah.

Examining his passengers with a satisfied expression, Harald set his hand on Hugh's shoulder. "Let's go, then."

The horses were only too eager to depart the uncomfortable, dangerous-smelling environment, and they took off in a brisk trot. The fire blazed with much less intensity now, giving out proportionally less heat and light. Marie watched, cold rain soaking into her hair and blanket, as Mother and Father faded into the shadows. She wondered how they would fare the night. A wave of exhaustion enveloped her as she cradled Julia's small hand within hers and, curiously enough, she found her thoughts drifting to Harald Hamsun and the way her own hand had felt in his.

CHAPTER THREE

"Oh, you poor dears!" Ida Olson's unmistakable voice penetrated to the very corners of Harald Hamsun's cozy house. "I came as soon as I heard. My goodness, Helen! You look as if you've been up all night!"

From her place on the bedroom floor, Marie sat up groggily and brushed the grit out of her eyes. Oh, she smelled awful, of smoke. Glancing around, she was surprised to see she was the only person remaining in the clean, neatly furnished room. When they turned in last night, Grandma and Rosemary had shared the bed while she and Julia had made a place on the floor. How could everyone have gotten up around her while she slept on?

With a groan she pushed herself up to a sitting position, her joints aching. Gray light filtered in from the curtained window. The events of last night seemed unreal, but the stench lingering about her and the sight of her grimy nightdress confirmed the fact that their house had indeed burned to the ground. Once again she offered up a quick prayer of thanks that their lives had been spared.

Ida Olson's piercing voice continued on, grating on Marie's nerves. Once she'd asked Mother if she didn't think Mrs. Olson was nothing but a loudmouthed busybody. Mother had said no, that there were good points to be found in everyone . . . just sometimes one had to look a little harder to discover them.

". . . so Lyle and I put a few things together for you," Ida continued, having scarcely taken a breath since she'd come in the door. "We stopped by your place for a look, and there's nothing left — I mean *nothing* at all. You were lucky to escape with your lives. My gracious, those chimney fires can sure go quick. A squirrel's nest, you figure? Why, we had trouble with squirrels one year, and my Lyle . . ."

The conversation continued with Ida dominating and Mother and Grandma Biggs getting only an occasional word in edgewise. Marie pushed herself to her feet, mulling over the idea of a squirrel's nest causing a chimney fire. That made sense, she supposed; she had heard of it happening before. But since the house had burned to the ground, there was no way to be certain. What was hard to believe, though, was how fast the house had gone up in flames. A shiver ran down her spine at the thought that their entire house had been consumed in well under two hours' time.

Was this Harald's room? she wondered, looking about. She had barely taken notice of her surroundings during the night when they came in. In the gray morning light she noted that the headboard and matching dresser were made of maple. A white tatted runner sat atop the dresser, on which rested a framed photograph of a man and woman. Walking over to the dresser, she examined the pair, deciding these had to be Harald's parents. The resemblance, especially the lines and shape of the man's face, was too strong for them not to be.

Catching her reflection in the mirror above the dresser, Marie shuddered. Her oval face was smudged with soot, and her normally glossy auburn hair, though pulled back into a braid, was dull and dingy.

The small, curtained closet in the corner of the room seemed to beckon her, and somewhat guiltily she found herself pushing aside the curtain to peek inside, telling herself there might be something she could wear until she . . .

Until she what? She sighed, beginning to realize the magnitude of her family's loss. She had no clothes — none of them had any clothes — except for what they wore as they fled the fire. What were they going to do?

She took in the well-ordered row of clothing hanging in the closet, a small trunk on the shelf above the clothes rod, and two pair of shoes sitting neatly on the floor. This must be Harald's room indeed, she surmised, looking at the size of the shirts and suit coat. Only two dress shirts and a single dress suit coat hung amidst the work-grade items. She wondered how many fine suits of clothing Chadwick owned . . . and if he even had a comfortable work shirt in his possession.

Harald Hamsun was certainly a simple man, not given to fineries.

Marie started at a knock on the door and let the curtain fall back into place. "I'm awake," she said, walking with haste to the place she'd spent the night. Bending over, she busied herself with tidying the blankets.

"Good morning, dear," Mother sang out, entering the room with a basket full of folded clothing. Marie observed that her mother had washed, brushed her hair, and dressed in an unfamiliar yet worn dark blue skirt and blouse that were slightly too big for her. Fatigue showed in her features, announced by the dark circles beneath her eyes. But her manner gave away none of her weariness. "I don't know how they managed it, but Myra Leonard and Coralee McGraw were here early this morning with food and provisions and clothes — even shoes — for just about all of us. Grandma's sitting on the sofa going through some items, and I thought we could sort through this pile together. Oh, and Ida Olson just dropped some things by, too."

"I heard," Marie said dryly.

"I was pretty sure she woke you," Mother added with a tired smile, setting the basket on the bed. "I just don't understand how word got around as fast as it did."

"Maybe people haven't *heard* our news so much as they've *smelled* it." Marie wrinkled her nose, then let out a sigh. "Well, all of Decoria Township knows about the fire; I wonder how long it will take for word to reach Chadwick in Mankato?" She imagined his distress at learning of their plight, how his fine team of horses would speed south over the eight-mile distance separating them once the report reached his ears.

"Give it a couple days, dear. It often takes folks in Mankato a while to learn what goes on in the country."

Marie nodded, anticipating Chadwick's arrival, hoping it would be soon.

"Would you like to wash?" Mother asked. "There's hot water on the stove. Some oatmeal for you to eat, too. All the men are over at our place, so you can get cleaned up in the kitchen. There's sure to be something to fit you in this pile. I'd guess Coralee's about your size."

"How is Father this morning?" Marie asked cautiously. To her surprise, her mother's eyes filled with tears.

"To be honest, I don't know."

"Well, what do you think is the matter with him?"

Mother closed her eyes for a long moment. "Oh, dear. Understanding the mind of a man is often a difficult thing." Wiping her tears with the end of one rolled-up sleeve, she gave Marie a watery smile. "But I've also heard your father say a woman's mind is beyond fathom, as well. In the first place, I think he's feeling guilty for not having checked the chimney sooner. He had intended to do that this fall, but he just hadn't gotten around to it yet."

"The fire wasn't his fault."

"No one is saying it was," Mother said, shaking her head, her small hands smoothing the white blouse atop the basket of clothes. "But you can't convince him otherwise. I'm also coming to see that he has a terrible problem with accepting charity."

"But he's always been so generous," Marie said.

"Yes, dear, but giving out of your plenty and receiving in need and humility are two completely different things. It all comes down to a matter of pride, Marie. I don't find it easy to accept charity myself, but I can look at it as the Lord providing for our needs. Your father's pride is keeping him from seeing it that way, or for being thankful for anything at all. I'm so glad Harald was able to talk some sense into him last night, or we'd have all spent the night in the barn."

"Will we stay here until we rebuild?"

"Well, there's another problem," Mother said with a deep sigh. "Your father chose not to buy fire insurance, so . . ."

"So . . . now what?" Marie asked, a feeling of dread growing within her belly. "Does that mean we can't build a new house?"

"I'm not sure what it all means yet, dear, but try not to worry yourself. We own the land, free and clear, most of the crops are in, and we have some savings tucked away."

"And the animals and outbuildings made it all right, didn't they?"

"That's my girl." Mother gave her a tired but approving smile. "See how much we have? We just need to look at things from that perspective and trust that the Lord has everything under control." Pulling half the pile of clothes from the basket, she set them on the bed. "And what a neighbor we have in Harald. He insists we stay with him as long as necessary, no matter that we more than fill his house. So in answer to your question, dear, yes, I believe we will be staying here."

"That's very generous of him." Oddly touched by their neighbor's giving nature, Marie felt a lump form in her throat. She remembered the special effort he had made last night to make her feel welcome in his home, and the gentle way he had treated Julia. She had never taken the time to know him very well, but it seemed that there was more to Harald Hamsun than she had previously thought.

The next few days passed in a blur for Marie. One of the neighbors, Coralee McGraw, had taken Sarah and Julia to her home to stay for a period of time, yet it still seemed as though there were too many things to do. Cooking, cleaning, washing clothes — it never ended. Marie, Rosemary, Mother, and Grandma scarcely quit moving.

And the donations poured in. Clothing, shoes, bedding, canned goods, meat, baked items, kitchen utensils, blankets. The list of items went on and on. Just this morning Joe Kinstrup had brought a bushel of apples from his orchard, and Lawrence Pickert a smoked ham. It troubled Marie to see how difficult it was for Father to accept these goodwill offerings from others. The boys had no such problem. Last night over a late supper Anthony and Raymond joked that they ate better now than they ever had.

Harald's house was quite a bit smaller than theirs had been, and it was a challenge to make do with so many people in tighter quarters. This was most evident, of course, at mealtimes and bedtime. Poor Harald, Marie frequently thought, having his home disrupted in such a manner.

But he didn't seem to mind one bit. His disposition never wavered from calm and steady, and he truly seemed to enjoy their company. He wasn't given to long discourses or even small talk, but he was kind with his words and generous with his compliments. And as much as he could, he helped Father and the boys with their farm work and with cleaning the rubble out of the basement.

Pausing while she packed a large basket of food for the men's lunch, Marie glanced outdoors at the glorious autumn day. The clouds and cold rain of the past few days had yielded to a sunny, more temperate offering. Was it just the weather that made her spirits soar? Nothing about their circumstances had changed, yet a burst of well-being suffused her. "I'll take lunch over to the house," she offered, eager to be outdoors.

"Thank you, Marie," Mother replied from the sofa, where she sat with Grandma Biggs, altering a donated dress for slender Rosemary. "Will you also pick eggs for me? I asked Hugh to do it this morning, but I doubt he remembered."

"What do you expect, Mother? He's only twelve," Rosemary interjected. She was seated at the table peeling tart, juicy apples for pie. For some reason she had adopted a manner worthy of a bossy eldest sister, though she was the second child born to William and Helen Biggs. Grandma always said it was because Rosemary was pleased beyond reason to be fifteen minutes older than Raymond, a fact she never let him forget. Only she didn't stop at Raymond. She played mother hen to all her siblings, save Marie.

"And you were never twelve?" Marie asked with a grin, taking rare pleasure in reminding her sister that she had been fifteen to her twelve.

"You tell her, Marie," Grandma Biggs spoke from the couch, chuckling. "And if that ain't enough, I can remind her about how I used to change her —"

"All right, all right," Rosemary conceded with a laugh. "I'll just peel apples, and Marie can pick eggs. It's better than picking a fight."

Carrying the weighty basket through the door, Marie thought how fortunate she was to have such a good friend in her sister. The two of them had always gotten along better than most sisters, she suspected.

Overhead a pair of noisy blue jays cavorting among rust-hued oak branches captured her attention. *What a perfect day to be outdoors,* she thought, the fresh fall breeze rustling the leaves and caressing her face and neck as she made her way down the walk to the drive. Looking up into a sky of such dazzling blue, it was hard to believe that anything could be wrong in the world. In fact, this day was much like the day before their house burned, the day she'd taken a ride through the countryside with Chadwick. It seemed like years ago, not just days.

Why hasn't Chadwick come to call? she wondered for the umpteenth time. News of their fire must have reached his ears by now. She felt hurt by his failure to rush to her side. People she scarcely knew had responded to the emergency, yet she had seen nothing of the young man she thought she knew so well.

"Can I help you with that?"

Stopping and turning, Marie watched as Harald took long strides to catch up with her, removing his hat as he approached. Blue work pants, held up by suspenders, hugged his sturdy form, and she noticed he'd rolled up his light-colored shirt sleeves, exposing muscular forearms.

Why on earth she should notice the way the sunlight shone upon the silky, golden hairs of those arms, she did not know . . . yet she did.

"It's lunch," she replied inanely, feeling suddenly shy.

Harald nodded, setting his hat back on his head and taking the heavy hamper from her arms. "Looks strange, doesn't it?" he commented.

"What — my lunch?" Marie forgot her

shyness, falling into step beside him. "You don't even know what I made."

"No, Marie, not your lunch." Harald smiled, his eyes crinkling up until they nearly disappeared. Einar Hamsun's speech had been heavily accented by his native Norwegian tongue, but only a hint of the lyrical intonation was evident in his nephew's deep voice. "See there?" he said, pointing across the lane to the copse of trees on the Biggses' property. "The empty place where your house stood."

"Oh . . . yes," Marie replied, taking in the vista — minus the farmhouse. Silently, she berated herself for her tongue-tied response. What was the matter with her? She never had any trouble holding a conversation with Chadwick. Even college-educated as he now was, he had told her more than once how much he liked talking with her.

Maybe her flustered feelings around Harald had to do with the fact that she knew he had once asked Father for permission to court her. And perhaps, also, because after the past few days she could no longer view him as a pleasant neighbor man whom she hardly ever saw. He was much more than that, she now knew.

So why, then, should she have these butterflies in her stomach as they walked along his drive, side by side? Having new knowledge of a man's depth of character most certainly should not cause one to feel agitated. And why, pray tell, did her gaze keep stealing toward him, to look him over more closely?

Pray tell.

Prayer. Why hadn't she thought of that before? In her mind she dispatched an urgent plea to the Heavenly Father that he might swiftly bring peace to this curious new anxiety that plagued her when in Harald Hamsun's presence.

"I would like to know you better, Marie."

Harald's direct words interrupted her prayer and nearly brought her heart to her throat. She had been seeing Chadwick Farrell off and on for the better part of four years, and he had never once said anything so forthright. Marie thought the gravel had never crunched so loudly beneath her shoes as it did now. Long seconds passed while her brain frantically tried to formulate a response.

"You would?" she said, finally.

"You are a fine woman." He nodded with certainty.

A fine woman.

There was something about the way Harald said those words that gave Marie a quiver deep down inside, and a resultant wave of warmth spread across her cheeks. Those three short words had conveyed appreciation and approval and manly interest all at once. Chadwick talked a lot, certainly, and he had told her how much he liked spending time with her, but such talk was always flowery, or in a teasing vein. He'd never directly or succinctly communicated any such heartfelt sentiments as she had just heard from this simple Norwegian farmer.

Or maybe not so simple . . .

Oh, Marie, now what? Clasping her hands together, Marie cleared her throat, missing the beginning of Harald's next sentence.

". . . not the best circumstances right now with both of us living under the same roof. During this time we can become better acquainted and later, if you wish, after you've moved back home, I will call for you."

Crunch, crunch, crunch.

On they walked, as the Indian summer sun beat down warm and steady. Good autumn smells filling the air. Father and the boys could now be heard easily as they worked to clear rubble from the burned-out cellar.

"You certainly are . . . frank," Marie ventured as they walked the short jog down the lane from the Hamsun driveway to the Biggs driveway.

"Just truthful." Harald looked over at her at the same time she chanced to take a glance at him. On his broad face was an expression of sincerity and earnestness, and his bright blue gaze sought hers.

Something about his expression caused another unknown emotion to run through Marie, strong and sweet and painful, completely unfamiliar. Dropping her gaze, she studied her clasped hands. "It's good to be truthful," she managed to say, nodding perhaps too much, her words sounding faint in her own ears.

But Harald had no such problems. His voice was as warm and deep as a pot of thick golden honey, making that peculiar feeling inside her grow even stronger.

"So what do you think, Marie? Would you like to know me better, too?"

CHAPTER FOUR

It was a long moment before Marie found
her tongue. "I . . . I . . . yes," she said, gulp-
ing, heart pounding, surprised to find that
she really did want to know more about
Harald Hamsun.

His only response was a smile and a nod,
eyes crinkling, and he continued walking.

Staying in step beside him, Marie felt her
mind whirl. The past few days at Harald's
house had only whetted her curiosity about
what sort of a man he was. Generous, that
was more than evident. God-fearing, to be
certain; he attended church regularly and
read from the Scriptures in the evenings.
And *truthful* — she had just learned first-
hand what value he placed on honesty. She
also had found him to be calm and kind and
gentle and . . .

Handsome?

For as long as she could remember, Chadwick Farrell's height and lean, dark-haired looks had meant *handsome* to Marie. Harald Hamsun, with his fair coloring, moderate height and broad, powerful frame could not possibly have been more unlike that. Why, his big hands could no doubt easily . . .

Span your waist?

Now, where on earth had a thought like that come from? Marie felt her cheeks burn once again and was glad Harald's attention seemed to be occupied elsewhere. He certainly had turned this day upside down with his straightforward declaration.

"Hey, Marie and Harald are coming with lunch," Hugh called from beside a pile of rubbish and burned timbers.

"This is *my* lunch. You'll have to get your own." A grin parted Harald's lips, revealing both a sense of humor and a row of strong, white teeth. His expression of mirth, eyes crinkled up so tight she was sure he couldn't even see where he was going, brought an answering smile to Marie's lips despite her tangled feelings.

A chorus of loud cries ascended from the foundation where their house once stood as Raymond and Anthony scaled the ladder that poked up out of the ground and brushed themselves off. Marie recoiled at the sight of her brothers, soot-black from head to toe, and even in her present state of distraction she couldn't help but wonder if those clothes would ever come clean.

Lunch was a pleasant affair. Marie was glad for the congeniality and banter that her brothers provided. It presented her the opportunity to nibble on a slice of bread and sort out her thoughts. Harald fit right in with the boys, and it was obvious that they thought the world of him. Though she tried not to, she found herself watching Harald through lowered lashes as his words rang through her thoughts, over and over.

When they were nearly finished eating, Father appeared from the barn, coming over only briefly to where they sat on the damp, autumn-browned grass. Unlike the boys, his appearance was clean, if threadbare. The donated garments of one of their neighbors hung loosely on his frame, accentuating a new leanness. He barely said hello as he reached into the basket and took out a single apple. There was a lifelessness in his normally animated brown eyes as he muttered something about having to go to the bank. A short time later, after hitching a team of horses to the wagon, he departed for town.

The conversation took a sober turn after Father's departure. Raymond was the first to speak. "I'm more than a little worried about him. He's been like that ever since the fire."

Anthony nodded. "He hardly says anything to anyone."

"Well, he said something to me yesterday," Hugh said, hurt evident in his young voice. "All I did was drop a bucket he handed up to me — it was heavier than I thought — and he called me stupid and yelled at me like he was never going to stop." He sighed, brushing crumbs from his sooty lap. "I said I was sorry. I didn't mean to do it."

"Well, it was full of rock and mortar, and you did almost drop it on his head," Raymond said with feigned disgust.

"Your father is a good man," Harald said, nodding, "but he's carrying many burdens . . . burdens none of you have ever carried."

Hugh responded in wounded bafflement. "But aren't we just supposed to lay our burdens at the foot of the cross? Pastor Price gave a sermon on that a few weeks ago."

"Don't you remember what else he said, Hugh? He also talked about the man who laid his burdens down, only to pick them right back up again when he finished praying." Anthony's attention to and quick recall of every detail of his life never failed to impress Marie.

"Mother says he feels guilty about the fire," she said, contributing what she knew to the conversation, "and that he's having trouble accepting charity."

"What other choice do we have right now than to accept charity?" Anthony's words were spoken matter-of-factly. "And if one of our neighbors had a fire, you know Father would be there to help in any way he could."

"He would, indeed." Harald reached for an apple and took a bite. Chewing thoughtfully, he added, "Give him some time. Acceptance is often a process."

"Well, the process is going a little too slow for me," Hugh retorted, still obviously smarting from his father's uncharacteristic temper and sharp words of the day before. "He never even apologized or —"

"Oh, Ma-riee," Raymond interrupted, drawing out the last syllable of her name on a sing-song note. "Lookie who's coming down the road."

"Chadwick the Ferret," Hugh pronounced with a snicker, recovering from his emotional ache in record time. "Grandma's right: 'Ferret' fits him better than 'skunk' because he sort of looks like a weasel . . . don't you think, Ray?"

"Well, I wouldn't say he actually *looks* like a weasel, but —"

Hugh didn't give Raymond a chance to finish his sentence before turning to Harald. "Marie wants to marry the ferret," he said with the brand of obnoxiousness only twelve-year-old boys possess, rolling his eyes in her direction. "Oh, Chadwick," he mocked, adopting an unnaturally high tone while he fluttered his hand over his heart, "come and take me away to your big fancy mansion in Mankato. I'm *madly* in love with you, and I want to —"

"Stop it, Hugh," Anthony said with annoyance. Waves of mortification billowed through Marie at their youngest brother's caricature of her. She had never once acted like that about Chadwick . . . what must Harald be thinking of her at this moment? Keeping her gaze directed downward, she busied herself packing the picnic items back into the basket.

In one motion Anthony pushed his tall, skinny body to a standing position and set his hat back on his head. "Your job is cleaning stalls this afternoon, Hugh; you'd better get to it. I would hate to think what Father might say to you if you don't have them done by the time he gets back from town."

"Come on, little brother," Raymond said

somewhat reluctantly as he also stood, "you don't really want to hang around here and watch Chadwick and Marie make gooey eyes at each other, do you?"

"I am free to help you this afternoon," Harald said to appreciative noises from all three of the Biggs boys. He handed his plate and cup to Marie as Chadwick Farrell's fashionable black buggy turned into the drive, led by the paired bays. "If we work hard, we can get the cellar finished this afternoon."

Marie felt sick. For all the promise the beautiful day had held, the afternoon was turning into the stuff from which nightmares were made. Not more than a half hour ago Harald had declared his interest in her . . . and for some reason still unknown to her she had responded accordingly. Was it just the shock of his direct words that had caused the strange, potent feelings within her as they'd walked along, or was it something more?

And why today, of all days, did her brothers seem intent on humiliating her before him?

If that weren't enough, at long last here came Chadwick, his handsome face a welcome sight on any other day. He liked her, she knew, but what was truly behind the inconstant nature of his courtship — if it could even be called that? What were his real feelings for her, his intentions? Over the past years, deep down, she had allowed herself to dream of being married to Chadwick, yet he seemed content to continue on as always, spending what time they were together waxing on about his plans and dreams for the future. She knew his family — his mother, in particular — didn't approve of his spending time with her, but what perplexed her was that he made no effort to take their relationship beyond its present state, despite the fact that she strongly sensed his romantic interest.

So why, today, didn't her heart leap as his carriage approached? Where was the usual thrill that coursed through her at the mere sight of him? Though she'd asked the Lord to remove her anxious thoughts, it seemed they had done nothing but multiply. Chadwick. Harald. What was she supposed to think? What was she supposed to feel?

And what on earth was she going to do with the two of them together?

Chancing a glance at the blond man, she saw that he studied the advancing carriage with an unreadable expression on his broad face. His eyes may have narrowed as he pressed big, work-roughened hands against

muscular thighs and pushed himself to a
standing position. Or it could have been just
a trick of the sunlight, Marie concluded.
Harald thanked her for lunch and went to
join the boys.

"Hello, Marie," Chadwick called, bringing his horses to a halt as he stood and
surveyed the damaged landscape. A long,
low whistled note escaped him, and he
gracefully alighted from the carriage, coming
to join her where she knelt over the picnic
basket. "I'd say it's true, then. I just heard
today . . . she burned right to the ground,
didn't she?"

Marie nodded, more ill at ease than she
could ever remember.

"But your family got out all right, didn't
they?"

"We're fine." She sighed, closing the basket. There was nothing more to pack, nothing more with which to occupy her hands.
She rose quickly, before he could offer his
arm to assist her. "Except that Father —"

"Say, I passed your father on my way out
here," Chadwick interrupted, straightening
the lapels of an understated but expensive
camel-colored wool suit coat. "He must
have been a bit preoccupied; he didn't even
wave.

"But I was preoccupied, too, Marie,

thinking that there are just plain too many fires," he went on, clearing his throat as he warmed to his subject. "People lose their homes, their businesses, their belongings, and sometimes their lives. In the city, whole blocks go up at a time. People simply need to be more widely educated on how to prevent fires. I've also been thinking about how I might someday implement a plan of public assistance to aid fire victims. . . ."

Marie nodded, thinking he looked like a politician as he spoke, hands clasped behind his back, pacing back and forth. Had he always talked so much? Thinking back, she realized that their time spent together had been largely consumed by the articulation of Chadwick's many concepts and beliefs. No wonder he liked to spend time with her; she rarely obstructed his abundant flow of words. She seldom had a chance to. With new awareness she contemplated Chadwick Farrell, drawing comparisons between his manner and Harald's.

". . . I said, where are you staying, Marie? And where did you get that dress?"

"Oh, pardon me," Marie said, pulling her attention from her thoughts to the man who stood before her, an earnest expression on his handsome features. "I've been a bit distracted . . . since the fire."

"Of course you have." Sympathy shone from his hazel eyes as he studied her appearance. "Despite your, ah, circumstances, you're looking quite lovely today. Your face seems to have a sort of radiance, a glow of its own."

"It does?" Why did he stare at her so? Marie brought her hand up to her face, thinking her cheek felt quite warm. Maybe she was really getting sick. The idea of spending a few days in bed, away from everyone and everything, suddenly had a great deal of appeal. There was just too much to think about.

"Hey, Chadwick," Hugh called, too innocently, from the ladder, "can you give us a hand down here?"

"I'd really like to," the tall, dark-haired youth replied, tucking Marie's arm in his own and strolling over to the edge of the cellar, "but I have to be going back to town. I'm very busy today at the bank. That looks like . . . quite dirty work down there."

The boys must have had a bet going about whether Chadwick would help. Marie could tell from the satisfied smirk on Hugh's face. Harald sent her a brief but questioning glance as he worked to loosen a heavy timber that had only partially burned, his shoulder muscles straining through his shirt.

"I must be going now," Chadwick called down. "But you'll have to ask Marie to tell you about the plans I have for assisting the victims of fires in the future. It's always been an idea of mine, but after hearing today of your misfortune, it's taken root and literally blossomed." Letting go of her arm, he gestured widely with both his hands. "Not only do I plan to unite the community with this effort, I will also educate the public on all possible ways to prevent fires from occurring. It's an exciting concept, one that I know will be of real help to all of Blue Earth County."

"Real help?" Marie heard Raymond mutter darkly, standing just below her with his shovel in his hands. "He wouldn't know what real help was if it bit him in the hind end."

"Well, I'm off," Chadwick called to his audience of laborers, evidently missing Raymond's observation. He touched the brim of his hat. "Good-bye, Marie," he said, skimming his knuckles in a light caress down the side of her cheek. His hazel eyes studied her face, his elegant brows lifted.

Marie cleared her throat, taken by surprise at his familiar gesture. At the same time Hugh snorted in laughter; whether in response to Raymond's remark or Chadwick's touch she did not know. Quickly she stepped away from the edge of the basement, away from Chadwick, and closed her eyes in embarrassment.

Why, today, had Chadwick chosen to touch her in such a manner in front of her brothers — and Harald, no less? She was never going to hear the end of it. Again she wondered what Harald must be thinking of her.

The sick feeling inside her grew.

"Are you sure you're all right, Marie? All of a sudden you don't look so well." She heard Chadwick's voice at her side; the spicy scent of his cologne filled her nostrils. "Can I give you a lift to . . . wherever you're staying?"

"Uh, no thank you." Opening her eyes, she forced a smile. "I'll just walk."

"If you're sure . . ."

"I'm sure."

"I'll be out to see you soon," he said in a concerned voice. "Now where is it you're staying, so I can find you?"

"At the Hamsun farm, across the road," she said with a sigh, knowing he wouldn't leave until he had received that information. "But I don't know if —"

"All right, then. You can count on seeing me soon." Having said that, he hesitated, as if there were something more he wanted to say. His eyes searched her face, and she could have sworn that he looked a little nervous. He cleared his throat.

"Good-bye, Marie," he finally said, patting her arm. With a jaunty step he walked toward his carriage, leaving Marie wondering what it was he had nearly said.

CHAPTER FIVE

The sun was setting as Raymond, Anthony, and Hugh trooped through the kitchen doorway of the Hamsun farmhouse, their spirits high. They had washed at the pump and had changed out of their filthy clothes. Their wet hair gleamed against their heads.

"We got it all done!" Raymond announced. "The foundation needs a little work yet, but thank goodness it's stacked rock. It won't take long, and we'll be ready to build."

"Thanks to Harald," Anthony pointed out. "We never could have done it without him."

"Yeah, you never seen anyone work like him," said Hugh. "He's worth three or four fellows and six horses all in one. I can hardly wait till Father sees it."

"That's wonderful news, boys," Mother called as she set the table. "I know your father will be very pleased."

Hugh padded over to the work table where Marie and Rosemary were putting the final touches on the evening meal. "What smells so good?" he asked, edging between them. "Mmm, fresh biscuits. How long till we eat?"

"We'll have the food on the table shortly," Mother replied, "so mind your manners until then. Say, speaking of your father, has he come back from Mankato yet?"

"Haven't seen him," Anthony replied. "Don't you think if he was just going to the bank, he should have been back hours ago?"

"He probably stopped at the lumberyard. That can take a while, as I recall," Grandma said with a snort. "Your grandpa always seemed to lose track of time whenever he went to town to look for lumber or hardware or machinery. Must run in their blood." She pushed herself up from the rocker where she sat crocheting. "Where's that Harald of mine?" she asked, making her way to the kitchen with the new walking stick he had fashioned for her the day after the fire.

Marie's heart made a funny leap when Harald's name was mentioned. All afternoon she had been looking forward to seeing him again — and dreading it, too, thinking of the way he had declared his interest in her. She had told him she wanted to know him better, too, but how was she supposed to act around him now? Maybe she had replied too hastily. Maybe she should have asked for time to think the matter over.

"*Your* Harald, Grandma?" Raymond grinned and snatched a biscuit. "He makes you a new cane, and now you've adopted him?"

"It's not a cane, it's a walking stick. You can go on and make fun of me all you like, but I'm comin' to love that young man like one of my own."

"Harald had a few things to do before he came in, and he said to go ahead without him," Anthony announced, assisting his grandmother to her chair at the crowded table. Both end leaves were extended, yet the distance between plates was minimal.

"Do you love Chadwick Farrell like one of your own, too, Grandma?" Imitating his eldest brother, Hugh light-fingered a biscuit and walked toward the table. "He came to visit Marie today, you know, and he touched her right on her face."

"What do you mean, he touched her right on her face?"

Marie felt the heat creep up her cheeks as she turned to the stove and lifted the lid on the stew. Giving the bubbling mixture in the big cast iron pot a stir, she realized Chadwick's uncharacteristic gesture had indeed been noted.

"You know, he kind of ran his hand down her face like this." Hugh demonstrated the caress in an exaggerated fashion on his own cheek, batting his eyelids and lolling his head back and forth.

"That's enough, Hugh," Mother said sternly.

Rosemary set down her spatula in exasperation and put her hand on her hip. "Oh, can't you just leave Marie alone, you little troublemaker? It's not nice to tease someone like that."

"Sure, Rosemary," he went on, "let's talk about you and Jason Gould holding hands after church last week — ouch!"

Mother had taken Hugh by the ear and now marched him out the door. Rosemary busied herself with piling biscuits in a napkin-lined basket while Grandma Biggs shook her head and pronounced, "That boy just doesn't know when to shut his mouth, does he?"

Hugh's overstated version of Chadwick's hand movement had caused more knots in Marie's stomach. Her restless thoughts shifted from Harald back to the banker's son, and why he might have chosen today to press his suit.

She had dreamed of such a moment. So where was her happiness? Her joy at Chadwick's familiar gesture? And why did thoughts of Harald keep intruding whenever her mind turned to the day's events?

After a long moment Mother reappeared, followed by an abashed Hugh, who asked his sisters' forgiveness.

"Let's eat our supper and put all this nonsense behind us," Mother said in a determined tone while the boys filed to the table. "Raymond, light that lantern over there, will you? Remember to put butter and honey on the table with the biscuits, Rosemary. And Marie, don't serve all the stew. Put some into the warming oven for your father and Harald."

Finally everyone was seated and the blessing asked. As the tasty meal was consumed, the tension fell away and the conversation turned to the day's events. Picking at her meat and vegetables, Marie found she still did not have much of an appetite.

Eventually the topic of Chadwick's visit came up again, and Grandma Biggs chuckled while Anthony gave an accounting of Chadwick's fine dress and appearance as he'd stood at the edge of the foundation, peering in at them. "You should have seen him, Grandma, going on about all the great and wonderful things he plans to do for 'fire victims' someday, yet he didn't even lift a hand when he saw a burned-out family right in front of his face."

"Hot air and horsefeathers." Grandma nodded. "I told you that boy was nothing but a pretty talker, Marie. No substance. Now take Harald —"

Marie was spared from responding as the door opened, admitting Harald and her father. Was it her imagination, or did the younger man seem to be supporting the older? Yes, Father was definitely unsteady on his feet, she noted with concern, and he looked terrible. His face was chalky — save the high color that stood in his cheeks — and his eyes were glassed over. Quickly she glanced at Mother, who wore a troubled expression on her face. The sounds of a meal being eaten dwindled away and conversation stopped.

"Did you spend the afternoon drinking, William Raymond Biggs?" Grandma's blunt question seemed to echo in the stillness of the room. "So help me, William, if you've been —"

"He hasn't been drinking; he's sick." Harald spoke quietly. "He's got a fever."

"Oh, my poor darling." Mother was out of her chair and at Father's side instantly. "You haven't been well all week, have you?"

"I didn't get the loan." Father delivered the words in a hollow monotone, casting a further pall over the room. "Herman Farrell won't loan me a cent to rebuild. He says he can't risk the credit."

"You're burning up, William. We can talk of loans another time. Harald, help me get him to bed."

"Well, why wouldn't that horse's patoot give us a loan?" Grandma Biggs demanded, outraged. "There's nothing the matter with our credit. The Biggses have always paid their debts on time, not that we've had that many of them. Help me out of this chair, Anthony." Irritation caused her voice to sharpen as she pulled herself to her diminutive height and banged her walking stick on the floor. "I smell Imogene Farrell's hand in these dirty dealings. And she calls herself a God-fearin' woman." Thumping her stick as she made her way to her son, she sputtered, "I know what this is about, William, and you should, too."

"Well, *I* don't know what this is about," Mother said, pulling on Father's arm, "but I know this man needs to be put to bed."

"It's a message to us, isn't it, Grandma?"

Anthony glanced at Marie as he spoke, his young face solemn.

"It sure is, sonny, loud and clear. Credit risk, my eye. Herman and Imogene Farrell have enough money to burn a wet mule. This is about Marie! That wretched Imogene can't stand the thought of her boy takin' up with a country girl, and she's tryin' to make us miserable any way she can."

"Surely Herman Farrell wouldn't let his personal feelings color his business decisions, would he?" Mother was aghast at such an idea. "That can't be true, can it, William?"

"True enough that he told Lawrence Bentz over at the lumberyard not to extend me any credit, either."

Mother drew in her breath. "Lawrence told you that?"

"I don't imagine he had to," Grandma Biggs replied for her son. "I told you those Farrells were trouble from the get-go, Marie," she added, shaking her finger for emphasis. "Now don't you wish you'd listened to me?"

The tears that had gathered in Marie's eyes finally spilled down her cheeks at her grandmother's condemning words. All eyes were on her. "I . . . I . . . don't know what to say," she finally said, her voice breaking on a sob. "I'm . . . sorry."

"Marie, this isn't your fault." Harald's voice was firm and even as he entered the conversation. Bending forward, he spoke to the incensed elderly woman before him. "Please sit down and finish your supper, Mrs. Biggs. We can talk about this calmly after we get William taken care of." Concern shone in his eyes as his gaze met Marie's over her grandmother's neat gray bun.

As Harald and Mother assisted Father to the bedroom, Grandma grudgingly stepped aside. Instead of returning to the table, however, she stomped toward the stove and filled a pot with water, muttering about Imogene Farrell's wickedness and about how on earth she was supposed to make a decent fever concoction with her herbals being burned up in the fire.

Fearing she wouldn't be able to control herself from outright weeping for much longer, Marie rose and excused herself, realizing dimly it was the second time within a week she'd left the table in such a state . . . both times over the mention of Chadwick Farrell. Rosemary laid a warm hand on her arm as she walked past her, but Marie let it fall away and stepped through the door.

Giving in to her emotions, Marie allowed

the tears to flow unchecked down her cheeks. How could so much have happened in less than a week? One day everything was fine, and just a few short days later absolutely *nothing* was right. Sinking to her knees on the grass near the grove of trees that lay between the barn and the stubbled cornfield, Marie cried out to God for mercy, for understanding, feeling every bit as desperate as the psalmist.

No immediate revelations came to her, no answers to the family's plight. Gradually the sobs that racked her chest abated; slowly and gently the tears stopped falling. She had no idea how much time she'd spent crying out her anguish, but twilight had long since slipped into velvety night. The moon was on the wane, allowing the points of countless stars to shine boldly in the vast sky.

How long had it been since she'd gazed at the stars? A peculiar quiet stole over her as she contemplated the beauty of the heavens, her eyes searching for and finding familiar constellations. How vast the universe, she marveled, how infinite the celestial bodies. A gentle wind stirred what few leaves remained on the branches above her and blew soothingly across her tear-ravaged face. Though the ground was damp with evening dew, the earthy smell of sod and fallen leaves mingled pleasantly, an aromatic balm for her troubled senses.

It was good to be out here by herself, alone with her thoughts. With a house full of people and activity it was all but impossible to spend private time in prayer, in contemplation. Sitting back fully on the grass, she relaxed, supposing that with all the unrest in Harald's house, no one would miss her for the time being.

God is our refuge and strength, a very present help in trouble. Therefore will not we fear. . . . Silently, she recited the Forty-sixth Psalm, reminding herself to have faith in God's power and protection, no matter what was happening. Her parents required all their children to memorize portions of Scripture, an obligation that Marie, as a child, had often fulfilled begrudgingly. Now she was thankful for her parents' firmness on the matter. Sighing deeply, she paused over the phrase *Be still and know that I am God,* resolving to spend more time simply being *still* before him.

"Marie, are you out here?" Harald stood at the back of the barn, holding a lantern aloft. A sphere of light surrounded him, illuminating the worry on his broad face. "Marie?"

"Over here, Harald," she called, knowing

it would be wrong to pretend not to hear or see him. "Near the trees." Only a short time ago she would have thought Harald Hamsun to be the last person on earth she would have wanted to seek her out, but now, curiously, she felt an unfamiliar pleasure as she watched him approach. The lantern swung in a wide arc as he walked, his strides sure and even, booted feet rustling the long grass.

Though the rational part of her told her it was dark and she was being silly, her hands flew to smooth her hair and wipe away any vestiges of tears. The pace of her heart increased the nearer he drew, a giddy feeling settling in her chest.

"Are you all right, Marie?" His voice was gentle as he squatted before her and set the lantern at his feet.

Squinting into the light, she nodded and attempted a smile.

"Can I walk you back to the house?"

"I . . . I'd like to stay out here a bit longer, if I'm not being missed too much."

A smile crossed Harald's broad face, causing his eyes to crinkle in a way Marie was beginning to find very endearing. "You're safe for the time being. Your father is in bed, your mother's got your brothers doing the dishes, and your grandmother . . . well, she's still all wound up."

Marie smiled shyly in return, dropping her gaze. "That's like her." Plucking at the grass near her feet, her mind returned to a more sober thought. "What do you think is the matter with Father?"

He shrugged. "Hard to say. When your spirit is sick, your body tends to follow suit."

Marie nodded, hoping nothing was seriously wrong with her father.

Small talk out of the way, an awkward silence dropped between them. Harald shifted on his haunches and cleared his throat. Marie glanced up at him and quickly turned away, but not before taking in the broadness of his chest, the size of his powerful shoulders. The tempo of her heart accelerated even further.

"What are you doing out here, Marie?" he asked, breaking the quiet between them. "You were very upset when you left the house."

"You'll probably think it's silly."

"You can tell me." Something in the timbre of his voice invited her to share her thoughts with him, and before she was conscious of forming an answer, she had already replied.

"Looking at the stars . . . and praying."

"Neither is silly, Marie." On his face was an expression of sincerity and earnestness, the same one he'd worn that day he'd walked down the driveway with her. "Do you mind if I sit with you?"

A thrill shot through her as she shook her head.

"You would prefer not?"

"No . . . I mean, yes . . . I mean, please sit down." She swallowed what little moisture her mouth contained and smiled ruefully. "If you still want to. I seem to have a good deal of trouble expressing myself around you."

"You express yourself just fine, Marie. That's one of the things I've always admired about you. That and your kind manner." Easing himself from his haunches, he sat cross-legged on the ground before her and blew out the lantern. In the darkness, he added, "And I would have to be blind not to notice your warm brown eyes and lovely smile. You are a beautiful woman, Marie Biggs."

His words, carried to her ears on a tender current of night wind, were both somberly spoken and deeply intimate. Even if nothing came of her acquaintance with Harald Hamsun, Marie knew she'd always remember this moment as the first in her life that she'd been genuinely courted. A part of her womanhood, until this time dormant, quickened within her, producing feelings both alien and exciting.

"Besides my . . . outward appearance, how well do you know me, Harald?" Her voice had a breathless quality when she spoke — was it from using his name? — but somehow the darkness enveloping them made it easier to speak the practical thoughts on her mind. "We've hardly had more than a passing association. Maybe I'm not the person you think I am."

His chuckle was easy. "You are. I know you from living here these past two years, from watching you in church, from sitting across from you at your family's dinner table . . . and I know a great deal of your character from your father, from the time he and I have spent together." He was quiet a moment before adding, "I've also prayed about you a great deal, Marie."

"Oh." Had she once thought his interest in courting her was due to loneliness? How wrong she'd been. Her mind worked to reconcile this new knowledge with the other mysterious elements of the night.

"What do you think about when you look at the stars?" he asked.

It was Marie's turn to clear her throat.

"Well, tonight I was thinking how long it's been since I've . . . looked at the stars," she concluded limply.

"They're surely plentiful tonight," he said. "Do you know what I think when I look at the stars, Marie?"

Her eyes now adjusted to the darkness, Marie could see the outline of Harald's broad face angled up toward the heavens. "What?" She was curious to know.

"That God made each and every one of them."

"I think that, too, sometimes."

Harald was quiet for a long moment, his voice serious. "I look at the stars when I have problems to be solved."

"Do you get the answers?"

"Not usually." Marie sensed, rather than saw, Harald's smile, imagining how his eyes would be crinkled.

"Then why do you keep doing it?"

"Because it reminds me that the God who is big enough to create the heavens and hang the stars in the sky can be trusted to carry me through whatever struggles I have here on this earth."

Lapsing into a comfortable silence, the two sat, occupied with their own thoughts while they looked at the magnificent display above them. Harald's words were food for thought for Marie, and she pondered the application of his practice, finding it sound. Now that she thought about it, she realized her mother almost never looked at the size of the problems before her — rather, she looked first to the Lord. Even with the predicaments now besetting them — the fire and destruction of all their wordly goods, Father's despondency and now illness, Herman Farrell's refusal to grant a loan . . .

The loan. Chadwick.

Marie had been so immersed in the wonder of this unexpected interlude with Harald that she'd pushed the issue of Chadwick Farrell to the back of her thoughts. To the front he now strode, his hazel gaze peering questioningly at her in her mind's eye. What was she going to do about Chadwick and his suddenly much-more-warm feelings for her? she wondered. And what about the loan? Did he even know that his father had refused hers the money they needed to rebuild their house? There had to be something she could do to try to repair things. Maybe she could go to Mankato and talk with Mr. Farrell herself. Surely he would be sympathetic if she explained their situation. . . .

What are you doing, Marie, looking at the problem or looking to the Lord?

Gazing heavenward, she willed her anxious thoughts to stop while she viewed the countless points of light. God was in control. He would carry her — and the entire Biggs family — through whatever lay ahead. Slowly, in her mind, she recited the psalm again, thinking on its words and God's sovereignty.

Harald shifted in the darkness, his clothing rustling. It seemed her nerve endings were on fire as his knee accidentally brushed her leg. She heard him breathe in deeply, then exhale. Had the touch affected him, too?

Her peace fled.

Why hadn't he asked her about Chadwick? Surely he had to be curious about her relationship with the banker's son, particularly after Hugh had painted such an embellished portrait of their romance. In fact, "romance" was not the first word she'd use to describe her on-again, off-again association with Chadwick over the past several years.

The evening before the fire Rosemary had asked her if she was in love with Chadwick, and she had replied that she wasn't sure. The stirring feelings she'd experienced over the years thinking about him and spending time with him were pale in comparison to what Harald Hamsun was now doing to her insides.

"Are you feeling better, Marie? Would you like to go back to the house now?" Harald's voice was rich with gentleness.

"Y-yes, I think I'm ready . . . oh!" A surprised sound escaped her lips as Harald's big warm hand unerringly captured her own and pulled her to her feet.

"You have some thinking to do, *min lille benn.*" The musical cadence of his native language flowed smoothly from his lips, his breath warm against her cheek.

It was a good thing Harald still held her hand, for her knees were in danger of buckling. The moment went on, sweet and terrifying all at once. Never had she stood so close to him before, her hand becoming intimately acquainted with the rugged texture of his, her senses to his unfamiliar, clean scent.

And then it was over . . . and she was disappointed.

"It's time to go back, Marie," he said, releasing her hand and bending to pick up the lantern. "There's much to be done."

Nodding, though she knew he couldn't see her, Marie fell into step beside him, thinking of the pile of problems that awaited her back at the house — and of Harald's reminder that God was indeed big enough to carry her family through their difficulties. That was true, she knew, but aside from that she wondered just how soon he could do something about the tangled-up mess she called her heart.

CHAPTER SIX

Father wasn't any better the next day, or the day after. The fever ate at him, devouring the remainder of his strength and any spare flesh it could find. Violent chills and episodes of profuse sweating visited alternately, causing him to cry out in misery. Both Mother and Grandma tried every remedy they knew, to no avail. Finally, Sunday night, Harald went to town for the doctor.

The respite of warm weather had passed, a blast of cold northerly air rushing in on its heels. It was well after nine when Harald and Dr. Camp returned, both heavily bundled against the chilly night. Dr. Camp nodded at the assembled family as Harald led him to the bedroom where Father lay. Mother had not left his side for hours.

Grandma Biggs rocked in her chair, doing more praying for her son than crocheting, Marie observed. The older woman frequently closed her eyes and let her hook rest in her lap. The rest of the family was gathered, as was the custom Sunday evenings, to take turns reading from Scripture and selected classical works, but tonight everyone seemed out of sorts.

Marie was lonesome for Sarah and Julia, but upon hearing of William's illness, Coralee McGraw had insisted on keeping the girls until he was better. She'd seen her sisters at church this morning; they seemed to be delighted with the idea of staying with Coralee's family a few days longer. They'd been having great fun playing with Annette and Bobby, Coralee had said, her children being nearly the same ages as the Biggs girls.

Marie had hardly seen Harald since their talk under the stars, and she hadn't seen Chadwick at all. With the older women spending so much time tending to William, the largest share of running the household had fallen to her and Rosemary. The boys had been busy, too, carrying on the day-to-day operations of the farm as best they could without their father's help or direction.

"What do you suppose is taking so long?" Hugh shifted impatiently.

"Patience, Hugh," Grandma Biggs replied without opening her eyes. "The doctor will be out when he's finished." Since her display of bad temper the night Father had come home sick, she had been subdued, even contrite. She had also apologized to Marie for blaming her for the family's misfortunes.

Finally Harald emerged from the bedroom, followed by Dr. Camp, who closed his bag with a sharp click. Scratching his balding head, he recited, "No injuries, no signs of infection, no rash, no pneumonia, no pain in the belly, no vomiting, no diarrhea. And no one else in the house has been ill, either." He shrugged. "I wish I could tell you what the matter is, but I can't seem to find a cause for William's illness."

"Well, something's the matter with him." Grandma sat forward in the rocker, recovering a little of her feistiness.

"Most assuredly something is the matter with him, Mrs. Biggs," the middle-aged physician agreed. "I just cannot find its cause."

"What can we do for him?" Harald asked.

"What you've been doing: Keep him comfortable as best you can and give him all the liquids he'll take. It appears he's in good hands." He started for the door and paused. "I'll be out to see him sometime Tuesday or Wednesday; by then he'll either be worse or he'll be better. Good night."

Harald thanked him for coming and accompanied him back outdoors. A helpless feeling engulfed Marie as the men exited the house, for a childish part of her had expected Dr. Camp to cure her father of whatever plagued him. For the first time she allowed herself to wonder if Father was ever going to get better. He was very ill indeed. When she'd gone in to see him just before supper, he had looked frighteningly old, much like Grandpa Biggs before he died. Tears welled in her eyes at the thought of losing him.

"What do you suppose Harald was doing all day yesterday?" Hugh asked. Sitting quietly seemed a nearly impossible undertaking for him. "He went to town early and didn't get back till late."

Grandma Biggs shushed him. "You'll learn someday, young man, the virtue of minding your own business. Harald is a grown man and isn't obliged to tell us of his whereabouts twenty-four hours a day."

Disgruntled, Hugh didn't press his point any further, but Marie had also wondered what occupied Harald's attention for an entire day. He'd acted peculiarly at church today, too, standoffish, and then had talked for a long time after the service with several men from the congregation. Perhaps he was trying to avoid her, regretting the things he'd said beneath the stars. She hadn't forgotten them, though. Not one word.

Despite her worry for her father, the things Harald had said and the memory of her hand in his burned in her mind as bright and hot as the flaming heavenly bodies that had shone down upon them that night. It seemed she had scarcely slept the past few nights for thinking of him and what the future might hold. One thing was for certain: She could never again think of Harald Hamsun as just a neighbor.

Marie was now very much aware of him as a man.

Morning dawned cold and clear and bright, the sky swept with the wispy cirrus clouds country folk liked to call "horsetails." Marie checked in on her father to find him in a deep sleep. Mother, too, was sleeping, the upper half of her body draped across the foot of the bed as she sat in the chair alongside.

Marie was relieved to see her parents in slumber. Softly closing the door on them, she made her way to the kitchen where Grandma Biggs sat at the table with a cup of tea, a week-old copy of the *Mankato Free Press*, and the Bible. The smell of breakfast hung in the air, yet the house was quiet, save the ticking of the clock on the chest.

"Good morning, Marie. Are your daddy and mama still asleep?"

Marie nodded, looking about. "Where is everyone?"

"Well, the boys are already doing chores, and Rosemary went along to get the eggs. There's a pile of griddle cakes in the warming oven for you, honey." Folding her hands across the open Bible before her, Ruth Biggs fixed her granddaughter with a keen look. "Harald was gone even before any of the rest of us were up." There was something in the way she said *Harald* that made Marie wary.

Nodding noncommittally, Marie moved to the oven for her breakfast.

"I notice we haven't seen much of him the past few days," the older woman continued on conversationally, but Marie wasn't fooled. Grandma was on a fishing expedition, casting her nets wide.

"Well . . . I'm certain he's very busy. He's got his own farm to run, plus he's helping out with ours as much as he can." Making her way back to the table, Marie sat down, spread her griddle cakes with Alice Kinstrup's fresh apple butter, and took a bite.

"I also noticed that you two spent a good

deal of time outdoors together the other night."

Marie stopped chewing and met her grandmother's penetrating gaze. She swallowed. "Well, he just . . . we just . . ."

Up rose those slender, snow-white brows while a satisfied smile stole across her lips. "Yes?"

"We looked at the stars, that's all." She felt her cheeks grow warm and dropped her gaze to examine her breakfast. Why did she have the idea that Grandma was delighted — rather than concerned with propriety — to know she had been alone in the dark with Harald Hamsun?

"The stars . . . hmm . . . yes." The satisfied smile broadened into a grin as Grandma closed the Bible and reached for the newspaper, allowing her attention and one lean index finger to skim over the front-page advertisements and columns of tight print. "My, oh my, I wonder what goin's-on I missed reading about last week while our house was busy burning down. . . ." Glancing up, her expression all innocence, she encouraged, "Eat up, honey. You don't want your food to get cold."

Marie took another bite of her cakes while her grandmother read on, humming. Though she eyed the older woman with suspicion, not another word was mentioned of Harald Hamsun, or anything, for that matter. As quickly as she could, she finished her breakfast and busied herself with the dishes while Grandma took her time over the newspaper.

"What on earth is going on out there!"

Lost in her thoughts of Harald, Marie nearly dropped the heavy bowl she was wiping when her grandmother cried out. Pushing aside the dark blue calico curtain, she was startled to see a flurry of activity on the lane and at their homestead. A full dozen wagons were parked about their property, and coming down the lane were two heavily loaded lumber wagons.

"Look, Grandma — they're turning into our driveway!"

"Well, get on with you. Go on over and find out what's happening, Marie."

In a trice Marie pulled on a cloak hanging from a hook near the doorway and half walked, half ran the distance to the Biggs yard, taking no notice of the nippy temperature. The lumber wagons had been brought to a halt a short distance from the open foundation and were being unloaded by several sets of hands.

What could possibly be the meaning —

"Hello, Marie! Good morning, Marie!"

Cheery greetings flew from neighbors and friends alike. Returning their hellos, Marie scanned the crowd, picking out her brothers among the men and youths busy unloading and restacking boards. She was about to make her way to them when she caught sight of Harald over near the pump with Lawrence Bentz, owner of Bentz Lumber. The two men pored over a sheaf of papers in Mr. Bentz's hands, then Harald nodded, took the papers, and wrote something across the top of them. After returning the papers to the older man, the two shook hands and rejoined the beehive of activity.

"Yoo-hoo, Marie, can you give us a hand over here?" Looking snug in a thick gray coat with a bright red kerchief tied over her curls, Nora Bromley smiled and waved from the back of her wagon. "Shoo, you kids!" she scolded, bending over her brood of well-bundled little ones. "Get back from the fire! Take a stick and go play fetch with Ace over there, away from everything. Go on, now."

The lanky mutt woofed, bounding along with his playmates as they went in the direction their mother had indicated. Cooking grates already had been set up over two large fires, and a neat stack of firewood sat ready to feed the flames throughout the day.

Marie saw that many families from their church were represented: the men working over near the exposed hole in the ground where their house once stood, and the women by the wagons, preparing food and drink to sustain them all.

It was a noisy, confusing scene. Children ran and played amidst all the activity, and the sounds of delighted shrieks and laughter rose in addition to the loud clattering of lumber striking lumber. Marie walked toward Nora's wagon, more than a little bewildered, trying to take everything in.

"We need to get the coffee going," Nora chirped, handing her three large pots. "Those men'll need plenty of warming this morning. Fill these up, and when you're finished with that, you can help Vanessa and Allison put the chili together. Allison said she let the venison stew all night, so it's nice an' tender. Bess fried a mess of donuts this mornin' to go along with the coffee, an' we got more cakes and pies than Sherman's army could eat in a week." Pausing in her discourse, she asked, "Are you feeling all right, doll? You're lookin' a mite —"

"Marie! Can you believe this?" Rosemary ran up to Nora's wagon and tugged at her sister's arm, causing the large coffeepots to clank together. Her dark eyes glowed, and she was out of breath. "They're putting up our house! Harald organized everyone yesterday after church. And guess what else?" She lowered her voice and indicated with her head where Marie should look. "Jason is here!"

Pretending to admire the young man of her sister's affections, Marie tried to make sense of everything. Harald had organized all this . . . in just two days' time? If Father hadn't been granted a loan — or even credit at Bentz Lumber, then who had paid for two enormous wagons full of boards and building supplies?

The answer, she suspected, was to be found with the broad-faced man who strode across the yard with a leather apron tied about his hips. As if he felt her gaze upon him, Harald glanced in her direction and tipped his hat, smiling almost shyly, it seemed, before his attention was captured by Josh Bromley and Howard Jensen.

A delicious shiver passed through Marie, leaving a strange warmth in its wake. *Harald did this.* Her step was light as she set off toward the pump, coffeepots clunking and clanging. Rosemary had already deserted her to study Jason Gould from a better vantage point.

"Pastor Price is here!" someone shouted,

as a team of horses pulled a plain carriage up the driveway.

"It looks good already — when do we eat?" the jovial middle-aged cleric called to the busy group of women. He set the carriage brake and dismounted, adding, "Joanne sends her regards; she's a little under the weather this morning. Speaking of which . . ." His eyes searched until they settled on Marie, and he walked toward her. "How is your father doing? Any better today?"

"A little, maybe. He and Mother were finally asleep, so we just let them be."

"Good! Glad to hear it. We'll keep praying, and in the meantime these good people will help you get a head start on your new house before the winter winds start flying."

Marie felt her eyes fill with tears. "I can't believe this . . . all of this . . ." she gestured.

A quiet smile stole over the pastor's face. "It's Christ's love in action, Marie."

"But how can we ever —"

"Shh, my dear. Don't trouble your heart with anxious thoughts. Here, let me help you with these big pots." His expression became animated. "We sure have a good showing, don't we? Stuart Goodrick and his boys couldn't come today, but they'll be

327

here tomorrow. And you know how the five of them can work. . . ."

The day took on the atmosphere of a festival. Smiles and laughter came readily, despite the autumn temperature, and the busy sounds of hammering and sawing filled the air. Several times Marie tried to single out Harald, but he was in the thick of the building operations, always in the company of several others. She wanted to thank him for all this — for all he'd done — but somehow a simple thank-you didn't seem sufficient.

She wondered how Father would take this. If he had difficulty accepting such charitable items as food and clothing, what would his reaction be to a *house?* Marie offered up another prayer for his recovery, asking that he also might be gracious about receiving this outpouring of assistance from Harald, their friends, and neighbors.

By mid-morning, Ed and Coralee McGraw arrived with their two children and Sarah and Julia. Both Marie and Rosemary were overjoyed to see their younger sisters, and Rosemary took them to Harald's house to say hello to their parents and Grandma Biggs. Somewhat guiltily, Marie remembered that Grandma Biggs had asked her to go over and find out what was going on this

328

morning . . . and she'd never returned to let her know. Oh, well, she'd know just as soon as Rosemary reached the door.

The morning passed quickly, and it wasn't until lunchtime that Marie was able to find an opportunity to speak with Harald. He had finished eating and was standing by himself at a chest-high pile of lumber, busy with a pencil and paper. Taking her bowl of chili, she walked slowly over to him, rehearsing what she would say when she reached him.

He saw her coming, though, and paused in his figuring, tucking his pencil behind his ear. "Hello, Marie." The smile on his broad face was for her alone, filled with welcome and affection and tenderness. "You've been busy this morning."

"I'd say you've been busy longer than that."

His expression became modest. "It's been no trouble."

"No trouble? Harald, you organized all this in just two days' time!" She gestured about the property with her steaming bowl of meat and beans, forgetting what she'd planned to say to him. "How can you . . . I just want you to know . . . I just want to tell you —"

He cut her off gently. "You don't have to

say anything, Marie." A light wind ruffled his blond hair as he gazed at her with eyes as blue as warm summer skies. Taking the tin bowl from her hand, he set it on the stack of fragrant lumber and cupped his big, work-roughened hands around hers.

"The other day I told you I would call for you once you'd moved back home," he began seriously.

Marie nodded, a flood of emotions skittering through her breast. Excitement. Nervousness. Longing. Joy. The sounds of people and activity faded into the distance as she yielded her hands to his touch, her very self to the volumes of affection and quiet adoration she read in that brilliant blue gaze.

The sense of joy and expectancy intensified inside her as a slow smile broke across his countenance, causing his eyes to crinkle in a most delightful way. "But I've been thinking on the matter, Marie, and I want to tell you —"

"There you are! I've been looking all over the place for you!"

The moment was abruptly broken as Chadwick Farrell stalked over to where they stood, his long stride making short work of the distance between them. "What is all this? What is going on here?" His hazel eyes flashed indignation while his arm swung in a wide arc.

Marie's stomach picked itself up and turned over with a *whump* as she realized how close she was standing to Harald, and that he continued to hold her hands within his. "They're rebuilding our house," she replied in as composed a voice as she could muster, pulling her hands from Harald's and taking a step backward. "It was all a surprise. . . . Harald arranged it."

"Harald arranged it," Chadwick parroted, his gaze sharp, as if Marie's movement had just registered in his mind. "Harald arranged what, Marie?" His tone was accusing, his lips pale with anger. "I can't believe this . . . any of this." Straightening the arms of his gray-on-black pinstripe suit, he glared at the rough-clad farmer before him.

"Your father refused William a loan." In contrast to the younger man, Harald's voice was calm, his stance relaxed. He met Chadwick's glower evenly.

"So you stepped in?"

"I'm just helping where I can."

"This looks like more than help to me. In fact, it looks to me like you're trying to buy something."

"Chadwick, you don't understand —" Marie began, only to be interrupted as the elegantly dressed man reached for her arm and pulled her to his side. The spicy scent of his cologne competed with the fresh-cut smell of wood that hung in the air.

Marie looked between Chadwick and Harald, one man angrily impassioned, the other seeming almost passionless. Yet Marie knew better. Just a short time ago she'd looked into a pair of bright blue eyes filled with more passion than she'd ever imagined possible.

"He's trying to buy *you*, Marie." Chadwick's lean fingers tightened uncomfortably on her arm, and he made no pretense of politeness. "Can't you see? He's only doing this to win your affections."

Harald organized all this just to obtain my favor? It can't be true . . . can it? Surely he isn't the type to take advantage of a situation for his own gain. Marie was silent a long moment, studying the high polish of Chadwick's shoes, recalling Harald's words as he'd held her hands. *He was about to declare his feelings for you, Marie, after spending roughly a week in your company. Doesn't that seem a little sudden?*

Extricating herself from Chadwick's grasp, she sought Harald's gaze. His expression was inscrutable, though she saw him take a deep, controlled breath. "Harald's not like that," she finally said, turning to Chadwick.

Where was the confidence in her tone? The assurance?

"Who have you known longer, Marie?" Not waiting for her to reply, he continued on, bending over so his face was at the level of hers. "And what about us?" He dropped the four accusing words before her.

With that, he turned on his heel and marched off, leaving Marie and Harald with an ocean of silence between them.

What is the matter with me, Lord? she prayed earnestly, wishing she had the moment to do over again. *I know Harald isn't like what Chadwick made him out to be. Why did I hesitate? What can I do now?*

"I'd best get back to work." Harald pulled the pencil from behind his ear and reached for his paper. "Don't forget your lunch." He handed her the now-cool bowl of chili. Though his tone of voice had not changed, Marie detected the hurt in his eyes. Her failure to speak up for him had wounded him.

Just then Pastor Price, eager to swing his hammer, declared mealtime to be over.

"Good-bye, Marie," Harald said politely, formally, as the men picked up their tools and resumed their places.

"Good-bye . . ." Her voice trailed off while he walked away. She ached to do *something* to repair the damage she had caused between them, ashamed of herself for not standing up for Harald's character. He was a godly man, a man of integrity. Of that much she had become certain in the short time she had spent with him.

And just what kind of character did Chadwick display today? she asked herself. *He was mean, rude, accusing, and even . . . jealous?*

Sick at heart and not knowing which direction to turn, Marie walked to the tall grass beyond the yard and dumped out the contents of her bowl. Mother had always said that if you weren't sure what to do, you should just pray on the matter and wait.

Well, she had prayed. Now it was time to wait.

CHAPTER SEVEN

"Marie, I owe you an apology," Chadwick said, regret written across his handsome face. "I'm quite appalled at my actions of yesterday and can only hope you'll find it in your heart to forgive me. If you'd be so kind to grant me a few moments, I'd like to explain some things to you." He sighed and gave her a repentant glance. "If you don't wish to speak with me, I would . . . understand."

The banker's son stood outside his carriage, parked in the Hamsun driveway a good distance from Harald's house. He was wrapped in a warm wool coat, one gloved hand nervously gripping and releasing the harness on the horse nearest him. It was barely nine o'clock in the morning. Marie thought that she certainly hadn't had to wait long for something to happen, but the present hollowness in her heart told her a visit from Chadwick — even his apology — wasn't what she'd been longing for.

"What would you like to explain?"

He glanced around. "Is *he* here?"

"Do you mean Harald?" A funny pang went through her as she said Harald's name. Almost an entire day had passed since the episode, and still she hadn't been able to find an opportunity to speak with him alone. "No, he's over working on our new house." Her breath made clouds in the bright autumn morning air.

Chadwick nodded, obviously holding his tongue in check. "First of all," he began after a long pause, "I wish to tell you that I found out what happened between my father and yours, and that I had absolutely no foreknowledge of it. My father and I . . . came to an understanding on some matters, and yesterday I drove out to offer your father my apologies — and a loan. My father, for reasons he thought good, treated your father unjustly, and I wanted to make it right. When I saw all the people gathered and stacks of lumber everywhere, I realized I wasn't going to be able to . . . well, I guess I just saw red, Marie. I am very sorry," he concluded, extending his hand toward her.

Marie frowned, recalling yesterday's

events. "The things you said to Harald were just plain spiteful," she said evenly. "He has been nothing but kind and generous to my entire family! Why, he took us in, Chadwick, in the middle of the night while our house burned to the ground, and he hasn't asked us *for one thing*. And as for those ulterior motives you accused him of . . . ooh!" Her voice rose as her anger spilled forth. "The last person Harald Hamsun thinks of is himself. So don't you dare slander his name within my earshot again!"

She'd failed to stand up for Harald yesterday, but today was a brand-new day, and she was determined not to repeat her mistakes.

"Marie —"

"Why don't you just tell the truth?" she interrupted. "You were angry because you saw him holding my hand." Taking a step toward the expensive carriage, she folded her arms across her chest. Then she took a deep breath, striving for a more composed tone in her voice. "I'm going to ask you to lay your cards on the table, Chadwick. What are your feelings toward me? Your intentions?"

"What? What . . . are Hamsun's?" The same note of jealousy she had detected in him yesterday was evident as he parried her questions with his own.

"I'm not talking about Harald right now; I'm talking about you. After more than four years of you coming and going as you please, I believe I am entitled to an honest answer."

A long silence hung between them. Chadwick looked uneasy, stunned, and a little sick all at once. Marie was surprised at herself, for she had never spoken so directly to him. Come to think of it, for all the talking he did, he had never spoken of personal matters in a forthright manner to her, either. But the simple act of asking for honesty, even if she didn't receive it, was oddly liberating. Her anger cooled somewhat with this discovery, and she looked past Chadwick to the brilliantly colored tree line beyond Harald's trim fields.

"Come on, Marie," came Chadwick's reply, pulling her attention back to his pleading countenance. "What do you want me to say?"

"How about the truth?"

"I . . . Marie, well, it's . . . it's a little complicated. You know I like you, Marie."

"And what of your parents' view of me? Or your father's 'good reasons' for denying our family a loan? They don't want you to see me, do they?"

"How did you . . . well, it doesn't matter anymore what they think. One of the understandings my father and I came to was that I would see whomever I wished." Chadwick seemed to recover his footing here. His voice lost the beseeching tone and regained its typical confidence.

"And I would like very much to pursue a . . . well, I would like to court you, Marie, if you would give your consent." Letting go of the harness, he stepped toward her with a handsome smile. "That's what you wanted all along, isn't it? You were just using Hamsun to force my hand." He uttered a low chuckle as he grasped the cleverness of his logic. "Oh, Marie. You're quite a handful after all. Shall I go in and speak to your father?"

By this time the anger had left Marie, and she looked at the man before her with dispassion. Once upon a time it would have meant a great deal to her to hear Chadwick Farrell declare himself, but now her heart beat evenly within her chest, and no thrills raced through her. *I'm not in love with him,* she thought. *Was I ever?*

"No, I don't think it would be wise to speak to Father," she said.

"Oh, that's right; he's still ill, isn't he? How forgetful of me, I —"

"I don't wish to be courted by you, Chadwick."

"You . . . what?" A perplexed expression appeared on the dapper man's face. "I thought you . . ." His voice trailed off, only to resume its jealous tone. "Hamsun? You can't be serious."

Marie nodded, meeting his gaze. Something burst free within her at the admission, filling her with joy and fright all at once.

"Oh, Marie," he spat with disgust. "He's nothing but a —"

"Stop right there!" She thrust her chin out. "I told you I would not listen to your slander."

"Then this conversation is over." Stalking back to his carriage, he hooked a long leg up on the step and swung into his seat. "You're not yourself today, Marie," he called, shaking his head. "I'll give you some time to come to your senses before I call again."

Marie stepped aside as he shook the reins and went up the driveway to the turn-around, his jaw clenched. He gave her a long look as he passed by on his way out, jamming his hat on his head. He turned out onto the lane, urged the horses to reckless speed, and soon he was out of sight on the gently rolling terrain.

Marie turned back to Harald's house with a sigh, feeling both relief and trepidation. Today she had done the right thing with Chadwick, she knew, but would she be given a second chance to do right by Harald?

The new house went up faster than Marie would have ever believed. By the time Dr. Camp returned to see his patient Wednesday afternoon, its spiny framework was visible from the windows of Harald's snug home. And even better, Father was sitting up in bed having tea and toast.

His face, especially his hollow cheeks and sunken eyes, spoke of the severity of his illness, but the fever had broken more than twenty-four hours earlier. Dr. Camp was delighted to pronounce him on the mend, lecturing him on the importance of making a slow and steady convalescence.

Grandma Biggs had threatened to take her new walking stick to her son if he so much as tried to pick up a hammer and go to work, to which the doctor had nodded approvingly.

Not long after the physician's departure, Marie peeked into the bedroom where her father lay. She had been in to visit him a few times since he'd taken a turn for the better, and it seemed to her as though his despondency had lifted along with the fever. He was still weak and very tired, but she could see no evidence of the gloom that had pervaded his outlook since the fire. All the Biggses had wondered how he'd take the news of the new house, but Mother said he had just lain back on the pillow and closed his eyes, tears squeezing out from beneath the lids, when she'd told him the rebuilding was well under way.

"Hi, Father," she said softly, seeing he was awake. "Can I do anything for you?"

"Come in, Marie, come in." His voice was weak, but the old genial tone was back. "I'm about ready to crawl right up these walls with boredom, but every time I think about it, I get tired and fall asleep again." He smiled with surrender.

"You need your rest; you've been very sick." Her heart squeezed painfully to see his tousled hair and thin, dear face, and to think that she had almost lost him.

"I was more than sick, Marie," he said, his smile fading. "Come and sit in the chair here, honey. I'd like to talk to you."

"What is it?" she asked, settling herself in the chair beside the bed.

"First off, I want you to know I don't hold you responsible for Herman Farrell refusing me the loan. No one does. Your

342

grandmother spoke out of turn that night. I hope you know she doesn't really blame you."

Marie nodded, a grin stealing across her face. "She apologized right away. Said she was just madder than a rained-on rooster to find out what Herman Farrell did to her boy."

"Her *boy*? I'm forty years old!" Father grinned back at her. "I have gray hair and seven children, and yet I'm still a boy to her."

It was good to share a laugh with her father, Marie thought, a little of her heaviness of heart melting away. She had not been able to speak to Harald alone since the other day, and that weighed on her mind. Whether he was simply too busy or deliberately sidestepping her, she could not say. Would he forgive her? she wondered. After the way she had behaved when Chadwick interrupted him, when he had been about to tell her . . .

When he had been about to tell you what? She had pondered that question many times over the past days. Countless times she had closed her eyes and recalled the way the wind blew through his hair, the slow smile that crept across his face, and the feel of his big, work-roughened hands around hers.

But it was the expression in his eyes that had shaken her to the core of her very soul — and shook her still.

"I told Chadwick I didn't want him to come around anymore," she offered, meeting her father's gaze.

"On my account?"

"No." Marie shook her head. "Though he did come to apologize for his father's actions. He said he didn't know anything about his father refusing you a loan until after the fact."

"That might be true enough." Father's brown gaze, perceptive as ever, searched her face. "What, then, prompted you to ask young Mr. Farrell not to visit anymore, if I may ask?"

"I don't . . . well . . ." she began and stopped, feeling self-conscious. "I just don't think my heart was right about him," she spoke up. "Besides that, his family was . . ." Mindful of her manners, she searched for a tactful way to convey her thoughts.

"I think we both know what you're trying to say, Marie. And I can't say I'm sorry not to be thinking of those folks as possible in-laws." A smile flickered across his face, and he directed his attention to adjusting the covers around him. "Would there be anyone else in your heart right now?" he asked in a seemingly offhand manner.

"Do you mean besides you?" she replied with more cheek than she felt, as warmth spread across her face. She knew her grandmother suspected her growing feelings for Harald, but to save Chadwick, she hadn't admitted those feelings to a soul. With her emotions so unsettled, she hoped Father wouldn't pursue this line of questioning.

"Listen to you, shamelessly charming your sick old father. Yes, I mean besides me. But if you don't want to talk about it right now, that's fine." Wrestling a pillow into position behind his shoulder blades, he lay back and waxed philosophical. "The heart can be a mighty troubling place at times, can't it? It's seldom a man has so much time to lie around and reflect on things," he continued, not waiting for an answer, "but I've had more time in bed these past days than I can ever recall. None of it by my choice."

"But you were —"

Holding his fingers to his lips, he gestured for her to be quiet and listen. "I was sick, all right, sicker than I can ever recall. But it took nearly dying for the Lord to get my attention — and break my pride — about the way I'd been behaving about the house burning . . . and show me what was really important in life. I hope you — all of you — can forgive me."

"Of course." Tears welled in Marie's eyes as she leaned forward and laid her head against her father's chest. His hands stroked her hair as he went on speaking, the sound of his voice rumbling in her ear.

"I'm not ashamed to say I've learned a great deal about humility from Harald Hamsun through these trials. He might be young, but he's got more wisdom and maturity than most men twice his age. You just don't run across many men in life like him, Marie."

No, I've never run across a man like Harald Hamsun, she silently agreed. A bittersweet pang pierced her chest, causing her tears to brim forth as she wondered if she would be given another chance with him. Listening to the steady thudding of her father's heart, Marie let her head rest fully against him, knowing he had done more than extol Harald's virtues.

He had just given her his blessing.

The moment went on, sweet and tender, until Grandma Biggs appeared in the doorway and cleared her throat. "Time for your daddy to get some rest, Marie. 'Sides, we need some more wood brought in, and everyone else is over at the house."

"Love you, Marie," Father whispered before he let her go. "Take heart, I have a feeling everything is going to work out for the best."

The wind was cold against Marie's face when she stepped outdoors for the wood. Intent on loading the split logs into the little cart and getting back inside as quickly as possible, she didn't hear Harald approach.

"Let me help you with that, Marie. I've been wanting to talk with you."

Startled, Marie turned to look up into a pair of sky-blue eyes. At the sight, she felt as though her lungs had collapsed upon themselves. All the things she'd been meaning to say to him flew right out of her head while she let the log in her arms fall into the cart with the others.

Lord above, he was *handsome*. Well-built, strong, and handsome. How could she have lived across the road from him for two long years and never noticed that? The broadness of his shoulders was evident through the work-grade red-and-black-plaid coat he wore, and Marie knew a well-muscled pair of arms joined with those shoulders. *What would it be like to be held in those arms?* she wondered. To lay her head against that chest?

Somehow she managed to breathe.

But where was his smile? The crinkles around his eyes? He seemed at ease, and his expression was kind as he gazed at her, but she had a feeling she wasn't going to like what he was going to say.

"Marie, I made an error in judgment about you," he began, confirming her worst fears and shattering her heart into tiny pieces with his words.

She no longer felt the cold bite of the wind against her face as numbness washed over her. Nodding, she dropped her gaze to the ground, wishing the earth could swallow her whole.

CHAPTER EIGHT

"I made an error in judgment, but I take the blame for it." Harald's rich voice was filled with regret. "With both of us living here, it just wasn't proper for me to . . . well, Marie, I need to apologize to you for putting the burden of my affections on you."

Burden? He thought his affections were a burden? In an instant the cold wind whisked away her numbness; hope leapt afresh within her breast. Was it possible he still cared for her? Was there a spark yet of that bone-melting warmth to be found in his gaze? Gathering her courage, Marie looked him full in the face, only to be disappointed.

It was Harald's turn to study the frozen ground beneath their feet. "You've been seeing Farrell for some time, I know —"

"But I —" she tried to interrupt.

"Let me speak, please, Marie. This is important for me to say." He cleared his throat. "I didn't keep my word to you, and that is why I need to ask your forgiveness."

"Didn't keep your word? What are you talking about, Harald?" she asked, puzzled.

"I told you I wouldn't call for you until you moved back to your own house," he said, lifting his gaze to meet hers. "In my . . . impatience, Marie, I rushed you. You have every right to wonder about the things Farrell said, but I hope, in time, you will come to believe they are not true."

Instead of the glowing warmth she had hoped to find, Marie read genuine distress in his eyes. Sorrow and compassion rose within her, and she ached with the need to relieve his suffering — pain he had endured on her account.

"Harald," she began, pulling off the battered, oversized leather mitts she had donned for her task. Tucking them under her arm, she stepped toward him and reached for his hand. His fingers were bare and icy cold, extending from the cut-away tips of the woolen gloves he wore. Warming them between her hands, she felt the roughness of his skin against hers and nearly wept at its sad state. Chapped. Cracked. A fresh, angry gash arced across his middle knuckle, while smaller nicks and cuts laced his thumb and other fingers.

This was the hand of a man who was trying to buy her affections?

What nonsense. She thought of Chadwick's smooth hands and long, lean fingers. His fine clothes and fancy carriage. Of all the intellectual prattle, eloquent speeches, and altruistic ideals she had listened to over the years. Chadwick's goals and generosity, she realized, extended only far enough to serve himself. Why had she never seen that before? And, worse yet, how could she ever have dreamed of marriage to a man like that?

Tears gathered in her eyes as she thought of Harald's selfless, giving nature. Of his care for others, his consideration for each member of her family. Of his integrity and character. His candor. Heavens, was it possible that she loved him already?

Swallowing past the lump in her throat, she saw that he was waiting for her to speak. "It's I who owe you an apology, Harald. I know you aren't . . . you aren't any of those awful things Chadwick said about you, and I'm sorry for not standing up for you when I should have. You're the most upright man I know."

A single tear traced its way down her cheek while the cold wind carried a sprinkling of the season's first snowflakes. "Can

351

you forgive me?" she whispered, her hands seeking to cradle his.

"Min skatt," he murmured, bringing her hands to his cheek while the distress in his eyes dissolved into liquid blue heat. Softly, he slid her fingers over his mouth and pressed a soft kiss against her skin before releasing her hands. Ever so gently, then, he wiped the tear from her face, the rasp of his rough skin — or was it his touch? — setting Marie's nerve endings on fire. Feelings she had never known raced through her, potent and sweet.

"Min scott? Wh-what does that mean?" Her words were breathy, her heart slamming against her chest.

"It means . . ." he said in a honey-rich voice, taking a half-step forward and closing the distance between them. His big hands cupped her shoulders, then slid down her upper arms. "It means I want to kiss you in the worst way, Marie."

"Oh . . . that's the . . . literal? . . ." Unexpectedly, a silvery ball of laughter escaped from her throat before the wild beating of her heart recommenced. "I don't think you're telling me the truth, Harald."

An answering grin lit the broad face so near hers, causing his eyes to crinkle in the way she would never tire of seeing. His nearness, combined with the fiery feelings coursing through her, made her next words husky and unimaginably forward.

"Then how do you say, 'I want to kiss you back'?"

"Jeg vil kysse deg tilbake," he answered lyrically, his words ending in something like a groan as he closed his eyes. His grip on her arms grew tighter before he released her, taking a giant step backward. His hands balled into fists and released once, twice, three times before he opened his eyes again.

"Marie," he began, his voice taut with an emotion she wasn't certain she could define. Had she displeased him with her shameless admission? Offended him?

His next words dispelled those fears, the passion in his gaze nearly singeing her with its intensity. "To be honest, I would like nothing better than for you to kiss me back, Marie. All day. All night. For the rest of my life. If you only knew how long . . ." he said, his words trailing off. With visible effort, he banked the blue flames in his eyes. "But for your sake, I want to do this properly. I will court you, Marie, when you've moved back home."

"But —" Though Harald's interest in her was unmistakable, disappointment shot through Marie at his timetable. He wouldn't court her till she'd moved back home? That could be weeks, maybe months!

"It's for the best, *kjære* Marie. Until then we will wait."

Marie nodded, joy and impatience warring within her. "How fast can you build a house?" she asked with impertinence, rapidly becoming acquainted with a heady sense of feminine power as she saw the resultant blaze of emotion in Harald's steady gaze.

"Faster than you're gathering this wood. Now in the house with you! I'll finish this."

With a last, long yearning look at the man vigorously tossing logs into the cart, Marie slipped on her leather mitts and began walking back to the house, hardly feeling her feet touch the ground. The snow was coming down at a quicker rate, filling the air with its frosty beauty and collecting in lacy white ridges against the irregular texture of the brown, frozen earth.

Being courted by Harald.

Spending the rest of her life with Harald?

I'm falling in love with him, she thought with a sense of awe. How on earth was she ever going to be able to wait for their house to be finished? It was like being six years old and thinking that Christmas would never come, only much, much worse. Surely the coming days and weeks would never pass.

But pass they did, and the work progressed steadily on the new house. A soft blanket of white covered the countryside, a quiet harbinger of the deep snows and bitter winds for which Minnesota winters were known. The geese and songbirds had long since departed for warmer climates, leaving behind their hardier kin: sparrows, jays, cardinals, dark-eyed juncos.

Father had recovered from his illness, his spirit as well as his body restored. Once again his easy laugh rang out, and his dark eyes brimmed with vigor. The younger girls had rejoined the family some time ago, and all the Biggs children, save Marie and three-year-old Julia, had returned to school. The boys had pleaded a strong case for staying out of school even longer so as to continue helping with the construction of their new house, but Father was insistent: to school they would go.

At the beginning of the day and again at the end, Harald's small home teemed with people and activity, yet he still seemed not to mind the disruption of his formerly quiet life. With his parents both gone and his only sister and her family living four hundred miles away, he said he considered it a blessing to share his house with the Biggs family.

As Christmas drew nearer, the notion grew in Marie's mind that perhaps the snow-sprinkled autumn afternoon with Harald had never happened . . . that his caressing voice and smoldering blue eyes had been a figment of her imagination. *Maybe it was nothing but a daydream, Marie,* she thought with increasing impatience and uncertainty, for since that day Harald had behaved no differently toward her than he did toward Rosemary or Grandma . . . or even little Julia.

She'd prayed for patience, she really had. But she'd never before known such feelings!

And how could Harald act so . . . so . . . *normal,* she wondered, when she did nothing but ache to spend a little time alone with him, to know more about him. How she yearned for the touch of his hand, to hear the intimate deepening in his rich voice as he spoke her name, gazing at her with enough warmth to melt every drift and flake of snow for miles around.

Chadwick had called for her twice before Thanksgiving. Both times she had politely but firmly turned him away, still somewhat amazed that his presence had no effect on her whatsoever. The last time he visited, he verbalized his unhappiness and disbelief that she had thrown him over for a simple Norwegian farmer. "I'm very disappointed in you, Marie," he had said before driving back to his fine home and position in Mankato. "You could have had a lot better than what you're settling for."

Settling for? Oh, but you're quite wrong about that, Chadwick. I feel anything but settled when it comes to Harald. . . .

"Isn't it exciting, Marie?" Her mother's animated words broke in on her thoughts. "Your father thinks we'll be able to move back home by Christmas. There will still be plenty of finish work to do, but at least we'll be home." She smoothed the boughs of fragrant, fresh-cut pine Anthony had brought in. "That being the case, I think we should make two advent wreaths instead of one. Then we can leave one here for Harald. Bring me in some extra wire, Anthony," she called, as her lanky second-eldest son prepared to step back out the door. "And tell everyone to come in for supper soon. We'll make the wreaths when we're finished eating."

The aroma of pot roast filled the cozy house, mingling with the yeasty tang of the bread Mother had baked earlier. Sarah and Rosemary set the table while Julia sat at the foot of Grandma's rocking chair, playing with her paper dolls.

"Marie, would you mix up a batch of sugar cookies for tonight, please? We'll bake them when the roast comes out. I've got a sack of white sugar there in the cupboard. Julia, my darling, will you come help Mama put this evergreen in a box? Then we need to find some candles."

"Do you suppose Harald ever had an advent wreath before, Marie?" Grandma Biggs asked, peering up from her crocheting.

"I . . . I couldn't say," she replied, striving for a nonchalant tone, though her heart had begun a rapid throb within her chest at the mention of his name. Why would Grandma ask her such a question?

"Einar's place has been without a woman's touch for a long time." She chuckled to herself. "Now he's got six women livin' under his roof. Yes, indeed. That's more than he needs. Just one ought to do him fine." She picked up her hook and work-in-progress. "Don't you think, Marie?"

Marie felt the heat begin in her cheeks. Did Grandma know something? She hadn't revealed her secret feelings for Harald to anyone — except Chadwick. She supposed it was humorous, really, that her erstwhile suitor should be the only person to whom she'd spoken of the state of her heart.

"You know what I think, Grandma?" nine-year-old Sarah piped, sparing Marie from having to answer. She set the last of the forks in place on the hopelessly crowded table. "I think Harald needs to have his own wife. He's going to be lonely when we go back home." Turning toward her eldest sister, she added in a loud whisper, "He's nice, Marie. I like him an awful lot better than I liked Chadwick."

"Me, too," Rosemary agreed. "I can't say I'll miss Chadwick Farrell."

"Amen to that, child," Grandma responded tartly. "I never did like that boy. Drivin' around in that fancy carriage of his, thinkin' he's so wonderful, his big head all swoll up like a kraut barrel. God willing, we've seen the last of him around these parts. I'm still tryin' to come to terms with his daddy refusin' us the loan, but I got plenty a'more prayin' ahead of me before I can do the forgivin'."

"Did Harald pay all the money for our new house?" Intense curiosity caused Sarah's young voice to drop in pitch. "He must be richer than Chadwick."

"I've been wondering about that, too," Rosemary declared with a grin, "only I didn't think it was polite to ask."

"Well, it certainly *isn't* polite to ask, and I would hope I've raised you better than that." Mother leveled a stern look at her adolescent daughter before softening. "But I can't see any harm in telling you that Harald did pay for the lumber and building supplies. He had some money put by from when his father died, which he was only too happy to pull out of Herman Farrell's bank. Your father and I consider it a loan, and we intend to pay him back every cent."

"But why do you need a loan? I thought you and Father had some money saved up." Rosemary's dark eyes were quizzical.

"We do, my dear, but we also have an entire household to furnish. Harald insisted we spend our money on that, and pay him back for the house at a later time."

"Thank the Almighty for Harald," Grandma exclaimed as the rocker ceased its motion. "Ain't many men like him, 'cept the ones I raised."

"You mean Daddy, don't you, Grandma?" Sarah said with a giggle. "You're bragging 'cause you were his mama."

"Of course I am, honey. I raised up your daddy and his brothers to be fine men."

Mother moved through the kitchen, a secret, knowing smile curving her lips. "And don't forget all our good friends and neighbors," she reminded her mother-in-law. "Without them, we'd be nowhere near as far along as we are."

The rocking chair resumed its steady rhythm, the crochet hook in the gnarled fingers flashing silver in the fading light. "Well, I still say men like Harald are few and far between. He's going to make some woman a dandy husband someday . . . don't you think, Marie?"

Really! Would Grandma never let the subject drop? Marie looked up from creaming the butter and sugar together, fruitlessly searching for some article of conversation so as to change the subject — only to see all eyes upon her. "What are you all looking at?" she snapped as a burst of giggles erupted around her. "Harald's got no time to pursue such nonsense."

There was fear in that admission, deep-down dread that perhaps Harald had changed his mind about things. About her.

And if he *hadn't,* well . . . she didn't know whether to admire him or throttle him for being such a man of his word. *I will court you, Marie, when you've moved back home. . . . Until then, we will wait.* The memory of his gaze made her stomach quiver. *I would like nothing better than for you to kiss me back,*

Marie . . . all day, all night, for the rest of my life.

"Nonsense?" Grandma Biggs's gaze was keen from where she sat in the far corner of the room. "If you say so, Marie. If you say so."

Chapter Nine

"Cut me a small piece of that red ribbon there, will you, Sarah? We'll give this little fellow a spot of color." Rosemary's slender fingers fashioned a tiny bird out of a pine cone and soft feathers.

"Where did you ever come up with an idea like that?" Father spoke with admiration as he leaned over her shoulder, obviously delighted with the craft his daughter's hands had wrought.

"Oh, it's not my idea. I learned it from Betsy Lira. She said her Aunt Mary Jo taught it to her when she came to visit from St. Paul last time."

"Well, I've never seen anything like it."

After a pleasant supper, the Biggses and their host had gathered again around the table, now spread with aromatic pine boughs, small branches of dried bittersweet, ribbons, buttons, thread, and snips of colorful fabric.

Harald sat next to Raymond, weaving greens into the wire forms he and Father had constructed. "You people make some handsome advent wreaths," he said. "I don't believe we ever put so much into it when I was growing up."

"We *always* make the *best* wreaths," Sarah averred. "Every year before Advent we have a party and make a wreath, and Mama gives us cookies and tea out of . . ." Her voice trailed off, only to resume thick with disappointment. "I guess we won't have tea this year, will we?"

"Of course we'll have tea, Sarah. Marie's already put the water on." Mother's voice was soothing, though touched with wistfulness. "We just don't have Grandma Perry's tea set anymore."

"It got burnded up," Julia added importantly, slipping down from Anthony's lap and padding over to Harald's side. She tugged on his sleeve. "Our house had a fire, and *everything* got burnded up."

"Yes, it did, little one. But we're still going to have tea, and we've almost got a nice, new house all ready for you . . . and that makes me very happy." Was it Marie's imagination, or did Harald's rich voice deepen with hidden meaning as he spoke to her sister?

Twisting the dishcloth in her hands, she paced back and forth between the stove and the worktable, waiting for the last pan of sugar cookies to finish baking. Then she'd have no reason to continue avoiding the happy gathering at the table. The large pot of water on the stove had almost reached a boil; a well-washed kettle, its bottom filled with loose black tea, stood ready to receive the steaming liquid. The kettle, plus a mish-mash of mugs and cups, would serve this year in place of her maternal grandmother's blue-and-white china tea set.

Marie sighed. She'd also had a sentimen-tal attachment to the dainty collection, but it wasn't only the tea set that had her heavy-hearted. In fact, it mostly *wasn't* the tea set . . . it was Harald.

He was a man of honesty, a man of his word. That she knew. And he had been very plainspoken about his intentions that snowy afternoon last month. But her spirits had been low ever since before dinner, when she'd been the object of her family's good-natured kidding about him. How could they all be so certain that she was right for Harald when *she* wasn't even certain any longer? Her intellect battled with the doubt that gnawed holes in the fabric of her faith.

I can't live like this much longer, Lord, she prayed, sliding the pan of lightly browned cookies from the oven. *I love him, I know I do, yet I'm miserable.*

"Mama, Harald's hand is bleeding! Look, right by his thumb!" Julia cried, prompting a flurry of movement and exclamations from the gathered Biggses.

"It's nothing, really," he protested, holding up his hand. "Just a few pricks from the pine."

Grandma Biggs stood and edged her way through her younger grandchildren to stand before Harald and examine his hand in an imperial manner. "Young man, your hands are in a sorrier state than my husband's ever were," she declared, turning them over, "and I thought his were the rawest I'd ever seen. I must've spent half our marriage applying salve to that man's cracked skin. Now you come on over to the kitchen and let me take care of this." Her tone brooked no argument, and she marched to the pantry. "I've got a little can of ointment all mixed up for such things."

Marie watched as Harald rose from his chair and stepped toward her, wearing a half-comical, half-uncomfortable expression on his face that said he was only doing this for Grandma Biggs's sake. He smiled as he passed her, nodding and lifting his eyebrows at the neat rows of cooling cookies.

See, Marie? He's more interested in the cookies than he is in you.

Work — and conversation — quickly resumed at the table. Anthony slid into Harald's chair and finished the last bit of weaving on the nearly completed wreath, while Raymond had already passed his neat-looking work on to the girls for decoration.

"Give me those paws, Harald," Grandma Biggs ordered, balancing her walking stick against the pantry and working open the lid of the tin with some difficulty. Taking a generous finger full of the puce-colored unguent, she applied it to the angry, chapped skin.

As she slid the cookies off the sheet with a shiny spatula, Marie covertly watched Harald's profile. What a man he was, she thought, her heart besieged with both yearning and discomfiture. How would it be, she wondered, to be held —

"Oh, my!" Grandma drew in a quick breath, as if in pain. "Marie, my rheumatism is acting up something fierce. Come on over here."

Marie started at her grandmother's request but moved obediently in her direction.

"Let me help you sit down, Mrs. Biggs."

Harald spoke with concern, his hands glazed with Grandma's ugly colored concoction. He stood helplessly before the older woman, wanting to help but not knowing how.

"No, stay put; it's just these old thumbs of mine . . . they don't work so well anymore. I'll wipe off and maybe go rock a spell while Marie finishes up for me." In a twinkling she had removed the salve from her hands with her apron, even before her granddaughter reached her side. "Now, Marie," she instructed, audaciously taking the younger woman's hands and setting them over Harald's. "This needs to be *thoroughly* rubbed in. And mind you pay extra attention to the badly chapped areas," she added sternly, her tone of voice belying the merriment in her keen brown eyes as she looked back and forth at the pair. "Now rub!"

Marie felt as if she had fallen into a trance the instant her hands covered Harald's.

Warmth.

Incredible warmth. That was the only thought on her mind as she began to move her fingers over the work-damaged skin. The emollient already had begun to soften the rough surface of the hands beneath hers, and Marie felt as though she were being drawn into a sumptuous tub of sleek, rich oils as well. But though her arms and legs grew languorous, her insides felt anything but.

Please, Lord, she appealed, *I can wait for as long as you say, but I just need a little reassurance.*

Her prayers were swiftly answered as, in a quick motion, his big hands closed around hers, nearly stopping her heart. Did his breathing sound a little irregular? Ragged, even?

"Marie," he said in a low voice, moving nearer, his fingers beginning a stirring caress of their own. "*Min kjærestet . . . min elskede.* Once again I find my honorable intentions flying out the window."

Holding her breath with both wonder and hope, Marie slowly looked up from those strong hands, up past the broad, muscular chest, into his face.

"*Jeg elsker deg,* Marie. I love you."

"I love you, too, Harald," she whispered in reply, pure joy pouring into her soul. "I was so worried you'd changed your mind."

"Never." A slow, certain smile curved his lips, filled with secret, unspoken promises, his eyes crinkling tenderly.

"Look! Marie and Harald are holding hands!" Hugh crowed from the table. "Hoo-hoo! And they're looking at each other all funny." He laughed with the innate hilarity of a boy straddling adolescence. His mother and sisters attempted in vain to hush him, unable to hide their own smiles.

"Well, it's about time someone got the ball rolling," Grandma Biggs muttered from the rocker, her flying crochet hook glinting in the lamplight. "Those two have been purely miserable for weeks on end!"

A burst of laughter rose from the assembled Biggses while Harald's hands tightened reassuringly around Marie's. With the smile continuing to crease his broad face, he turned his gaze toward Father. "I love Marie," Harald declared, "and it is my hope that —"

The older man interrupted, a pleased look on his countenance. "If you're asking for my blessing, Harald, you had it long ago."

"Does this mean Marie is going to marry Harald?" Sarah piped innocently.

An explosion of exclamations, conversation, and delighted laughter burst out in the snug house while Harald pressed his lips against Marie's ear and asked her to wait in the kitchen.

Helen and Rosemary sprang from their chairs to embrace Marie while Harald wiped his hands on a towel, handed the cloth to Marie and disappeared into his bedroom. A few moments later he returned with the small trunk she had once noticed high on the shelf of his closet.

"Don't pour that water yet," he cautioned the women in the kitchen, setting the trunk on the table and whetting everyone's curiosity. "I have something here Marie may want."

"What is it?" Julia asked with wonder while her family gathered around. Marie's heart beat with excitement as she was all but whisked to the table by her mother and sister.

"It was something of my mother's . . . something I remember with great fondness."

Crisp, yellowed tissue paper. A half-dozen slim, leather-bound volumes bearing foreign text. A neatly folded, daintily woven woolen shawl of red and white. As Harald removed the items, one by one, the air of expectation around the table grew.

At the bottom of the trunk sat an oddly shaped bundle, wrapped with a plain ivory-colored towel.

"What's that?" Sarah asked, her voice filled with intense curiosity.

"It's Marie's, if she would like to have it." Harald's gaze met hers, drawing her to his side. "Open it, *min kjærlighet*," he urged.

Marie's fingers hesitated over the soft

cloth as she tried to guess at the gift Harald offered. Finally, she unwrapped the towel to discover an exquisite china teapot with six matching cups and saucers. "Oh . . . Harald," she whispered, tears filling her eyes. The Biggs women crowded closer, each straining for a glimpse of the fragile, beautifully decorated vessels.

"May I serve you tea?"

Nodding somewhat dumbfoundedly to Harald's tenderly spoken query, Marie found herself being assisted into a chair at the table while many hands made short work of clearing away the residue of the wreath construction. Anthony arranged the two laurels side by side in the center of the table, ten tall candles standing at attention amidst a profusion of lush greens. He gave her a shy smile and a pleased wink as he stepped back.

It seemed only a moment before Harald, Mother, and Rosemary returned from the kitchen bearing the tea and a tray of cookies. Setting a dainty saucer and cup before her, Harald paused with the teapot in his hands.

If his expression weren't so earnest, devotion shining from his brilliant blue eyes, Marie might have laughed at the incongruity of the fragile porcelain container in his wide, weather-beaten hands.

"There's one more thing of my mother's, Marie," he said, nodding toward her cup. "It's yours, as well . . . if you will accept it." He smiled then, his eyes crinkling delightfully.

A hush fell upon the room as Marie slowly reached for the cup, her fingers beginning to tremble when a small clink reached her ears.

"There's a *ring* in Marie's cup!" Sarah cried.

"Oh," was all she could say, pulling the cup toward her, seeing for herself that Sarah's words were true. The delicate band of gold gleamed with quiet elegance, its feel smooth against her probing fingertip. Looking up, she met Harald's gaze and silently dispatched a prayer of gratitude to her heavenly Father for the great treasure he had given her. Love — and thanks — welled up inside her as the troublesome tears began once again.

"Well, Marie?" Grandma Biggs queried. "Our tea's going to get cold if you don't stop your dillydallying and give him an answer."

"I'd be honored to accept your mother's ring, Harald." Marie smiled through the wetness tracing its way down her cheeks.

The room exploded in cheers while

Harald set down the pot, took her face in his hands, and tenderly wiped her tears.

And then he poured her tea.

RECIPE

Dear reader,

This recipe was given to me by my friend's mother, who was Norwegian to the bone. These cookies have always delighted me because of their rich yet delicate flavor. You won't be able to stop at one!

Peggy Stoks

SUGAR COOKIES

Cream together:
1 cup powdered sugar
1 cup oil
1 cup sugar
1 tsp vanilla
1 cup butter
2 eggs

Sift:
4½ cups flour
1 tsp soda
1 tsp salt
1 tsp cream of tartar

Blend dry ingredients into the first mixture. Roll into balls, place on ungreased cookie sheet, and flatten each ball with the bottom of a glass dipped in sugar.

Bake at 350 degrees for 9 or 10 minutes. Makes 6 to 7 dozen.

GOING HOME

Katherine Chute

CHAPTER ONE

1876, Near New Orleans, Louisiana

Ancient oaks lined the way to Devereaux, their branches intertwined to make a canopy over the road. Charles Foster Devereaux rode slowly, enjoying the glints of sunlight that broke through the shelter. Fall leaves in reds, browns, and yellows swirled at his horse's feet.

He drew in a breath of the fragrant Louisiana air. Rain threatened, and he could smell smoke from a nearby fireplace.

"Thank you, Lord, for bringing me home," he murmured. "It's been such a long time." He felt the years fall off his shoulders as he drew closer. Devereaux had been home to his family for three generations. That is, until it had become his — and he had lost it.

Avalanche, the fine chestnut Charles had bought with six months of hard work, shook his head restlessly as Charles kept him at a walk. It had been a long journey, but now Charles wanted to savor the moment. He didn't know what lay ahead, but for now, each step brought healing to his soul.

The road turned, and there was Devereaux. Its white columns, badly in need of paint when he left ten years before, now glistened in the morning sun. As Charles drew closer, he saw no signs of broken windows or battered doors. His home — his former home — had been restored.

A man and two young women on horseback were approaching the house from a side path. Taking notice of Charles's progression toward the house, the man turned and said something to the girls as he dismounted. The younger of the two started toward the rear of the house — toward the stable, Charles knew. The other girl stayed at the man's side.

Probably the man's daughters, Charles thought. *He's afraid I'm a vagabond up to no good.* In a few short paces he would have to explain himself.

He allowed himself one more look at the house. Magnolia trees swayed in the breeze, framing the house with gentle limbs. He had dreamed of the fragrant blossoms that came in the spring. Now, with fall, the dark green leaves were accented with light brown edges.

His thoughts were cut off by frantic barking, a whinny, a scream, the pounding of hooves in the dirt. A horse raced past him with the younger girl clinging desperately to its back. Terror in her face, she had dropped the reins and was trying to hang on to the mane.

As the terrified horse and rider headed toward high ground, Charles urged Avalanche to a gallop. He knew how to head them off.

He circled around to the back of the house and onto a path he had known since childhood. Between the trees and down the hill, he emerged ahead of the girl, just as he had always been able to do when he and his brothers had played in these fields.

Coming alongside the runaway, Charles reached out to grab the dangling reins. Missed. He pushed close enough to feel the horse's flank on his leg and tried again. Got them.

Reining both mounts to a halt, Charles slung his leg over his saddle and jumped to the ground.

"Are you all right, miss?" he asked.

"Please help me down," she said unsteadily. She had a China doll look, with long blonde curls, big blue eyes, and fair skin. He guessed she was about sixteen.

When he lifted her to the ground, she burst into tears.

"Are you hurt?"

"No, I'm not hurt. I was just so scared."

"Mary! Are you all right?" The man arrived, jumped off his horse, and rushed to the girl's side. "What happened?"

"That dog scared him, Papa. He got spooked, and when he bolted, I dropped the reins. I thought he'd never stop." She buried her head in his side as she sobbed, and the man put his arm around her.

"Well, he might never have stopped if it hadn't been for this gentleman," he said. "I thank you, sir."

"I was glad I was here. She was fortunate she wasn't thrown."

"How did you know about the path?" asked a voice behind them. The older girl reined her horse to a stop and leveled a stare at Charles. She wasn't as striking as the other girl, her features less delicate, her hair light brown. She looked at him now with her gray eyes narrowed.

"Just lucky, I guess," Charles answered. "I saw that was my only chance to catch the horse."

"The luck was ours, I think," the man said. "Why don't we all go up to the house so we can thank you properly? Come on,

Mary, you can ride with me." He helped the younger girl onto his saddle, then climbed up behind her.

"I'll bring Butter," the brown-haired girl said. She reached over and picked up the now-docile animal's reins.

As the four of them slowed in front of the house, another man appeared, evidently one of the estate's hired hands. "I'm sorry, Mr. Jackson," he said, taking charge of Butter. "That scroungy little dog from up the road just came out of nowhere and scared the daylights out of him. Is Miss Mary all right?"

"The Lord was looking out for her, Frank," Mr. Jackson answered. "She's fine, just scared. And we owe this man a debt of gratitude. Please see to his horse also."

"Yes, sir," Frank said, leading the horses to the stable.

"Please come in, Mister —" Jackson hesitated.

"Foster. Charles Foster." These people didn't need to know he was a Devereaux, not with what he had come to ask.

"Mr. Foster, I'm Tate Jackson. This is my daughter Mary, whose life you just saved, and this is Charlotte, her sister. I'm sure my wife has something refreshing to drink, and I know she'd like to thank you herself. Won't you join us?"

"Why, thank you, Mr. Jackson. I'd like that."

Charles followed the Jacksons up familiar steps to the front door and into the entry hall that had haunted his dreams for years. A spiral staircase ascended directly in front of him, graced by a solid-oak stair rail that his grandfather had made by hand. The chandelier that his father had imported from France had been polished till it sparkled.

"Devereaux is a beautiful place," he said, almost to himself.

Charlotte turned to him in surprise. "Devereaux? That was the name of this house when we bought it."

Charles frowned. *Was?* "But someone down the road —," he mumbled.

"Oh, I know," Charlotte said. "The locals here have long memories. They still call this place Devereaux, even though we renamed it Jackson Manor. When we moved here from Philadelphia, we wanted this house to have our name, not that of some family we never knew. But you are right. Jackson Manor is a beautiful place." She turned and followed her father into the sitting room.

Charles contemplated this news as he too entered the familiar room. So Devereaux was no longer Devereaux? It had never occurred to him that such a thing could happen to his old home. But maybe this was what he deserved. He had been the one to sell the plantation. Stricken with grief at the time, he hadn't even inquired about the prospective buyers. *Yankees?* His father and grandfather must be turning in their graves.

"Agatha!" Tate called. "Come meet the day's hero!"

Agatha Jackson emerged from the small adjoining study with her needlepoint still in hand. "What's happened?"

"Mary's horse ran away, and Mr. Foster came along just in time to save her," Tate said.

Agatha's eyes widened and her face paled. "Oh, Tate! I told you that horse was too spirited!"

"Nonsense," he replied. "Mary handled herself very well, under the circumstances. But we do have Mr. Foster to thank for her safety."

Agatha turned toward Charles. "Naturally, we are indebted to you for being so quick to resolve the situation."

"Not at all, ma'am." Charles gave a small bow.

"He was very gallant, Mama," Mary added. She smiled at him with dimpled cheeks.

"I told Mr. Foster you might have some refreshment," Tate said. "I imagine he's thirsty after his morning's adventure."

"Of course," Agatha replied. "Hattie has just baked some cakes, and the tea won't take but a moment. Girls? Can you give me a hand?"

"Mr. Foster, that horse of yours is fast," said Tate, as the women left the room. "He was most impressive. I'm always looking for good horse stock, if you're —"

"He's not for sale. We've been through some rough scrapes together. I named him Avalanche — because he saved me from one once out west."

"I see. Well, you're a fortunate man indeed."

Agatha returned with the tea tray, followed by Charlotte and Mary carrying plates of cookies and cakes. "Here we are, Mr. Foster," Agatha said. "I hope you like the tea. It's a special recipe I make only when we have the fruit available. Tate works with the shipyards, and he can get them for me when a shipment comes in. So, you see, you came at a very good time."

She poured him a cup and waited for him to take a sip.

"It's good," he said. "Different. Reminds me of Christmas." He noted the satisfaction in her face and reached over for a cookie.

"As a matter of fact, that's what we call it — Christmas tea," she said. "But I couldn't wait."

"Are you from this area?" Charlotte asked, her eyes fixed on his face.

"Originally. I've been gone for a long time," he answered.

"And where have you been?" she asked.

"Charlotte!" Agatha chided her daughter. "Really, he's going to think we have no manners at all."

"Yes, ma'am. I beg your pardon, Mr. Foster," she murmured.

"Women!" Tate grumbled. "All fuss! Please leave us so Mr. Foster and I can talk. He obviously had business at Jackson Manor before Mary found herself in distress."

"Of course," Agatha replied. "Mr. Foster, please let me know if you need anything."

Tate turned back to Charles as the women retreated. "Was there something I could help you with, Mr. Foster? You were coming to us, were you not, when Mary's horse ran away?"

"I was looking for work, and I was hoping to find some at Dever— at Jackson Manor. I grew up on a large estate like this, and I thought I could be of help to you. I know it's not easy to keep up with all the responsibilities."

Tate fingered his chin and considered Charles for a moment before answering. "I'm sorry, Mr. Foster," he said at last. "I'd like to help, but I really have no . . . On second thought, I do have a job, if you don't mind keeping crops. One of our tenant farmers left some time ago, and we have his house available, if you're interested."

"I'll take it."

As the men left the parlor, Mary turned away from the door of the small study and smiled at her sister. "Sounds like Mr. Foster is staying for a while, Charlotte," she whispered.

"Mary! Were you eavesdropping?" Charlotte scolded. "Papa should be able to conduct business without you prying. That's most unbecoming for a lady."

Mary was silent for a moment, and then her mouth turned into a playful smile. "I saw you looking at him, Charlotte. Don't you think he's handsome?"

"Of course not!" Charlotte retorted. "Besides, he's much older than I!"

"Maybe, but his hair isn't gray," Mary pointed out. "He has curly black hair and wonderful blue eyes. And he's so dashing."

"Just hush, Mary."

"I wonder where he's been. Did you hear him say he was from this area originally?"

"You are far too curious. It'll get you in trouble one day. Anyway, you've said quite enough about Mr. Foster."

"A little speculation can't hurt," Mary scoffed. "You're too serious, Charlotte. Papa says so — and that's probably what keeps the beaus away. I already have three, and you're four years older. Why, you probably wouldn't know how to catch a man if you wanted him!" She paused. "I know! I'll teach you! Mr. Foster won't even know what hit him."

"Mary, please!" Charlotte laid a hand on her sister's arm. "You know Mama says God has someone for everyone. When the right man comes along, he's going to like me just as I am! I don't need to play games. Besides, I'll be going to Aunt Gertrude's soon. Being a governess to her children is far better than getting mixed up in your schemes."

In her bedroom, Charlotte gazed at her reflection in the dresser mirror. No, she didn't have her sister's looks. Her eyebrows were a little too thick, her lips a little too full. It had always been her lot to hear how beautiful, how sweet, how vivacious her sister was.

She sighed. It was all true. Her sister was all that — and Charlotte loved her.

Still, Charlotte had her own qualities. Her biggest distress was that no one seemed to notice them. Black lashes framed her gray eyes. Her chestnut hair did have a nice shine. Still, she knew she was much too serious for the local boys. They, in turn, were so immature.

Charlotte rose and looked out the window to see Papa and Mr. Foster walking toward the tenant houses. *I wonder where he came from,* she thought. It seemed their guest had known just where to find the path that had enabled him to rescue Mary. He looked somehow familiar, too. And, she had to admit, he really was handsome.

Her thoughts were interrupted by a knock at her door.

"Charlotte, it's me. Please let me come in," Mary called as she pushed open the door. "I'm sorry, really I am. I didn't mean to tease you. Forgive me?"

"How could I stay mad at you?" Charlotte sighed, turning away from the window. "Maybe I do need some lessons. But you can't tell anyone. Promise?"

"I promise." Her sister giggled. "Oh, this is going to be fun, Charlotte."

"Now don't get carried away," Charlotte replied, trying to look stern. "This has nothing to do with Mr. Foster."

CHAPTER TWO

Charles stood back from the plow to survey his field. In the days that had passed since his arrival, he had been able to turn under most of what remained of the previous season's crop. Apparently, the former tenant had reaped the corn and left, not bothering to prepare the land for the spring planting.

It had been so difficult to sell Devereaux — the hardest decision he had ever made, even though there really had been no decision at all.

The place had been in ruins, and there was no money, no help. The Northern states boycotted the South after the war, so that meant there was no market for the cotton or the crops. High taxes, imposed to repair the damage in bankrupt Louisiana, took every cent he had, so he couldn't afford to hire the workers necessary to keep up such a large plantation. His family had all been gone by then — his father dead of typhoid as the great war between the North and the South broke out, his brothers killed in battle, and Melinda — a lump rose in his throat even now — had died with their baby in childbirth.

He remembered how hard he had worked to save the place. But the grief he felt when Melinda was gone had broken him. It had been his decision to let Devereaux survive under someone else's hand rather than see the plantation die. He had loved this land too much for that. And now he knew the decision had been right.

He pushed his hair back off his forehead with the heel of his hand. Farming was hard work, but it was welcome. He was home. He was at Devereaux — no matter what those Yankees wanted to call it.

He leaned on the plow handle and thought about the Jacksons for a moment. They had treated him fairly since his arrival, he had to admit. But he was glad they hadn't met him before now. The sale of Devereaux had been arranged by a family friend, so there would be no reason to connect him with the past. Being a common worker on the land wasn't the life he wanted, but it was better than being away — better than having a hole in his heart.

Avalanche shifted restlessly and whinnied. Charles had pressed the animal into service as a plow horse, even though it seemed beneath him. Maybe by next season he would be able to afford a mule.

Charles pushed once again on the plow, watching with satisfaction as the earth turned the black soil to the top. It was good land — always had been. He would have no trouble with his crops if the weather co-operated.

As though in answer, Charles felt a few raindrops on his face, and then it was pouring. The rain was cold and looked as if it might set in for what was left of the afternoon. He unhooked the harness and began walking the horse to the shelter he used as a barn. He was already soaked to the skin, and he still needed to rub the animal down for the night.

From the shelter of the porch, Charlotte watched as Charles ran toward his house. He splashed through the water that already had gathered at the foot of the steps and climbed to the porch two steps at a time. He stopped in his tracks at the sight of her.

"What are you doing here, Miss Jackson?" he asked.

Charlotte bit her lip. She was soaked to

the skin. Her clothes clung to her and dripped in puddles on the porch. Her bonnet, fashionable moments before, trickled green from the velvet trim down the front of her dress. Even the basket of food she had brought to Mr. Foster was ruined. Water streamed from the bottom, and she could see that the bread was a soggy mess.

"I was bringing you some dinner, sir," she answered. "As you can see, I was caught off guard by the storm."

Charles stared at her.

"You'd better come inside while I start a fire."

"It's not proper," she said. "I must leave at once."

"I won't be responsible for you catching pneumonia." He took the basket from Charlotte's hand and set it on the porch. Then taking her by the elbow, he guided her to the door. Once inside, he lifted a blanket from a chair and draped it around her shoulders.

"Sit here while I start the fire," he ordered. "Haven't you noticed these storms come on suddenly this time of year?"

"Of course," Charlotte replied. "I was just . . . I only . . . I just got caught in it, that's all."

"So I see." Charles busied himself with

the fire. Soon he had kindled a crackling blaze, and warmth began to ease into the room. He backed up to the heat and studied her. "I appreciate you bringing the supper. But, frankly, I'm at a loss. I have no clothes for you to put on, and I don't have a carriage to take you back to your house. Do you have any suggestions?"

She straightened in the chair. "I'm sorry to have inconvenienced you, Mr. Foster," she said. "I don't recall asking you for anything. I was bringing you a gift. Perhaps that wasn't such a good idea. Maybe you'd prefer your own cooking."

He looked down at his feet. "You're right, of course," he said. "Thank you for thinking of me. And you're right on another count. It probably wasn't a good idea. You don't know anything about me, Miss Jackson. It may be better that way."

As a carriage splashed through the mud outside, he looked away from her and strode to the door.

"Mr. Foster, I was looking for Miss Charlotte," Frank called from the carriage. "Her ma seemed to think she might be up this way."

"She's here," Charles shouted above the torrent of water that rushed off the roof. He turned back into the room without looking at Charlotte.

"I suppose you'd better go."

"I think I shall," she retorted as she flounced out of the room — as much as she could flounce in her soggy dress. "Thank you for your kind hospitality."

Charles said nothing else.

From the carriage, Charlotte didn't look back.

CHAPTER THREE

The rain lasted for a week. Water seemed to be everywhere — standing in pools, dripping from roofs, blowing in the cold winds that came with the storm.

I don't mind, Charles thought as he sat in front of a fire and listened to the thunder. He left only to care for Avalanche, taking extra time to brush the chestnut's coat and spoil him with treats. "You don't make as good a conversation as Melinda used to," he told the horse. "But we'll make it just fine. When this rain stops, we'll go exploring like we used to do."

The first morning he saw sunlight instead of gray skies, Charles went out and saddled Avalanche. Anxious to be out of such close space, the horse stamped his hooves in anticipation.

"Don't worry, boy," Charles said. "We'll be out in the air soon."

Charles let the horse run when they reached the main road. Avalanche was glad to oblige, stretching his legs into long strides as he left Jackson Manor behind. The cold air felt like fingers in Charles's hair. He, too, was glad for a reprieve from days spent inside, from the often claustrophobic feeling that seemed to go along with trying to be someone else.

It was harder than he had thought it would be. Yes, he could enjoy the land, but he had to have his guard up all the time, never letting his past slip, never giving a clue to who he really was.

The road ended at the church. Charles climbed off Avalanche and dropped the reins as he looked at the small white building.

He and Melinda had been married here. He could imagine her now in her grandmother's wedding gown of Irish lace, carrying a bouquet of flowers from the garden. His whole family and hers had been there — a happy time. He could almost hear the laughter as they celebrated together.

"I've given you my forever," Melinda had whispered to him. "I'll always be yours."

"And I yours," he had answered, putting his face against her cheek.

But forever hadn't been long enough.

He looked toward the cemetery at the back of the church. They were almost all there now — his mother and father, his brothers, Melinda, their baby daughter, most of her family. He walked to their graves and saw the names, rubbed his fingers over the tombstones. His family. His whole life.

"Hello, Mr. Devereaux," said a quiet voice behind him. Charles whirled around, surprised.

"Reverend Miller." Charles nodded his head in respect to the older man. "How did you know I was here?"

"Saw you ride up, but I know that's not what you're talking about," he said. "You ought to know what the grapevine is like around here, Charles. Word got around that the Jacksons hired a new man — Charles Foster. The folks around here are curious about newcomers. I heard a full description. Fact of the matter is, your coming here saved me a trip to verify my suspicions."

"I'd appreciate it if you wouldn't tell what you know," Charles said. "I don't know how long I'll be here. I just had to see Devereaux again — even if I had to come as a hired man, a tenant farmer. The Jacksons don't know who I am. If they find out, they're likely to think I'm up to something."

"And are you?" The minister arched his

white eyebrows. "The Jacksons are fine people. They've been good for the community. Tate Jackson is looking at ways New Orleans can bring the big ships to port, and that's going to help the economy in this whole region. I'd hate to think you were here to trouble them."

"No. Don't worry. I won't hurt them."

"Then I'll honor your request," Rev. Miller said. "I've known you long enough to know you wouldn't lie to me. And your secret should be safe. A lot has changed, people have moved on — I'm probably the only one who would remember your face, although your name might be a different story."

Charles turned away, back toward the graves.

"They were solid people," Rev. Miller commented. "You can be proud you were part of them. Miss Melinda was a fine lady. But it's been ten years, Charles. Has there been anyone else? Have you remarried?"

"No. How could there be anyone else?"

"Forgive my frankness, son," the minister said. "But I was serving in this church when you were born. I saw you grow up and become a man. What I see now disturbs me. You need to get on with your life."

"Get on with my life?" Charles said, without emotion. "I think that's what I'm doing. I still walk, I still breathe. I think that is getting along with my life, Rev. Miller. God saw fit to keep me here without them, and I don't know why. But I pray every day that he'll help me get through it. And he does — one breath at a time, one step at a time, one day at a time. It's been that way for ten years, and I guess it'll be that way the rest of my life."

Rev. Miller smiled. "The healing will come in God's time, Charles," he said. "In the meantime, you're in my prayers. Just remember that God gave you your past. He's given you your future, too."

Charles shrugged.

"Usually there are flowers on these graves," Rev. Miller went on. "At least, when flowers are available. The weather's been a little nasty for that lately."

"Really?" Charles asked, his eyebrows raising in surprise. "Are some of our friends still in the area? I thought you said they were all gone."

"They *are* all gone," Rev. Miller answered. "Agatha Jackson puts the flowers there. She says it's her way of paying her respects to the family that once owned her home. Feels like she has a kinship to them, I guess. It's a nice thing to do."

"Yes," Charles agreed. It was a nice thing to do. So even these Yankees could sense the loss of his family at Devereaux–Jackson Manor. Somehow, that was comforting.

Charlotte had calmed down considerably since the incident at Charles's house. It had been a disaster, and she had been quite agitated about looking so foolish.

Once her initial anger and humiliation had passed, though, she was able to be more objective. Why had she been so upset? Getting caught in the rain was something that could happen to anyone. She had been taking him supper — that had been a real mission.

"Be honest with yourself, Charlotte," she told herself aloud in her room. "You didn't do anything wrong." She thought about how she must have looked, standing on his front porch in total ruin — probably not at all like the women he was used to. Obviously, he was a man who had been places, seen things.

She laughed to herself, shaking her head in disbelief. Yes, she had been quite a sight. Now she put the final touches on her riding habit. William Beaumont would arrive at any moment for a morning ride.

Mary poked her head into Charlotte's room and watched for a moment as Charlotte smoothed the last stray hair under her hat. "William is here," Mary said, looking confused. "Charlotte . . . is there anything you want to tell me?"

"Tell you? I don't know what you mean."

"Well, I mean — riding with William? I thought — is he a beau now?"

"Of course not," Charlotte replied. "You know we're just friends. And we're only going for a ride. Friends can do that."

"Have you reformed?" Mary asked. "Could it be that my sister is suddenly going to become the belle of the parish? I mean . . . really, Charlotte, what's going on?"

"Nothing's going on — can't I ride if I have a mind to?"

"Y-yes." Mary looked doubtful. "You're doing this to make Mr. Foster jealous, aren't you?"

"Of course not!" Charlotte cried. "I'm not interested in Mr. Foster, and the feeling is clearly mutual. Why would I want to make him jealous? It wouldn't serve either of us."

"I don't know, Charlotte. I guess it would be silly, wouldn't it?" Her eyes said it would be perfect.

Any young lady in the parish would love

riding with William Beaumont, Charlotte knew. He already had broken several hearts. But, for Charlotte, he really was just a friend. The two had spent countless hours exploring the grounds at Jackson Manor. The morning ride — while not something they did often anymore — was merely an outing for both of them.

William had retrieved Charlotte's horse, Taffy, from the stable and was ready to go. "Good morning, Charlotte," he called as she walked down the slope from the house. "Hurry up! Let's ride!"

Charlotte was barely in the saddle before William had his horse at a full gallop, heading toward the back pastures. "Try and catch me!" he yelled.

Charlotte urged Taffy to catch up. "Faster, Taffy, faster," she shouted as the horse began to close the gap. Trees and fences flew by in a blur. But approaching Charles's house, Charlotte couldn't resist a sidelong glance. Was he outside today? Would he be watching from his house?

Her concentration briefly broken, Charlotte didn't notice Taffy slowing her pace — didn't see that William was increasing his lead.

No sign of Mr. Foster, she thought to herself. Of course, if he were watching from the window, she wouldn't be able to see.

"Charlotte!" William called. She turned her attention back to her companion, who had stopped at the other end of the pasture. She spurred Taffy in that direction.

"What happened?" he asked as she drew abreast of him. "You were catching up with me, and then you slowed down. Why?"

"I guess you're just too fast for me, William."

"I doubt that," he observed. "But let's pretend it's true. Let's ride toward the bayou. The water's nearly over the banks."

The morning passed quickly. Charlotte and William rode along the bayou, stopping to wade in the cold water. They explored the wooded areas near the house, surveyed the fields, raced again down nearby roads. They returned to the house the same way they had come — through the back pastures.

Once again, Charlotte couldn't resist a look toward Charles's house.

"Who lives over there?" William asked.

"Just one of the tenant farmers," she said. "No one special."

"Ah, yes," he said. "I heard about him. Is he as old and withered as the last tenant you had? Or is he overrun with children like the man at our place?"

"Neither, really," Charlotte answered.

"He's older but not withered, and he's not even married."

"Really?" William teased. "Then he should be interesting fodder for the single ladies in these parts."

Charlotte ignored him and took off once again across the pasture. She tossed her hair in the wind, knowing she was looking her best and hoping Charles was watching. This time she won, with distance to spare.

William rode with her as far as the stable before he headed home. Charlotte handed Taffy over to Frank, then she walked around to the front of the house. There was just time for a bath and her new perfume before dinner.

She had just reached the porch when she heard a horse approaching and turned to see Charles riding up the main road toward the house. Charlotte lifted her hand in greeting, and he nodded in return.

Charles slowed Avalanche and stopped at the foot of the steps.

"Miss Jackson. So you've been riding in the sun, too, I see."

Charlotte felt deflated. Charles hadn't been home when she and William rode by — and he hadn't been looking out the window, either.

"Yes, I —"

There was a shout from the house, followed by the sound of running feet. "Charlotte, Charlotte! Come quick! The puppies are here!" Mary rushed out onto the porch. "Oh, hello, Mr. Foster. You can come, too. They're just adorable. Come on!"

She disappeared back into the house. Charlotte smiled.

"You'll have to excuse Mary," she said. "She hardly ever walks anywhere. . . . Would you like to see the puppies? It's our dog, Pearl. They must have just been born."

"Sure," Charles answered. "Where are they?"

"On the back porch, I believe. Let's walk around this way. I think it'll be faster."

The puppies had attracted the whole household's attention. Even Tate Jackson was part of the small crowd gathered around Pearl's bed. Pearl herself showed no animosity toward the observers. She seemed to sense they were all family, there to admire rather than to harm. She held her head proudly, surveying her litter of thirteen to make sure all was well with them.

Charles bent to look at the tiny creatures struggling for a place at their mother's side. Pearl was aptly named, he could see. She was solid white, with the look of a good hunter. If that was true, the pups would be in demand in these parts. He had owned a dog with the same coloring once. In fact, Max had looked a lot like Pearl.

The Jackson family laughed and whispered, trying to keep the noise down so the new mother wouldn't be disturbed.

"They look like a bunch of rats, don't they?" Tate said. "But they'll be fine dogs, if we can keep Mary away from them so Pearl can raise them properly."

Charles looked up and saw that Agatha had her left hand in the crook of Tate's elbow, her right hand placed gently on his forearm. She laughed and looked adoringly at her husband. Mary held one of the pups, petting its tiny ears as it huddled against her.

"Come on, Mary," Charlotte admonished. "Put the puppy down so he can get his dinner. You don't want him to get cold."

"I think I can keep a puppy warm," Mary retorted. "I'll put him down in a minute." As if in answer, Pearl whined from her place on the porch.

"See, Mary," Tate said. "Pearl wants her pup." Mary walked over and put the puppy back down with the others. He burrowed his way in and promptly went to sleep.

"You'll have to forgive us for making such

a big fuss over a litter of puppies," Tate said. "Pearl is rather special to us. Her daddy wandered up right after we moved to Jackson Manor. He was a sorry sight — skinny, hungry. I don't know where he'd been, but he was nearly dead. We nursed him back to health, and he stayed with us until he died in his sleep last year. He was a good dog and a great hunter. He sired Pearl with a neighbor's dog, and she was the pick of the litter. These pups are his grandchildren."

Her daddy? A great hunter? Could it be? Selling Max was one of the last things Charles had done before leaving Devereaux. There had been no food, and Max already was too thin. Charles had wanted to make sure the dog would be taken care of. Could it be he had traveled back home? All those miles?

Charles felt sick at heart. This was all too much for one day. First, the cemetery and Reverend Miller, now this. He needed to go home and be by himself.

"I understand," he told the Jacksons now. "Looks like Pearl is a pretty good dog herself, and she has a fine litter of puppies. You have a right to be proud. Now if you'll excuse me . . ."

He turned and walked with a heavy step

down the porch to the yard. He had so much to think about.

Rather than mounting Avalanche, Charles led the big chestnut down the path to the house. He looked around at the familiar buildings and trees. He could see curtains at the windows of the house blowing with the gentle breeze. He looked at the window that once had been his and Melinda's, and memories flooded his mind. He looked away, toward the barn, and saw himself playing games with his brothers.

He remembered Max as a puppy, his companion as he rode across the estate. It hurt to think of him almost starved to death. And yet — Max had done just what Charles had. He had come home.

Charles gave Avalanche a perfunctory grooming, with a silent promise that he would do it right later. Then he went into his house and built a fire in the fireplace.

As he watched the flames, he thought about Devereaux and all the things that had happened to make him leave, about Max and the new life he had made in a familiar place. He reflected on his life for the last ten years and on all the things Rev. Miller had said to him. And he thought about the Jacksons standing around the new lives on the back porch, laughing and enjoying a moment that was important to them as a family.

"That's what I really miss," Charles said aloud. "It's my family, not the buildings, not the land. It was Mama and Papa, Will and James . . . my Melinda. They were Devereaux to me. Now they're gone — and so is Devereaux."

Charlotte still sat on the back porch with Pearl, even though the rest of the family had gone about their business. Trying to sort out her tangled thoughts, she acknowledged that she didn't understand herself sometimes. Lessons in feminine wiles? Dressing in her finest clothes with the threat of rain overhead? Looking to see if Charles Foster might be watching as she rode with William? What did it all mean? Life had become so complicated in the past few weeks.

Certainly, Mr. Foster was intriguing. She wanted to know all about him, to understand why he looked so sad with the puppies today, to resolve the mystery that seemed to hang around him.

But that was her head talking. Maybe her

heart was trying to say something, too. Maybe she really was attracted to Mr. Foster . . . Charles. Mary seemed to think so. But then, Mary was always trying to stir up something.

No, she wasn't sure. But there was one thing she was certain about. She wasn't playing any more games. No more trying to look like something she was not. No more making things look like they weren't. From now on, she would be Charlotte Jackson. Just plain, serious Charlotte, who attracted no attention. She would only find out if Charles Foster was the man God intended for her by being the Charlotte whom God had made. That, she knew, was something she could do well.

CHAPTER FOUR

Charlotte found herself too busy preparing food for the Thanksgiving feast to think much more about becoming governess for Aunt Gertrude's children. She and Mary baked breads, brought out canned fruits for pies, and helped Mama plan the menu for the meal they would serve. Mama surveyed the meat in the smokehouse and sent Frank out for a wild turkey.

The dinner had become an annual event, a family tradition that Charlotte enjoyed. The Jacksons invited the hired help and their families, as well as several nearby neighbors.

It was Papa's job to issue the invitations, and Mama sent him on his mission well before the dinner to make sure it wouldn't conflict with any other event. She needn't have worried, Charlotte reminded her. The same people were invited every year, and they waited in anticipation for Tate to invite them again.

***

Charles looked up from mending fence to see his landlord approaching on horseback. "Mr. Foster, I see you have things well in hand for this time of year," Tate remarked, looking around the plot of land. Firewood was neatly stacked, waiting for the next cold spell. A rotted porch rail had been replaced, and the horse shelter's door had a new hinge.

"I hope so," Charles said. "We don't have much winter around here, but you've got to be prepared."

Tate nodded his head in agreement. "I came by to invite you to our Thanksgiving dinner next week. It's a tradition — we invite everyone within shouting distance. Agatha and the girls have been preparing for some time now, so you know the food will be good. You don't have other plans, do you?"

"No, sir," Charles said. "I'm honored to accept your invitation."

"Fine, then," Tate said. "I'll tell Agatha to expect you." With that, he rode off to the next house on his list.

Thanksgiving dinner. The memory of holiday meals at Devereaux made Charles's mouth water. It would be good to be part of a tradition again.

When Thanksgiving Day came, Charles arrived to find Jackson Manor crowded with other guests. They were a varied sort. Small children played in the yard; older ones amused themselves by climbing the oak trees or skipping stones off the pond. Men gathered on the porch for conversation, and the ladies visited among themselves inside. Some were dressed in fashion's finest; others wore patched and worn clothing. It didn't seem to matter. For one day, everyone came together to enjoy themselves. In Charles's mind, the dinner was already a success.

When everyone had been ushered into the dining room, the meal was served to a chorus of *oohs* and *ahs.* Then conversation paused as Tate Jackson stood before the group.

"Thank you all for coming," he said. "It's always a pleasure to have you in our home. We Jacksons look forward to this time every year, and we hope you do, too. Let's give thanks." He bowed his head, and his guests followed his example.

"Dear Lord, we come to you humbly today to thank you for all the blessings you have bestowed upon us. Thank you for all our friends here today. You have truly made this our home, and we appreciate your bounty and all the blessings you have given us. Thank you for this food and for the hands that prepared it. Amen."

"Amen," said the guests in unison. While the children went off to their own table in the kitchen, Agatha, Mary, and Charlotte served the food. This day, Hattie, the Jacksons' cook, was among the guests.

"At Thanksgiving, everyone is our guest," Charlotte recalled her mother telling Hattie the first year. "It will give us pleasure to serve you, for once." And so, each year, Hattie and her family sat with the other guests, enjoying Thanksgiving as one of the Jacksons' neighbors.

Their weeks of hard work were evident, Charlotte noted with satisfaction as the guests sampled each dish. The meats were tender and juicy. Roasted potatoes turned golden with melted butter. Corn, peas, and beans were prepared just right. Muffins, yeast bread, and corn bread were still warm from the oven.

The guests ate until they could eat no more, finally pushing back their plates. Dessert would have to wait until there was more room.

"Sure was a fine meal, Mrs. Jackson," Charles said to Agatha as the women began to clear the table. "The finest I've had in a long time. Thank you for including me."

"You're very welcome, Mr. Foster," she answered. Then she winked. "Just wait until Christmas."

He laughed. "With Christmas tea, right?" She nodded and turned to take some dishes into the kitchen.

The men and the women separated again, the men going off to the parlor, the women to the front porch to watch the children. The conversation lasted until Charles was sure there was little more to discuss.

He saw some familiar faces, but no one he knew well. Rev. Miller must have been right — all his family's old friends had moved on. Certainly, a lot of people left after the war. And although a few men cast curious glances in his direction, Charles had successfully diverted all questions about his background, steering the talk toward crops instead. If anyone had recognized him, they hadn't said so. That was a relief, although he didn't want to keep up this pretense forever.

The pie was served, and little by little, the guests began to leave. Charles lingered while good-byes were said, in no hurry to return to his empty house. Finally, when everyone else had gone, he realized he needed to be off. But as he started toward the front door, Agatha laid a hand on his arm.

"Mr. Foster," she said. "I wonder if you could give me a hand before you go. I mentioned Christmas to you earlier. Tomorrow I need to dust off our old Christmas things to start decorating. We only have a month, you know. Would you mind helping me carry them down from the attic?"

"Now, I can do that, Agatha," Tate said. "Let Mr. Foster go home. It's been a long day."

"I don't mind at all," Charles assured him. "Where are the decorations? I'll be glad to carry them down."

Agatha smiled and steered him up the stairs to the attic. "These three trunks," she told him as they entered the dim loft. She lifted their lids to reveal crocheted angels, Christmas linens, and brass candlesticks.

"All of these things must go up before the pine boughs are brought into the house," she explained. "You can see how busy we'll be." She picked up a small box filled with crystal, leaving him to wrestle with one of the trunks.

Charles had hoisted the trunk and started

out the attic door before he noticed his surroundings. He looked around in amazement. There was his mother's settee, his father's riding saddle, an old bureau that had been in an upstairs bedroom, trunks his mother had brought to Devereaux when she married his father. The baby cradle that had been his, his brothers', and would have been his own baby's. The box of baby clothes, a pile of quilts. He recognized all of it. He hadn't realized these things still existed.

When he turned his back on Devereaux, he had left it all. There had been nothing else to do, nowhere to take anything. He had assumed the new owners had burned the things or sold them. He had left it for them to do, because he knew he could not.

Now, here it all was in the attic. Lowering the trunk to the floor, he opened the bureau and found linens and clothing. Tablecloths his grandmother had made, and clothes he had worn as a boy. He fingered a small wooden box that had been Melinda's special case for her treasures. His hand smoothed dust off the top so he could see her initials carved there. He hesitated, then opened it, his hand trembling as he lifted the lid.

Inside was a stack of letters tied with a faded blue ribbon. He thumbed through them and recognized them as letters she had written and saved for him during the war. Under that was a scarf he bought for her right after their marriage. The colors were as brilliant as if it had been worn yesterday. And there was her diary.

He remembered the evenings she had spent huddled over its pages before going to bed. He had teased her then, wanting to know what she wrote, if she talked about him.

"It's none of your affair," she'd tell him. "This diary is just for me, to help me remember." She would finish writing and put the diary back in its place in the box. It never occurred to him to try to read it. But here it was now, its leather cover curled at the corners from years in storage. He turned a few of the pages, and their musty odor drifted up to him.

Charles looked toward the door. He could still hear voices downstairs. The Jacksons would be waiting for him. No use giving them reason to wonder what was taking so long. He put the letters and the diary in his coat pocket, and then carried the trunk downstairs.

Agatha sprang on the trunk's contents like a child opening a gift, while Charles went back to retrieve the next one. It was difficult, going up and down the stairs with the trunks, acting like he had nothing better to do. All he really wanted was to go home with his newfound treasures and read — and remember. He had to act calm, or his hosts would sense something was wrong. They might even think he was stealing from them.

Was he? They had bought the house lock, stock, and barrel. But Melinda's diary, her letters. No, those would never belong to the Jacksons.

"Guess I'd better be heading home," he said when the last trunk was down. "Avalanche will be wanting his oats." He thanked Tate and Agatha again for their hospitality and took his leave.

At home, Charles put the letters and the diary in a safe place and got busy doing anything he could find. He was itching to sit down with them, to read Melinda's words, but he also dreaded feeling the pain of her loss again. After rubbing Avalanche down and giving him an extra brushing, he swept the front porch and brought in a fresh supply of firewood.

At last, when he could think of nothing else to do, Charles retrieved the letters. He sat with the stack between his hands for a long time, looking at the ribbon that had once tied her long, thick hair. Finally, he pulled the bow loose and let it flutter to the floor.

Melinda had written him often during the war, then simply kept the letters when she had nowhere to send them. He remembered coming back to Devereaux when the war was over. Melinda had given him the letters then, and he had read each one. He hadn't known what became of them after that. Melinda must have packed them away.

He began reading, and he read until darkness fell and he had to light the lamp. "I don't like this war," she had written. "It has taken you away from me for so long. There is killing and hurting on both sides — the North and the South. And what will it amount to? What will be gained by killing our Christian brothers? The Scriptures say that in Christ there is no east or west. There shouldn't be a north or south, either. Please come home to me safely, my darling."

Another letter begged him to be kind to others he met on the road.

"You never know what the circumstances are, so try to help those you can. I like to think that someone would help you, if you were in need. I don't think there would be a war if only we were more concerned with those around us."

And about his father's death: "Typhoid

has affected so many. We tried to keep him cool, to keep the fever down. But there were no doctors, and he slipped away from us. We buried him next to your mother at the church. Oh, how I wish you were with me now."

The letters brought it all back, all the torment that began with the war. The losses, the death. When he was finished reading, he tied the bundle with the ribbon once again. It made him too sad. She had made life bearable, and then he had lost her, too.

He set the letters aside and picked up the diary. It was late, but he had to go on. In a way, he welcomed the pain he felt now. It was so much better than the numbness that had surrounded him for so long.

He opened to the first page and began reading what Melinda had written only for herself. She had begun the diary on their wedding day, and she wrote about feelings he didn't even know she had experienced, about events he had long since forgotten. It was like seeing her again, like finding a missing piece of himself.

It was nearly dawn when he finished. He stirred the fire and stretched his aching body, enjoying the quiet peace of daybreak. How amazing that he had found the letters and diary. "One of God's little miracles," he told himself. He thought about one of the last entries in Melinda's diary:

"It won't be long before the baby is born. Charles is so excited. I hope it is a boy for him, but I know he would love a little girl just as much. Either way, I pray the baby is born healthy.

"I love Charles more than I ever thought possible, more every day. I can't help but worry what might happen when the baby comes. Of course, if something does happen to me, I'll know it was God's will, and he will take care of my loved ones. But my main concern would be for Charles and the baby. It's hard to think about him with someone else, but I do hope he wouldn't mourn for me too long. I wouldn't want him to. A man as wonderful as Charles shouldn't be alone. I hope he would find someone else, someone kind who would love him as much as I do."

Oh, Melinda, that's so hard, he thought. *I loved you, too. And being without you has been the toughest part of all. How could I find someone to take your place?*

But he was lonely. The past few weeks had told him that. For years, he had fooled himself into thinking he liked the solitude, the moving about from place to place. And, coming to Devereaux, he had thought

425

his heart would heal.

It had, in a different way than he had expected. Reliving old memories had opened old wounds and made him remember why the hole in his life was so large. What was it Rev. Miller had said? *Just remember that God gave you your past. He's given you your future, too.*

Maybe the minister had been right. Maybe it was time to get on with his life. Whether that meant God had someone else for him or not, he had to move forward and not look back. He had spent too much time in the past.

He closed the diary and placed it on the table next to his chair, leaving his hand on it for another moment. *Thank you, Melinda,* he thought. *Thank you for letting me go.*

Charles knelt by the chair and bowed his head. "Lord, thank you for giving me the time I had with Melinda," he prayed aloud. "Help me to get my life back and do whatever it is you want me to do. Amen."

Standing, he reached for the letters and the diary. Looking down at them, he considered for a moment, then set them gently on the fire. Then he rose and strolled out the door to watch the sunrise.

CHAPTER FIVE

The last crocheted angel and the last pine bough were in place at Jackson Manor. Charlotte stepped off the chair she had been standing on and admired their work.

Christmas was her favorite time of year. The decorations looked so festive she wished they could stay up all year.

"Oh, that's beautiful, girls!" Mama exclaimed. "Now all we have to do is find our Christmas tree."

Outside, branches swayed in the wind, brushing the windows of the house. The wind whistled in the corners, and thunder sounded from a distance.

"I guess we won't be doing that today, from the sounds outside," Mama said. "Goodness! We've been so busy, I hadn't even noticed the weather had turned."

"More rain." Mary sighed as she watched the storm approach. "We're going to have a river around our house before spring comes."

"Never mind about that. Good rain now will bring good crops in the spring," Mama chided. "Just remember that if we were in Philadelphia, it would be snowing instead of raining. Be thankful the winter is milder here."

"Maybe so," Mary acknowledged. "I guess I'll go visit Pearl and the puppies." Charlotte smiled. Mary visited Pearl every chance she got. Mary enjoyed the puppies, loved playing with them. Charlotte could picture her sister sitting on the porch, which seemed to be covered in puppies, now that they were bigger. They always jumped in Mary's lap and tried to lick her face, sending the sixteen-year-old into peals of laughter. She even had them all named, although Mama had warned her not to do that. In due time, the puppies would have new homes.

Charlotte looked out the window at the limbs swaying and the dust blowing across the road. She liked this kind of weather, and it would refresh her after being in the house all day.

Running upstairs, she picked up the quilt off her bed and ran back down, calling to her mother. "Mama, I'm going outside. I'll be back in before the rain starts."

Before Mama could answer, Charlotte was out the door. Away from the house, and facing the wind, walking was a little slower than Charlotte expected. She made her way to the edge of the pasture and shook the quilt to spread it on the ground. As soon as it touched the grass, the wind picked up the quilt's edge and rolled it back to its middle. Charlotte spread it again, this time holding the edge to give herself time to sit down.

The wind blew at her hair, loosening the pins that held it in place. Charlotte removed the pins and let her hair blow behind her. She lifted her face to the wind, feeling its coolness and the promise of rain.

Lightning crackled in the distance, and she knew it would be raining soon. Ah, but this felt so good. She would wait a little longer.

Charlotte looked around her, watching the weather change the appearance of Jackson Manor. On one side of the sky, black clouds rolled along ominously. They faded to lighter patches toward the other horizon, where the sun still shone in ribbons across the land.

She could see Frank bringing the horses in from the pasture as some of the other men hurried to finish repairing a hole in the stable roof. Hattie ran from the kitchen to the smokehouse, probably to retrieve food for the evening meal. Charlotte could see her father's carriage coming up the road in the distance.

"Miss Jackson, I do believe you enjoy the rain," said a voice behind her. "Could it be the excitement of trying to get to dry ground at the last minute, or do you just like getting drenched?"

She jumped, startled at the unexpected interruption. Turning, she saw Charles Foster standing with a cloth over his arm.

"You scared me to death!" she cried. "Do you always sneak up on people like that?"

"Only young ladies who dare the rain to catch them," he answered. "Here. I brought you this to put over your head." He tossed the cloth onto her quilt.

Charlotte felt red heat creeping up her neck and flushing her cheeks.

"I'm not going to get wet, Mr. Foster," she informed him. "I just came to enjoy the breeze. Believe me, I'm close enough to my own house that I can run if I need to."

"Seems to me you were surprised once before." He smiled. "It could happen again. Anyway, there it is if you need it."

"Thank you, but I'm sure I'll be fine."

He hesitated for a moment and began to walk away. She watched his retreating figure for a moment, his black hair tousled by the wind.

"Mr. Foster!" He turned and looked back, one eyebrow raised.

"You'll have to come see the house, now that it's decorated for Christmas," she blurted out. "All we need is a Christmas tree. Are you going to put one up at your house?"

He considered her question for a moment, then shook his head. "It's been a long time since I had a Christmas tree. In fact, it's been a long time since I celebrated Christmas, other than in here." He tapped his chest. "I remember whose birthday it is, and I praise him for that. But . . . well, my wife died at Christmastime, and I just haven't felt . . ."

"I'm so sorry. I didn't mean to . . ."

"No, don't feel sorry. It was a long time ago. It's just that when you're by yourself, there doesn't seem to be much need to go to all the fuss."

"Then you need to go to some fuss this year," Charlotte insisted. "You aren't by yourself anymore. There are all of us." She looked at his eyes and was touched by the softness that appeared in them. Somehow, he didn't look as sad as he once had.

"I'm a hired man here, Miss Charlotte," he said. "You don't need to include me in your plans."

"In Christ there is no east or west," she quoted. "And at Christmas, especially, there should be a proper celebration."

Before Charles could reply, Charlotte's attention was distracted. At first it looked like dust rolling toward them, but she quickly realized it was rain. Leaping to her feet, she rolled up the quilt and thrust Charles's cloth back at him.

"Looks like you might need this yourself." She laughed and began running toward the house. Bounding onto the porch, she turned just in time to see the rain sweep over the place where she had been sitting. Charles stood in the rain where she had left him, watching her retreat.

***

The next afternoon, Charlotte went with her father to "find" the Christmas tree. It wasn't that they had to search for one; they just needed to find the one the family had chosen months before. It was a Jackson tradition. As soon as summer began to fade, the family trekked into the woods to pick out a

Christmas tree. It had to be perfectly shaped and tall enough to reach the ceiling — but not too tall. The rule of thumb now was to make sure the tree was no more than twice as tall as Papa. One year they had misjudged, and the tree had been much too tall even to get into the house.

They had marked the tree with a red bandanna, and Charlotte spotted it first. Papa cut it down with an axe, and they took it to the house. Upright, it looked to Charlotte like the most perfect tree yet.

Mary clapped her hands in delight. "Oh, it's going to be beautiful!" she said. "I can't wait until the star is on the top."

"We'd better start decorating then," Charlotte remarked. "All the ornaments have to be on before Papa can put up the star."

Mama handed Mary the first ornament and reached in to the trunk for another one. Soon they all were engrossed in the task, pausing occasionally to admire ornaments they hung year after year. For Charlotte, each year brought new excitement when the Christmas tree went up.

"Oh, I forgot to give you this," Papa said, climbing off his ladder for a moment. He handed Mama an envelope. "It's from Kate McPhee. I saw her and Jim on my way to the shipyard this morning."

Agatha opened it and read the note. "Oh, it's a Christmas party!" she announced. "The first one of the season! And we're all invited. We'll need new dresses for this."

Papa groaned. "That means you'll have to consult the dressmaker, I suppose. What a chore!"

Mama laughed and threw a strip of ribbon at him. "Yes, but first we'll have to decide on fabric."

Charlotte and Mary started talking, both at once.

"What color do you think I should choose?"

"Do you think it would be too cold for sheer fabric on the sleeves?"

"When can we go to the mercantile, Mama?"

"Hold it, hold it!" their father ordered. "Let's just finish the tree for now. I'll take you in the morning, I promise."

"I just hope all the other girls don't get there first," Mary fretted. "I want to find the prettiest fabric for myself."

"I don't think you should worry," Charlotte assured her. "They won't sell it all by morning. Besides, even if someone else picks the same fabric, your dress won't look the same. That's the best part of hiring the dressmaker — she'll know what everybody is wearing."

The mercantile in New Orleans was well prepared for the season's parties, with bolts and bolts of colorful fabric and rolls of ribbon in a rainbow of colors. Charlotte gave her father a peck on the cheek when he left them to check on a saddle he had ordered. She knew he had learned early in his marriage not to get involved where fashion was concerned.

Mama weighed fabric in her hand, trying to decide between a blue taffeta that would go well with her hair and a more serviceable green velvet. Mary went straight for the ribbon, dangling pieces from her hair in front of the mercantile mirror.

"I always start with my hair first," she told Charlotte. "If the color looks good around my face, then I know what to choose for my dress."

Charlotte stood and pondered for a moment, then walked over to the bolts of red. It was a Christmas party. Why not choose Christmas colors?

Papa returned to find Mama still trying to decide between the taffeta and the velvet.

She draped one piece over her shoulder, then the other.

"Take both," he suggested. "Two new dresses won't hurt." Charlotte smiled at their exchange as she waited for her fabric to be cut. To her right, she could see Mary still trying to decide.

"You'd better hurry, Mary," Papa said. "I think your Mama and Charlotte are about finished, and you still have to see the dressmaker."

Mama hurried over to assist her youngest daughter, and soon the decision was made. The women left the store with their purchases in hand.

Papa went to the hotel to have a cup of coffee while the dressmaker was consulted. As the woman pinned and tucked, the Jackson women could visualize their fabric in various styles. They were a happy group, Charlotte realized, when the final decisions had all been made and they went to meet Papa for lunch.

As they sat in the restaurant, Mary chattered happily about her new dress. It would be apricot satin, with a velvet cloak to match. She had taken considerable care to select just the right lace, the most appropriate ribbon. And her gloves would match her dress. She already had decided to allow

James Conrad to be her escort.

Charlotte sat in silence, listening to her sister. The idea of an escort had not occurred to her. In previous years, she had gone alone and had a wonderful time. There had been conversation with other women and the occasional dance with a man. But now . . . she longed for someone to think her dress beautiful and to dance every dance with her.

Just someone? she scolded herself. *I think you really mean Charles Foster.* She remembered his eyes yesterday — they had seemed bluer against the gray sky, and they had pierced her heart when they looked into hers. At the memory, she shifted in her chair.

What if she asked him to be her escort and he said no? She knew there would be talk if he said yes. Most of the neighbors knew he was a hired man at Jackson Manor. Yet, she knew he was like no other tenant farmer they had ever hired. He was so proud — almost like he belonged there. He walked with his back straight, his head held high. He had been right. She really knew nothing about him, but she did know how he made her feel.

All right then, she thought. *I'll ask him. I'll ask in the name of celebrating Christmas.* With a smile, she began to eat her meal.

When the family returned from town, Charlotte made an excuse to go for a walk. She found Charles cutting firewood behind his house. Approaching cautiously, she tried to form the words in her mind. He looked up and smiled.

"Why, Miss Charlotte," he said. "What brings you here?"

Miss Charlotte. At what point had he stopped calling her Miss Jackson? She wasn't sure.

"I-I was thinking of our conversation about celebrating Christmas," she began. "I was wondering if perhaps you would care to escort me to the McPhees' Christmas party next Saturday?" Her words were coming faster. "It's the first one of the season, and —"

"I'd be delighted," he said. "Thank you for asking."

She stopped. "Really?"

"Yes, really," he said. "I haven't been to a party in years. You're right. It would be an excellent way to begin the Christmas season. I'd be pleased to escort you, Miss Charlotte."

Her shock began to wear off, and she couldn't suppress a smile.

"All right," she said. "I'll see you on Saturday." She turned and left, while she still had the strength. Even as she walked, her legs felt wobbly under her.

My goodness, what have I done? she thought. *Mr. Foster is escorting me to the McPhees' party!* At the thought, she felt the excitement well up in her stomach. She thought of the way his eyes had crinkled as he smiled at her. Would she know what to say, how to act? She scoffed at her fears. Of course she would! She had been trained properly. Even so, it would be an interesting evening. A most interesting evening.

CHAPTER SIX

The day of the party dawned to find the Jackson women already up and about. There was much to do, and the McPhees lived a distance away by carriage.

They scurried around, washing hair and tying it up in rags. The dresses had arrived from the dressmaker the day before, but Charlotte remembered there was always a bit of lace or ribbon that didn't lie quite right and had to be pressed.

"Mama, should the bow be on the left or the right?" Mary asked. Both Charlotte and her mother busied themselves with that and a dozen questions just like it. At last, all the dresses met their collective approval, and they began to anticipate the moment they could put them on. But after lunch, they would all nap before it was time to dress. The evening would be long, and they wanted to be refreshed.

Charlotte felt amazingly calm when she awoke. After some lighthearted teasing from Mary about Charles Foster, the two young women settled into choosing dance slippers and planning hairstyles. Charlotte tried her hair several different ways before deciding how she would wear it for the party.

When it was time, Charlotte slipped her red velvet gown over layers of petticoats. Her mother helped her fasten the long row of buttons in the back and slipped the gold ribbon through Charlotte's curls, which hung in ringlets around her shoulders. Then she was ready, and she felt confident — like she could face anything.

"Oh, my dear," her mother said breathlessly. "You look lovely."

And she did. Charlotte could see it in the mirror. Plain Charlotte was gone, replaced by a woman with sparkling eyes and flushed cheeks. Her mother and sister, too, were even more beautiful than usual, and every bow, every hair was in place.

"Are you ladies ready?" Papa called up the stairs. "The men are all here waiting, and so are the carriages."

"In a minute, Tate," Mama called down.

"Are we ready, girls?" she asked them. They nodded and smiled at each other.

"Then let's go greet our men."

Descending the stairs, Charlotte glanced down to see Charles waiting for her. He didn't look the same without his work clothes. Instead, he looked every bit as fashionable as her father did, with a starched white collar and black coat and trousers.

His face was relaxed, his eyes traveling over every detail of her dress. He smiled as she reached the bottom of the steps.

"You look lovely," he told her. "Like the red berries on Christmas holly."

Charlotte had never stood so close to him before. Looking up at him now, he seemed so tall, so debonair. "You're very handsome, too, sir," she declared. "And I'm not sure looking like a red berry is much of a compliment."

"Only to point out that you're going to stand out at the party," he explained. He offered his arm with a flourish, and she took it self-consciously.

The couples went outside to the waiting carriages and began the journey to the McPhees' estate. Charlotte had worried about what she and Charles might talk about, but Mary kept them all entertained. Soon, they were involved in word games, and the time flew quickly by.

At the McPhees', Charlotte felt in a daze

as she introduced Charles to her neighbors and friends. She held his arm as they made their way through the crowd, conscious of the whispers and raised eyebrows. He was handsome, she knew, and people no doubt wondered that she had arrived with an escort. Labeled an old maid years before, Charlotte always came to parties alone. Tonight she was giving them something to talk about.

If Charles was aware of the stir, he didn't act as if he noticed. He nodded and greeted the other guests with a finesse she didn't know he possessed.

"Charlotte, everyone's talking about you and Mr. Foster," Mary whispered, after pulling her aside. "They think you make a most striking couple."

Charlotte's heart skipped a beat, but she smiled at Mary and said nothing. She felt happier than she had in a long time.

The McPhees had spared no expense in preparing food for their guests. Long tables were laden with treats of all kinds, and the guests indulged as much as they dared before the dancing began.

As the first chords of the opening song began, Charlotte slid into Charles's arms. Shivers of delight seemed to reach all the way to her soul as he guided her across the dance floor. It was just as she had hoped it would be.

They danced and danced, with no sense of the time. Sometimes they were locked in intense conversation, and sometimes they laughed at some small, silly thing. At times, their eyes met and there was no conversation — no need for words at all.

At last, Charles stopped and guided Charlotte to an outside balcony. "I'm a bit out of practice at dancing," he said. He stopped to brush a stray lock of hair from her cheek. "You are so beautiful."

Beautiful. It was something she never thought anyone would call her. A word to describe her sister, yes. And yet he had used it for her.

She looked into his eyes — eyes that somehow seemed familiar. Why did they? Or was it something in those eyes she recognized?

His lips drew near to hers, brushing them lightly. Her vision blurred, and she felt dizzy. Was she dreaming? He kissed her then, tenderly at first, then harder, as if he had found something he once lost.

"I've wanted to do that all evening."

She put a finger over his lips. "Hush," she said. And she kissed him back.

They returned to the party to finish the

last numbers. Then it was time to go home. It had ended all too quickly, as far as Charlotte was concerned.

On the journey home, Charles reached for her hand and held it to his lips. "Where do we go from here, dear Charlotte?" he asked in a voice so low only Charlotte could hear. "How do we proceed when we're back at Jackson Manor?"

"Proceed?"

Mary and James were paying them no attention, laughing at something funny they had heard at the party.

"What I mean is that I'm a hired man back there. You're the young lady of the manor. If you're feeling what I'm feeling, then what do we do now?"

"Behave like two people who like each other very much," she replied.

They held hands in silence, listening to the clip-clop of the horses' hooves, feeling no need to talk until they arrived at Jackson Manor.

Charles helped Charlotte from the carriage, then bowed, suddenly aware of her parents' presence. "Thank you for a memorable evening, Miss Charlotte." He took her hand and kissed it softly. "I'll see you again soon," he whispered, and disappeared into the darkness.

Upstairs, Mary was replaying the party as her mother helped her untie her sashes. "Oh, Mama! It was just the most perfect evening! James was so charming, and everyone said he was the best dancer there. I think I might ask him to the next party as well, and maybe even caroling."

Mama raised her eyebrows.

"You're a little young to settle on one beau, Mary," she warned. "Wait a season or two. But I'm glad you had a good time." She turned to her older daughter, who was already in her nightgown. "Charlotte, did you enjoy the party?" she asked.

Charlotte looked up from her mirror, where she was combing her hair. "Oh yes, Mama," she said with a little smile. "I did."

Mama opened her mouth to speak.

"Mama, do you think we could have our own Christmas party?" Mary interrupted, catching Charlotte's eye. "It would be so much fun!"

"No, my dear," Mama answered. "We're organizing the carolers this year, and we'll be responsible for the refreshments. I think that's enough — and quite in keeping with what the season is really about."

"But, Mama," Mary said. "You know . . ."

The conversation drifted out of her

thoughts as Charlotte sighed in relief. Mary was skillfully distracting Mama before she asked too many questions. Charlotte wasn't ready to talk about the evening just yet. She wanted to hug the memory of the party to herself for a while. It was all so new, so wonderful, that she didn't even have words for the way she felt. The way Charles had looked at her, his kiss, the whispers as they said good-bye. It had all been like a dream.

CHAPTER SEVEN

Charlotte woke the next morning with the sun shining in her face. She climbed out of bed, pulled on a robe over her nightgown, and looked out the window.

White fluffy clouds drifted across a blue sky. From her window, she could see the magnolia branches swaying in the breeze. What a beautiful day! It didn't look like winter at all. But Charlotte felt the chill at the window and knew that appearances sometimes were deceiving. It would be cold enough today to wear her cloak.

She strained her eyes toward Charles's house. From her vantage point, she could barely see the smoke curling from his chimney. *Oh, he was awake!* "I wonder if I'll see him today," she said to herself aloud.

"Probably," her mother answered from the doorway. "He is likely to be at church, and Papa has asked him to dinner."

Charlotte whirled around, blushing.

"I just wanted to make sure you were awake," her mother said. "Breakfast is ready, and we'll be leaving soon." She hesitated, then moved toward her daughter. "I know you're taken with Mr. Foster, Charlotte, but do be careful. You're so inexperienced. I'd hate to see your heart broken."

"Thank you, Mama," Charlotte replied. "But don't worry. I'll be careful." Mama gave her a quick hug and hurried off.

Charlotte threw open the doors to her wardrobe. What would she wear today? Somehow, Charles made it matter. She wanted to look her best.

Deciding on her rose-colored silk, Charlotte wasted no time dressing. She twisted her hair into a knot and fastened it. People had always said it was a style becoming to her, and she wanted her hair to look a little different than it had at the party. After a final inspection in the mirror, she picked up her cloak and went downstairs, where the rest of the family had gathered.

At church, Charlotte saw Charles's horse tied to the hitching post when they arrived. Inside, she saw him seated at the back. She nodded to him as the family brushed past on the way to their pew at the front. He lifted his fingers in greeting and grinned at her.

The Christmas hymns seemed especially joyous to Charlotte this morning. She was so happy she barely could keep her voice steady. And she had to force herself to listen to Rev. Miller's sermon, aware all along that Charles must be watching her from the back of the sanctuary.

As the final prayer was being said, she prayed her own prayer. "Dear Lord. Please forgive me for my inattentiveness this morning. You've blessed me so mightily that I can hardly keep my wits about me. Please keep me calm and let me know if Charles is the right man for me. I want only to be in your will. Amen."

Charles was waiting for her at the door.

"Good morning, Charlotte," he said. "Nice day, isn't it?"

"Oh, yes, it is," she answered. "I see you survived the evening. And I hear you're joining us for dinner. Is that right?"

"Yes, I did, and yes, I am." He smiled. "Your papa was kind enough to send me an invitation this morning. Hattie is about the best cook I've ever known. And I never turn down good cooking."

"Well, maybe sometimes you do," she teased him. "As I recall, you were less than happy to see me with dinner on your porch one day."

He chuckled at the memory. "All right," he admitted. "Maybe I do sometimes. But never when the food is dry." They both laughed then, and Charles offered her his arm as they left the church.

Outside, he paused on the walkway. "I look forward to seeing you this evening, Miss Jackson," he said, bowing. "However, I promised to see Master Smith safely home. His mama isn't feeling well today."

She could see eight-year-old Davey Smith astride his horse, waiting for Charles.

"Duty calls then," she said. "I'll see you tonight."

He leaned forward one last time. "I'm looking forward to it." Then he mounted Avalanche and followed Davey out to the main road.

"Charlotte." Mama placed a hand on her daughter's shoulder. "Papa's expecting a visitor, so he's taking Mary home. He loaded up some pine boughs in the carriage for me this morning so I could take them to the cemetery. Can you help me? We'll only be a minute."

"Of course, Mama," she said. "But I still don't understand why you feel compelled to keep up the Devereaux graves. They aren't family. You never knew them."

"I know," Mama said. "But I feel like I do. I see signs of them everywhere in the house. In the notches they carved in the door to mark their children's growth. In the few pieces of furniture they left that we still use. In the attic every time I go up there."

She loaded Charlotte's arms with the pine branches, which had been wrapped in paper to prevent the prickly needles from damaging their skin and clothes.

"Besides," Agatha continued, "we've been fortunate. We don't have any family in this cemetery. They're all in Philadelphia. And you know our friends tend the graves for us there. It's the Christian thing to do."

Charlotte thought about that as they walked toward the cemetery. Mama was right. It was the Christian thing to do, she supposed. And anyway, what did it hurt?

She stopped at the first grave and stooped to unwrap the pine bough to put it in place.

Thomas Lee Devereaux, she read. *May 1, 1810–July 10, 1863. Husband and father. May his soul rest in peace.*

She turned over in her mind the facts she knew. Thomas's parents, Jesse and Annie Devereaux, were over there. Mama always started with them, because they were the ones who had built Devereaux–Jackson

Manor. *Margaret Elizabeth Foster Devereaux,* the next tombstone read. *December 8, 1817–February 2, 1851. Beloved wife and mother.* This was Thomas's wife, she knew. She walked on, unwrapping a pine branch for the next grave as she went.

Melinda Beauregard Devereaux. April 9, 1848–December 23, 1866. And next to her a baby's grave. *Eugenia Bethany Devereaux. Died at birth, December 23, 1866.* Christmastime. How sad. Charlotte wrinkled her brow. That sounded familiar, but the memory seemed wrapped in a fog. She moved on to her mother's side, her branches all gone now. Her hands were cold, and she rubbed her fingers to warm them.

Mama bent to place the last of the branches.

"Caroline Haley Foster," Charlotte read aloud.

Agatha glanced back at her daughter.

"Caroline Haley Foster?" Charlotte mumbled.

"Yes, dear," her mother said, turning to look at the tombstone. "Rev. Miller says that was Margaret Devereaux's mother. Look, she died after Margaret did. Life can be so sad sometimes, can't it? It must have been hard on her to outlive her child."

Caroline Haley Foster. Margaret Elizabeth

Foster Devereaux. Charlotte felt a need to go home.

"Mama," she said. "Can we leave now? I'm really very cold." She tightened the cloak around her shoulders, but that didn't stop her heart from pounding in her throat.

"Certainly, darling," Mama answered, gathering up the paper from the pine branches. "We're finished here. Goodness, you are trembling. Let's get you home, where it's warm."

It seemed like ages before the carriage pulled up in front of the house. Charlotte tried to keep her thoughts calm until she and Mama were inside. Forcing herself to walk slowly, she went up the stairs, as if to go to her room. Instead, she continued until she reached the attic.

Lighting a candle just inside the door, she surveyed the room. Trunks here, a rocking chair there. She knew what she was looking for. But where?

Winding through the remnants of someone else's past, she reached the windows, and she no longer needed the candle. The light of day would show her what she had come to see. There they were, stacked against the wall.

The Devereaux portraits had hung on the walls when the Jacksons arrived in New Orleans. They had meant nothing, until Mama started tending the cemetery. Then she had made it her business to find out who the people in the portraits were.

"I don't want strangers in my attic," Mama had said. So they always dusted the portraits carefully when they cleaned the attic each spring.

"One of the Devereaux clan might show up one day to claim them," Agatha said. "I'd feel terrible if they were all dusty."

Charlotte knew them herself now. Thomas and Margaret Devereaux on their wedding day. Jesse Devereaux on his horse. Melinda Devereaux, looking so young. And Charles Devereaux with a white dog that looked a lot like Pearl. *Charles Foster Devereaux.*

She sat down on the floor in dismay, forgetting her dress. Charles Foster. Charles Foster Devereaux. There he was. Much younger then, but unmistakably Charles. The blue eyes that had seemed so familiar. They looked at her now, mocking her, yet piercing her soul.

Confused thoughts flooded her mind. He had looked so familiar. At the party, he had held his head high, like he belonged there. Like he belonged *here*. He hadn't seemed like any tenant farmer she had ever known.

And the path he had used to rescue Mary — of course he had known of the path.

Why? Why was he here? Why was he pretending to be someone else?

Charlotte sat for what seemed like hours, thinking, sorting.

Finally, she put her face in her hands and wept, deep anguished sobs.

When she was finished, Charlotte dried her tears and stood, brushing the cobwebs off her dress.

She knew what Mr. Charles Foster Devereaux was up to. He was trying to get his family home back — and he saw Charlotte as the way to accomplish the task.

"Well, he's wrong," she said to herself, trying to rearrange her disheveled hair before she left the attic. "Mr. Devereaux is tangling with the wrong person. I won't be used like that."

With purpose in her step, she left the attic, closing the door behind her.

My prayer's been answered in a strange way, she thought as she entered her bedroom. *God has just shown me that Charles is not the man for me. I should be thankful to know that now. If it had gone any further . . . if I had learned to love his smile . . . if I had let him look at me any longer with those eyes . . .* She cut herself short. No! She had been deceived.

Charlotte Jackson had looked foolish once in front of Charles Devereaux, but it wouldn't happen again. He had preyed on her inexperience, but now she saw him for what he was. She would make sure he realized it, too.

Charles walked to the house that evening with a spring in his step. Charlotte. She was wonderful. Why hadn't he seen it before? The way her eyes sparkled when she smiled, her hand on his arm, the way she had held her head at the Christmas party.

Though he had tried to ignore the stares and whispers, he had enjoyed seeing Charlotte receive so much attention. The party had transformed her. He could see it, and he knew the other guests did, too. He hoped he had a little to do with that.

Charles looked forward to this dinner, to seeing her again. Tate had done him a favor by inviting him. Otherwise, he would have had to invent an excuse to call on Charlotte.

Nearing Jackson Manor, he looked up at the windows where his and Melinda's bedroom had been. He could see the white curtains tied back neatly and imagine her waiting there for him. The memories were still present, but they were softer — not causing the anguish they once had. His years with Melinda had been good, but he knew she wouldn't want him to go on living in the past.

"Good evening, Charles," Tate said as he opened the front door. "I'm glad you could come. Please come in."

Agatha hurried to Tate's side, smiling when she saw Charles. "Yes, please come in, Mr. Foster," she said. "Dinner will be served momentarily."

"My nose tells me I'm in for a treat," Charles observed.

"I hope so," Agatha replied. "Hattie says she's preparing something new, and she won't even let me in the kitchen. I usually like to serve familiar foods to guests, so it'll be a surprise for all of us. Excuse me, and I'll see where the girls are."

Charles followed Tate into the parlor.

He saw Mary hurrying down the stairs just as her mother started up.

"Mary, slow down!" he heard the older woman warn. "We have a guest. Act like a lady, and don't tempt an accident on these stairs."

"All right," Mary agreed, then abruptly changed the subject. "If you're looking for

Charlotte, her door is closed, and she won't answer me. I think she must be busy getting ready for Charles." She drew out his name, fluttering her fingers at her throat for emphasis.

"Don't be so dramatic!" Agatha chided. "I'll see about her. Now go downstairs and help Papa entertain Mr. Foster."

Charlotte lay in bed when her mother knocked on the door.

"Darling, it's me," Agatha called. "Mr. Foster is here."

Charlotte said nothing. Finally, the door opened slowly, and Mama peered in at her. "My goodness!" she said in alarm. "Are you ill?" Bustling into the room, she put cool fingers on Charlotte's forehead.

"I think so," Charlotte responded wearily. "I think I caught a chill this morning."

"You do feel warm," Mama pronounced. "You'll stay in bed, of course. Don't worry. We'll look after Mr. Foster. You get some rest."

"Thank you, Mama."

Charlotte watched with relief as her mother retreated. She had been convincing, she knew. It wasn't really a lie, either. She did feel ill. Ill at her stomach, and the cause was downstairs. It was a much better idea to stay in her room than to face him just now.

"Charlotte is ill and won't be joining us," Agatha announced. "She caught a chill after church this morning, I think. It was awfully cold. We should have come straight home."

Charles started to speak.

"Oh, don't worry, Mr. Foster," she said. "I think bed rest is what Charlotte needs. She hardly seemed warm, so I think we caught it in time. I'm sure she'll be much better tomorrow."

"Well, then, let's go see the puppies until dinner is ready," Mary suggested, jumping up from her chair. "They've grown so much! Why, two of them are spoken for already."

The puppies had outgrown their pen on the porch, and they whimpered and jumped up the sides. Mary leaned down to pick one up.

"This is my favorite." She handed a squirming ball of fur to Charles. "His name is Lucky."

Charles petted the puppy's ears and let him nibble at his hand. Could anything serious be wrong with Charlotte? Was he only letting himself in for more pain?

"I know!" Mary squealed. "Mr. Foster, why don't you take Lucky? You don't have a dog, do you? I'd keep him myself, but

Papa says Pearl is enough for us. This way he'll be close so I can still see him."

Charles lifted the pup with both hands and stared into its eyes. Something he saw there triggered a familiar, affectionate feeling. It wouldn't be a bad idea to keep a dog at the tenant farm.

"All right," he agreed.

Mary picked up each of the other pups and told him their names. Charles was relieved when Agatha called them inside for dinner.

The meal was good — Hattie had cooked a shrimp jambalaya — but the evening was dampened with Charlotte's absence. Charles knew the Jacksons were trying hard to entertain him, but he didn't feel much like company. At the end of the meal, Agatha went upstairs to check on Charlotte, in the hopes, he knew, that she at least could say good-bye. But her mother returned alone, saying Charlotte was asleep.

At last, Lucky in tow, Charles went home.

The day for caroling arrived, and Tate, Frank, and Charles worked during the morning, filling the wagons with hay. Neighbors would arrive after lunch, and they would travel from house to house singing Christmas carols.

461

They all knew that once the neighbors arrived, there would be hardly anyone left in the community to carol to. But that was part of the fun. All who were able joined in, stopping at each house for Christmas treats.

Charles was still concerned about Charlotte. It had been days since she had been too ill to join them for dinner. His inquiries about her health were met with "She's just not herself right now." He looked over at Tate as they were spreading hay in a wagon bed. Tate had said nothing about Charlotte all morning.

Once everyone arrived, Charles helped the ladies find seats in the hay and gave the men a helping hand into the wagons. With everyone else aboard, Charles helped Mary up, then Agatha, then . . . Charlotte. Here was Charlotte, at last.

Relief flooded through him. "Charlotte. Are you really feeling better?"

She spoke without returning his glance. "I'm fine, thank you." Finding a seat, she turned to the woman beside her and began a conversation in low tones.

Charles watched her for a moment, his disappointment giving way to anger. Charlotte Jackson was obviously playing some kind of female game. So much for thinking they had a special relationship. Maybe he had scared her, and this was her way of backing away. Perhaps her parents had intervened.

Charles didn't feel much like singing. He just couldn't seem to open his mouth when the others launched into the familiar carols. Each time the group went into a house for refreshments, he stayed outside with the wagons, making the excuse that the horses needed to be looked after.

Charlotte didn't look at him once, as far as he could tell. She climbed off and on the wagon with ease, laughing with the others, singing every song.

When the carolers arrived back at Jackson Manor, everyone crowded into the house, ready for something warm to drink. But Charles remained outside to help Frank with the wagons and horses.

The guests stayed long after the hay was out of the wagons and the horses had been groomed and fed. Charles could hear their laughter, see them walk past the windows. Smoke curled up through the chimneys as the fireplaces warmed the rooms inside. He could imagine the warmth, the happiness of belonging and celebrating together. He longed for that. Perhaps it had been stupid for him to walk away. He could have been a part of it. Yet he couldn't bring himself to join the group. He would have felt like an intruder, with Charlotte acting the way she was. Saying good-night to Frank, Charles walked over and sat down under one of the expansive magnolias, his back to its trunk. Maybe Charlotte would come out.

The cold ground had chilled him to the bone by the time the guests began to file out, bound for home. He stood and stretched his body, watching them as they all said their good-byes, waiting for his chance. Agatha, Tate, Mary, and Charlotte stood on the porch, wishing their neighbors a Merry Christmas, waving to them as they departed.

The last guest left, and the Jacksons walked inside together, closing the door after them. Charles kicked with all his might at a stick lying at his feet. "Women!" he spat as he started for his own house, kicking the stick again for good measure.

CHAPTER EIGHT

Charlotte sat in the parlor, her hands busy with needlepoint. Her mind was somewhere else, and she hardly noticed Mary watching her from across the room.

"Charlotte," Mary spoke up. "Charlotte, please tell me what's going on."

Charlotte looked up at her sister. "I don't know what you're talking about."

"Oh, I think you do. The night of the party, I thought you would swoon from happiness. And now — Charlotte, you haven't said two words in days."

"I've been thinking."

"About what?" Mary demanded.

Charlotte laid the needlepoint in her lap and sighed. "If you must know, I'm thinking of going away."

"Going away? But where? And why?"

"You know Aunt Gertrude is anxious for me to go to Philadelphia and work as her children's governess," Charlotte said, her eyes cast down. "I've just been thinking maybe it's as good a time as any. Why should I wait?"

"Why should you be in such a hurry?" Mary countered. "It's nearly Christmas. You can't go now."

"Yes, I can," Charlotte answered. "There's nothing to keep me here."

"Nothing to keep you — Charlotte, I don't understand. What about you and Charles?" Mary frowned. "Please tell me what happened."

Charlotte folded her hands in her lap, trying to hold back the tears. Why not tell Mary that Charles was really Charles Devereaux? Wouldn't it be best to expose him to the whole family? Somehow, she couldn't do that — not yet.

"I can't," she whispered. "Suffice it to know there's good reason for me not to see Charles anymore."

Mary looked at her in bewilderment. "Charlotte, I won't tell a soul. You know you can trust me. Maybe I can help."

Charlotte bit her lip and said nothing.

"Charlotte? Please?"

Charlotte thrust her needlepoint aside and stood up. "I'm too restless for needlepoint today. I think I'll go for a walk. I'm sorry I can't talk about this right now, Mary. Please understand."

Charles watched Mary approach from his front porch, where he sat with Lucky at his side. "Hello, Mr. Foster," she called. "Hello, Lucky!" The puppy greeted her by jumping up on her leg and pawing her. She reached down and petted him, then leveled her gaze at Charles.

"I need to talk to you," she told him. "I hope you won't think it's none of my business, but I'm worried about Charlotte. I thought you could help."

"I'm listening."

"Well, surely you know something's happened," Mary began.

"That seems obvious," he agreed. "And do you know what it is?"

"No, I don't," she acknowledged. "That's why I'm here. I wanted to find out from you so I can help Charlotte. Will you tell me? She won't."

Charles looked at her for a moment, then turned away.

"I don't know. One moment, everything was great. The next moment, she wouldn't even speak to me. If you can discover the reason, I wish you'd tell me."

"But surely there was something —"

"Nothing that I know of," Charles interjected. "I've tried to talk to her, but I can't even get close. She manages to avoid me every time."

Mary was silent for a moment. "Perhaps now would be a good time," she said. "Charlotte's gone for a walk. I think you'd find her in the back pasture. It would be hard to avoid you there. But, Mr. Foster . . ."

"Yes?"

"Please find out what is troubling her. Charlotte is planning to leave, to go to Philadelphia for good. Please try to set things right." Mary's brow was wrinkled with concern. "She's my sister, and I don't know what I'd do without her."

Charles nodded and rose from his chair. "I'll do what I can — if she'll talk to me."

Charlotte walked across the pasture, aware of the coolness of the day. She should have brought a wrap. *Louisiana has spoiled me,* she thought. *Winter is much colder there in Philadelphia, and I won't be able to forget my wrap.* A flock of geese flew overhead, and she watched them until they were out of sight. As she moved on, a hand caught her arm. Whirling to face her attacker, her gasp of fear turned to surprise.

"Charles! Let go of me, please."

He didn't loosen his grip. "Not until you tell me what's wrong. You've been avoiding me for days. I think you owe me an explanation."

"I owe you nothing."

"Charlotte, the party. Remember how we were, there? What's changed?"

"Nothing's changed. I needed an escort. That's all. I'm sorry if you imagined otherwise." She pulled away from him, trying to loosen his fingers from her arm.

"Imagine? I don't think I imagined anything." He pulled her against him, holding her shoulders to look her in the eye.

"Look at me and tell me it didn't mean anything," he demanded.

"I don't know what you're talking about . . . Mr. Devereaux."

He dropped her arms and stepped back. "Devereaux?"

"Yes, Devereaux. Did you think I wouldn't find out? Did you think I was so stupid? Now leave me alone." She turned and began to run, leaving Charles standing in the pasture. She had to get home, to her own room. She had to pack.

Avalanche was beginning to tire when Charles spotted the little church at the end of the road. Reining to a halt, he leapt from the saddle. He looked inside the church — no sign of Rev. Miller. Ducking out the back door, he ran up the path to the little house where the cleric lived. The front door opened before he could knock, and Rev. Miller stepped out.

"Charles. What's wrong? I saw you ride up —"

"Reverend, tell me what you told Charlotte about me. She's going to leave. I must know."

"Wait a minute. Take it easy, Charles." The minister eyed his visitor. "Come in, rest a spell." He took the younger man by the arm and led him inside, gesturing toward a chair.

"Let me get you some tea."

"There's no time for tea," Charles said. "Please, Rev. Miller. Talk to me."

"All right," the older man said, sitting down opposite his guest. "Now tell me what the problem is."

Charles took a deep breath and began. "Charlotte realizes who I am," he said. "The only way she would know is if you told her. I need to hear what you said to her, so I can know how to talk to her. She's so angry. . . . She won't let me near her."

Rev. Miller leaned forward in his chair. "I haven't said anything to anyone, Charles. I made a promise to you, and I've kept it. You can depend on that."

"How then —" Charles began.

"I don't know of anyone else in the community who would remember you," said Rev. Miller, leaning back. "The Tylers, the Carters, the DuBois family — they all sold out and moved away after the war. It just got too hard, the taxes were too high. And the others — Jeb White and his wife, Tallulah, Andrew Simmons — they died and left their places to their children. As near as I can recall, they were all too young when you left to remember what you looked like. I don't think any of them —"

"How then?" Charles demanded, almost to himself. "How would she know?"

"There's a more important question than that, Charles," Rev. Miller said. "And that is: What must she think? Think about it. Even I wondered what your intentions were. I heard you've been seeing Miss Charlotte. If she knows you're a Devereaux, what conclusions might she draw?"

Charles looked at him for a moment, then

groaned and put his head in his hands. "I've got to see her, talk to her. Even if she doesn't want to, I've got to talk to her. I have to explain, before she's gone for good."

"Then do it, Charles," the minister urged. "Go back and talk to her. Make it right." Charles was already out the door before the minister finished.

Dusk had fallen by the time he arrived at Jackson Manor. Lamps inside the house had been lit, and light from the windows fell across the porch as he climbed the steps. The door swung open at his touch, and he stood for a moment wondering why the Jacksons would leave it unfastened.

Faint scuffling sounds came from within. He listened but heard no voices, no footsteps. The scuffling subsided, followed by a low moan.

Charles inched his way across the great entry, looking all around for signs of danger. The parlor was empty, and he could see no one at the top of the stairs. He moved down the hallway a few steps at a time, pausing to listen, then moving another few steps. If there was an intruder, he needed the element of surprise on his side.

I wish I had my pistol, he thought. *What good will I be unarmed?* He went back to the parlor and picked up the poker from the fireplace. Tiptoeing across the room, he turned the doorknob to the small study and eased open the door.

"So you've found us, sir," a gruff voice said. "How cunning of you. Now tell me your name, rank, and who you fought for."

Charles was looking down the barrel of a pistol, and the man who held it didn't look like he was joking. Dark, dirty hair lay unkempt around his face, and his mouth was fixed in a scowl. His clothes were tattered. He stood in the middle of the room, feet apart, with his full focus on Charles.

Risking a glance to the side, Charles saw a second man standing in the corner of the room with the Jackson women huddled behind him. He was thinner than the other, with limp yellow hair, and wore the uniform of a Confederate soldier. He, too, was holding a gun.

Another moan. Charles pushed the door open further and saw Frank, tied in ropes, with a large bloodstain on his trouser leg.

"I repeat. Your name and rank, sir," the dark-haired man growled. "Speak up, or I'll shoot."

"Captain Charles Devereaux," Charles answered, looking at a white-faced Charlotte. "Captain Charles Foster Devereaux."

"And what side did you fight on?" the man demanded.

"For the Confederacy, sir," Charles said. "The Mississippi Twenty-third Infantry Division. If you're from Louisiana, you know the fighting didn't come here until later. I went to Mississippi so I could help."

"You related to Will Devereaux?"

"He was my brother. He died in the Battle of New Orleans."

"I know," the man said, lowering the pistol. "I was there with him. Name's Carson. Will was a good man. He told me about this place. He loved it, you know. Told me about your grandpa and your pa building it up. Now you don't own it anymore, do you? Nah, I asked around. I know these Yankees have it now. I oughta shoot you for lettin' 'em have it."

"I didn't have a choice," Charles said. "Devereaux was a proud place. You know how it was right after the war. There lots of damage. Men came back from the war and found what hadn't been burned was rotting. It took money — money I didn't have. I was starving. I had to leave. If I had stayed, Devereaux wouldn't be standing today."

He paused.

"Well, we're here to get it all back," Carson said, raising his pistol again. "You can help us or not. We're going to get Southern soil back into Southern hands — if we have to do it one place at a time. You with us?"

"You mean you're going to rob and pillage and murder? No, I'm not with you. Didn't you have enough of that with the war? When I left Devereaux, I left the South. I had to get away, because I couldn't stand the destruction that was left. These people — they came to help. Mr. Jackson works with the shipyards. It's going to bring the South back, make it a good place again. And this woman and her daughters — they put flowers on my mother's grave when I wasn't here to do it. No, they came to help, and they renamed this place Jackson Manor. It's a good name, because they succeeded where I failed. Leave 'em be."

Carson glanced at his partner, who shrugged. After considering Charles for a moment more, he put the gun inside his coat.

"All right," Carson said. "I'll do what you ask out of respect for your brother. But remember this. We aren't the only ones. There are others like us that want the South back the way it was. And next time you might not be here to protect 'em. Next time, they might not be so lucky. Come on, Davis."

The blond man pushed past Charles and followed Carson out the door. For a moment, no one said anything. They listened to the footsteps across the porch, listened for the sound of horses leaving Jackson Manor. Then they sprang into action.

Charles knelt beside Frank, untying him. Agatha was there moments later, with a basin of water and rags to staunch the wound.

"He's unconscious," Charles said to her. "We need a doctor."

"Charlotte," Agatha responded. "Go get one of the boys to find Doc Kelly. Tell him to hurry." Charlotte ran out of the room without a word. Agatha turned to Charles.

"Thank you, Mr. Foster," she said. "You've come to our aid again. And with Tate gone — I shudder to think what could have happened."

"Actually, the name's Devereaux, Mrs. Jackson," he answered. "But please call me Charles. I think you've known me long enough."

"Yes . . . Devereaux," Agatha looked at him as she finished the bandage. "I'm sure it's an interesting story — why you came back, why you're here now. And as soon as we get Frank taken care of, I'd like to hear it."

Charles nodded. Then he lifted Frank onto the sofa. "I think he'll be more comfortable up here," he said, placing a pillow under the injured leg.

Charlotte appeared, a little breathless from her errand. "Jimmy's gone for the doctor. How's Frank?"

"He's still unconscious, Charlotte," her mother answered. "I hope the doctor hurries." She looked from Charlotte to Charles and then to Mary, who had not moved since the men left.

"Mary? Are you all right?"

"Yes, Mama," she answered, her voice quivering.

"Come with me to the kitchen, then," Agatha said, taking command of the situation. "I think some tea would do us all good." Without a word, Mary followed her out.

Charlotte sat down in a chair near Frank. "At least you were honest about who you are to those hooligans," she said, looking down at her hands.

"If I'd been honest before, would your papa have hired me?"

She looked up at him. "No. He would have turned you away, just as he will probably turn you away now. How did you think this would end, Charles? What were you going to do? Shoot us all so you could have your home back?"

"Of course not."

"No, I know you wouldn't," she said. "You didn't have to shoot us. All you had to do was prey on an innocent girl who didn't know enough to protect herself from your charms. If I hadn't realized who you were, it might have worked."

He half rose from his chair. "Is that what you think? That I was after you because of this house, this place? It's not true." She continued to stare at him. She seemed about to speak, when the doctor arrived.

Doc Kelly knelt over Frank and examined his leg. "He's lucky," he said after a long moment. "The bullet went clean through. I'll need to clean the wound and stop the bleeding. I hope you have plenty more bandages."

"Yes, Doctor," Agatha answered, rushing to his side with the rags she had gathered earlier. "What else will you need?"

Seeing that Frank was being taken care of, Charles took Charlotte by the arm and ushered her out into the parlor. "I need to talk to you," he said. "And I want you to listen to me. Will you do that?"

"It depends on what you have to say," she replied, raising her chin. "I'll give you five minutes."

"Devereaux was my home," he began. "I lost everything I had here. I lost my parents, my brothers, my wife . . . and our baby. The night Melinda died, I just went crazy, and I left the next day. I went out west, working any job I could find, getting close to no one. Any time I felt the least bit comfortable, I left." He paused to catch his breath.

"Finally, I got tired of running, and I came back here," he continued. "Just to work — not to take back Devereaux. I came because it's the only thing I knew to do. I came back home, even though it's really not my home anymore. It was the only place I knew of where I might find some peace and some comfort — and I was right. Only the comfort didn't come from Devereaux — not from a bunch of dirt and buildings. It came where I didn't expect it, from a woman who made my heart come home. You helped me find myself again, Charlotte." He paused, fighting to maintain control of his surging emotions. "I know you don't believe me," he began again, "but I'm telling you the truth. My heart wasn't missing Devereaux.

It was missing something much bigger. And I found it."

He looked away for a moment. "There's your five minutes' worth." He stopped, running his fingers through his hair, his emotions spent. When he looked again at Charlotte, she was trembling, and tears rolled down her cheeks.

"Charlotte?" he reached out to touch her arm, and she didn't resist. "Please forgive me for deceiving you."

"I do forgive you," she said in a small voice. He took her hand and touched it to his lips.

"My dearest," he said.

"Kiss her, Charles," Mary whispered loudly from around the corner, peering in at the two of them with mischief on her face.

"Mary!" Charlotte cried in dismay. "Are you spying again?"

"Mary, I could use your help in here," Agatha ordered from the study.

"Yes, ma'am," Mary replied, rolling her eyes and disappearing from view.

Charles turned back to Charlotte. "Her idea isn't a bad one," he said. "Do you mind?"

Charlotte shook her head. He took her face in his hands and kissed her on the cheek, on the corner of her mouth, and finally on her lips. It was a kiss to make up for all the ones he had missed. At last, he drew back and looked into her eyes.

"Now you need to tell me one thing," he said.

"What's that?"

"How did you find out I was Charles Devereaux?"

She smiled and took him by the hand, leading him into the entry. They climbed the stairs to the attic, and she showed him the portraits. His heart was in his throat as he looked at Melinda's portrait, at his parents' — faces he hadn't seen for so long.

"I just knew I had seen you before," she explained. "Helping Mama in the cemetery, I saw the Foster name on the tombstones. That's when I remembered these portraits. I guess you should have thought of another name. I might never have put it together then."

"I'm glad you did," he told her. "I never want to try being someone else again. Although Charles Foster is my real name — I just left off the last. Anything else would have been dishonest." They both laughed.

"I tried being someone else myself, so I guess I've been a little dishonest with you, too," she admitted. "Remember the day on your porch, when I got soaked to the skin? I was taking lessons from Mary on how to get your attention. I guess it never works when we try to be someone other than ourselves."

He grinned at the memory, then nodded and took her hand as they climbed back over the trunks, the cradle, a broken chair.

They stopped at the attic door, and he looked back over the things from his past, shaking his head in wonder. Then he turned his back and closed the door.

Downstairs, Frank was awake, and the doctor had gone.

"Frank, I'm glad you're all right," Charles said. "You gave us quite a scare."

Frank managed a weak grin. "I don't remember much," he said. "I heard screams, so I came in and saw those ruffians. I don't remember anything after they shot me. Must've hit my head when I fell."

Agatha hushed him. "Don't talk any more," she said. "You've had quite an evening. Just rest. We can discuss this tomorrow. I know Tate is going to want an accounting, too. In fact, there's a lot for him to hear about." She looked at Charles and Charlotte.

"Mr. Devereaux — Charles, I'd like for

you to stay tonight, if you don't mind," Agatha said. "I'll make up the guest room for you. Please. Tate will be home tomorrow, but we're pretty defenseless if those men come back tonight."

Charles nodded his agreement and wondered just how pleased Tate would be when he heard everything that had happened.

Chapter Nine

Charlotte watched from the porch as her father arrived the next morning, his wagon loaded with boxes. Her mother rushed out the door to meet him.

"Tate, I'm glad you're here," Mama said. "So much has happened since you were away."

"Tell me about it, darlin', while I unload the wagon," he said, kissing her hello. "I've got special surprises for you."

"No, I want you to sit down and listen to me and Charlotte," she insisted. Taking his arm, she led him to the porch. Papa shrugged and sat down on the step as Mama began to relate the previous day's events.

At first, Charlotte thought, he seemed amused at his wife's intensity, her seriousness. But his eyes widened as he heard about the intruders and how close his family had come to harm.

"We need to notify the sheriff," he said, rising to his feet. "My family has to be safe in our own home."

"The sheriff just left," Charlotte assured him. "Charles gave him a full description of the men. They have caused trouble before, and they're already wanted in town. We'll just have to take extra precautions around here. If there are others, like they said, then we need to be prepared."

"Agreed." Papa nodded. "Now what's all this about Charles?"

Charlotte took a deep breath and then recounted how she had discovered Charles's true identity. Her father stood quietly until she had finished.

"So Charles passed himself off as Charles Foster when he's really the former owner of this plantation? I don't like that," Papa said somberly. "Deception never comes to good."

"He had his reasons," Mama told him. "But I'll let him tell you about it. He's here, and he's ready to talk to you, to explain why he did what he did."

"Looks like you need help with that wagon, sir," Charles said, coming around the house. "Let's unload it while we talk."

Walking over to Charles, Papa looked into his tenant's eyes. Charles gazed back, raised his eyebrows, and gestured at the boxes.

"Shall we?"

The two men unloaded the wagon, talking all the while. They placed some of the boxes under the Christmas tree, and Papa warned the women to "stay away until Christmas." Papa asked questions while they carried other boxes to the stable; Charles gave more answers while boxes were delivered to the kitchen pantry.

At last, when they had finished unloading the wagon, they walked down the path toward Charles's house. Charlotte watched them in dismay.

"What if Papa sends him away?" she whispered to Agatha. "I don't think I could bear it."

Mama patted Charlotte's hand. "Don't worry, my dear," she said. "Your Papa is a fair man. Everything will be all right. You'll see."

Charlotte waited at the window, watching for Charles and her father. She longed to see them coming back down the road, Papa's arm around Charles's shoulders.

After an hour, Papa walked back alone, and her heart sank. She was standing at the door when he came in. "Papa?" Charlotte said, her voice trembling.

"Charles is leaving Jackson Manor," Papa

said. "We can't have the former owner of the estate planting crops for us. I appreciate his circumstances, but I never would have hired him if I had known. He understands that."

Charlotte looked at him, unable to speak as tears gathered in her eyes.

"I'm sorry, Charlotte." Papa's voice was gruff. "I didn't have a choice."

"Where will he go, Papa? He has no one to turn to."

"I'm sure he will be fine. He's survived a long time on his own."

Charlotte turned and went to her room, not even looking at Mary when she passed her on the stairway.

By the end of the day, Charles had moved his things from the tenant house and had packed them in a wagon that Tate loaned him. Charlotte, watching for some sign of him from her window, ran down the stairs and out to the front porch to see him go. He passed without looking at the house, his shoulders slumped as the wagon pulled out onto the road.

CHAPTER TEN

Charlotte felt as if a rug had been pulled from beneath her feet. Although she tried to go on as if nothing had happened, she often found herself crying for no apparent reason — except that she had a good one. Charles was gone, and she didn't know when — or if — he would return. Her mother and Mary seemed not to know what to say, so silence became a way of life within a day or two.

To make matters worse, visitors called frequently to wish the Jacksons a merry Christmas. Charlotte was anything but merry, and she found it difficult to fake the emotion. Instead, she took it upon herself to serve the tea, to bring in the treats, to collect the plates. She welcomed the monotony of such tasks.

On Christmas Eve, with only the family present, Charlotte found she could no longer pretend to be cheerful. Worse yet, she felt she was spoiling Christmas for everyone else.

The Jacksons traditionally opened one gift apiece on this night, and this year it was Charlotte's turn to begin. She sighed and started to reach beneath the tree for a package when a loud knock on the door startled everyone.

"Who could that be?" Papa grumbled.

Glad for the distraction, Charlotte went to the door and pulled it open. *"Charles!"*

"Merry Christmas!" Charles greeted her cheerily. "May I come in?"

Stunned, Charlotte stood aside to let him pass, then slowly followed him to the living room. *Charles is here!* She wanted to pinch herself to be certain it wasn't a dream. But there he stood, smiling at her parents, winking at Mary. Without a word, Mama stood to pour him a cup of tea.

Charles took the cup and sipped its contents, obviously savoring the taste. "Christmas tea will always be special to me," he said to Charlotte. "I'll always remember the first time I tasted it — the day I first laid eyes on you."

"Then you should have it every Christmas," Charlotte replied, as warmth flooded her cheeks. "It can be a tradition."

"Speaking of traditions, I have a gift for

you," he said, taking a small package from his pocket. "I hope you'll forgive such a small present. You know I haven't had much money."

She started to protest, but he shook his head.

"No, you need to know," he said. "This was a present I bought for Melinda the Christmas she died. I never had the chance to give it to her, and it stayed wrapped up in the attic all this time. I want you to have it now, because I want you to know how much you mean to me. I think she would have wanted that."

Charlotte took the package from him with trembling fingers, loosening the string that held it together. The paper fell away, and a gold locket on a fine chain dropped into her hand. She opened it and read the inscription: "My love, my heart, my life. Love, Charles."

"Oh, Charles," she whispered. "It's beautiful."

"I hope you like it. I had it engraved especially for you." She leaned over to give him a hug, and he whispered so only she could hear: "I love you so much, Charlotte."

"It's perfect. Help me put it on." She smiled as he fumbled with the chain's clasp. Papa grinned at her as she waited. The locket gleamed against her dress, and Charlotte touched the necklace self-consciously.

Charles looked at Charlotte's parents. "With your approval?"

Papa nodded, while Mama's eyes filled with tears.

Charles shifted to face Charlotte. "I want you to be my wife, Charlotte. I want you to be there for all my Christmases so you can make me Christmas tea."

"Christmas tea?" she asked in mock surprise. "Is that the only reason you want me to marry you?"

"I think you know better than that," he said, kissing her tenderly. "Please say yes. I've already asked your papa's consent. He knows I can support you, because he recommended me for an overseer's position at the docks."

"Yes."

He raised his eyebrows. "You mean it?"

"Yes, I do," she said. "I've never meant anything more. I love you, Charles."

He whooped with joy, and she laughed, enjoying the moment, basking in his love for her. Charles stood and took her hand, pulling her up to stand with him. Mary squealed with delight and ran over to kiss her sister on the cheek.

"I'm happy for you both," Mama said.

"Now we have a wedding to plan." She reached over and took Charlotte's hand. "You'll be a beautiful bride, my dear," she said, wiping a tear from her eye.

Taking another sip of tea, Charles looked around the room at the family that had become his. Agatha and Tate, sitting hand in hand. Mary, with tears in her eyes, congratulating her beloved sister. And Charlotte, who had filled such a void in his life. His heart had truly come home again — and the future had never looked brighter.

RECIPE

Dear Reader,

This special tea recipe was given to me (after much begging!) by my college roommate, who comes from an old Louisiana family. The origin of the recipe has long since been forgotten, but Christmas Tea has been a favorite for generations. My own family has adopted it as our own, and so I pass it on to you. Enjoy!

Katherine Chute

CHRISTMAS TEA
(serves 6 to 8)

6 cups water
2 tbs lemon juice
1 tsp whole cloves
½ cup sugar

1 inch stick cinnamon
2½ tbs black tea
¾ – 1 cup orange juice

Combine the water, cloves, and cinnamon. Heat to boiling. Add tea; cover and steep for five minutes; strain. Heat orange juice, lemon juice, and sugar to boiling; stir into hot tea.

The employees of Thorndike Press hope you have enjoyed this Large Print book. All our Large Print titles are designed for easy reading, and all our books are made to last. Other Thorndike Press Large Print books are available at your library, through selected bookstores, or directly from the publishers.

For more information about titles, please call:

(800) 257-5157

To share your comments, please write:

Publisher
Thorndike Press
P.O. Box 159
Thorndike, Maine 04986